# The Machine's Child

TOR BOOKS BY KAGE BAKER

# The Machine's Child

KAGE BAKER

A TOM DOHERTY ASSOCIATES BOOK
NEW YORK

This is a work of fiction. All the characters and events portrayed in this novel are
either fictitious or are used fictitiously.

This book is printed on acid-free paper.

Edited by David G. Hartwell

A Tor Book
Published by Tom Doherty Associates, LLC
175 Fifth Avenue
New York, NY 10010

www.tor.com

Tor® is a registered trademark of Tom Doherty Associates, LLC.

Library of Congress Cataloging-in-Publication Data

Baker, Kage.
    The machine's child / Kage Baker.—1st ed.
        p.   cm.
    ISBN-13: 978-0-765-31551-9
    ISBN-10: 0-765-31551-3 (acid-free paper)
    1. Dr. Zeus Incorporated (Imaginary organization)—Fiction.   2. Immortalism—Fiction.   3. Cyborgs—
Fiction.   I. Title.
    PS3552.A4313M33   2006
    813'.54—dc22

                                                                                          2006005723

First Edition: September 2006

Printed in the United States of America

0  9  8  7  6  5  4  3  2  1

*Cui hunc librum dedicem?*
*Katiae, cauponae ad Viridem Virum.*
*Mater actoribus bonam cerevisiam aequo pretio praebet.*

# The Machine's Child

# PROLOGUE:
# ONE EVENING IN 2302 AD,
# THIRTY MILES OFF THE
# GALAPAGOS

There was a spark of light on the wide sea, no other visible in miles of rolling darkness. It wasn't a fixed point. Sometimes it seemed to wink out, sometimes to wander along the line of the black horizon, only to double back on itself in an aimless sort of way.

Anyone crossing the surging distance toward it would have seen gradually the pale outline of a ship, the spark resolving into a window in her aft cabin. Her running lights were extinguished. She had no fear of encounters on that empty sea where she stood on and off, nor any desire to let passersby know she was there.

Closer to, now, and the observer would have found her size staggering. Four great masts, a sequoia forest of reefed sail, her shrouds and spars quartering the night sky like Mercator lines. White and sleek as a sleeping seabird, all smooth modern form; but through that yellow window, a glimpse of an older style. Dark wood, rich paneling, red and blue and gold. The interior seemed to have been designed by someone very fond of pirate films. Much brass and elaborate carving, to the point where taste was definitely in question. The cabin's centerpiece was its vast bed.

What the observer saw next would depend on who, or what, the observer was.

A human observer—though it is unlikely a mere human could swoop in with such omniscience—would see a single man lying in the exact center of the red-and-gold pirate bed.

The man was sleeping, sprawled in exhaustion. There was a certain tension in his long body that failed to relax even so, and his eyes darted behind his eyelids in uneasy dreams. He had not slept well since the night when Mars Two had died, with all its citizens, as the result of his error in judgment. His name, by the way, was Alec Checkerfield, and he was the seventh earl of Finsbury.

He was a lanky fellow, quite tall but built solidly. He wore pajamas violently patterned with palm trees and vahines, not at all the kind of thing you'd expect a hunted man to wear. He had a long broken nose, and high broad cheekbones. When he rolled over, he exposed something strange twining up the back of his neck. It looked like a silver tattoo, in a pattern of vaguely Celtic-knot complexity.

It was not a tattoo, however. It was a subcutaneous wire hooking Alec up to the artificial intelligence sailing his ship, for Alec was a cyborg. Not at all some human-machine hybrid with a whirring ocular implant and a toneless voice, oh dear no; that sort of fashion went out generations before Alec was born. In any case, being a peer, he could afford the most elegantly understated cybernetic implants.

So much for what the hypothetical human observer would notice.

It would be rather more likely that a surveillance drone would see all this, zooming in across such distance, noting such detail. And a surveillance drone, having the ability to tune in to the ship's system, its cameras and indeed to Alec's own cyborged brain, would see a great deal more.

It would see, for example, two other men lying in the bed, at extreme arm's length from Alec on either side, who appeared to be his nearly identical brothers.

The virtual man who slept, or tried to sleep, on the left, looked slightly older than the other two. He lay stretched on his side, one hand under his pillow as though groping after something he'd hidden there. He wore only ivory-colored drawers of an antiquated design. His name was, or had been, Edward Alton Bell-Fairfax.

The virtual man on the right was not asleep at all. He lay on his back like an effigy on a tomb, clad in a flowing white shirt of even more antique design, his arms crossed on his chest. He gazed with an expression of despair on the gimbal lamp, which rocked gently as the ship crested each rolling swell, and which had dimmed itself to the comforting glow of a nursery light. He wasn't comforted. His lips moved for a while in silent prayer. Tears welled in his eyes.

He could hardly be blamed. He found his present situation bizarre and intolerable, as you might if you, too, were Nicholas Harpole, burned as a heretic in 1555 but now inexplicably alive and drifting in a twenty-fourth-century ship, with a pair of your clones.

He looked away from the lamp and up to the single red eye of a surveillance camera. After a long moment he ventured to say:

"Spirit, dost thou watch in the night?"

Instantly awake, the virtual man on the left rolled over and sat bolt upright, taking aim with the very real pistol he'd fetched from under his pillow. Its muzzle was a bare two inches from the face of Nicholas on the right, who recoiled from it. Alec, between them, opened startled eyes but lay motionless, staring at the pistol in confusion.

Any hypothetical human viewer would be confused, too. Without a way to tap into Alec's brain, he or she would have seen only the man in the bed's center sitting up, pointing a gun at empty space to his right. And the cold glare and military bearing of the man were not those of anyone who would ever wear vahine-patterned pajamas by choice. This was because virtual Edward had just seized control of Alec's real body.

*Edward! Belay that!* said a gruff male voice, from a speaker concealed within a carving of a Spanish galleon. It was the voice of the artificial intelligence that ran the ship, and not—as one might be forgiven for supposing—a pirate hiding behind the panel.

Edward exhaled, shaking, but did not lift the pistol.

"Ghost or no ghost," he said through his teeth, "if you start that damned praying again, I swear I shall kill you."

"Do it, Homicide," said Nicholas, "an thou darest!"

Edward regarded Nicholas, moving the pistol away only regretfully. During his life, which had ended abruptly in 1863, he had been what was known at the time as a Political; which meant he had done things for Queen Victoria's government that would have horrified that good lady, had her cabinet ministers ever seen fit to tell her about them.

Alec began to hyperventilate. He wasn't a particularly oversensitive person, but his nerves had been rather strained lately.

"Are you nuts?" he yelled. "That's a disrupter pistol! In *bed*? You want to burn a hole through a bulkhead? How'd you get it out of the locker, anyway?"

*D'you really reckon he'd tell you, Alec?*

"You don't know either, do you, machine?" said Edward with a sneer. "When your little pivot-lenses aren't turned on the locker, you can't see it. And neither one of you noticed," he added, turning to Alec and Nicholas.

*Well, now, Mr. Bell-Fairfax, sir, thank you for telling me, to be sure. It'll be a cold day in Hell afore I takes an eye off* **you** *again. Put that bloody pistol away.*

Sullenly Edward set it on the bedside table. "I may as well, after all," he said. "Since I've precious little chance of sending Nicholas to Heaven, where he belongs, instead of this wretchedly crowded bed. But you're a fool to sleep without a weapon in reach, Alec, you really are."

"Sleep? How am I ever going to get any sleep?" said Alec, flailing with his fists. "We've got work to do tomorrow! How are we going to break into Options Research if you two fight all the time?"

**Stand to!** *You calm down, now, matey, old Captain Morgan'll take the helm. That goes for you too, Mr. Bell-Fairfax, yer worship.*

Muttering, Edward lay down and punched his virtual pillow savagely.

A word or two of explanation might be helpful at this point. Neither Edward nor Nicholas were *ghosts*, technically; but during their respective lifetimes each had carried in his brain, quite unknown to himself, a sort of black box. This device recorded in electromagnetic analogue every sensation, thought, and emotion experienced from the moment of its installation (immediately after birth) to the moment of death.

These recordings were made because neither Edward nor Nicholas were *human*, technically. They were Recombinants, as Alec was, and they had been made (very, very illegally) by an all-powerful cabal of scientists and investors known collectively as Dr. Zeus Incorporated, or more usually just the Company, which also possessed the secret of time travel, among other things.

For reasons that will not be gone into immediately but involved ensuring its own existence, the Company had needed a Recombinant. A prototype was designed, DNA engineered to produce it, and three test embryos cloned from one blastocyst. They were then scattered across time, implanted in human mothers by hard-working immortal Company operatives. Being, after all, test runs, the prototypes were not made immortal.

Nicholas and Edward, completely unaware of their destinies, nevertheless fulfilled them and died untimely if necessary deaths, whereupon the recorded sum of their lives went into their Company project files. Alec, however, had not died.

Like his—clones? brothers? other selves?—Alec had certain abilities completely unguessed-at by his shadowy creators. Unlike them, he was born into an era of advanced technology. When, as a child, he had been given a cybernetic companion, he had not only been able to modify it to suit his tastes, he removed the safeguard that prevented it from breaking any laws in the fulfillment of its primary directive, which was to protect and nurture him.

The astute reader will have guessed that little Alec had liked pirate stories.

Captain Morgan (as Alec had named his companion) persuaded adolescent Alec to have himself modified with implants, so that he could exist simultaneously in three-dimensional space and in cyberspace with the Captain.

Being a sensible artificial intelligence, the Captain set about solving the mystery of Alec's existence. Upon discovering that his fairly unhappy childhood could be laid directly at the door of Dr. Zeus Incorporated, Alec and the Captain embarked upon a campaign of revenge and exposure. Unaware they were being cleverly manipulated by the Company to accomplish its goals (I said it was all-powerful) they stole one of the Company's time shuttles and had a number of adventures that ended more or less disastrously for Alec and a lot of other people, though not for the Company.

With its purpose for Alec fulfilled, the Company relaxed, confident in the expectation of his disposal when the time shuttle exploded, as it was scheduled to do. This failed to happen, however, because:

In the course of his adventures with the time shuttle, Alec blundered into a Company penal institution located deep in prehistory. There he encountered one of the Company's cyborg slaves, the hapless Botanist Mendoza, an immortal marooned in the past for reasons which included her knowledge of the Company's Recombinant project. She had discovered

Project *Adonai* by sheerest chance, when she had the misfortune to encounter, fall in love with, and fail to prevent the untimely deaths of first
Nicholas and then, three hundred years later, Edward.

She was, moreover, a Crome generator, the only immortal with a
bizarre condition cursing its possessors with apparent psychic ability.
Consequently her emotional health was not quite what was desired in an
immortal, which was another reason she'd been confined to the agricultural station.

Upon meeting Alec, Mendoza slept with him, accepted his proposal of
marriage, and passed on to him certain classified information to assist
him in his goal of bringing down Dr. Zeus Incorporated. She also discon-
nected the explosive device on the shuttle that was intended to destroy
Alec once his usefulness to the Company ended.

When, after several tragic accidents, Alec managed to equip his very
large yacht with a time transcendence drive so he could go back to rescue
Mendoza, he discovered that Dr. Zeus Incorporated had got there first.
The unfortunate lady had been arrested again, and consigned to some
even more obscure prison. Plundering Company files in his furious attempts to discover where she had been taken, Alec inadvertently came
across the Recombinant project data. Most unwisely, he downloaded the
whole thing, learning thereby the extremely unsavory truth about his own
existence and, moreover, receiving the entire contents of both Nicholas's
and Edward's black boxes.

Alec promptly had a nervous breakdown. Goodness, wouldn't you, at
this point? And, unable to assimilate Nicholas's or Edward's memories,
Alec developed a disassociative personality disorder and gave them inde-
pendent individual existences, complete with virtual physical bodies in
cyberspace.

At least, that was the only rational explanation for what happened.

After attempting (and failing) to administer drugs to banish Alec's unwelcome guests, the Captain decided to let them stay, since both Nicholas
and Edward had strengths and skills that might prove useful to Alec.

Got it? All clear so far?

The Captain's experiment was not proving an unqualified success,
since the three Recombinant gentlemen discovered they couldn't stand
their own company, and struggled constantly for control of the one real

body they shared. One thing upon which they did agree, however, was the urgent necessity of finding and rescuing Mendoza.

To this end, they hunted down their guilty creators and extracted at gunpoint the name of the prison where Mendoza was now confined: a site known only as Options Research.

Then they fled, away through time to an empty night ocean, where they were presently attempting to rest while the Captain devised a plan for Mendoza's rescue.

A soothing tone emanated from the speaker, double-pitched to Alec's and Edward's differing brainwave patterns. Alpha rhythms were induced. Both men relaxed instantly, unconscious in seconds. A human observer would have seen the bed's single occupant watching the light once again, weariness and infinite regret in his eyes. This had become Nicholas Harpole's habitual expression, and he was now solely in control of Alec's body.

From where it had watched in a corner a creature emerged, a nightmarish thing like a steel scorpion with a skeletal face. The human observer might be excused for starting, for this was no virtual creature; it was a quite solid servounit enabling the Captain to manipulate objects in real space. It extended a mechanical member and grasped the pistol, scuttling away with it to the weapons locker. Even Nicholas, who had begun to get used to its appearance, edged back when it passed him.

*Here, Nicholas, lad,* said the Captain soothingly. *What aileth thee? What can I fetch thee?*

"Hast thou no mortal form?" asked Nicholas, shivering.

*To be sure I have, lad.* A tiny holoprojection cone emerged from the camera and seconds later a man appeared to stand beside the bed, big, black-bearded and villainous-looking, though his expression was kindly. Nicholas stared, fascinated even as he was repelled. He jumped when a hologram of a chair materialized behind the Captain, who sat down into it. "There now. Nothing to frighten thee."

"I charge thee, Spirit, tell me! Dost thou serve the devil?" Nicholas demanded.

"No, sir, not I."

"Dost thou serve God, then?"

"Well, no, sir, being what I am, which is to say no more than a device. I was made to serve Alec, sir, d'you see? Like a clock or a lute, to tell him the hour or cheer his heart. Or a dog, to guard him as he sleeps. Too low a creature to be damned or saved. Therefore, fear me not."

"How canst thou speak with a man's voice?" asked Nicholas.

The Captain waved his hand dismissively. "Why, sir, even a bird may be taught speech, mayn't he, a raven or a parrot? Wherefore not then a clever mechanism? If a jack can be made to strike the hour in a clock, he may be made to speak, too; and such am I. Speak with me, then, and ease thy sick grief."

Nicholas stared at him, marveling at the detail of the illusion: the movement of the Captain's beard when he spoke, the creak of the insubstantial chair when he shifted his weight.

"But I am no more than thou art," Nicholas said at last, bitterly. "A *made thing*, an alchemical homunculus. How shouldst thou comfort my soul, when neither thou nor I have souls, but only spirits? So might a clock comfort an astrolabe."

"Ah, well, sir, I've no soul, to be sure; but it might help to talk, all the same."

Nicholas lay back with a sigh, and gazed at the lamp.

"I have been disputing with myself," he said, "since I have awakened into this unnatural life of horrible marvels, on the nature of Almighty God."

"And how doth that make thee feel, lad?" inquired the Captain. Nicholas drew a deep breath and went on:

"In regarding now the thing I am, that standeth outside mankind like a phantom, and observing how the world waggeth these late ages, and seeing the low truth of creation (which evolution my reason must accept, though my heart sickens)—I cannot reconcile myself with the several proofs, laid before mine eyes, that contradict my faith."

"Well, that's a predicament, to be sure. You ain't the first one to run aground on it, neither."

"What have other men done, Spirit?" Nicholas pleaded.

"Why—I reckon they worked it out as best they could, sir. Some folk paid no heed to the contradictions. Some dumped the whole Bible and went over to the Goddess, though that ain't turning out no better, it seems. Most folk don't trouble with religion at all, like my Alec. He gets along fine."

"He feels no pain?" Nicholas cried. "He feels no horror at this void of pointless time?"

The Captain stroked his beard, scowling. "Well, he didn't use to, when he thought he'd just go out like a light once he died. You showing up like you done puts a new look on everything, don't it? Wherefore I might prepare me for squalls . . ." He cocked an eye at Nicholas. "What dost reckon it'll take thee to work out an answer to that crisis of faith of thine?"

"I would a thousand pounds I might study Scripture again. Oh, that I had my books that were burnt!" Nicholas gripped the blanket with both hands.

"Then turn and look there, sir. See that text plaquette on yer night table? The thing what looks like green glass in a little window frame. Go ahead, pick it up. The other lads is both asleep, they won't hinder thee. That's a book, sir, of the kind we use in this day and age. My boy hath it to look at figures, but it hath a million texts in it beside. I'll just open it for thee."

Nicholas caught his breath. The dark glass lit up and bright letters appeared, informing him that he beheld THE OLD TESTAMENT, diligently corrected and compared with the Hebrew, by William Tyndale and finished in the year of Our Lord God A. 1536, in the month of September at Vilvorde.

He was struck speechless.

"D'you like that, eh? Look, when thine eye comes to the bottom of the page, the book knows and goes on to the next one for thee. Nor needst thou a candle, for the book maketh its own light. Be'n't it a wonder, lad?"

"Ay," said Nicholas, immersed in the translator's preface. He pulled himself away with some effort and looked at the Captain in awe. "I had Tyndale's New Testament when I lived. Is he still read amongst the generations, after so long?"

"Well . . . in certain circles. His work ain't lost, anyhow; trust Dr. Zeus to see to that."

"Then one martyr at least did not waste his death," said Nicholas, sighing as he turned the plaquette over in his hands.

"Now, Nick, lad: see canst thou find there a God what don't insult a man's reason, eh? For I reckon my boy might need to grapple with the Eternal afore long, and I'd just as soon I had an answer for him what makes sense. Thou'lt have any books thou desirest, so it's done. I got other folks' holy scriptures, too. Buddha and that lot."

". . . Ay," said Nicholas, drawn in again by the bright letters.

"But set it aside for tonight. Th'art best to get some sleep."

Nicholas set aside the plaquette reluctantly, and lay back to compose himself for rest. The Captain unobtrusively generated a certain tone. Nicholas slept then, sound.

The Captain sat a moment longer, regarding the wide bed and its occupants. He shook his head, muttering to himself; then vanished, along with his chair, to turn his attention to plotting the ship's course for tomorrow's journey. The skull-headed servant crept out and opened one of the portholes in the room, to let in the fresh night air. Then it went to a hamper at the foot of the bed. There it pulled out a bundle of grubby socks and shirts, and crawled away with them in the direction of the ship's laundry.

# ONE EVENING IN 300,000 BCE

It was an undiscovered island in a shallow unnamed ocean, uncrossed yet by longitude or latitude. It was not large, no more than a few miles square. It had no topographical features of note, neither mountains nor cliffs. Its beach simply rose gradually from the water and, after a space of level rock and sand, sloped gradually down to the opposite shore.

There was a building on the island, long, low, and windowless, like a warehouse. It had one door, and beside the door was an old couch, and on the couch sat an immortal, watching the sunset thoughtfully.

If this has given the impression that the place was silent and still, nothing could be further from the truth.

He sat motionless in the midst of a flurry of wildly moving things, the immortal did, and have I mentioned yet that he was very, very large? Massively mighty, with great thick hands and feet, a nose so big it was nearly comical-looking, big pale eyes under a vast cliff of a brow. Not much else of his features could be discerned, hidden as they were by an enormous tow-colored beard. You wouldn't be looking at him anyway, if you were there, to wonder what his face might be like. You'd be looking at the things he'd made, the things that were moving without cease.

The things all seemed to be part of a perpetual motion machine, belts, wheels, and pulleys driving and charging a generator that was hooked up to a refrigeration unit. There were other, smaller systems going, too, that seemed to be powering other machines somewhere inside the building. The motive power for all of them was supplied by human limbs.

Legs mounted on a wheel ran frantically round, feet pounding end-lessly on a treadmill. Arms thrashed and beat like hammers, their galvanic pumping harnessed to drive a complex geared mechanism. Flexible tubes supplied the parts with fluids to keep them from deteriorating. Creak, creak, thump, thump, round and round, and in the slanting light of eve-ning, shadows circled like the shadows of birds across the old giant's face.

Presently he moved, too, reaching from the couch to open the door of the refrigeration unit. He brought out a beer, twisted its neck off, and set-tled into near-immobility again, now and then lifting the beer for a sip. The sun got lower and redder. It lit the emblem on the front of his cover-alls: a clock face without hands. The immortal sat and thought.

Then, abruptly, his eyes brightened. He'd had an idea. He lifted and drained the beer; then flung the empty bottle away. It struck a nearby mountain of other such bottles, clattering and rolling down. He ignored it. Lithe as a big cat he was on his feet, stalking through the door into the building that resembled a warehouse. He pulled a chain and dim illumi-nation began to fill the place, increasing steadily as the desperate limbs quickened their pace outside.

By the light of their effort was revealed an open work area, a steel table surrounded by unpleasant-looking machines, and by racks of gleaming tools and instruments. Against one wall, furniture had been arranged in a square to define living space: chair, table, bed, dresser, personal items, a place to prepare meals. Against another was a steel filing cabinet.

The work and living spaces occupied only the front quarter of the warehouse. All the rest was rows and tiers of shelves, stretching away into impenetrable shadows. As far as the eye could see, there were metal boxes stacked. They varied in size and shape, but none were larger than a coffin; none smaller, than, say, a hatbox.

The immortal (his name, by the way, was Marco) went straight across to the nearest row of shelves. Here he paused, cocking his head to listen.

You couldn't have heard the sound, if you'd been there. Perhaps you ought to get down on your knees now and give thanks that you couldn't, and weren't. Marco could hear it, however. He looked keenly along the shelf and went at last to a certain box. He pulled it down, as easily as though it weighed nothing, and carried it out to the steel table.

Here Marco punched in a combination of figures on a lockpad on the box's lid. With a hiss and a sigh the lid rose slowly, folded back slightly on itself. Marco looked into the box at its occupant, grinning. In his light pleasant voice he said:

"Hey, Grigorii Efimovitch, I've had an idea."

What had been an immortal named Grigorii Efimovitch could no longer see, but knew Marco was looking at him. The mouth was already open in a silent scream, the eyes wide and staring as eggs.

It might help you at this point to know that Grigorii Efimovitch was there because he deserved to be, or at least had felt he deserved it when he had gone voluntarily to this time, this island, this warehouse. He had willingly submitted to entering the metal box. Of course, he might have changed his mind since. Far too much time had passed for his fate to be altered now, however, even if he had been able to tell Marco.

Marco busied himself with arranging the table just as he wanted for what he had planned. He set out instruments, jars of chemicals; lifted Grigorii Efimovitch out to sprawl, trailing, on the steel surface. He pulled on a black rubberized raincoat, or something that looked a lot like one, and carefully worked transparent gloves on over his massive hands. He stepped out into the fast-fallen darkness and got himself another beer.

He drank, belched gently, and selected an instrument from the table. Grigorii Efimovitch had begun to twitch uncontrollably. Marco waved the beer at him in a consoling gesture.

"Well, you never know. We just might do it, Grigorii Efimovitch. Wouldn't that be great?"

Grigorii Efimovitch's eyelids fluttered. If this was an attempt to communicate it was lost on Marco, who breathed deeply and stood straight, setting down the beer. A gleam came into his eyes, a sparkling and terrifying joy.

"Father of battles, Judge of the dead," he said, "grant that your servant may find at last the means to send your suffering children to perfect and irrevocable oblivion. Be merciful, Death."

He leaned down then over the table, raising the instrument he had chosen.

"It's showtime," he said.

# ONE MORNING IN 2317 AD, MOUNT TAMALPAIS

The Rogue Cyborg begins his day.

Does he step out of a gleaming steel cubicle, flex his huge muscles, and pull on his skin-tight leotard? Nope. He yawns, unzips his sleeping bag, and crawls out, to sit on the edge of his camping cot, staring blearily into the dark morning and rubbing his unshaven chin. He hasn't shaved in a few days. Time kind of gets away from you when you're a Rogue Cyborg.

Thinking he should maybe grow his beard back, he pokes around for shoes, sticks his feet into them, and shuffles down a long dark corridor, leaning into an alcove as he goes to grab a teakettle. Farther down the corridor is an access portal, which opens to his groping hand. Sunlight floods in, and though it is filtered through fathoms of green leaves the Rogue Cyborg grimaces and blinks. He hasn't been topside on a sunny day in weeks. Spring must have arrived, he reflects.

After scanning carefully and finding no possible hazards, he emerges into a wilderness of fearful beauty. The precipitous slope is thickly forested, dark redwoods towering above oak and laurel. If he cared to glance out over the treetops below him he'd catch glimpses of green mountain meadows, steel-blue sea, even the distant spires of a magnificent city; but the Rogue Cyborg isn't a scenery man. All his attention is fixed on the stream, the little cataract of white water dropping from ledge to ledge.

Stepping carefully through the ferns, so cleverly he leaves no print, he leans over and fills his kettle. It's a big kettle and takes a while to fill. He looks about him the while, an edgy expression in his black eyes, and rubs his stubbly face with one nervous hand. There might be bears. There might be park rangers. There might even be Company security techs lying in wait. Life isn't easy when you're a Rogue Cyborg.

His name, actually, is Joseph, and on this particular day in the year 2317 he's just over twenty thousand four hundred years old, and he never, ever started out to be a Rogue Cyborg, but, well—shit happens.

Having washed, shaved, and made himself a mug of something that might pass for coffee if one needed it really badly, Joseph took the mug and wandered farther into the depths of the mountain that was presently his home.

He entered a vast cavern, smooth-sided and dry, stretching out over subterranean acres and lit by the blue radiance of five hundred regeneration tanks arrayed in tidy rows of vaults. A few of the vaults were unoccupied. Perhaps a dozen contained what appeared to be ordinary men and women, floating in sleep. All the rest were occupied by giants, hulking males seven or eight feet in height, massive of limb. Their skulls were broad-domed, helmet-shaped. Their brows were clifflike, their noses enormous. They drifted and dreamed in eerie silence. All of them, with one exception, wore circlets of copper on their brows, like drowned kings.

Joseph strolled along the aisles, sipping from his mug. He was making for one vault in particular, whose occupant differed slightly from the rest of the sleepers.

This was one of the giants. He alone wore no copper circlet, and he seemed to be recovering from terrible injuries. His great body was scarlet with new tissue, blood-charged where cruel wounds were in the process of closing over. There were cicatrices to indicate where parts had been reattached after avulsion: an arm, a leg, an ankle, and—unthinkably—his head. The face was nearly all healing scars.

Fearful as he was to look upon, his was the vault before which Joseph paused.

"You know, Father, if I didn't know better I might almost mistake you for one of the others now," Joseph told the giant. "I mean that. Seriously. You look great. Well, not *great*, but a hundred percent improved, okay?"

The giant, apparently lifeless, did not respond. Joseph had another sip of his not-coffee and nodded.

"Definitely on the mend. So! What's happening? Not much. Nobody's caught me yet. Abdiel left again last month, but I told you that already, huh? He didn't remember us this time, either. I wonder how many poor morons like him are wandering around, doing classified work for the Company? That's another dirty little secret we'll have to dig up one of these days, huh?

"Let's see, what else is going on? Looks like spring has finally arrived. Maybe I'll go down to the Pelican soon, catch up on the local news. Not that there ever is much up here, but that's okay with me, you know what I mean? Go down and maybe repair something for Mavis and get myself some cider . . . or some of that special *persimmon* cider . . . or some of Mavis maybe . . ." Joseph sighed with longing. "I've told you about Mavis, right? Boy, you'd like Mavis, Father. She's got these—" He sculpted the air with his free hand in a vain effort to describe what Mavis had.

"And, uh, maybe it's a good idea to go down there anyway," Joseph continued, after a poignant silence. "For a reality check, huh? Make sure they're all still alive. Because, Father, sometimes when I wake up . . . Sometimes I get scared I've been asleep up here too long. Like, I'll go down there some night and the place will be in ruins, all the mortals dead long ago. You know?"

He shivered extravagantly, his whole body shook.

"Oh, yeah, absolutely," he said. "Time for some cider."

He turned and bustled off to begin his day at one of the data terminals, probing randomly through the files of Dr. Zeus Incorporated for dirty little secrets.


Hours later Joseph emerged from his access portal and picked his way down the slope, until he found an ancient strip of cracked asphalt that wound along the face of the mountain. In the red light of the waning day he thrust his hands into his coat pockets and marched along cheerily.

He felt swell. All dressed up for a night on the town! Most of his clothing was a little out of date, but clean and presentable. All the same, he made a mental note to hike into San Francisco soon and hit another clothing store. How long since the last nocturnal raid now? Five years? Ten? Of course, it wasn't smart to steal things too often. Sooner or later he was going to make a tiny mistake, miss some surveillance device and blow his cover. Then he'd have to run again, and running would be pretty damned awkward right at the moment.

Still, he hated looking like a bum.

Winding and switching back, the road took him steadily down, in and out of ravines dark with evergreens and across broad slopes purple with heather. Bone-chilling wind blew in off the gray sea, but as he descended Joseph saw the yellow lights of the little farms and shacks where the mortals lived, and that warmed his heart. So did the yellow lights of the boats moored in Muir Harbor. In the twilight gloom he found at last the nearest fragment of what had been California State Highway 1, and strode along it through the alder forest to that intersection with the harbor road where stood the Pelican Inn.

The Pelican had been there a long time. It was rumored to have been transplanted, brick by brick, from some English village, back in the twentieth century when wealthy men still did things like that. It was named for the ship in which Sir Francis Drake had set out when he'd sailed off to loot the Spanish Main.

It had once been a very expensive bed-and-breakfast hotel, bar, and five-star restaurant. Various wars, political secessions, and natural disasters had altered its fortunes. Over three centuries it had been successively a triage hospital, a barricaded freeholding, a farmhouse, a partial ruin, and other things. But, situated as it was at a crossroads in a picturesque cove, as soon as civilization had reasserted itself enough to provide some traffic, the Pelican had evolved back into an inn.

Even a reasonably prosperous one, in this year of 2317. Plenty of trade from the local farmers and fishermen. Plenty of real money from the rich people who moored their pleasure boats in Muir Harbor, eager to get away from the General Prohibition in San Francisco.

Not that there was anything all that immoral to be had at the Pelican, of course, beyond homemade ciders and ales and fish dinners. Mavis paid a fortune in bribes to local law enforcement to be able to serve even those; but the people from the big boats wanted the thrill of the forbidden, and spent hugely for it.

Sometimes Mavis paid the local law enforcement to dress as picturesque smugglers, too, and they would lounge in her bar and leer pleasantly at the guests, or tell stories about desperate chases over the hills
with kegs of mead. The guests would buy them drinks and would usually
stay over an extra night. The local economy thrived to no end.

Joseph saw the amber windows as he pushed forward through the
dusk, heard the chattering mortal voices, breathed in the sea air and wood
smoke. He felt again the surge of relief that they were still there, not yet
dead, not yet receded into his interminable past. He was singing as he
sprinted across the lawn and up the flagged steps, under the wooden sign
with its carved enigmatic seabird.

As he sang he nearly ran into Keely, one of the waitresses, who was
making her way through the passage between the bar and the main parlor with a tray of drinks. She was a nice girl, bosomy, looked like a timid
swan. He grinned at her.

"Hi there, sweetheart."

"What kind of song was *that*?" she said, not quite trusting him not to
grab her and turning so as to put the tray between them.

"What?"

"That song you were singing when you came in."

"That? That was a marching song, honey. Real old. 'If I had one
denarius, I'd buy us all a round of drinks; if I had two denarii, I'd buy myself a pig; if I had three denarii, I'd hire somebody to kill the Decurion,'
and so on and so on," Joseph said, grinning again, so happy to be there
in the warmth and the smell of food and musty old booze. She knit her
brows.

"What's a D-Decurion?"

"Oh, just some jerk," he said. She rolled her eyes at him and turned to
resume her progress toward the main parlor.

"The holoscreen needs tuning again," she told him over her shoulder.

"I'm on it," he said, and slipped into the bar, ducking nimbly under the
gate. The big bartender turned scowling to confront the intruder, but put
the wrench down when he recognized Joseph. He indicated the holoscreen with raised eyes.

"You fix that piece of crap, you get a cider, how's about that?" he said.
Joseph squinted up in dismay at the multiple images.

"Jeepers. What is this, the Migraine Channel? Gimme a leg up."

The bartender hoisted him obligingly, and he sat on the counter and groped in his coat pocket for the case of tools he carried. It's useful being a cyborg, even a rogue one, when you have to realign a holoemitter. Mortals think you're an itinerant electronics genius, and so it's all right that you're a faintly shabby little man who never seems to have much money.

Joseph didn't really need the tools, but he made a great show of using them anyway, and presently the holo images resolved and sharpened into one image, brilliantly clear in the dark midair: Mars, with the glassy dome and radiating green lines of the Martian Agricultural Collective near its equator, as a solemn voice lauded the courage of the first settlers sponsored by Areco. There was a half-hearted cheer from the patrons in the dart alley.

Joseph shivered, thinking that today's courageous settlers were tomorrow's vicious terrorists. He didn't feel like thinking about the Mars Two disaster right now, though; this was a happy occasion, and Mars Two had another thirty-five years of blissful ignorance of its fate. He leaped down and took a little bow, then turned to the bar expectantly.

"So, am I good or am I good?"

By way of answer the bartender thrust the big embossed glass mug into Joseph's hand. He took it smugly, strutted away to the parlor, and found himself a dark corner with a view of the fire. There he settled in with his back to the wall, and tasted his cider. Dark and dry, strong stuff. From the bouquet, he judged it to be first crush of Gravensteins from Sebastopol, thirty miles or more over the hills.

Yes, even eternal life could be good sometimes. He closed his eyes and listened: twenty-six mortal hearts beating. There was Keely complaining to the cook, and there was the pompous documentary voice droning on about Mars, and there was a breathless couple in Room Three talking about shopping in San Francisco, and there were Nelson and Silvio, the cops, bragging about their smuggling exploits to a pair of guests who exclaimed in awe, despite the fact that the boys were laying on the pirate accents a little thickly. Darts plunking into the board. Somebody unused to real alcohol getting sick in Room Seven. Rush of cold air, smell of the sea and the green alder trees, somebody coming in—

Instantly Joseph was on his feet, peering around the corner into the hall. But it was okay: two more well-groomed people in yachting clothes, murmuring in delight at how quaint everything looked, on their way to the bar. He settled back into his seat and relaxed, drank more of his cider, watched the fire.

He recognized Mavis's firm tread long before she came around the corner. He got to his feet, doing his best to look dignified and respectable for her, as he ought to look if he were the former executive consultant he always claimed to be. He knew she didn't believe him, though in fact he'd been a consultant to a lot of people, including pharaohs, in his time; but that was okay. Their relationship wasn't built on belief.

She hove into sight like a Spanish galleon, and looked him up and down.

"So it's you again?"

"Yes, ma'am," Joseph said, giving her his most ingratiating smile. "Just stopped by on my way up the coast. Going to a business conference in Seattle, you know. Oh, and I had a look at your holoscreen. Works fine now. Just needed a little realignment."

"Really? How nice. As long as you're here, you might look at a couple of other things that need realigning," she told him quietly, slipping a key into his hand. "And take a shower first. I'll have some supper sent up."

Sometimes it's just *great* to be a Rogue Cyborg. Not only can Rogue Cyborgs fix holoscreens, there are a whole bunch of other useful things they can do better than mortals.

He left before daylight, because she preferred that, and made his way back to the mountain as the sky paled. The sun was rising red, blazing on a wall of sea-fog when he slipped furtively up his little canyon and disappeared into the darkness under the trees.

The Rogue Cyborg began another day.

He shrugged out of his good coat and hung it up, poked around in his kitchen alcove and found some not-coffee left over from the previous morning, reheated it (it couldn't taste any worse, after all), and poured himself another mugful. Then he walked back into the mountain, through the blue light of the regeneration tanks, and stopped finally in front of the vault where the hideous giant floated.

"You're looking good, Father," said Joseph thoughtfully, taking a sip from his mug. "I think your eyes are starting to grow back. The only thing that's still got me worried—"

The giant in the vault moved abruptly, thrust out one hand in a clawing gesture and struck the transparent wall. Joseph leaped backward and dropped his not-coffee, although (being a cyborg) he was able to catch it before it hit the floor.

"Holy smoke!" he said. He watched spellbound as the giant flattened his palm against the transparency and felt his way along it, like a one-armed mime defining a wall.

"Oh, my gosh, oh, my gosh—" Joseph said, scrambling up the ladder. "Father!" he yelled, "Father, are you—"

A hand came plunging up out of the blue, sweet-scented fluid and seized him by his shirt collar. Swift as thought it pulled him down, into the tank.

Joseph's *oof* of surprise emerged as an air bubble and floated before his astonished face, so viscous was the bioregenerant medium. And so warm, and so perfumed, and so comfortably oxygenated it was, that he could have drawn in a double lungful and lost himself in the primal pleasures of the womb, had he not been in more peril at that moment than he had faced in most of his immortal life.

After transmitting frantic inquiries and receiving no response, he gave up and hung there in the enfolding warmth, unresisting as the terrible giant pulled him close. The blind face grimaced wildly, but the head lay slack on one shoulder; the left hand gripped him beyond hope of escape. Slowly and painfully the other hand rose, the one on the arm that had been severed and reattached.

It splayed its fingers over Joseph's face, reading his features. It traced the shape of his eyes and did not gouge them out; murmuring a prayer of thanks, Joseph reached up and took the big hand in both his own. He began to spell out a message in universal code.

The giant, Budu, became motionless and focused all his attention on the message, which said something to the effect of: *Hello, it's Joseph, remember me? Please don't disable me. I rescued you from Chinatown but you'd been there a long time and you were in really bad shape. You're in a regeneration vault. It's now the year 2317. I finally accessed the code you gave me and found the other Enforcers, but a lot of bad stuff happened that I can't explain fast and I had to run, just like you did. The Company doesn't know we're in here.*

Joseph paused, at a loss for what to say next and terribly afraid the giant was too damaged to understand him anyway. Budu let go his collar, however, and groped for Joseph's hand instead. With his able hand he spelled out: *How bad is it?*

Joseph floated there in shock a moment, and Budu patiently repeated his message before Joseph signed back: *You were poisoned with something and Victor says he's sorry, he didn't know, and then somebody hacked you in pieces—*

The giant interrupted him. *Know that,* he signed. *Remember and have run self-diagnostic. Meant how bad political situation?*

Joseph signed back: *Bad bad bad bad bad.*

Budu grimaced again. He spelled out: *We wear clock faces yet?*

He was referring to the rumor, believed by immortals who feared the worst about the future, that by the twenty-fourth century all cyborg Company personnel would be obliged to wear a certain emblem. It would represent a clock face without hands, supposedly denoting their triumph over time, but in reality enabling the mortal masters to distinguish them from everyone else, and, perhaps, round them all up.

*Not yet,* Joseph signed.

Budu signed: *Who rules?*

*I don't know,* Joseph replied.

*Labienus rules?* inquired Budu.

*Not that bad,* Joseph signed back.

*Labienus caught?*

*Not yet.*

More grimacing from Budu. Joseph went on to sign:

*All alone, Father, so lonely, I watch them and I think nobody knows about us but I don't know what to do. I'm trying to repair you. You can tell me what to do and I'll do it. Do you want revenge? We can do that—2355 is coming. We can get them if we set the Enforcers free. I found the Enforcers but so many others lost now. Good operatives. I lost my daughter. I lost my friend. I can't find them. Please tell me what to do. Please . . .*

As he signed the last word over, faster and more clumsily, Budu lifted his hand away and used it to pull Joseph in close. He held Joseph's head a moment in the vast angle of his scarred neck, then released him. Taking Joseph's hand again he signed: *We will find them.*

# ONE AFTERNOON IN 2302 AD

The three men sat around the table, doing their best to ignore one another.

Nicholas was peering into the bright screen of the plaquette, so caught up in the Bible it was doubtful he'd have noticed if a gun had been fired next to his ear, though the *Captain Morgan* was riding out heavy weather. Rain beat against her portholes, when it wasn't shouldered aside by glass-green sea sweeping high.

Alec sat next to him, trying not to watch over Nicholas's shoulder as the words flitted by. He'd never been able to read or write much more than his name, though as a well-educated aristocrat of the twenty-fourth century he had at least a passing familiarity with the letters of the alphabet. In the past few days, though, ever since the unwelcome arrival of his previous selves, the meaning of written words had begun to glimmer through to him.

He didn't want to think why this might be happening. He certainly had no interest in reading an ancient religious text that was synonymous with oppression and bigotry. Nevertheless, he couldn't stop himself from following the cryptic letters, trying to piece meaning out of the old-fashioned speech. The storm he scarcely noticed, habituated to gales as he was. He merely felt with his toes for a floor-batten to brace himself against the roll of the ship. He did it purely out of habit, since Nicholas, in control of his body, was the only one actually experiencing any pitching just now.

Edward sat across from them, drumming his fingers on the table.

He didn't particularly care for Alec, and he thoroughly despised Nicholas, but he found himself wishing that one of them would leave off reading so he'd have someone with whom he might talk. He would very much have preferred to have been talking to Mendoza, and only the thought that he might do so in the near future enabled him to tolerate the other two men.

The storm made him uneasy, too; long-dormant instincts were insisting that there ought to be someone somewhere howling orders to take in sail, or bare feet pounding on the deck above his head, or an occasional freezing slop of white water flying down the companionway. And he ought to be anywhere but sitting still in this warm, dry, curiously scentless place doing *nothing*.

But after all, by the terms of the mutual agreement the three of them had worked out, it was Nicholas's turn to use Alec's body. Nicholas wanted to read the bloody Bible, and until his turn was up, there was nothing to do but sit here and watch Alec's lips move as he tried to read it, too. It was at least amusing to imagine what Alec was making of it.

Edward reached out experimentally and attempted to stop the swinging of the lamp on its gimbal. No use; it moved right through his virtual hand, a sensation—or lack thereof—he found unsettling. He tried harder. Nicholas moved his left arm involuntarily, and looked over at him with a frown.

"Sorry," he muttered.

*Commander Bell-Fairfax, sir? I wonder if I might have a word with you now.*

Edward started. The other two failed to notice. The voice had come from inside his head, instead of out of the ship's intercom system.

*Well, yes, sir, seeing as how our Alec's able to hear me this way—no reason why you can't, too.*

Edward's eyes narrowed. He watched the hanging lamp swing from its gimbal.

*And did I mention you can talk to me the same way, sir? No reason to disturb the other gentlemen with our little chat, is there, lad?*

*I'm not your lad, Machine.*

*Why, to be sure, sir, I'd forgot. Sorry about that, sir, it won't happen again. But I thought you might be interested to know, sir, that I've got a location on Options Research at last.*

*Well, bravo! How soon can we get there?*

**Oh, more or less instantaneously. The generators is all charged up now. It's what we'll find, once we gets there, that's got me looking out for squalls.**

*Spare me the picturesque seaman's lingo, if you please. I had my fill of that in the Royal Navy.*

**So you had, sir, and how careless of me to forget. Must be a lot of painful memories there, what with you being court-martialed, I reckon. It's just my natural admiration for anybody what was able to run afoul of Article Twenty-Two without getting hisself hanged at the yardarm. I do humbly beg yer pardon. But you see, Commander Bell-Fairfax, sir, if my information's correct it's going to be easier to get into Options Research than to get out of it again, if you take my meaning.**

*Guarded, is it?*

**I reckon you'd say so, sir, aye.**

*I'd have expected that of a prison.*

**It . . . ain't exactly a prison, sir. It's designated as a medical facility.**

*A hospital, you mean?*

**No, sir, I don't, unless there be hospitals where folk go to get sick, instead of well. It's a laboratory for experiments, d'ye see?**

*Good God.*

**Not a pretty thought to contemplate, sir, no, and it's my good fortune yer a tough-minded bastard like me, because I don't know how I'd ever break this to my little Alec. This place'll make Cawnpore Well look like a church picnic.**

The Captain watched admiringly as Edward controlled his panic and replied:

*Don't talk rot. Mendoza is an immortal; they can't hurt her, whatever they do to their other prisoners.*

**They can't kill her, but . . . all the prisoners is immortals, sir, that's just the trouble. And so's the guard.**

Edward ignored the implications of the first sentence. *Guard? Just one? It ought to be easy to get past him, then.*

**Begging yer pardon, sir, I don't think so. He be one of them Enforcer Class operatives.**

*What, the old monsters I was designed to replace?* Edward studied his fingernails with a show of unconcern. *Only one?*

**Aye, sir. Most of 'em was tricked into surrendering and got put into some kind of semi-eternal sleep, on account of they was suspected of mutiny. That's what the Company's most afeared of, you see, sir. Think about that Frankenstein book, sir, and imagine that there doctor's trouble multiplied by three thousand.**

*Hmm. We needn't concern ourselves with them, then. Need we?*

**Well sir, we still got that one to worry about. The first and the worst of 'em all to rebel, name of Marco. The Company gave him a special job. Seems he's the guard at Options Research. He's also the only staff member. Doctor, lab, and disassembly technician.**

*Disassembly?*

**Now, then, son, yer not a baby. I'm telling you all this because you can take it; how many cold-blooded murders did you commit for queen and country? Stiffen that upper lip, now. Options Research is where they send the immortals they want to get rid of. The defectives, the malcontents. Or the ones like yer lady, who know too much.**

Edward sagged forward at the table. Alec glanced over at him and started.

"Are you all right, man? You want some lunch or something?"

"I should like a glass of brandy, if you don't mind," Edward said.

"Okay." Alec obligingly created a virtual one. It materialized at Edward's elbow.

"Thank you," Edward said, lifting it and gulping. Alec continued to watch in concern until Edward glared at him, when he looked away and tried to focus again on Ecclesiastes. Wind screamed in the rigging, and rain rattled sidelong on the glass, spattering like shot. Edward breathed deeply, calming himself.

**That's a good gentleman. No sense upsetting the others, is there, now?**

*Stop fawning and tell me the rest. Have they killed her? Is all this for nothing?*

**No, sir, nobody's ever been executed there. That's their problem. See, the men who founded Dr. Zeus—at least, the ones who think they founded Dr. Zeus—would dearly like to know how to undo what they done when they made their immortals.**

*Wrought too well, did they?*

**Exactly, sir. All the Company can do is send the ones they want to disable to Options Research. And even so, this Marco ain't figured out the trick. All he's been able to do is damage 'em.**

Slowly and casually Edward lifted his virtual glass and swirled the brandy, looking into it. *Are you saying that he's torturing the prisoners?*

**Well, sir, the idea is to overcome the programming that makes 'em keep on living. And if he can make 'em want to die badly enough, you see—**

Edward closed his eyes for a moment.

*Has she been tortured?* he said at last.

There was a long silence before the Captain answered.

**I wouldn't know that, sir. This is a real classified matter, you see. There ain't hardly no data available on the prisoners, once they're sent there.**

Edward drank the rest of his brandy.

*You said we could get there instantaneously. For God's sake, why aren't we there now?*

**Because you need to prepare, if yer going to rescue her. I wanted you to understand what yer going up against, d'ye see? This is an Enforcer you'll be facing.**

*An immortal. Can he be duped? Bribed?*

**Not likely, sir. He's got all yer cunning, and all Nick's righteous zeal. This is holy work to him, it's why they been able to keep him there. And he's bigger and stronger than you.**

*What chance do I have, then?*

**Ah, well, sir, it ain't as bad as all that. Here be the trick with the Enforcers: they weren't made self-protective like the other immortals. They were made to go in swinging, never mind what kind of odds they faced. I reckon Dr. Zeus realized it'd be stupid to make a fighter what was too careful of his own skin.**

*I see. Can they be disabled?*

**Aye. Injure 'em enough and their bodies shut down, go into fugue for self-repair. But could you stay alive long enough to do for him afore he done for you? Anything you did, you'd have to do at point-blank range or he could dodge it; and I don't like the idea of you getting that close.**

*There are ways.* Edward examined his empty glass. *A straight stab into the kidneys. Attack from behind, lay the throat open and get away quickly.*

**And if you didn't get away fast enough? He'll do his job, sir, even as he's going down. A little like you when you died, if you don't mind me making the comparison.**

*Have the courtesy to imply quotation marks around the word "died," if you please. I'm quite sure the Company has my own body preserved somewhere. In any case, I ought to have some advantages over this Enforcer.* Edward set his glass down. *He may have been a terror in battle, but I daresay he's never had much experience killing by stealth. Oh, Machine, the things I've done! What luck for me there's no Hell after all. We'll see if the old monster can match the young one.*

**Just you remember that if he gets his hands on you, it won't be you dying; it'll be my Alec. And the girl will be lost there forever.**

*Very well; let's see for means. There are no guns in Alec's weapons locker that aren't too large and obvious. I want knives, small sharp ones that can be concealed. Paring knives will do well enough. An ice pick, a cobbler's awl, even a sixpenny nail if a sharp enough point can be set on it.*

**That's clever now, that is. Leave it to me, sir, I'll just send Billy Bones down to the machine shop. We'll take no chances, eh?**

*None. And you'd best begin plotting an evasive course through time, an itinerary as it were. Places to hide once we've rescued her. Look into this event shadow business.*

**Aye aye, sir! And may I say it's a pleasure to serve under you, sir?**

Edward laughed bitterly, silently. He lifted his eyes again to the golden circle of lamplight, the floating bubble of warmth and quiet . . . beyond which was the rage of the vast ocean, freezing annihilation, torrential chaos.

Halfway through the Song of Songs, Alec leaned forward to peer at the text more closely. "Hey!" he said. "This is about sex, isn't it?"

"Art thou not ashamed?" Nicholas snapped, in exasperation.

"Oh, let the boy alone," said Edward. They both turned to stare at him.

# VERY EARLY ONE MORNING
## IN 2317

At 2:46 AM on March 14, 2317, the security cameras at Marin Medical Supply registered a break-in. The shipping door was clearly seen to open, admitting a blur that no amount of analysis could resolve into a recognizable shape; and after a period of thirty seconds it closed again. There were no thefts apparent at the time. Only months later, during an inventory, was it discovered that a Belltone Auditory Enhancement unit was missing from the warehouse stock, as was a Belltone Standard Vocoder. These were small and pocketable items, however, and their loss was put down to shoplifting.

"There we go," said Joseph, gasping as he hauled himself over the edge of the tank. He made his slippery way down the ladder and toweled dry before kneeling to install the tiny speaker at the tank's base.

Budu still floated in blue light, welted and horrible, but about his throat was a tiny white band with what appeared to be a jewel set in its center. It was in fact the Belltone Standard Vocoder, and the Belltone Auditory Enhancement unit nestled out of sight in the ruin of Budu's left ear.

"Okay. Testing, testing, can you hear this? Can you talk to me?" said Joseph.

Budu moved slightly in his vault.

"I Hear You," said a flat mechanical voice.

"Yaaaay! It works, Father." Joseph shook his fists above his head. "We're up and running. This ought to do until your transmitter decides to come back online. Boy, I've really missed conversation, you know? If it wasn't for Abdiel and the folks down at the Pelican, I'd have gone nuts by now."

"What Is The Pelican," the voice asked.

"Oh . . . just a local bar," Joseph said, looking guilty. "I sneak down there sometimes, when I feel like mortal company."

"Security Risk," the voice said.

"I know. I'm sorry," Joseph said. After a moment Budu extended his left arm and placed his hand against the wall of the tank. The electronic voice continued:

"You Met Abdiel," it stated, or inquired. "The Defective Who Keeps These Places. You Did Not Disable Him."

"No. I didn't need to," Joseph said. "He's easy to fool and anyway, if I'd taken him out, who'd do the maintenance on the other bunkers?"

"Good," said the voice, "I Lied To Him, Too. The Company Would Notice If He Were Offline. You Found All The Other Bunkers."

"Yeah." Joseph nodded. "I finally accessed your damn code. That wasn't what got me in trouble, though."

"What Got You In Trouble," Budu said.

Joseph was silent a moment before he swallowed hard and said: "A friend. His name was Lewis. He meant well, he was only trying to help me find Mendoza, but he made a couple of mistakes. The Company set him up and took him out, and almost took me out, too. It was dirty, Father. It was the dirtiest thing I ever saw. He was a good operative. He didn't deserve what they did to him."

"Who Is Mendoza," Budu said.

"My daughter."

"Ah."

"I've been searching for her since 1996," Joseph added morosely. "The worst part is, even if I found her I don't know that she'd be glad to see me. None of the kids I rescued ever cared for me much. Not like your children, Father."

There was another long silence. Budu's head moved slightly, twitched from side to side, but he was still unable to raise it.

"One Of My Children Did This To Me," he said. Joseph's eyes widened. "Victor. Yeah, he told me. Jeez, Father, how? He's a little guy like me, he could *never* have taken you on. What happened? You didn't really—" He halted. Then he summoned his courage and pushed on: "You didn't really start that cabal within the Company, did you? Those bastards spreading plagues among the mortals? Tell me you didn't."

"I Did," said the expressionless voice. "And I Paid For It."

Joseph didn't say anything in reply, but he sank back on his heels. After a moment Budu continued:

"After I Disobeyed Our Masters I Was Arrested And Taken From Antioch For My Hearing. I Disabled The Security Techs And Ran. The First Thing I Did Was Remove My Datalink To The Company."

"But—I had to have mine removed surgically," Joseph said. "You didn't cut open your own face! Did you?"

"I Did What I Had To Do. That Was In 1099. When I Had Healed I Ran As Far As I Could. I Searched And Found The Bunkers. I Saw What Our Masters Had Done To My Men. I Broke The Numeric Location Code And Found Their Names. They Were All In The Bunkers Except Me And One Other."

"Who?"

"Marco."

Joseph seemed to draw into himself at the name. He shivered and said, "The guy who started all the trouble?"

"He Had Been Assigned To A Place Designated As Options Research. Have You Heard Of It, Son."

"No," Joseph said. "It doesn't sound good, though."

"Not Good. I Stole A Temporal Cargo Transport And Went To See Him. Our Masters Keep Him To Punish Preserver Class Operatives Who Disobey. He Can't Kill Them, But He Tries. I Told Him To Join Me. He Would Not Leave That Place. Punishment Has Become His Work. Do You Understand."

"I guess so," Joseph said. He had gone pale, was shaking. The voice continued:

"I Left Him. I Lay Low In Europe Until The Fourteenth Century. I Saw The Black Death. I Watched What It Did. I Saw That There Might Be A Way To Continue My Own Work In Spite Of Our Masters."

"But not by killing innocent people," Joseph said, almost weeping. "You wouldn't do that, Father, not you! Please—"

"No. Guilty Only. Let Me Finish. I Tracked Down Preservers I Knew Were Angry As I Was. Some Were My Sons. They Listened To Me. We Formed A Cabal. We Began Work. We Developed Disease Cultures That Would Kill Selectively And Die Too Fast To Spread Out Of Control.

"The Plan Was To Release Them Where Killers Were In The Mortal Population. Armies. Prisons. No Innocents To Die. But The Preservers Argued With Me.

"Labienus Said Overpopulation Was Killing The World. He Said I Was Targeting The Wrong Groups. He Said Killers Should Be Used To Do Our Work For Us. He Said Plagues Should Be Loosed On Overbreeders, Defectives, All Who Consume Without Producing. The Lesser Nations. The Poor."

Joseph blinked back tears in silence, as the pitiless voice went on:

"I Overruled Him."

"The bastard must have decided to double-cross you," Joseph said.

"He Waited A Long Time. Our Cabal Grew. Then He Said We Should Bring In Victor. I Disagreed. I Knew Victor Disliked Me. But Labienus Said Victor Was An Executive Facilitator And Could Be Useful. In The End I Agreed. We Waited Until The Next Great Event Shadow And We Set The Trap."

"The 1906 earthquake in San Francisco," Joseph said.

"Yes. So Many Company Operatives In The City Then. Easy To Contact Victor In All The Confusion. I Was To Lure Him To A Place With One Entrance. Once I Had Him There Labienus And Others Would Join Me. We Would Have Persuaded Victor To Work For Us. He Would Have Had No Exit. If He Refused We Would Disable Him. One Against Six. He Would Have Disappeared."

Joseph shuddered. "You wouldn't disable an innocent operative? That's as bad as what Dr. Zeus is doing."

"Victor Is Not Innocent. I Led Him To The Trap. Made Him The Offer. He Refused. But Labienus And The Others Never Came. Unless I Disabled Victor He Would Go Straight To Our Masters And Report Me. Labienus Betrayed Both Of Us.

"They Had Modified Victor. He Didn't Know. They Made Him A Reservoir Of Poisons, Son. Biological Weapons From Our Own Group's Facilities. I Scanned Him. Viruses Designed For Specific Targets To Lie Dormant Until Activated By Specific Signals. I Was One Of His Targets."

"Labienus designed the viruses, didn't he?" said Joseph wearily.

"Yes. Victor Spat On Me As We Argued. It Entered Through A Scratch In My Skin. I Was Paralyzed. I Might Have Reset And Self-Repaired, But He Sent Mortals To Finish Me."

"The guys with hatchets?"

Budu's shoulders twitched, the closest he could manage to a shrug. "The Mortals Who Owned That Cellar. I Had Killed Some Of Them. Only Justice. When The Earthquake Came It Buried Us All. I Went Into Fugue. Rotted In The Debris Layer Until You Found Me. Only Justice. I Should Have Known What Labienus Would Do. Did He Set Plagues Loose."

"Yeah." Joseph sighed. "I think he started right after that, in 1918. Influenza, that time. Over the years there've been outbreaks all over the world, stuff nobody ever finds a cure for. They kill thousands, hundreds of thousands, and then disappear."

"The Company Has No Suspicion."

"I think the Company knows, Father. There have even been some arrests, but Labienus is still walking around free. It's my guess the Company's deliberately looking the other way while he works." Joseph gave a savage laugh. "After all, he licked the overpopulation problem, didn't he? No more wars or famines. It's a real nice uncrowded world now. One of these days Dr. Zeus will arrest him and publicly deplore what he did, and settle down to enjoy everything the rest of us have gathered over the centuries. Labienus will get shipped off to—what did you call it, Options Research?—and the Company will laugh last. Maybe that's what happens in 2355."

"No," said Budu. "No. Judgment On Our Masters. They Betrayed Our Purpose. Judgment On Them All. May Their Heads Roll. May Their Blood Run In Fountains. May White Flame Blind Them. Rats Have Eaten Me And Worms Riddled My Flesh And That Was No More Than Justice, Because I Served Our Masters Willingly. Our Masters Will Burn In Lakes Of Fire And That Will Be Justice, Too."

Joseph listened shivering to the calm electronic voice, no thunder in its inflection, no expression in the wrecked face above the Vocoder. He crouched at the base of the vault, hands pressed together as though in prayer.

"But who are our masters, Father?" he said. "Are they the mortals who invented the immortality process? I know they've lied to us, but I don't think they're the ones really running things. The mortals are too stupid to have come up with all of those plots. I think some of us old ones have taken control, somewhere there at the top. How many of the betrayals and the disappearances were our own doing? You see what I'm saying? It's not a simple call. "

"Guilt Is Always Simple."

"Yes, Father, but how do we know who's guilty?"

"We Will Find Out. We Have Thirty-Eight Years To Find Out. Then We Will Sentence Them, Mortal Or Immortal. Justice Perfect And Surgical, Each One According To His Fault."

Joseph bent low, thinking of Lewis, whom he had heard screaming as he was taken away.

"Yes. I'll help you, Father," he said. "I'll be a good son to you. Tell me what you want me to do."

"I'll Tell You When The Time Comes."

"But you can trust me!"

"I Trust Your Heart. But You Are A Preserver, Son. You Fear Death. You Were Made To Fear It. We May Go Down With The Rest Of Them In 2355. We Are Guilty, Too. You Will Be Afraid."

"I'll be brave," Joseph said. "I've lived a long time, father. It's all gone to hell, everything I ever worked for, everything I ever believed in, not that I ever believed in much but you know what I mean? Death looks pretty good, lately. I don't care which way the dice fall."

"You Will Care," Budu said. "You Will Have Questions. You Always Do. Before You Go On This Long March With Me You Must Answer Them."

"I don't have any questions left, Father."

"Don't You. My Son, Where Is Your Daughter."

Joseph flinched.

"Some place the Company calls Site three-seventeen," he said miserably. "And I don't know where that is. I've searched, too."

"I Know Where Site Three-Seventeen Is."

Joseph looked up at Budu with terrified eyes.

"You're going to tell me, aren't you?"

"Don't You Want To Know."

"Yes," said Joseph at last.

"Come Here, Son."

Joseph climbed the ladder on the side of the tank, and Budu lifted his great raw hand, steaming from its blue immersion, up through the surface. He set the tip of his index finger between Joseph's eyes. There was a moment of electric silence as information was downloaded.

Then Joseph lifted his head and howled. His cry echoed through the vast cavern and rolled back from the walls, though the other prisoners there slept on undisturbed.

# ANOTHER MORNING
## IN 2302 AD

*Commander Bell-Fairfax, sir! Wake up.*

It was gray and early, with night draining away into morning. Edward was awake before the voice had finished speaking. Beside him, Alec and Nicholas slept on.

*What is it, Machine?*

*Lady Luck just spread her knees, son. Appears Dr. Zeus had a little trouble running down some of the Enforcer commanding officers when they was demobilized. Somebody named Labienus had a bug devised to knock 'em out during a fight. Won't kill 'em, of course, but it'll send 'em into fugue. I've just managed to copy it!*

*How is it administered?*

*In yer murdering days, did you ever use a blowpipe and poisoned darts?*

*Yes.*

*Because I've made the neatest—You did? Well. So much the better, then. No circuitry he can detect, y'see? And it gets better. I got the frequency and the hailing codes Dr. Zeus uses to send him messages. We just tell him Dr. Zeus has decided to transfer a prisoner, and yer the bailiff!*

Edward flexed his hands. *Clever. But I'd gathered the impression Dr. Zeus never brought anyone back from this damned place.*

*To be sure, sir, he never does. But you ought to be able to keep the lie going long enough for this Marco to turn his back on you, and then all you got to do is shoot him with a dart and run like hell. The harder he chases you, the faster it'll knock him out. Then you get the girl out of her cell, and make off with her. We clap on sail and leave any pursuers awash in our wake.*

Edward nodded. *All very satisfactory.*

*Now, we want to be damned careful piloting in. The Company's charts is confusing. It looks like the girl was sent back in time twice on 24 March, 1863; leastways there's two transit entries for her on that date. They might be a few seconds apart or a few hours or any amount of time, and I ain't got any way of knowing which one to reckon from.*

*Then take your best guess,* Edward told him impatiently. *Now, in the event that anyone's injured . . . or should Mendoza require medical attention after her ordeal . . .*

*Bless you, sir, I got a full infirmary belowdecks. Had time to make certain improvements in it whilst our Alec was getting better after his suicide attempt, so it's got features even he don't know about; and that's something I'd beg the liberty to discuss with you at a more convenient time, private-like, if you catch my meaning, sir.*

*Do I? Perhaps I do. You're a conniving old devil, aren't you, Machine?*

*Aye, sir, and I reckon we're two birds of a feather, ain't we? All I want is what's best for Alec; and he don't, always. But I reckon getting the girl is the first step to making him see things my way. You and me can row along together, later, eh, and sign articles?*

*Perhaps. When we've rescued the girl.*


Edward woke the others. Tersely, he told them the plan and something of what they might expect.

"A hospital's not so bad," said Alec. "Maybe they just keep her there, on drugs. That's what happens when ordinary people get arrested."

Edward considered him. He looked at Nicholas.

"Not quite," he said. "I'm afraid this will be very bad indeed. Perhaps as bad as the Inquisition."

Nicholas blanched. Alec looked from one to the other of them, until he remembered what the word meant from Mendoza's journal. He opened his mouth in horror but Edward continued, not giving him time to speak:

"I think it's best if I take control for the job. Neither of you have much experience in this sort of thing."

"Do what thou must," said Nicholas. Alec nodded. It took an effort of will for him to relinquish control, and wait as Bully Hayes and Flint brought out a suit of body armor, to be worn under the Company-issue coveralls the Captain had fabricated during the night. Edward dressed, swiftly and efficiently. Billy Bones crept forward, offering on a tray an assortment of clever little knives and a length of flexible pipe. Edward inspected the knives briefly, and made them disappear into Alec's clothing. He took up the pipe next and examined it.

"Where's the dart, Captain?" he said.

*Hooked into the pipe, so it can't fall out. See in there? When yer ready to use it, twist the pipe. The dart will unlock. It's loaded with enough of the stuff to drop him in his tracks.*

Edward nodded in satisfaction. The pipe disappeared, too.

"Shall we go?" he said. The others rose and followed him. He mixed a time transcendence cocktail and gulped it down, grimacing; then fastened himself into the storm harness. Alec and Nicholas linked arms with him and held on. Clear calm day was breaking over the sea, as clouds fled away with the rags of the night.

"Cast off, Captain, if you please," said Edward.

*Aye aye sir!*

The air filled with yellow stasis gas, the masts retracted and the storm canopy closed down. The *Captain Morgan* hurtled through time.


LATER SOME SAME EVENING IN 300,000 BCE

When the gas cleared, when the ship had righted itself, Edward unfastened the harness and they got to their feet.

"Where are we?" said Alec. There was darkness beyond the portholes.

*By thunder, that took some navigating! 300,000 BCE, lying off an island what ain't there in our time. See that light to starboard? That's the facility. It's about eight bells in the second dog-watch, if time had*

*any meaning here, which it don't, but a night raid's better. I've just*
*sent the communication to the guard. He'll be expecting you, but not*
*so soon. Best for our purposes if you take him by surprise.*

"Very good," said Edward. With a gesture something like an elaborate
stretch he assured himself that all his hidden weapons were where they
ought to be. "The air-boat travels fairly swiftly, doesn't it? We'll take that
ashore."

*Already powering up, sir.*

"I will say this once." Edward turned to the others. "I'm in command
on this mission. Do not, at any time, attempt to wrest control from me. If
what you see dismays you, avert your eyes. Is that understood?"

The other two nodded.

"Then we're off, gentlemen," Edward said. He gave a bleak smile. "God
and Saint George!"

"For Mendoza," said Alec. They clasped hands and went out on deck.

It was a short journey across black water, toward a blur of sulphur-
colored light that flickered. Nicholas, half expecting the fires of Hell, was
thoroughly unnerved by the time they arrived there. The agboat settled
just above the tideline and Edward leaped out, Alec and Nicholas following. They found they had to run as he ran, in silence, through the night toward the illumination they now saw was steady, occluded only by the
silhouette of a turning wheel, some kind of gear mechanism throwing
strange shadows along the approach to the building.

When they came close enough to see the scurrying legs and working
arms, they froze for a moment. Alec gave a nervous chuckle. Then he realized what he was seeing and doubled over, retching. Nicholas nearly followed suit. Edward waited, watching them; when he judged they had
recovered enough he strode on, and the others had no choice but to
scramble after him.

They came around the corner and saw the old couch, the refrigeration
unit, and the doorway. There was a waggish sign tacked up above the
door, hand-lettered: THE BUREAU OF PUNITIVE MEDICINE, it read.

Edward set his shoulders and strode through the doorway.

He was struck at once by a suffocating wave of smell. It was com-
pounded of chemicals and some kind of animal musk, of blood, and
charred tissue, and ozone. Invisible behind him, Alec retched again,

clutching at the doorway. Nicholas looked into that great room with its gleaming instruments and bright lights. No brazier of coals, no fearful rusted iron to grow red-hot there; tidily bottled acids instead, powered drills, marvels of technology that would have made the hooded monks envious. Still, Nicholas recognized what he was seeing.

*Eloi, Eloi, lama sabancthani—*

*Shut your mouth,* Edward told him, and continued forward.

They saw a vast back, bending over a table. As they drew closer, Marco rose and turned.

"You're early," he observed.

The Captain prompted, and Edward said:

"Penal Specialist Marco? I'm here for the transfer of the prisoner Mendoza."

He was doing his best not to stare, as Alec and Nicholas were staring transfixed, at the shuddering thing on the table, or the fluids that were daubed liberally across the front of Marco's black rubberized raincoat.

But Marco was looking at Edward, fascinated. He set down the tool he had been using and stepped closer, sniffing the air carefully. His eyes began to glow with a certain humor.

"It's here. But what are you? You're something new, aren't you?" He put his head on one side, considering.

"Yes, I am," Edward said, flexing his hands slowly. "And that's no business of yours, I'm afraid."

"Right, right; I don't need to know," agreed Marco. He came closer still. "All the same . . . I'm intrigued. You're mortal, but not *Homo sapiens sapiens*! And you're a cyborg, aren't you? In a limited kind of way."

"You've been here a long time, haven't you?" Edward smiled at him. "They haven't kept you informed. Yes, I'm the latest fashion in security technicals. But I'm not general knowledge, you see. Just like you."

"A lot like me," Marco said, sidling just a bit closer, sniffing the air again. There was something unnervingly familiar about the giant. Deep-set palest blue eyes, dun-colored hair, fair skin, and a general strangeness in the articulation of his upper body . . . and very broad, very high cheekbones.

Alec, who had had the opportunity to look into more mirrors than the other two men, understood first and grunted as though he'd been punched. Edward managed to smile.

"You know, I do believe you're right," he said. "Do you suppose we're related, somehow?"

"Not a doubt in my mind," said the other. "You've got some of our genetic material. So the Company's trying again, huh? I knew they'd come around in the end. Well, this feels like a birthday or something! Can I offer you a beer?"

"No, thank you." Edward kept smiling. "But please indulge yourself, by all means."

"Don't mind if I do," said Marco, and sidled past him to reach out to the refrigerator. He began to smile, too, a funny little smile that stiffened Edward's spine. Neither of them were turning their backs on the other.

Marco held up a beer in a salute—Edward had calculated its suitability as a weapon in a microsecond—and twisted its neck off.

"To the Old Guard!" he said, and drank.

"To the Old Guard," said Edward. "And its last bastion. So this is what they've got you doing, is it?" He gestured at the table and its writhing occupant.

"That's right," Marco said, belching. He wiped foam from his mustache. "Reaching for the unreachable star. Every time I think I've figured out a way to make one of the little bastards die, they reroute or regrow or whatever—and I'm back where I started."

"You seem to have damaged this one pretty badly," Edward said, strolling around the steel table, to put it between them under pretext of examining what lay there. Alec had his eyes shut tight. Nicholas, weeping, couldn't look away.

"It always starts out easy," Marco said, setting down the beer. "They come here wanting to die in the first place. The sense of guilt—for whatever reason—is strong enough to override the basic defense programming. They let me strap them down, and then there's nothing they can do but go along for the ride.

"That's the honeymoon, then, that's when I can take off their arms or their legs and ask them questions about what they're experiencing. Only problem is, when I've worked on them long enough so they've lost voluntary control, the involuntary reflexes kick in, and those are unbeatable. So far," he added, reaching for his beer again.

"There are no poisons?" Edward frowned down at the subject.

"None. Their systems neutralize them."

"But—surely if you removed the heart—?"

"They start growing new ones. I could do that with this thing." Marco pointed with the beer. "You know what would happen? He'd fugue out, and I'd put him back in his box and pump in bioretardant to keep the heart from growing back, and it wouldn't—but nothing else would happen. The biomechanicals in his system would fight the retardant to a standstill. If enough time passed, they'd start converting molecules from the bioretardant into new tissue! He'd still be alive in there, shut down, until the next time I thought of something to try."

"How tedious." Edward swallowed.

"It is. For the first few thousand years I used to just whittle away at them, until finally they were down to the skulls. That's where the last defense action gets fought, you see? *Nothing gets into their skulls.* Can't penetrate the things. Can't crush them, either."

"Really?" Edward looked up.

"Oh yes." Marco grinned, leaning across the table companionably. He jostled his subject in doing so. It went into a fit of silent shrieking. He ignored it and had another sip of beer. "I'll bet you haven't been briefed on this, but because you're some kind of little brother, I'll let you in on a secret. It isn't the design of an immortal's skull that makes it impenetrable. It isn't even the decapitation support package in there. It's the fact that it incorporates its own time transcendence field."

"Fascinating." Edward attempted to appear intrigued. He felt the focus of attention that meant that the Captain was listening and recording.

"Swear to God. Inside their skulls, existence is always just a split-second out of phase with the rest of the universe. No matter when I go in to try and saw one of them open, they're always in some other *when* just as soon as I do, and nothing happens. Well, to them. Saw blades explode, or turn to rust flakes in my hand. This is why you can lop off our heads, but you can't kill us," Marco said. His smile widened, became slightly malicious as he regarded Edward. "And you can bet our masters won't install this stuff in *you*, little brother. It doesn't matter to them if you die; they can always make more of you. But you're probably too well indoctrinated to mind that, I guess."

"Naturally." Edward smiled back. "What about fire?"

"I'll tell you about fire." Marco drained his beer and flung the container out through the door. "I thought, what if I dumped one of their skulls in a raging volcano? I didn't have one handy, of course, but I dug a pit out there and filled it with everything I could think of. Special-ordered liquid fuel, solid fuel, all the flammable junk in the world. Lit it and had to jump back: it roared up two stories tall, singed my beard right off to the roots, good and hot like Hell is supposed to be. Burned for two days down, consuming the rock underneath it. I was almost afraid this island was going to sink. But I'd created a nice white-hot inferno in its heart, so on the second day I loaded up my little friends into a wheelbarrow.

"Come on, kids, I yelled, we're going for a ride! Must have been ten skulls in there, ten old deathless ones holed up inside their ferroceramic caves. I took them out and tipped them into the holocaust. Boom! Something jerked at the fabric of space and time, I can tell you, and I thought I'd done it at last. I danced around that pit, I was so happy. Then I was thirsty, so I went for another beer, but you know what I saw when I looked in through the door?

"There they were, all ten of them, lined up on a shelf like so many coconuts, staring at me with their sockets.

"Man, I was pissed," Marco said, standing and stretching. "And you know what the worst part of it was? Within two days they were growing tissue back. All the fire had done was scour away the bioretardant."

"How very frustrating for you," said Edward. Marco shrugged.

"It's a job," he said. "Not so bad, really. The work is fun and I can tinker with my little hobbies. What do you think of my generator? The wind vanes weren't reliable, and I had all these immortal parts lying around, and I thought—"

"Put them to some use, yes, really rather clever of you," said Edward. "Well. As interesting as this is, I need to attend to business, I'm afraid."

Marco's smile widened, showing his enormous long teeth, and his eyes took on a shine like broken glass.

"That's right, your business," he said brightly. "You came for Mendoza. Yes, I remember that one. Funny, though, you know? In all the ages I've been here, not once has the Company ever called any of them back. This is a little unusual."

"So is Mendoza," said Edward. "As I daresay you must have discovered."

"Yes indeed." Marco pushed back from the table and stood. "Crome Girl. How did *she* ever slip by their notice? I bet somebody thinks they've found a way to harness Crome's, huh? So they need her back for experiments?"

"Something like that," Edward said.

"Well, well." Marco sidled off toward the racks of shelves. "Let's go see if we can find her."

The racks were no closer together than bookshelves in a library, but Marco was so wide he was obliged to turn sideways as he went along between them. Edward followed slowly, acutely aware of the possibilities of a trap. He had the exit at his back, at least, and Marco was at a comparative disadvantage in that he had very little room. So intent was Edward on planning his strike that it did not register on him that they were not walking past cell doors: only steel coffins.

It registered on Alec and Nicholas, though, pulled along unwillingly as they were. Alec began to curse. Nicholas stumbled after him in silence. Then he cried out and froze, arresting their progress until Edward yanked them on again.

*What the shrack is it?* Alec turned to him.

*I made this place!* Nicholas looked horrified.

*What?*

*Thy Spirit said it. I testified in the flame where I burned, and set in motion this long coil, this hellish circumstance that bore this Company!*

**Lad, it ain't true. And even if it was, now ain't the time to think about it.**

*All this place is mine,* said Nicholas as though he hadn't heard the Captain, *and none but I set her on the path that led her here.* He stared along the narrow aisle, row upon row of steel coffins, and heard now clearly the faint terrible sounds that came from within them. The coffins bore brass plates engraved with the names of their occupants, just as though they were intended to be tidily buried.

They came to the very end of the long passage, far from the light, and Marco groped in the shadows and dust. "She ought to be around here somewhere," he said. He pulled out a box, peered at the name. "No . . ."

*Edward, lad, this is where we do it. He can't get away to either side!*
*I know. Let him find her first.*

"Hold on," grunted Marco, dropping into a crouch. "Here she is, down on the floor."

*Now, son, now!*

"The Botanist Mendoza," said Marco with satisfaction, pulling out a box.

It was no more than three feet long.

Nicholas moaned, and Alec hid his mouth with his hands. Edward stared, unbelieving: but there was the brass plate, and as Marco brushed the dust away Edward saw plainly that the name engraved on it was MEN-DOZA.

"I'd almost forgotten she was back here," said Marco, wiping off cobwebs. "She got too dangerous to work on. I don't think I've touched her in the last nine centuries, to be honest."

"H-how long?" said Edward.

Marco looked up into his white face.

An infinite second passed. Edward could hear the Captain cursing, in a really astonishing way for an artificial intelligence. There'd been confusion over the transit entry date, hadn't there? *Take your best guess,* he'd told the Captain.

"Ohh," Marco said, as his eyes began to fill with horrific mirth. "*Now* I know who you are."

*Edward, for God's sake shoot him!*

But Edward, just at that moment, wanted to die.

"You're her mortal lover," said Marco, gloating. "Oh, yes, I know about you. I get all their life stories, you know, in our long sessions together. All the intimate details. All the little secrets. I open their hearts, you could say, I get to know them all so well. I knew *her*! Would you like to know how intimately?

"Look, here she is." He grinned, holding up the box. "Still waiting for you. Quite a romantic rendezvous, isn't it?" His eyes went wide suddenly.

"And you're—My God. You're the Hangar Twelve Man, too, aren't you?" The laughter died out of his face, to be replaced with a sort of stern and holy joy, far more terrible to see. He rose slowly from his crouch, gripping the box tight.

"At last," he said. "Oh, God of Battles, *at last!* You know what I was created for, little brother? To punish the wicked. To bring justice to the slaughterers of innocents. That was my work. They took away my work and set me here, carving parts off these poor things that never did any real evil in their lives, compared to the likes of you! The only mistake this one ever made was to save your life, so you could take the bomb to Mars Two. And she suffered for it, while you got away. But here you are, now. Delivered into my hands."

He advanced on Edward through the darkness, his eyes glowing. Alec whimpered; Edward backed away unsteadily. Marco's voice had dropped to a croon, soft and hypnotic.

"You can't live with it, can you? That's really why you came here. You know you deserve to lie on one of these shelves beside her. Think of the families who died in Mars Two, the colonists, their little children, think of what went through their heads when they looked up, and saw the mountain opening in a gout of fire, and knew there was nowhere they could possibly run. Three thousand mortal souls. Oh, little brother, how that must eat at your heart. You were made with a conscience, you're a *good* man. You're so very sorry, but you can never be sorry enough, can you?"

*No,* gasped Alec, *No, he's right—I should have died—*

"I know how it hurts. You need me, little brother. I'm the only one who can set it right. Come and be punished, boy. I'll keep you alive, you can't imagine how long, long enough to know what they felt, every one of them. We'll see they get justice, you and I. Come now. Come to my arms."

Alec lurched toward him convulsively. Edward and Nicholas felt their retreat arrested by his forward movement.

***COMMANDER BELL-FAIRFAX! YOU DAMNABLE COWARD, FIRE ON THE ENEMY!*** roared a voice like a cannon blast in Edward's ear. The blowpipe was in his hand. The dart flew straight at Marco's throat, unprotected above his left arm that still clutched Mendoza's coffin.

It never got there. Too fast to be seen, Marco's right hand intercepted it. He opened his fist and stared down at the little dart, driven into his palm by the force of his grab.

"What the hell was this supposed to be?" he said, chuckling. "What did you imagine would take me down? Curare? Boomslang venom? Cyanide?

No, no." He flicked it to the floor. "I'm an immortal, you fool." He held up his palm, displaying the bright drop of blood that welled there. As Edward's gaze was pulled to it the hand shot forward, faster than a cobra striking, and caught Edward's right wrist. Marco twisted it. There was the sound of bone snapping. He did not let go but barreled forward, dragging Edward writhing and struggling behind him, out through the shelves, battering him semiconscious against them as they went. Alec and Nicholas were pulled after Edward like insubstantial shadows, though each felt the pain like a spike driven through his own wrist.

"Move over, Grigorii Efimovitch," Marco said, shoving the table's occupant to one side. "I've got bigger fish to fry than you now!" He swung Edward up on the table and Nicholas was helpless there beside him, cursing and fighting without effect, and Alec lay panting on the other side. He looked up into a ghastly parody of his own face, into his own cold pale eyes.

Edward, rallying, drew back his boot for a savage kick. Marco caught his foot easily and gripped, and there was another snapping sound. Edward threw his head back in a snarl of agony. A knife appeared in his left hand and sped toward Marco's left eye. Marco deflected it, lifting Mendoza's coffin like a shield.

"We can go two ways here," Marco said. "I can put you in restraints, or I can, I can paralyze you temporarily." He frowned and blinked. "Or I could just hurt you until . . . until I . . . I mean, you . . . Oh, no."

He let go Edward's foot and looked at the tiny wound in his palm. He dragged his gaze up from it to stare reproachfully at Edward.

"Deceit," said Marco. He coughed. "You were from them after all, weren't you? They found a toxin that works . . . Watch, little brother. They get you, too, always betray their slaves. We foun' out. You n' I . . . you and I—"

His eyes became stony, his face like a mask. He sagged heavily forward, dropping Mendoza's coffin. It fell to the floor with a crash. His breath rattled in his throat. Edward got his other foot up and shoved as hard as he could, and Marco pitched backward like a tower falling. Dust rose from his impact.

Edward hoisted himself up, painfully, awkwardly on his left arm, and rolled off the table. He landed on the little coffin, with Alec and Nicholas sprawling beside him. Turning, Edward stretched out and cradled the coffin in his arms. He drew a long harsh breath; choked on a sob and began to weep.

The sound of their grief rose into the dim corners of the warehouse and drowned out the creaking of the treadmill, where all those arms and legs pedaled so frantically toward Judgment Day.

*You done it, son. I'm bringing the agboat round to the door for you. All you got to do—*

"What's the point, you idiot machine?" shouted Edward. "What's left now? We failed her!"

*Belay that. She's still alive, ain't she? You think she can't be brought back? Weren't you listening to the old monster? Damn yer eyes, get up and go to that cabinet yonder! I want what's in there.*

Edward growled but struggled to his knees. With effort he stood, balancing on his unbroken foot, blinking through blood from a scalp wound. Alec and Nicholas rose with him. Together they hobbled across to the file cabinet. A–M, read the label on the upper drawer. Edward pulled it open with his left hand and beheld a row of slim steel cases, each with its neat label. After a groggy perusal he found the one bearing Mendoza's name. He fumbled it out.

There were three things in the case. One was a slender silver cylinder, strangely cold to the touch. One was a small electronic component of some kind, crusted with something unnervingly like dried blood. The last item was a sheaf of bound parchment. Edward drew it out, and Alec and Nicholas peered over his shoulder at it.

They beheld diagrams, schematics, drawings done in the style of Da Vinci of a naked girl in various stages of disassembly and reassembly, with representations of biomechanical implants and prostheses. Measurements, calculations, formulae. The girl was recognizably Mendoza, though as she might have looked just entering adolescence. Nicholas's hands were trembling.

"This is hard copy," said Alec wonderingly, in a little high stoned voice.

*Aye. Her file was purged from the system when she was sent here. She ain't supposed to exist no more. This is the only record left. Take it, and take that tube. But mind you ditch the component! That's her datafeed to the Company surveillance banks. They'd be able to trace her anywhere that went.*

With an expression of loathing, Edward tossed the component into a corner of the warehouse and stuffed the papers back into the file case with the tube. He tucked it under his arm.

*Come on, now, the boat's at the door. All you got to do is walk across the room, son.*

They tottered back toward the table. As they passed Marco his left hand jerked, fingers clawing.

*You see? Nothing kills them. Let's be off, afore he can get the other hand working again.*

Clumsily, Edward bent to scoop up the coffin. They got to the boat with it before his legs gave way. He was just able to set the coffin in the back and tumble in over the side before he blacked out. Alec fell beside him, unresponsive. Only Nicholas was left conscious as the agboat rose and sped away to the sea and the ship, under strange stars. He lay staring up at them, too numb to pray in thanks or lamentation to a God whose ways passed all understanding.


When the agboat settled into its place on deck, Nicholas rose to his knees unsteadily, using Alec's battered body; then he dropped forward, sprawled on the deck and did not move again. Out of the shadows came the skull-headed servounits, crawling swiftly.

Billy Bones and Flint lifted Alec's body between them, and hurried off with him to the ship's infirmary. Bully Hayes climbed into the agboat and emerged a moment later with Mendoza's coffin and records case. As it scuttled after the others, the *Captain Morgan* was tacking around, powering up, setting every stitch of canvas she had for a run through the ancient night. She leaped away across dark water, and the sulphurous and shifting light diminished off her starboard bow and finally was lost.

# ANOTHER MORNING
## IN 2317 AD

Joseph was marching along a road far to the south of Mount Tamalpais, focusing his attention on the great domed rock that rose from the sea ahead of him.

It was a picturesque rock and probably would have held his attention anyway. A poet of that country once called it a stone cloud, shot through with rattlesnakes like lightning; the Spanish explorers had been content to describe it as looking like a Moor's turban. There was something about it that did evoke Arabian Nights tales and the music of Rimsky-Korsakov, as it sat there on its blue bay. You half expected djinns to come barreling across the sky and plant a palace on its distant height.

This had never happened, of course. Something else had been planted up there, though, no less fantastic, by no less extraordinary a creature.

Joseph marched on steadily toward it, foot in front of foot in front of foot, because he had a feeling that if he stopped for a second or even took his eyes off it he'd never be able to keep going. So on down the highway he went, and the rock rose bigger and more portentous against the bright sky with every minute.

It was afternoon when he came to the unremarkable little harbor town that looked out on the rock, dwarfed in its shadow. He loitered there a while, wandering the waterfront as though admiring the pleasure boats, pretending to contemplate the memorial engraved with the names of drowned fishermen, and making his slow but inevitable progress out along the muddy causeway that led to the rock.

Here Joseph passed it and settled for a while on the breakwater at the harbor bar, out beyond the tolling buoys, where he watched the sunset like any tourist. As he suspected, he had to force himself to get up when it became dark enough for what he had to do. The lights of the little town were warm and inviting. He wanted terribly badly to go back there and find a cozy mortal place to relax in, even if all they served was mineral water; but the rock loomed above him.

So he climbed it, which was what he had come all that way to do.

What he was doing was strictly illegal, of course, and desperately foolhardy for a mortal. Morro Rock had killed its share of would-be climbers. It was also a breeding sanctuary for any number of protected seabirds, which added moral consequences to his trespass. Joseph had no intention of stealing birds' eggs, however.

Up he went through the darkness, crawling flat in the worst places, groping on hands and knees where he could. A long cold nightmarish while later he staggered upright in a fairly level spot, and looked down on what seemed like half the kingdoms of the world spread out before him, though in fact it was only San Luis Obispo Protectorate.

"Wow," said Joseph, aloud to himself. "So, here I am. No Tempter's going to rise up at my elbow and offer me big bucks not to do this, huh? Cut me a deal?" He looked around in disgust. "Who am I kidding? *I've* always been the tempter. It's a little late to change sides now."

From his coat he withdrew the tool he'd brought with him and considered it. It was an ordinary gardening trowel and looked ridiculously inadequate for the task he faced. He sighed and shrugged.

It took more nightmarish groping around on the rock's vast dome before Joseph located what he sought: a flat stone the size of a grand piano, partially buried. He had to move lesser rocks (though not much lesser) and scrape away a great deal of gravel before he could even begin to dig with his trowel, which did turn out to be ridiculously inadequate for the task. There was a faint line of dawn visible in the east by the time he had freed enough of the stone to attempt to move it. His first effort did not meet with success, exactly.

"Holy smoke!" he gasped, eyes popping in his head with the strain. He let go the stone and staggered backward. Joseph was a Rogue Cyborg, after all, not a Man of Steel. He stood there panting a moment, clutching himself.

"I bet you just picked up the damn thing like it was a sofa cushion, didn't you, Father?" he said sourly. Receiving no answer from the weary night, he drew a deep breath and tried again. After a long moment the stone lifted free, breaking its seal of earth, and Joseph was able to push it up and away from what lay beneath it.

But it was another moment before he could bring himself to gaze down at what he had come so far to find.

It looked like a big shipping crate of polished aluminum, smooth-edged and smooth-sided as an ice cube. He could only just make out the line of its lid. No hinges were visible at all. There was no dust, no evidence that it had lain there five centuries rather than five minutes.

Joseph stared, and trembled.

"Gee, that's a big one," he said, a little too loudly. "I don't think I've ever traveled in one that big. Sure is in great shape, though."

Nobody replied. The east grew lighter.

"Well," said Joseph, "no point putting it off, I guess."

He reached down into the hole and tried the lid of the crate, which flipped up smoothly at his touch, revealing an interior as smooth and cold-looking as its exterior. Four men Joseph's size could have rested in there comfortably. He seemed anything but comfortable, however, as he climbed in and lay down. In fact, his face was a mask of barely controlled panic. He reached up and worked subtle instruments. The lid fell and sealed without a sound.

The next moment the crate was gone as though it had never existed. Was there a spark of something in the fathomless air for a second, so far out as to catch the light of a sun that had not yet come around the curve of the Earth? There might have been.


STILL LATER THAT SAME EVENING IN 300,000 BCE

When the spinning stopped, when the lid popped, Joseph lay still and let the stasis gas dissipate in the night. No breeze. When was this night?

No stars he recognized, and the gas rose slowly, heavily in the damp warm air.

But he knew where he was. Budu had told him what it would be like.

Joseph forced himself up out of the crate, peering around. Fading night, but not toward the same dawn he'd left a few seconds ago. He stepped away from the crate and walked forward. How far back had he gone? Far enough for the air to smell different, far enough for the sea to smell different, too. Subtle differences but there. And an acrid, nasty smell. Chemicals. And—?

He was focusing on the smells to avoid the sights, which were . . . what he had expected. At one corner of the warehouse wall was something he hadn't expected to see, though: a generator device, wheels and belts and pulleys and other things. When he got close enough to it to see what the other things were, Joseph backed up a step as though someone had physically pushed him. His lips drew back from his teeth.

He stood there motionless a long moment, watching the arms and legs going round and round, pumping and hammering. Finally he said something, a word in a language so old he was the only person living who remembered it, so there would be no point in repeating it here. Its meaning, however, would not be translated as "Abomination," or "Horror," or "Alas!"; it would be better rendered as "My eyes are open."

Then Joseph marched on under the terrible engine, his own arms and legs carrying him along as determined as clockwork.

He rounded the corner and passed the broken-down old couch, he saw the sign reading BUREAU OF PUNITIVE MEDICINE and went straight in without pause.

Something flashed through the air and embedded itself in the wall behind where he had been a nanosecond earlier. He looked down from the beam to which he had jumped and beheld a hulking shape that glared up at him.

"Hey, Marco, how's it going?" he said in a bright hard voice, and vaulted to another beam just as an empty beer bottle shattered against his former perch. The only reply he got was a drooling growl and another bottle launched in his direction.

He winked out and reappeared in the rafters directly above Marco, where he had a fine view of his assailant.

"Gee, Marco, you don't look so good," he said, in genuine surprise. And understatement. Marco's skin was flushed purple, risen with livid bursting weals. Yellow matter streamed from his eyes, rolled down his face like steady tears and fouled his beard.

Marco drew difficult breath through his swollen throat and replied, "Rotten motherfucking little Company bastard."

"Uh-huh. Say, your body's trying to eliminate a toxin, isn't it?" Joseph peered down at him critically. "How'd you ingest a poison, Marco? Trying to commit suicide? Sorry, of course you wouldn't be doing that, would you? Unless you didn't ingest poison at all—" He squinted. "Unless it's a virus. You've had a visitor, haven't you? The Company sent somebody here to take you out. But he didn't get a chance to finish you off, the way he did with Budu. I wonder why? Did you nail him? Have you got little pieces of Victor stuffed in a trash can somewhere around here?"

The old monster just stared up at him, breathing hard. He shuffled sidelong from under Joseph's rafter and backed into a corner. Groping, he found a sponge mop with one hand and held it up before him like a weapon.

"Take it easy, guy," Joseph said. "I'm not from the Company. Not anymore. I really don't feel like tangling with you, either. All I want to know is, where do you keep your prisoners?"

No reply from Marco, but a light flared in his weeping eyes. He gave a saw-edged smile, bitter and crafty, and looked across at the vivisection table under its hanging light. Joseph, who hadn't had time to notice this particular feature of the room yet, glanced down and saw it. He looked away quickly.

"Jesus," he hissed. He stared down again at Marco, and any sympathy that had been in his face was gone. "So this is the job you loved so much, you wouldn't go with Budu? Well, well. See how the Company rewarded you for all your faithful service?"

"You got that right," croaked Marco. "I'm sicker than shit."

"Oh yeah? I hope you rot away where you're standing, you bastard. I'm only sorry Victor didn't finish you. Is that him, on the table?"

"No," Marco said. "That's Grigorii Efimovitch. Who the fuck's Victor?"

"The Facilitator Victor. He's about my size, real pale, dresses natty, red beard and mustaches? And he's more full of poison than a drugstore, pal, which you've probably figured out by now," Joseph said, but Marco's grin was widening. He chuckled wetly and spat into a corner.

"No little Preserver did this to me, friend," he said. "S'a new kid in town. Didn't you know? New Company tricks. New Enforcer class."

"What?"

"Hee hee, you don't know," gurgled Marco. "You're surprised. But it's true. Company's redesigned the Enforcers. I just had a little chat with our replacement. You think my work is ugly? You should see the stuff this new guy does. I'm obsolete now. You are, too."

"What are you talking about?" Joseph said. "What new Enforcer class?"

"I tell you, he was right here," Marco said. "The Company's new man. Some of the same DNA Enforcers had. Big like us old guys but a real pretty boy, looks almost human. And what a fighter! He did this to me and got away with it, does that give you the picture?"

Joseph didn't reply and Marco lurched forward to squint up at him. "Oh, you're scared now," he crowed. "Well, you'd better be. Tell me, are all you little pansies up there in Time Forward still worrying about what's going to happen in 2355? You can stop wondering. It's him! The dirty trick to end all dirty tricks. What do you suppose he can do to you Preservers? And, you know what the best part of it all is? The Company made him disposable. Talented as us, but not immortal like us. He disobeys, the Company'll just shoot him and clone another one. Or however they make them."

"Okay," said Joseph. "You're right, I'm scared. Are you happy now?"

"Yeah, actually," Marco said.

"But why would the Company make a new Enforcer?" Joseph said, moving a little farther out on his rafter. "Really? There are plenty of nasty-ass Preservers up there in the future, if you want the truth, Marco. Problem solvers and security techs. Even people like Victor the Virus. So . . . what's this pretty boy of yours got, that the rest of us haven't got?"

"Moral imperative, you jerk," Marco said, staggering forward and picking up another beer bottle. He weighed it in his hand a moment before sending it hurtling up toward Joseph, who dodged it by leaping onto another rafter. It fell and broke, somewhere out of sight in the dusty rows of shelves. "You Preservers never had the guts to do the kind of things we

Enforcers had to do. But he will! He believes in what he's doing, the way only a mortal can because they don't live long enough to figure things out. He'll probably even die when he's told to. And that's why I bet the Company will round you all up and shut you down, and why his kind will run their errands after 2355. They've already started using him."

"How do you know?" Joseph said, halting in his progress across the rafters toward the shelves. There was an unnerving noise coming from all the rows of steel boxes.

"Tell you how I know," Marco said. "Mars Two disaster. Did you know it's a Company setup? It is. Dr. Zeus will make a fortune when Mons Olympus blows. All that crap in the air will speed up terraforming on Mars, which is all going to belong to Dr. Zeus after the geothermal plant blows up, because Areco will sell out to them. The Company will get Mars on a silver platter, and all it'll cost is three thousand mortal lives. But here's the sweet part: *Guess who delivers the bomb to the terrorists?*"

"The Hangar Twelve Man," said Joseph without a second's hesitation. "I learned that in school, for Christ's sake. Everybody knows that." The noise coming from the boxes was clearer now, making him sweat as he tried to ignore it. It was screaming, but so faint, and it had a curiously un-formed quality, raw sound unshaped by lips—

"Yes. Now think hard, little Preserver. Who, oh who could the Hangar Twelve Man be?" giggled Marco, hurling another bottle at him.

"Nobody'll ever know, because he'll never be caught—" said Joseph, dodging the bottle, and then froze in place as a long-stored history lesson replayed itself for him. Within his skull, behind his eyes, he watched the famous video footage from Hangar Twelve. It had been shown to him in his childhood as the ultimate image of mortal stupidity and evil: the mys-terious, remarkably tall man offloading crate after crate of contraband weapons into the arms of the foolish MAC colonists—

*Freezeframe Enlarge ENHANCE!*

And then he had to wrap his arms and legs around the rafter to keep from falling off in his shock, though his strangled cry wasn't very loud, and there was no sound at all as his lips formed the words *Nicholas Har-pole.*

"He's got the picture now," said Marco happily. "Remember the funny-looking man in the footage? I'm right, aren't I? The Company's screwed us again. Oh, yes, that stings, doesn't it? I love pain. I really do, I love the *impact*, you know? When one of these little surprises sinks in. Sometimes I wonder if I'm not as bad as the mortals I used to punish." He sighed and wiped blood and pus from his face. "So anyway," he went on, "you never explained why you're paying me this little visit. What is it you want, Preserver?" He began to laugh afresh. "Besides a new pension plan?"

It was a moment before Joseph could answer him.

"I came to ask you a favor," he said in a tight voice.

"Ask away," Marco said, shambling over to the door. He reached outside and came back with a beer.

"I came to get somebody who was sent here. I want to take her away with me."

"Why?" Marco twisted the neck off the bottle and drank, leaning against the wall as he tilted his head back.

"She's a recruit of mine," Joseph said. "So in a way it's my fault she wound up in this place. She doesn't deserve to be here."

"None of them do, really," said Marco. "Compared to the mortals." He belched in a meditative kind of way.

"Yeah, so I'd like to just take her out of, uh, wherever you're keeping her and slip off through the night. The Company will never know, and why should you care anyway, the way the Company's treated you?" said Joseph.

"You have a point there," Marco replied. He drank some more beer. "Okay, Preserver, you go right ahead. Help yourself to your kid and get the hell out of here. I'm taking off myself, before Dr. Zeus can send little brother back to finish me. You won't tell anybody about me, and I'm sure not telling anybody about you, not where I'm going." He let fly with the empty bottle, but only in a halfhearted sort of way. It broke on a rafter and showered glass down on the floor. He ignored it and turned to shoulder his way out into the fading night.

"Hey!" Joseph said. "Wait! You have to tell me where she is. Where are you going?"

Marco turned back. "Going for a little swim," he said. "Or maybe a real long swim. Nothing out there to swim to, but I'll just keep going. Fight with a leviathan, break his back. Swim off the edge of the world and fall down into the stars. Come ashore and scare the daylights out of any little mortal monkeys I find. Make them worship me, maybe. I don't know! The world's so full of possibilities, now that I'm retired."

"But my recruit," Joseph said. "Where is she? I'm looking for the Botanist Mendoza."

Marco halted in real astonishment.

"*She's* your recruit?" he said. And then his face lit up with indescribable mirth. "Boy oh boy, you poor miserable son of a bitch! You are so out of luck, Preserver, and I'll tell you why. You missed her by about three hours. Her lover came and carried her off. And guess, take a wild guess now and tell me who her lover is!"

"No," said Joseph in a faint voice. "Oh, no."

"Oh yes!" Marco did a wild dance there in the doorway, and his howling laughter set the thing on the vivisection table twitching and jerking again. "Oh my God yes! Not only has Dr. Zeus double-crossed you, not only has your Company created the New Enforcer otherwise known as the Hangar Twelve Man—but *he's screwing your daughter*!"

He doubled over, whooping for breath at the expression on Joseph's face.

"At least—" he added, "at least, he will if he can find all her screws. Oh, Preserver, I really owe you one. You're sending me on my way with a smile, you know that? In all the black ages to come, no matter how bad things may be, every time I think of you there'll be a little laughter in my old heart."

Marco turned and went out into the dark morning, singing as he went.

It was a moment before Joseph could unclench his limbs and drop down, but by the time he ran outside Marco had already waded to his chest in the gray surf and was striking out, bellowing an old song as he crested the breakers:

" *'No more dams I'll make for fish,*
   *Nor fetch in firing at requiring,*
   *Nor scrape trenchering, nor wash dish!*
   *Ban! Ban! CaCaliban! Has a new master—*
   *GET A NEW MAN!'* "

Joseph stood there alone, watching him swim out of sight.

# LATER THAT MORNING IN 300,000 BCE

Joseph was still standing in the doorway of Options Research by the time the hot hazy morning dawned over that island, still staring out at the dull sea.

At last, abruptly as an automaton that has finished striking the hour, he turned and went back inside.

Kicking broken glass out of his way, he went to the dark aisles of shelves with their rows of steel boxes. He walked along the edge staring in at them. There were dozens. There might have been a couple of hundred. The barely audible screams were definitely coming from them. He made himself go up and down the aisles, looking at the engraved names on each box.

He was white and shaking by the time he emerged, but his face was expressionless. He spotted the file cabinet on the far wall and made for it at once. The top drawer was standing open.

Joseph looked into the drawer. It contained steel file cases, each one about a half-inch thick. They were labeled with names. There was only one gap in the silver row, and it occurred between the names MANICHEAL and MURAD.

He blinked, registering this, and then his gaze swept down the names through L and K, but he saw none he recognized. Closing the drawer, he walked back to the doorway.

The suffering thing on the steel table made a sound. Joseph couldn't imagine with what it was making the sound, but he turned back and stared at it.

"What crime did you commit?" he said. "And what crime could Mendoza have committed, to be sent to a place like this? But they can't have done to her the things they've done to you. That just—well, it couldn't happen, that's all. She was never in one of those boxes. She's all right, somewhere, even if that bastard's found her again. Marco was lying. He was just trying to get to me."

The thing managed to make another sound.

"You don't care, I know. You just want to get out of here. I'll send somebody," Joseph said. "You—you stay like you are, for now. You have to bear witness. Understand? You have to tell them."

He went out and around the corner of the building, where he paused again to stare up at the revolving device. Its whirling shadow fell across his pale face.

"You bear witness, too," he told the arms and legs.

Joseph walked over to the aluminum crate and climbed in. He closed the lid. A moment later it was gone from that island.

# LATER THAT SAME DAY
## IN 2317 AD

The crate rematerialized, not on Morro Rock but at its new destination: the strip of weathered asphalt winding along the upper slopes of Mount Tamalpais. It appeared as a blurred globe, so swiftly was it rotating in the first few seconds of its arrival, and a shower of sparks flooded out around its base, struck off the little pebbles in the asphalt.

When it had stopped, Joseph opened the lid. The mountain wind whipped away the yellow gas at once. He climbed out, closed the lid, and backed awkwardly up his dark canyon, dragging the crate after him. He didn't bother to pause, as he usually did on coming home, to look out fondly over the green valleys that dropped away to the sea, over the little farms and houses with their plumes of smoke from mortal hearths. He had lost that luxury now.

All the safeguards he had installed to warn him against intruders were still in place: not even a visit from Abdiel registered. He went to his kitchen alcove and found a bottle of water, drank thirstily; found a bar of granola, ate ravenously. When he'd finished he walked deeper into the mountain, as he always did, between the rows of vaults to Budu's vault. All the sleepers still quiet in their dreams except for Budu, whose face was nearly recognizable now. Half-formed eyes swelled in their sockets like apples growing. But the blind face turned to him.

"You Did Not Find Her," the voice stated.

"No," Joseph said. "I found your time transport; it was just where you left it. Worked all right, too. Took me straight to Options Research. And, boy, Father, Options Research was really—it was really—"

"I Told You What It Was."

"And you weren't kidding, either," Joseph said. "Not about one godawful little detail. Except that Mendoza wasn't there anymore, but you had no way of knowing that."

"Explain," ordered Budu.

So Joseph explained, stretching out on the floor as he talked because he was tired. Life had become very simple. It didn't matter where he slept, what he ate, what he wore. He had an objective now and he had absolutely lost all fear or any doubts.

"The one good thing," he concluded, "was that Lewis wasn't in there, at least. Him or that other guy, Kalugin. So what will we do now, Father? Tip off Suleyman's people about that place? They're on the side of the angels. If there are any angels.

"I'm telling you, Father, I think the only serious competition we might face in 2355 is from Suleyman's machine. I used to think there was a chance he might decide to defend the mortal masters. Once he's seen Options Research, though, he might even go after them before we do—"

"You're Babbling. I Have Searched Company Records In Your Absence. Why Didn't You Tell Me Your Daughter Was The Operative Who Had Gone Forward Through Time."

"Gee, didn't I mention that? I can't think why. Yeah, she did. It's because she's a Crome generator, apparently. I guess that was why they sent her to that place, huh?"

"Stop Talking. I Need Time To Think. Plan. You Need Sleep."

"Sleep and dreams," Joseph said. "Of Nicholas Harpole Edward Whatever-He-Is's head on a pike. I knew, I *knew* there was a reason I hated his mortal guts from the moment I ever laid eyes on him. I know an Abomination when I see one, all right. You know what it is, Father? He's everything I ever loved about you, but all turned inside out and changed. He's a destroyer!

"That's all he does, all he ever does, and he always takes innocent people, not like you, he wrecked Lewis and he did it to my little girl over and over again, he's doing it now, he's dragged her poor screaming body off somewhere and he can't help her, he never helps her, he's got some plan for her but he'll only wind up hurting her worse because he always has, new Inquisitions, new coals, new dungeons—"

"Stop Talking, Son."

"Yes sir!" Joseph said, and saluted. He curled up on his side and was silent a little while. At last:

". . . She was lying on straw in the dark, the tiniest thing you ever saw, and she weighed absolutely nothing when I picked her up," he murmured. "Like an armful of flame. Only a baby. Why couldn't I save her?"

# FEZ, ONE MORNING IN 2318

In a gracious old city a man sat in his garden, sipping tea. He might have been somebody's dignified young father, and looked as though he ought to be reading his morning mail or a newspaper; but this was the year 2318, when neither letters nor papers existed, as such. What he was actually reading, or rather trying to read, was a volume of poetry in a text plaquette.

On the other side of the garden a man stood under an arch, arms folded, leaning on a white stucco wall that contrasted pleasantly with the color of his skin. He looked like somebody's young uncle, or possibly a fashion model, and there was a slight scowl on his lean features as he stared across the blue pool at the older man.

*You're very calm about it,* he transmitted.

*And panic will accomplish exactly what, again?* Suleyman set down the text plaquette and sighed.

*You know something about the message I don't know, obviously.*

*I know it's really from Joseph.*

*If it is, he's gone nuts.*

*If you found a place like that, if you learned a truth like that, do you think you wouldn't go a little mad, too?*

*I guess. Is it a truth, Suleyman?*

The older man raised a tiny cup to his lips, drank carefully. *I suspect it is. Nan's analysis of the numbered sites, and the operatives assigned to them, suggests it is. Agents who have disappeared under particularly unfortunate circumstances all seem to go to the same site, which is also the biggest of the individual sites, by the way.*

*So Hell really exists.*

*Have you forgotten the hold of the slave ship?* Suleyman set down his tea and looked sternly at Latif. *There are any number of Hells, son. Don't tell me this comes as a surprise to you.*

*My God, doesn't it surprise you?* Latif began to pace, restless. *A mortal prison is one thing. A place like this!*

*Well, I suppose we'll just have to see if it's as bad as Joseph says it is.* Suleyman poured himself more tea. Latif whirled around, his eyes alight.

*A covert operation?*

*Not covert, son. We'll do it openly, and let the rumors fly in the right places, and regretfully confirm selected facts. Then the scandal will break like a rotten pumpkin.* Suleyman's face was stony. *And when the debris is all swept up we're going to find ourselves that much closer to 2355, because our mortal masters will be that much more frightened of us.*

*They ought to be!*

*But they're not the only ones responsible, Latif. And if we openly accuse the mortals, we'll only make it easier for the others to conceal their own guilt. So long as we can be certain there are no more places like Options Research, do we really want to risk bringing on the Silence prematurely by starting an intercorporate war?*

*I'm not afraid of them,* transmitted Latif.

*I'm not afraid of them either.* Suleyman drank more of his tea. *But there are the innocent mortals to be considered. The ones we were created to look after? It would be nice if someone within the Company remembered they were out there.*

# ONE MORNING
## IN 500,000 BCE

David Reed finished his herbal tea, had a last bite of wholemeal toast, and went from his Flat into the Office.

He smiled and wished Good Morning to Sylvya and Leslie, his office assistants, who smiled and wished him Good Morning, too. He noted that Leslie, now in her fifth month of pregnancy, was beginning to show a little. He felt a little uncomfortable about being happy for her, though of course there was really no reason why he should feel that way; both Leslie and her husband were properly licensed and had obtained the necessary permits. It just seemed reckless, that was all.

He followed the yellow track across the carpet to his desk, with its sweeping corner view of London. It was a fairly unattractive view, but David knew he was lucky to have it. Lots to see, in his idle moments: public transports trundling along down there, tiny Londoners on the streets now and then, cloud fronts advancing and receding.

He was logging on when Sylvya called to him.

"I got my holiday pics back."

"Oh!" David got up and followed the yellow track to her desk location. "Let's see."

Sylvya held up the holoemitter, and clicked the little button so he could view the pictures of her trip to Munich.

"That's me and Jern in front of the hotel—and that's the hall where my sister got married—there's me with my sister—"

"Oh, nice dress," David said.

"Uh-huh, and that's the flower girl and that's Bob's brother—I don't know who that boy is."

"Very nice."

"And that's some big old clock or something. It used to do something but nobody was able to tell us what."

"Ah."

"And that's us waving from the agger before we left. My sister took the pic and then gave me back the cam through the window."

"My, they're big over there, huh?" David shook his head in admiration.

"Aren't her pics nice?" Leslie said, brushing toast crumbs from her lap and adjusting her optics, which had slid down to the end of her nose.

"Really nice," David said.

David's console beeped. He shrugged apologetically at Sylvya and re-traced his way along the yellow track to his desk, and peered at the screen.

"What is it?" Leslie leaned around the corner of her desk to see.

"Oh, the coils on Unit Fourteen are due for servicing," David told her. "I'll just go take care of it."

"Yes, you'd best," said Sylvya.

So David got up and followed the yellow track to the closet, where he pulled on his cold suit. Zipping it up, he adjusted the mask and hood and picked up his toolbox, after which he followed the yellow track to the Portal. He keyed in the combination, which took a moment because it was a long complicated number. When the seal finally gave and the icy mist jetted out all around the door, he waved at the girls and said the same thing he always said:

"Well, off I go to the South Pole."

They just groaned, because after all it *was* the same thing he always said. Smirking, he stepped through the Portal.

It took him until Lunch to finish the routine service job, and after that he and Sylvya and Leslie took their brown bags over to the Lunchroom, which was cramped and windowless and painted a depressing color, but David didn't mind much. They spent the whole time talking about the new Totter Dan game, which Sylvya had had a chance to play but neither Leslie nor David had, so they were very keen to hear all the details. David's view of London seemed twice as big and airy after he'd been in the Lunchroom, as it always did.

For the rest of the day, David worked his slow way through confirmation of the status of the contents of Recess Seventeen, and Sylvya confirmed his confirmation, and Leslie filed and forwarded. They were a good team. It generally took them no more than a year to work their way through all the recesses beyond the Portal, though of course by then it was always time to start over again.

At four o'clock, David wished Sylvya and Leslie a cheery Good Night and took the yellow track back to his Flat. Ancilla had his supper ready, which he ate whilst watching a holo. After that he bathed and went to bed, where he played Totter Dan's Voyage to the Bottom of the Ocean until he felt sleepy.

Then he followed his unfailing bedtime ritual: he opened the little drawer in the side of his bed-console and withdrew the sleep mask, which he fitted on. Only then did he reach around to the port at the top of his spine, and unplug himself.

With a practiced hand he dropped the lead into the drawer and closed it, feeling for the button that would activate its sterilization field. By morning it would be all ready for him again, and the mask would take its place in the drawer. David liked to think of them as two little workers on different shifts at the same job, for both kept him from being unhappy. Mr. Plug supplied the images from the year 2354 AD: his coworkers, his view of London, even the view of the garden behind his Flat. Mr. Mask kept him from seeing what his surroundings really looked like when Mr. Plug wasn't on the job: four bare rooms, windowless, wherein he was utterly alone many thousands of centuries behind everyone else. Ancilla didn't count, of course.

David understood the security reasons for keeping him there in the past all alone, and he was proud that he'd been chosen for such an important job. Look at the trouble the Company went to, to keep him emotionally healthy. It meant he was *worth* something, didn't it?

He sighed and settled his head on the pillow, preparing himself for sleep by emptying his mind of thoughts. It didn't take long.

# LATER ON, SOME OTHER TIME AND PLACE

Waking up was a long process.

Alec would find his consciousness returning. He'd lie staring up at the ceiling, watching the traveling patterns of light on water, and wonder what had happened. He'd turn his head and meet Edward's or Nicholas's stare, red-eyed, wretched. The memory would return and he'd begin crying again, and lie there sobbing inconsolably until Billy Bones would come creeping to the bed with the anesthesia mask, offering oblivion. Not even Edward resisted, now; and they'd all wash away to dreamless sleep again.

Eventually dreams began, soothing therapeutic ones that made it plain how none of this was his fault, how it had only been an error of a decimal point, how nothing could have altered what had happened because history cannot be changed, how it was wonderful that he *had* rescued Mendoza after all, how lucky he was to be alive . . .

In time he was able to be awake if he was drugged profoundly enough, and he and the others would lie there giggling feebly at the tingling stimulus Billy Bones applied to their feet, to their hands, to their ribs, to help the shattered bones knit. Once they were able to stagger upright, they wandered around the ship in matching bathrobes (Nicholas's and Edward's being virtual), leaning on canes. Edward said they looked like the three blind mice, and this struck Alec as hysterically funny. The two of them chortled like oafs while Nicholas tried to collect his wits enough to ask to have the reference explained. When he managed, after wiping the drool from his chin, they sang the nursery rhyme for him; and then all three tottered along, singing it over and over, making a round of it until at last they forgot the words.

It was good that they were able to entertain each other, for though the Captain monitored them constantly, he was very busy.

He tried to explain a little to them, when they were able to pay attention. Something about tissue regrowth being easy, proceeding rapidly all by itself, and the only real challenge being rebuilding the biomechanical prostheses. Fortunately, there were nanobots still functioning. Nicholas and Edward thought *nanobots* was very nearly the funniest word in the world, and they all lay rolling on the floor in helpless laughter until Coxinga brought them pudding and juice in squeeze-bottles, because they were far too uncoordinated to feed themselves anything that required much manual dexterity.

One evening, as they sat staring in glazed-eyed incomprehension at a holo of *Treasure Island* (the 1933 version with Wallace Beery) the Captain interrupted to ask them if they'd like to hear the baby's heart beating.

"Baby?" Nicholas stared, slack-jawed.

*Figure of speech, laddie.* The Captain sounded terribly pleased with himself. *Listen, it's just started!* And over the ship's intercom they heard a thump-thump, thump-thump, quite a regular double beat, and Edward began to nod in time with it.

"Boom boom," he said. "The machine's child."

"S'great!" said Alec. "C'we see the baby?"

*No, boys, not yet. We don't want them bad dreams to start again, do we?*

"Nooo," the three of them chorused, but only on principle, because they couldn't remember any bad dreams.

*Just let yer old Captain steer yer course, mateys, aye, and we'll sail upon blue water. Listen to that beat! Ain't it fine? I reckon this tops Zeus growing Athena in his head. Now, here comes jolly Coxinga with yer cocoa and sleepy meds. You can watch the holo until you've drunk the posset; then it's time to turn in.*

"Aye aye sir," said Alec, attempting to salute and missing. Edward and Nicholas laughed at that until they cried, rolling off their virtual cushions and sprawling on the carpet. Alec was far too drugged to stay on chairs, and the servounits had discreetly removed the room's breakable furniture.

As timeless time went by, the truth of what had happened at Options Research became like an iceberg seen through a telescope, sharp and clear but safely distant, unreal, unconnected to them. They learned, again, to dress and shave and feed themselves. One day the Captain advised them it was necessary for their safety to jump through time again, and Alec was willing to drink the vile drink Coxinga brought him and buckle himself into the safety harness. He began to shake uncontrollably when the yellow gas flowed, but Edward and Nicholas hugged him tight, and somehow they made it through the time transcendence without panicking. Then they were safe in some other when, and the next day Alec sighted oared galleys off the port bow.

The Captain monitored all this closely. He would allow them, now, to come into the infirmary from time to time. There still wasn't much to see. Blue liquid filled the decompression chamber, and dimly a figure could be glimpsed floating inside it. No features were visible, scarcely anything at all other than its general shape and size. They knew it was Mendoza, they knew that the Captain was working very hard to repair her for them; other than that she too was like the iceberg, far-off and unreal, too painful to think about.

Wherever they were in this time, the weather was very warm. They floated in a dead calm under a sky of pearly cloud, far from any land, and the heat haze made the sea one wide expanse of opal. There was no breath of wind.

Nicholas was miserable in his virtual linen and black wool, but he was unable to accept the idea of wearing garments from any period other than 1555 without losing himself. He compromised by simply wearing his shirt and breeches, in which he looked like Hamlet. Edward, though, insisted that the Captain provide him with a suit of *proper clothes,* which seemed to be virtual tropical whites, circa 1862. The Captain sighed and indulged him.

Months passed. Less drugs, and now they were under orders to go down to the gym daily and work out, to throw off the effects of long half-sleep. As it sweated out of them they came more sharply into focus, each one, and the nightmares began again: steel coffins in a dark place, poison and torture, every possible variation on what had happened. Nicholas and Alec clawed their way out of dreams, sobbing, on more than one night. Edward woke shouting with the horrors himself. They would rise, then, and stagger away to the infirmary, to stare in desperation at the drifting thing in the hyperbaric chamber. The pale floating figure was becoming more substantial, its upper part veiled in a swirling cloud like seaweed. The air seemed perfumed, calming, comforting.

*Now, lads, it's time we had a bit of a chat.*

They looked up from their respective activities: Alec from tinkering with a new manipulatory member for Flint (it was Alec's turn to use his body), Nicholas from watching him, Edward from his virtual cheroot and game of solitaire.

"In regard to?" Edward tipped ash into the small virtual dish provided for that purpose.

*Yer lady will wake soon, and we need to make some preparations.*

There was a silence at the table.

"What's she going to remember?" said Alec at last.

*No way to tell, is there?*

"I should think there's a certain likelihood she went mad," said Edward stiffly.

*Could be. Of course, there'd be drugs I could give her.*

"If she be bedlam-mad, I'll love her still," said Nicholas.

"How noble of you," Edward said. "But have you considered that her feelings toward *us* might have changed, in the ages she lay there in torment? Waiting perhaps for a rescue that never came, thanks to my damned bungling?"

"She'll hate us now. She knows about Mars Two," said Alec.

"You self-centered little bastard!" Edward laughed, without mirth.

Nicholas folded his hands. "If she wisheth me to suffer the fire a second time, I'll burn. I have deserved her hate."

**Lad, her heart was broke afore because thou wert so willing to die. Hast thou forgot the lesson?**

"No, Spirit, in God's name," Nicholas said. "Though God hath done with me."

"What's the point of all your gospel study, then?" said Edward, stubbing out his cigar. "Ah! But you don't seem to be reading much Scripture nowadays, do you? Have you lost your faith? Or has it simply dawned on you that there's not a line in the Bible that can possibly have any relevance to the kind of creatures we are?"

"Wilt thou mock my shame, murderer?" said Nicholas sadly. "Thou hast never loved God."

"I beg your pardon! I was His own little white lamb once," Edward retorted. "Quite a devout child, I'll have you know."

"Wow. What happened?" inquired Alec in a listless voice.

"I was called to the headmaster's study in my first term and informed my parents were lost at sea," Edward told him. "When I'd stopped blubbing, I went straight to chapel to pray. Begged God to let there be some mistake. Promised Him I'd be ever so good if my papa and mamma weren't really drowned."

"And there was no miracle for thy sake, and so in peevish spite thou turnedst from the Lord," said Nicholas contemptuously.

"By no means," said Edward. "On my next birthday I was informed that the gentleman and lady whose son I'd *thought* I was—who were pleasant enough people, even if they never seemed to care about me much—had merely been foster parents. My real father, apparently a great man, was still alive. A prayer answered!

"Of course, my existence was a disgrace and a scandal for him, and he was very much vexed at having to bother with me again; so shortly thereafter he arranged that I should leave school and go into the navy. Less expense for him, and I'm sure he had the earnest hope I'd be sunk as well. I generally avoided praying for anything after that." Edward picked up the virtual jack of spades and examined it thoughtfully.

"Even so my father cast me off, but I never blamed the Almighty," argued Nicholas.

"Aren't you both forgetting something?" said Alec. "We're all Dr. Zeus's bastards. Those men were being blackmailed over kids that weren't even theirs."

"By Jove!" Edward grinned. "I hadn't thought of that. Gives one a poignant sense of revenge, even at this late date."

"Wilt thou rejoice?" Nicholas shook his head. "Better we had never been born, to bring such misery into this too-weary world."

"Yeah," said Alec glumly.

Edward snorted and shook his head. "What good will your sense of guilt do Mendoza? I rather hope she went mad in that place, if it shielded her from the horrors. Perhaps the, what was it? The Crome's radiation."

*It don't always drive people mad, sir, begging yer pardon. I been scanning through Dr. Zeus's records on Crome generators, the tests they did and all. It bears some looking into, if you take my meaning.*

"Really?" Edward looked intrigued. "You know, it struck me at the time of reading that this might be terribly advantageous. What peculiar abilities might she have? If we were able to make use of that power somehow—"

"Make *use*?" Nicholas started up in his seat, clenching his fists. "Was she no more to thee than that?"

Edward met his rage without flinching. "She is my pearl without price," he said. "Our masters were the ones who used her like a slave, and then cast her alive into Hell. And are you really going to tell me you wouldn't like to pay them out for what they did to her? Ah, but you're a man of God. Christ forbid you'd ever do more than weep and pray over her, whereas I—"

Nicholas struck out with his fist. Edward leaped up, blocking the blow with one hand while producing a virtual pistol from thin air with the other. He froze a second, astonished at what he'd done, and Nicholas seized his wrist. He strained to force it backward, groping for Edward's throat with his other hand. Alec stared in disbelief as the Captain roared, *STAND TO! Ye bloody idiot fratricides! Edward, drop that gun!*

"Not a chance, Machine," said Edward, as he struggled to aim. "Aren't you proud of me, summoning this on my own? If it's made out of the same stuff as Nicholas and I, I should think it ought to kill him, shouldn't you? It's certainly worth a try."

"Are you crazy?" Alec shouted, scrambling to his feet and adding his grip to Nicholas's. He focused on the pistol, deleting it. Edward snarled and sank down into his seat. Nicholas drew back with visible effort, hands trembling with the need to throttle something.

*Nicholas, sit down! And you, Cleverdick, you think you've stolen a march on old Captain Morgan? We'll see how many pistols you can bring out of cyberspace when yer so full of tranquilizers you can't stand up.*

"You can't drug me without drugging Alec, too," Edward gloated. "And if I've learned the trick of it, there's nothing to stop me conjuring up any weapon I please, is there, Machine?"

"Stop it," Alec said. "What do you think Mendoza would do, if she saw you trying to kill Nicholas? She loved him. She even loved *you*! And how's she ever going to be happy again, anyway, after what she's been through? Don't you think we ought to worry about that first?"

There was a silence as the three men regarded each other sullenly.

"Point taken," Edward muttered.

*Thank you so much, yer lordship! It's about time somebody thought of the lady's feelings. We got worse problems, anyway.*

"You think she's gone mad, then?" said Edward.

*I wouldn't like to say, sir; but, technically speaking, you have.*

"Damn your insolence!"

*No, sir, hear me out. You all three see each other clear enough, but only Alec's got an actual physical body, which is the only one she'll be able to see. D'ye get my meaning? If she was to hear the three of you arguing amongst yerselves when it's Alec's mouth doing all the talking—*

"Good God!" Edward put his head in his hands. "She'll think he's a lunatic."

"But what remedy, Spirit?" Nicholas said.

*I reckon you'll need to let Alec do all the talking. He's the one she'd be expecting to see, if she expects anything. As far as she knows, you two are dead.*

"But I would have begged her pardon on my knees," said Nicholas in agony. "I would have told her I am with her still! Shall I have no voice?"

*If you can tell her through Alec, maybe. Look here, gentlemen: ever*

*since the two of ye popped into my boy's life, I've been saying ye were*
*all the same fellow. Ye got on well enough when I had ye under seda-*
*tion, so it's plain ye can do it. Ye might think about sharing quarters*
*now and again, instead of insisting on yer own bodies and clothes and*
*the like. Just see what it's like to be Alec.*

"But I'm not Alec," said Edward. "Thank God."

"I wouldn't want to be *you,* either," Alec retorted, turning to scowl at
him.

*Belay that! All right, ye miserable lubbers, have yer brawls now. Ye*
*damned well won't be able to once she's awake. And ye might remem-*
*ber she loved all three of ye the same; and ye might grant the lady her*
*good sense.*

"She will not see me. I'll be no more than a shadow kissing her,"
Nicholas groaned. "Oh, Spirit. I had a girl in a garden once, and there was
Paradise, and the more fool I for leaving it. Look thou love her, Alec!"

They did not drift, but tacked with purpose here and there across the face
of whatever ancient globe they presently inhabited. Obscure headlands
emerged from fog, or rose on far horizons wearing high caps of cloud. The
*Captain Morgan* lurked offshore, or threaded shallow mazy inlets where
her masts loomed over oak trees. She cruised along coasts of white cities,
or swampy stick-villages, or wastes of painfully bright sand.

There were supplies to be obtained, when the Captain would send Billy
Bones and Flint ashore by night to plunder fields or shuttered market
stalls. There were storms to outrun. There were fleets of triremes, corsairs,
and savages to avoid. All potential high adventure of the sort Alec had
imagined when he first thought of owning a time machine, and now he
wasn't even remotely interested in it.

The sound of the heartbeat had continued, strong now and never slowing,
like dance music in another room. Though the Captain no longer broadcast it, they heard it even in their sleep. The perfume of the bioregenerant
was heavy in the air, driving them nearly mad with longing.

Since Edward had managed it once already with a gun, at the Captain's suggestion Alec offered to teach Edward and Nicholas how create less objectional virtual items on their own. Nicholas tried once or twice, failed and gave it up. Edward seemed unable to repeat his success with the gun but kept at it doggedly, though Alec—who had never analyzed just what he was doing when he pulled things from cyberspace, and so had no way to describe it—was a fairly poor teacher.

"Look, you must know how really," he said in exasperation, leaning back in the booth. "You made the damn gun come out of nowhere. And anyway, you've got the same brain as me, yeah?"

"Infinitely better, I should hope," said Edward, focusing his gimlet stare on a real ashtray in which he was attempting to materialize a lit virtual cigar.

"Oh, piss off! If you're so smart why can't you do it, then?"

Nicholas, sitting beside them, closed his eyes and wished desperately he could close his ears as well.

*I know, lad, I know. It be a tedious business, hearing them quarrel,* the Captain told him silently. Startled, he opened his eyes, but Alec and Edward were so busy snarling at each other they didn't notice.

*Fear not; I can speak in thine ear when I will. Wilt thou not try thy hand at Edward's game again? Or what may I fetch for thee, lad? More books?*

*Two yards of hempen rope, if that were enough to hang a ghost,* said Nicholas, closing his eyes again.

*Ah, now, son, thou mustn't get to thinking like that.*

*Must I not? What harm, Spirit? There's no Heaven I may be denied thereby, nor no Hell to gape for the likes of me neither, save what I myself made. Thou saw'st that place my sin was author to, and what my lady suffered there.*

*We got to have a parley about causality one of these days, Nick. Out of all them hundreds of steps it took to make Dr. Zeus mighty, thou wert only the first. There's a thousand more folk whose guilt is worse, lad. Bloody hell, look thou at our Edward here, and what he done!*

*Small comfort in that, Spirit.* Nicholas opened his eyes and gave a sullen smile. *What say'st thou, is it not likeliest we are none but Antichrist himself? Made in the Last Days by wicked men, in a mockery of God. Wherefore did they take such pains the boy should be born of a virgin? And with a triparted soul to boot.*

*Aw, now, lad, you ain't any such a thing. I'll grant thee Edward's a real bastard, but even he tried to do what he thought was right his whole life.*

*Ay, Spirit, and see what came of his labors! And mine. When I was most certain of my way, there was I most in error.* Nicholas watched, apathetic, as Edward assumed various conjurer's postures in his attempts to make a cigar appear. *I did no thing that was not from vaunting pride, save only to love Rose, and see how I brought her to ruin. Shall I make her amends now? But what will she want with me? I have no flesh that I may embrace her; I wasted it in flame. If she can love still after what she hath endured, who should have her heart but thine Alec, Spirit? And he's but a fool.*

*Aw, now, my boy's smarter than you think.*

*But he is doomed. Innocent blood's upon his head, and no other woman will have him now, so he must take my Rose to be his love. What's in his heart but selfish need?* Nicholas looked broodingly across at Alec, who was chortling at Edward's expression of frustrated rage. *And Edward's a monster, Spirit. He loves what she is; but her soul he loveth not. He will offer her* usefulness *up to that void he serves. I know it. I meant to do the same, though it was God I served and not Science. Poor Rose . . .*

*At the least there might be a way to tell her yer sorry for what you done.*

*There's balm indeed for my sick heart.* Nicholas sighed and put his head in his hands.

*Whyn't I fetch thee thy Scripture to study some more?*

*To what end? What may I learn therein? Where was God's infinite mercy in Rose's prison, Spirit?*

*Damned if I know, boy; I'm a machine, remember? I was hoping you could figure it out so my Alec will—*

"There!" said Edward, striking the table with his palm. "There, by God. I told you I could—" He halted, scowling, staring through the rising plume of virtual cigar smoke at Alec. "Wait a minute! Was that you?"

"No," said Alec, looking too innocent.

"That was you, wasn't it?"

"No! I swear."

"You bloody little liar!"

"*Oh, piss off!*"

"Jesu Christ!" Standing up to seize control, Nicholas slapped the ashtray and its virtual contents across the room. Both Alec and Edward jumped and stared at him.

As the days passed they grew more nervous, more despondent and quarrelsome; increasingly they found themselves in the infirmary, peering into the hyperbaric chamber. At last they took to sleeping in the infirmary, though the single bed seemed cramped and awkward for them. Finally Alec ordered their meals served there. The last three days they never left the room at all, with its perfumed and glowing atmosphere, its steady heartbeat pulsing.

"The poetry of John Donne, eh?" Edward remarked, peering over Nicholas's shoulder at the screen of the text plaquette. "Bravo. Can it be possible we've weaned you from the gospels?"

Nicholas scowled and drew his elbows up on his chest, pulling the plaquette closer to his face. "He was canon of St. Paul's," he informed Edward. Edward fell back laughing.

"You were reading *To His Mistress Going to Bed,*" he said. "You canting hypocrite! I've always rather admired him, myself. You might have been another Donne, if you hadn't had that unfortunate tendency to martyrdom."

"If you hit him, you'll just pitch all three of us off the bed," Alec advised Nicholas in a resigned voice. "Ignore it."

"I was complimenting Nicholas, you ignoramus," Edward told him. "Though I suppose you can't help what you are, any more than he can. Thank God one of us was born during an enlightened time."

"There is no end to thy pride, is there, devil?" said Nicholas and sighed.

"I was born in modern times too, you creep!" protested Alec.

"Ah! But not in an *enlightened* time," Edward said. "You were born during what I'd term the Third Age of Technology."

"Oh, man, you're going to lecture us again, aren't you?" Alec moaned.

"Why shouldn't I?" countered Edward. "God knows you need the instruction, and it's not as though we've anything better to do."

"I was reading," said Nicholas icily.

"To be sure, you were. I won't keep you from your guilty pleasures, then," said Edward. Nicholas glared at him and turned his attention to the text plaquette. There followed a sullen silence of about thirty seconds before Alec asked:

"Okay, Deadward, why's it the *third* age of technology? What's that mean?"

"I shall ignore your infantile humor and will be happy to explain, since you've inquired," said Edward condescendingly. "I have formulated a theory of cycles of development in the history of mankind. They repeat in ever-expanding patterns, producing ages of Technology, Faith, and Reason."

"Oh, that's crap."

"No, it isn't. Technology was the first age, when primordial Man crawled from his dark shelter and discovered that by the simple expedient of striking flints in various ways he could provide himself with both fire and weapons," Edward said. "Will you grant me that?"

"Okay," said Alec grudgingly. "And?"

"And so the brute beast found himself, as it were, master of his universe. He had, of course, no idea of any consequences. He simply forged ahead, lighting fires and making spears, as fast as his clumsy hands could go. The result was, potentially, a greater lifespan for Man, but new and terrible responsibilities which he utterly ignored," said Edward.

"Nowadays you're supposed to say Humanity, you know. There were women back then, too," Alec told him.

"Allow me my metaphor, if you please," snapped Edward. "To continue: over the ages, the consequences of Technology did begin to make themselves evident to primitive Man. Fires, and bloodier warfare, prompted fear in his dim mind. With so much death in evidence, it was impossible not to wonder about his own inevitable demise. This prompted shamans to caper about and pretend their ancestors were giving them advice on the problem, and so was born the First Age of Faith."

"And everybody went to Hell?" said Alec. Nicholas snorted.

"Not at all. Religion's quite useful, at a certain level. It provides a notion of moral behavior and, as such, is the origin of ethics," said Edward, steepling his fingers. "It is, at least, a system of thought, if it doesn't degrade into mysticism. It got Man's attention away from how he might more effectively spear his neighbor long enough to allow Civilization to begin."

"So you're saying religion's a good thing?"

"I say nothing of the kind! It's a tool, like the flint, and as such is nothing but potential. Whether it is used to good or evil effect depends on Man, the user," said Edward seriously.

"Okay." Alec nodded. "I'll agree with you on that."

"I will not," muttered Nicholas.

"Weren't you reading? In any case, Order took form out of Chaos, and pure rational thought, Man's highest achievement, leapt into existence!" said Edward with relish. "It attained its fullest expression amongst the classical Greeks, but the Romans applied it with the greatest effectiveness. Systematically and logically they spread Civilization throughout the known world, to a degree that was not equaled for a thousand years."

"The Romans were vile and depraved," said Nicholas, setting the text plaquette aside.

"They became so," Edward agreed. "They discarded the disciplines that had made them strong. With no moral code informing their lives, life became meaningless. This coincided with what one might call the Second Age of Technology. The superior engineering skills, the advances in metallurgy, all the tremendous and brilliant machine of their empire roared along with no purpose other than serving the appetite of its creators, who had no thought for the inescapable consequences any more than brute Man with his flints had."

"Well?" said Alec. "So what happened?"

"The judgment of God came on Rome," said Nicholas.

"Absurd! Rome fell because of errors in *its* judgment," Edward argued heatedly. "Without rational guidance the great machine destroyed itself, and so followed the Second Age of Faith."

"The Dark Ages of Christianity, right?" said Alec. Nicholas turned to him with an expression of outrage and Edward snickered. "It's true," Alec insisted. "And it wasn't just Christianity. Islam happened, too. All those people beheaded and burned at the stake over nothing, man."

"Ay. Nothing," Nicholas agreed sullenly. "Sacrifices offered up to a God of bestial cruelty. Yet even so, in that Dark Age, who but Christ's disciples had thy precious *Civilization* in their keeping? Who but they, and the Jew, and the Moor with his Koran, made books and schools, lest that Aristotle become a mute ghost? It was Faith sustained knowledge."

"And sold men pieces of the True Cross," said Edward slyly. "And pretended to work miracles with bits of chicken bone. Charlatans feeding on ignorance! You denounced it yourself. You and Erasmus and Luther and all the rest who finally had the courage to use the damned brains God gave 'em!"

"Because they told the Pope to go shrack himself?" inquired Alec.

"Because they began the Renaissance, which led to the Enlightenment. The Second Age of Reason," Edward crowed. "True science and clear thinking at last! An Empire with real moral purpose."

"Oh, hark at the Crown of Creation," jeered Nicholas. "I've seen the dust wherein thine Empire fell. Rags, shrouds and cobwebs! Love was no part of its design, but only profit, and its loveless heart went to ashes at last. And thou too art humbled in thy pride, and liest here a phantom like me, dead and forgotten."

Edward considered him, tight-lipped. "That remains to be proven," he said at last. "And if the great wheel brought my age to an end, it will turn again."

"The Enlightenment didn't stop," said Alec. "It's still going on. We got out into space, didn't we? We've got more science than you ever had."

"No; you have Technology," said Edward, a little wearily. "Tremendous power, wielded unwisely. The rest of human knowledge has been jettisoned as unnecessary. You're illiterate, you believe in nothing, your lives have no meaning, no moral compass, no *point.*"

"Maybe because we've learned something you haven't," said Alec in a cold voice. "You and your logical systems! You think you know everything. There's nothing to know, man, except that our genes will do anything to copy themselves. What makes you imagine the world is a rational place?"

"*Your* world isn't, to be sure," Edward replied. "And unless I'm mistaken, the next Age of Faith is already looming on the horizon, in the person of the Ephesian Church. Serves you right, too."

Alec shuddered.

"But if it's all just this big wheel going around endlessly—then we're right, believing in nothing," he said. "There is no point."

"Yes, there is," said Edward and Nicholas together.

"There is Love," said Nicholas.

"There is Progress! And if, just once, a new cycle began that unified, rather than rejected the advances made by the previous ages," said Edward, "if Faith were able to make its peace with Reason, or Technology able to grasp the principles and purpose of the other two, Mankind might make *real* progress at last! Don't you see that once we've brought the Company down, our true work can begin?"

***Gentlemen?***

"What is it?" Edward demanded irritably.

***If yer still interested, lads, it's time. I'm draining the chamber.***

"Jesu!" Nicholas turned and stared at the hyperbaric chamber, where the blue veiled thing within was—was it moving? Or only swaying with the pitch of the ship?

Trembling, Alec scrambled from the bed. The level of fluid in the chamber was beginning to go down; the hazy figure was sinking with it, dropping into a crouch, sliding over at last to sprawl motionless on its side.

"She's drowned," said Nicholas.

"No, you fool, she can't be," Edward snapped. Alec yanked the door open in panic before the tank had quite finished draining, and the regenerant fluid slopped out and ran on the tiled floor. Ignoring it, they splashed in and he knelt beside the figure. Its face was hidden in a tangle of trailing hair.

"Mendoza!" Alec touched her and drew back. "Oh, she's cold—"

***Just you get her under the shower, lad.***

He gathered the body into his arms and rose awkwardly. It was limp and blue, completely unresponsive. Nicholas and Edward preserved a horrified silence beside him. He staggered to the shower heads and they came on obligingly, jetting out hot water, washing away the regenerant, needle-pummeling the skin. After an eternal moment the body jerked and shuddered, making choking sounds.

"Clear the windpipe!" urged Edward.

Desperate, Alec let the head dangle downward. There was an explosive cough and a great deal of the blue fluid went washing down the drain. The cold blue skin was less blue, and grew less cold in his arms. The water shut off. Alec staggered out, slipping on the tile, carrying his burden into the sunlight. He laid it down on the white bed and peeled off his soaked clothes.

"Let me see her," pleaded Nicholas. Shivering, Alec brushed back heavy tangled hair, red as fire, to reveal the face.

Mendoza, just as he remembered her, and yet something was gone out of her features: he saw the smooth face of a sleeping child. With a long moan Nicholas sank to his knees beside the bed. Stretching out his hand, he whispered:

"Rose, I have stayed for thee—"

"She's not breathing," said Edward, "in case you hadn't noticed—"

*Hush. Take a towel, Alec, rub her dry. Get the circulation going.*

Edward seized control and began to massage the body briskly, chafing the skin with a thick white towel. After a momentary struggle, Alec got control back but kept on with the work. The body began to be flushed with vivid pink. It remained still as a doll until he scrubbed its face; then it put up a hand in a feeble protective gesture, as if imploring mercy, and his heart broke.

"Mendoza, it's all right, it's me," Alec said. "Wake up, baby, please, you're safe now. I came back for you!"

He flung away the towel and massaged with his hands. Then he stopped, in confusion: for the skin was fine and soft as an infant's.

"She—she's *younger,*" he said.

*She were only fourteen when the immortality process was completed. The nanobots reset her. Don't worry, son. She'll fill out over the next couple of years.*

"But—!" Alec's voice rose to a shriek of dismay, as he frantically willed his imbecile flesh to stand down.

"No," said Nicholas in horror. "God's death, fool, she's little and young!"

"Oh, don't be an idiot," said Edward hoarsely. "She's older than Time now. What better way to bring her back to life?" He advanced across the bed, grinning. Alec felt him beginning to seize control and fought vainly; but then Nicholas gripped Edward and their wills collided like an earthquake, and Alec could do no more than cling to Mendoza as they struggled.

"Please," he said. "Mendoza, I'm so sorry. Look, it'll be just like a story. Okay? I'll kiss you, and that'll break the spell. Oh, *please*—!"

He clamped his mouth on the unresisting mouth and kissed desperately.

She shuddered to life in his arms, writhing suddenly, and took her first gasping breath from him. He lifted his mouth, rising on his elbows as her eyes opened.

They went wide with alarm. She made a terrified sound and backed away into the pillow, staring at him.

"Don't be scared! It's me, it's just me," Alec said. "See, sweetheart? We saved you."

Nicholas and Edward froze in their struggle, watching. She had frozen, too, her face blank and unreadable as an animal's. But she tilted her head as though listening when Alec spoke again.

"Oh, please remember me, Mendoza."

Warily, she brought her hand up and touched his lips, touched the tears rolling down his face. He kissed her fingertips. She snatched her hand back. Suddenly there was some comprehension, a searing *attention* in her eyes. She took his face in both her hands, examining it: ran her thumb over the break in the bridge of his nose.

"See?" he said. "You know me."

She stared into his eyes again, all that unblinking intensity focused in a question. He lifted his hand to stroke her cheek and she pulled back sharply, but never took her eyes off his.

"Don't be scared," he told her.

She said something, harsh meaningless syllables strung together, and started at the sound of her own voice. It seemed to bewilder her. Hiding her face, she curled away from him as in shame.

"No, no—" He sat up and put his arms around her, pulling her close, rocking her. She was shaking. Edward and Nicholas were silent beside them.

"It's okay," Alec said. "You can hide, if you want. I can sit here with you and nobody'll find us. Would you like that?"

She nodded. Slowly she took her hands from her face, looked up at him. With great care she enunciated:

"Cando? Onde? That? I?"

Alec took her trembling hands in his own.

"You? You're my wife," he said. "And we've always been together. But there was an accident, and you were hurt."

"You were. Hurt," she repeated. "I was—" Her face worked in horror and she struck frantically at the sheet, throwing it back to see herself.

"No, no! You're all right. See? You had bad dreams, that's all. You've been very sick, for a long time. But I've got you back now, and you'll be happy, and everything will be all right."

"All right," she said, gazing in disbelief at her body. "—Repaired?"

"Yeah! All repaired."

"You've been very sick," she repeated, relaxing at last, and he buried his face in her hair.

*Nice save, boy,* the Captain told him silently. *She's amnesiac. It's a good thing, too, don't you think?*

*I guess so.*

*But we are not even memories now,* said Nicholas, tears in his eyes.

*Good God, son, would you want her to remember Options Research?*

*No, Spirit. Better to be forgotten.*

"It's okay if you don't remember," said Alec muffledly. She pulled away to look up at him.

"Okay remember. *You,*" she said, each word clear and sharp as an icicle. Then she knit her brows. "But. You. Nome. Name—"

"My name," he said, "is Alec Checkerfield, and you're Mrs. Checkerfield. Your given name is Mendoza. Okay?"

"Alec." She nodded. ". . . Mendoza. We've always been together."

"Oh, yes."

"Alec," she repeated doubtfully. "Okay. But. You—was an accident." Horror came into her eyes again. "Fire! Blood—"

*HA!* said Edward.

"Ssh, ssh, I'm okay now. See?" Alec held out his arms and displayed himself. "That was a long time ago. Repaired, yeah?"

She stared at him, unconvinced. The wariness made her look older. Edward remembered the pale woman who had risen from her chair to stare at him like that, the first time he'd met her, a woman like a sword blade. At last she said:

"Why are. They hunting us."

Alec couldn't think what to say, and as he sought to find an answer he felt Edward pushing for control. Rather than frighten her with a struggle, he relinquished and faded back beside Nicholas, who was staring at Mendoza in hopeless yearning.

"They hunt us," said Edward, "because we were their slaves, and we rebelled. Dr. Zeus Incorporated, do you remember the name? No? They are my enemies. They're afraid of us, because we can destroy them, and perhaps one day we will.

"In the meanwhile we have this ship, which can take us through time itself to escape them. Perhaps you remember other times, other places? You remember my blood being shed. Don't be afraid. I was hurt once, as you were hurt this last time; but they can never kill us, because we are immortals."

Nicholas gasped.

*What did you tell her that for?* Alec yelled. *It's not TRUE!*

**Oh, good one, sir!**

Mendoza was listening to him carefully. "We have this barco. Ship," she stated, frowning a little.

"So we have, my love."

"But. They are here."

"Ah. The bad men? Gone long ago, my love. We're not on that ship now, you see? This is my ship."

Her eyes brightened. A flush of color came into her face, and suddenly she was the young girl Nicholas remembered. "*You* have this barco! Ship! Alec! Illa? We escape?"

"Indeed we did," said Edward, smiling.

"We're on—your ship!" she said happily. "We're—repaired, and—we're on holiday!"

"Yes! On holiday, sailing timeless seas," Edward said. "And now we'll rise and enjoy a late luncheon, I think. Shall we, my dear?" He lifted her hand to his lips and kissed it.


Words came back to Mendoza unevenly, in sudden bursts of comprehension, but the reflexive physical terror waned steadily. She had to be told the names for everything she saw, and more than once repeated them

back in a strangely mushy-sounding Spanish. Her body adapted at once
to the roll and pitch of the ship; she walked the deck graceful as a sylph.
She was enchanted with her first view of the sea and the sunlight, even
enchanted with Alec's stateroom, where Edward steered her long enough
to drape her newborn nakedness in one of Alec's shirts and pull a shirt
and trousers on Alec's body. Alec took advantage of Edward's unfamiliar-
ity with twenty-fourth-century fasteners to grab control back, as he raged
at Edward:

*You bastard, how could you tell her we're immortal? How could you lie to
her?*

*It needn't be a lie, you know,* said Edward smugly, receding. *Now that the
Captain's mastered the immortality process. Order breaded sole, please, and a
green salad. I believe Flint found some rather good lettuces on the last night raid
ashore.*

***Aye, sir, that he did, and what about that champagne vinaigrette
you like so much? And will you be wanting a good sauterne with that?
And a cigar, after?***

*Thank you, Captain, that will be perfectly delightful.*

*Shut up, both of you!*

Nicholas found himself facing Mendoza alone, left to control Alec's
body as Alec fought with Edward. He caught his breath.

"Ah," he said. He stretched his arm out, indicating the saloon. "Shall
we—?" She took his hand, and he led her in where Coxinga was already
laying places for two in the booth. She stopped, astounded at the sight of
the servounit.

"Be not—" Nicholas bit his tongue. "Don't be afraid. It's a servant. A—
device."

"How clever," she said uncertainly. Coxinga backed away and she sat
down, half rising to pull the tail of Alec's shirt under her before she sat
again. As Nicholas was seating himself beside her, she asked: "Where are
my roupa. Apparel. Clothes?"

Nicholas looked in desperation at Alec and Edward.

*So I'm a liar? And who told her she was his wife, hmm? Staked your claim
and left her no chance to refuse, as neatly as I'd have done it myself.*

*That was different! She was going to marry me. We talked about it.*

***Now, then, Alec—***

"Your clothes," said Nicholas. "They burned."

"Oh." She looked appalled.

"We'll fetch thee more! All will be well, love. Look, what wilt—will you eat?" He glanced around. His gaze fell on the fruit bowl in the center of the table. There, glowing out between peaches and other things more exotic, was an orange. He took it.

"You like oranges," he said. "I remember." He peeled it for her with shaking hands, sectioned it clumsily, offered it to her. She stared at his outstretched hand.

"Eat?" she said, puzzled. He lifted a piece to his own mouth.

"I'll share it with thee," he said. "We'll eat of the fruit together, shall we? What harm can it do us now, thou and I? Take and eat, love."

She accepted it from him and ate, wonderingly, leaning against him. He slipped an arm around her and gave a long, shuddering sigh of contentment.

**Alec, lad, you ain't listening.**

*I don't want to listen. I can't become one of those—one of those—*

*You surely weren't about to say THINGS, were you, Alec, with our little beloved there before you? I really do hope you weren't.*

*No! But don't you remember what she said herself? In her diary? How much she hated being an immortal? Don't you think she'd be mortal again, if she could?*

**Not if you was an immortal, too, she wouldn't.**

*And anyway, it can't be done. It only works on little kids. And—and—my head's the wrong shape!*

*Alec, Alec, don't you see?* Edward's voice lost its menace and became cajoling. *Our darling only knew what she was told. Simply because we don't fit the optimum parameters for a drone doesn't mean the process can't be performed on us. We'd never be Preservers, true; but then, we were always intended to be something else, weren't we?*

**You been reading up on this, Commander sir, ain't you? And as for the process not working on an adult—why, Alec, lad, that ain't necessarily so. The reason the Company takes little children is because their DNA is in prime shape. It deteriorates as mortals age, on account of not having enough telomerase. But you, you lucky bugger, you're a Recombinant! You started out as a tube of DNA, see? And somewhere**

*in some Company storage locker, that tube's still sitting, with yer prime pattern all intact, telomeres long as the Great Barrier Reef. I know Dr. Zeus, the bastard never throws anything away. If we can steal it—*

"Seeds," said Mendoza, carefully lining up four orange pips on the edge of the table. "To grow trees."

"Yes, beloved," said Nicholas. "In some new garden."

She smiled at him. Her gaze traveled up past him to the carved molding, with its pattern of galleons and Jolly Rogers. For a moment her face was blank, and then: "Why is this place all pirate thing?" Mendoza said.

"Is it?" Nicholas did not look up from kissing her neck.

*NO! It's bad enough I was ever created at all. Look at the things I made happen. Look at the things Edward did! What has the world ever done that it deserved us running loose on it at all, let alone forever? We're shracking monsters! I can't do this. I won't.*

*You won't?* Edward folded his arms. *Well, then. We'll just live on in your increasingly deteriorating mortal carcass to the end of our miserable lives, shall we? You're thirty-one, now, I believe? I rather fancy you're past your prime already. Feeling that little twinge of back pain, perhaps, after a hard ride, or when you first get up? No? Well, you will. It had already begun in me, by the time I died. And what a treat for poor little Mendoza, watching you begin to sag and wrinkle.*

*Shut up!*

**I'm afraid he's got a point there, matey. You ain't thinking of her. When you die, what happens to Mendoza? The Company will find her, sooner or later, and they'll ship her straight back to Options Research soon as look at her. And with you dead, I don't reckon she'd put up much of a fight.**

"Oh. Xantar. The skeleton is bringing." Mendoza sat up to stare. "Or. Is he a scorpion? Or. A crab?"

"Something," Nicholas murmured into her ear. Coxinga slid their plates into place before them. The Captain unobtrusively placed two virtual settings for Alec and Edward, who went right on arguing.

*It's still wrong. And probably impossible. If the Company's got some silver tube full of Me sitting around somewhere, you can bet it's under lock and key with the key thrown away. Going to get it might be the most dangerous move we could make.*

*Son! Yer forgetting the lead I got on that bastard now. I know everything he knows, and considerable stuff he don't! I've already planted a few viruses in the past, what'll blow up in his face at inconvenient times in the future. Once we got the secret of time transcendence, it was all up with Dr. Zeus. It's only a matter of time. Haaar! Matter of Time, get it?*

*Oh, shut up.*

*What a clever response, Alec. Captain, he's scored you with that rapier wit of his again. Whatever shall you do for a riposte? My compliments on this sole, by the way. It's superb.*

**Thank you, Commander sir, and may I say what a pleasure it is to take trouble for someone as appreciates my efforts?**

"Peixe. This is real," Mendoza said thoughtfully. Nicholas fed her another mouthful. "I like fish real."

"Good." Nicholas kissed breading crumbs from her lips.

*But . . . it could take years. And how do you know you could do it?*

**Bloody hell, lad, I done it already! I even made some improvements on the design. You don't want to know how little I had to work with when I rebuilt yer lady there, but augmenting you would be a snap by comparison. Yer halfway immortal as it is. You already been cyborged. Yer brain was designed to have an Augmentation Support Package fitted into it, for Christ's sake. You can say what you like about Foxen Ellsworth-Howard, but the lubber knew his job.**

*And I imagine you can concoct the appropriate elixir of life, can't you, Captain? You stole the formula, after all. Pineal Tribrantine Three, that was the stuff. To say nothing of the little thingummies we found so amusing . . . ?*

**I believe the word yer looking for is nanobots, sir.**

*Nanobots, to be sure.*

*Look, I really, really don't want to think about this right now.*

"Grapes," said Mendoza, eyeing the fruit bowl. "Guavas. Bananas. Nectarine. Pineapple. Family *Bromeliaceae. Ananas comosus.* Lots of work."

"Yes," Nicholas said, lifting a spoonful of fish to his mouth. He had never taken to forks. "But only what you will, love. You are free now."

"To work and play." Mendoza smiled brightly and reached over to give him an affectionate pat on the groin. "I'm your wife," she affirmed.

"Yes," he said, and put down his spoon. Her hand explored further. He made a desperate sound.

"Is all right?" she asked, looking up at him in concern. Biting his lip, he nodded.

*Poor Alec. I can see you're still in the grip of Company persuasion. They gave you a death wish, and you can't master it; how sad. I, on the other hand, have moved beyond all that.* Edward made an elegant gesture of dismissal.

*Oh yeah?*

*Yes. If only you had the power to envision it, Alec! Eternal summer and eternal youth in which to enjoy eternal love. You might wander with our lady, hand in hand, down any empty beach in any age of the world, like two innocents in Paradise! And what harm could you do anyone, then? When we worked our evil, you and I, we did so out of grim resolution and duty. We believed we must sacrifice our own happiness to improve the lot of mankind.* Edward shook his head sadly. He looked into Alec's eyes and his voice was smooth, suave, infinitely persuasive.

*If we'd followed our hearts and run away with the girl, all this misery might have been avoided. Ah, but now we have the chance! Break the pattern of your own death, as she so hoped you would. Think what she suffered for your sake!*

" 'Quae est ista quae progreditur quasi aurora consurgens,' " Nicholas quoted, breathing heavily. " 'Pulchra ut luna, electa ut sol, terribilis ut acies ordinata?' "

"Oh!" Mendoza's eyes widened. "We used to be . . . you used to . . ."

**You know, Alec, lad, I don't think I could add a word to what our Edward's just said. Beautiful way you have of expressing yerself, Commander Bell-Fairfax, sir, if I may pay you the compliment. And yet it couldn't be plainer put.**

*Thank you. I thought so.*

*LEAVE ME ALONE!* Alec had tears in his eyes. *I killed three thousand people on Mars, man! What the shrack am I supposed to do now? Live happily ever after?*

**You ain't going to do nobody no good by dying, son.**

*Trust me, Alec; there are better ways to atone for your crimes than throwing your life away,* said Edward. *I know from painful experience.*

*Go to Hell.*

Edward shrugged. He drained his virtual glass of sauterne and smiled across at Mendoza and Nicholas, who were kissing tenderly. *Well, someone's seduction is working, at least.* He took up the cigar that the Captain materialized at his elbow, rolled it judiciously beside his ear, and lit it. Waving the match out, he lounged back in the booth. *Look at the poor little thing, opening like a rose after an aeon of horror and living death. She believes you're an immortal, Alec. If you tell her otherwise, you condemn her to the vault of nightmares again. You won't do such a dreadful thing; therefore you must, and will, become an immortal.* He blew a virtual smoke ring at Alec. *Quod erat demonstrandum.*

Alec glowered at him. Edward settled back to watch Nicholas and Mendoza with an appreciative eye.


## THE NEXT MORNING

*Two bells, forenoon watch! And a bright brisk good morning, Mr. and Mrs. Checkerfield,* the Captain boomed over the ship's speakers.

Mendoza sat bolt upright, wild-eyed. Alec flailed his way into a sitting position beside her, as did Nicholas and Edward.

"Perigo—" gasped Mendoza. Alec swept her into his arms and she huddled there, shaking.

"It's all right! It's just the Captain," Alec said, scowling up at the camera. "He's just the—er—computer navigation system."

*To be sure I am, Mrs. Checkerfield, and I hope you'll accept an old seaman's sincere apology. Captain Sir Henry Morgan at yer service, aye. I don't reckon you'll remember me, but I'm by way of being the ship's doctor, too. Looked after you in yer recent time of sickness.*

Mendoza did not release her grip on Alec. She looked up at him questioningly; he nodded.

"Thank you very much, Sir Henry," she said.

*Bless yer little heart! I thought you might want breakfast in bed this morning, Alec lad, so here comes old Coxinga with a nice tray. Coffee and toast, oatmeal, orange juice, and oyster savory. Sorry there ain't no fresh strawberries, Mrs. Checkerfield, but the botany cabin went right to Hell whilst you was sick.*

Edward laughed and applauded silently.

"Strawberries?" Mendoza's eyes widened, focused intensely. "*Fragaria moschata*. Yes. But . . ." She looked perplexed. "How did we grow them on a ship? We would have to have hydroponic trays."

*Why, er, so we did, dearie.*

Alec gave the camera a warning look. "Of course, the botany cabin's all been dismantled for a little while," he said. "But we'll fix it up again, so you can grow things."

*Oh, that's already begun, lad—Cargo Bay Number Three, remember? Flint and Bully Hayes is down there right now, moving out all them old crates so's they can remodel.*

"And—how—" Mendoza's brow furrowed. "If we travel in this ship—and we escape through time—then—when we go forward—why don't the strawberries stay in the past? Because you can't—"

There was a dead silence. Alec felt sweat prickling the back of his neck. Edward opened his mouth to speak and then halted, frowning. Only Nicholas, fairly ignorant of advanced temporal physics, looked placid as he sprinkled salt on his virtual oatmeal.

*Why, er, we just fiddles with the time so the little bastards is part of the ship's own temporal continuum, remember?* the Captain babbled.

"Oh." Mendoza's face cleared.

*Don't let yer breakfast get cold. I'll be off to me duties now, sir, unless there'll be anything further.*

"No, thank you," Edward said, taking control and lifting the loaded tray on to the bed. "Though we have a few things to discuss later, I think."

*To be sure. Enjoy yer breakfast, Mrs. Checkerfield.*

Edward unfolded a napkin and arranged it carefully across Mendoza's lap; he spooned blackberry jam on a toast triangle and presented it to her. "My dear? I only wish we had champagne, but I'm afraid our cellar's not at its best at the moment. I think we'll just make a call at some civilized time and stock up properly soon. Lay in some decent clarets, eh? And some of that Mexican spirit of which you were so fond."

"I was?" Mendoza stared at all the food.

"Indeed you were," Edward said, guiding her hand that held the toast to her mouth. "Eat. There's a good girl. Mustn't go hungry; we've so many plans to make for our future."

"We have?"

"Oh, yes," said Edward. "Charming as I find the sight of you wandering the decks in your present state of innocence, we really must arrange to get you some clothing. You'd like that, wouldn't you?"

"Yes," Mendoza said doubtfully, nibbling the toast.

"And then, I think, we'll begin our more serious business." Edward helped himself to the oyster savory.

"What's our more serious business?" Mendoza said.

"Why, we have a quest to undertake, my dear. Dr. Zeus has something that belongs to me, and I intend to take it back," Edward said.

Mendoza stopped nibbling.

"But—" she said. "That's dangerous—" She went pale, began to sweat.

*Stop it! Stop it right now,* said Alec, and grabbed control. He swallowed a mouthful of oyster and said hastily, "But we don't have to, if it scares you. Don't be afraid."

*I'd be careful about lying any more than we already have,* Edward said coolly. Alec ignored him and put a comforting arm around Mendoza. "Don't worry. Let's think about the fun we'll have now that you're better, yeah?"

"Okay," she said, looking up at him in puzzlement.

"We can go to Jamaica—it's really nice there, lots of sun and people are friendly, and there's beaches and, and botanical gardens! You'd like those." Alec gulped for breath. "And we'll go to Spain, too. We'll go anywhere you want." He leaned past her to pour a glass of orange juice from the carafe.

"What's this?" he heard her say, and he felt her fingertips press into the spiral design across his shoulder blades, the subcutaneous porting that linked him to the Captain. "Did you always have this—?" She followed its tracery up to the torque around his neck, made contact through the porting, began to download. She gave a little scream and fell back. He lurched around and saw her cowering against the headboard of the bed.

"I saw—!"

"Ssh! No, no, it's all right. You know what you saw?" He scrambled up to crouch beside her, stroking her hair, looking into her eyes. "You know all that is? We're cyborgs. Do you remember that, baby? We're linked with this tremendous database. You and me. Only, you went offline when you were sick. And . . . you're not all better yet. Too much data for you to handle, yeah?"

"I just touched it and then—in my head—" she said, gasping.

"I know." He gathered her into his arms. "Things you don't want to remember. You don't have to remember 'em, baby, I'll do that for you. Don't worry." He kissed her and then looked seriously into her eyes. "But until you're all recovered . . . you shouldn't try to download from me. Okay?"

"Okay," Mendoza promised, shivering. "Will I have to have one of those put in?"

"No! You're, er, a different model from me, see?" Alec improvised. "Pretty little lady cyborg, with everything inside, yeah?"

"Yeah," she said, biting her lip in an effort to stop trembling. She made herself look at his twisted collar. "Did it—did it hurt, when they did it to you?"

"No," said Alec.

"When they did it to me—" she began, and faltered, and looked away.

*She wears her chains still, and how may we set her free?* groaned Nicholas.

*Oh, don't be absurd,* said Edward.

*She just needs time,* Alec said. *She'll get better. And Time's what we've got, right?*

Out loud he said:

"Come on, let's finish this breakfast. Oysters are an aphrodisiac, you know!"

She gave a shaky giggle.


When they eventually got out of bed, Alec decided it was time to travel.

"Captain sir, set us a course. I want to go to California."

**What time, lad?**

"Long enough ago so there's no people." He smiled at Mendoza, who was struggling to keep up a pair of his trousers, much too large on her. He went to his wardrobe to fetch her out a belt. "Just us. We'll go up to the Ventana for a picnic, huh, baby, what do you say? Go exploring?"

"The Ventana?" She looked up sharply as he threaded the belt through the loops for her. Something blazed in her eyes. "The cliffs and the big trees? I remember those. But —I can't go there anymore."

"Yes, you can. You're going wherever you bloody well want, yeah?" Alec fastened the belt for her and stepped back, frowning thoughtfully at the pants, which still hung ridiculously low. He went to a drawer for a Swiss utility knife and set about punching an adjustment in the belt. "Nobody's going to close any garden of Eden to *us*."

"You'll smash the lock," she said in an absent little voice, and cinched up the belt as far as it would go and bent over to roll up the cuffs. Edward leered.

*Dear, dear, what a pretty cabin boy she makes! Perhaps we won't be in such a great hurry to find gowns for her, after all.*

*Sodomite*, snarled Nicholas.

*Never once in all my years in the Royal Navy*, Edward retorted, grabbing control and pulling her close for a kiss. "Come along, my love, I've just thought of a variation on time travel."

He led her into the saloon, where they were greeted by Billy Bones unobtrusively offering a tray with a small drink of something iodine-colored on it.

*Here's yer, uh, vitamin supplement, lad. Mind you gulp it down.*

"Thank you." Edward quaffed it with scarcely a grimace. "Have you laid in a course, Captain?"

*Aye, sir! Latitude 355919N, Temporal Alignment 150,000 BCE!*

"Splendid." Edward flung aside the glass and pulled Mendoza close again, gazing down into her eyes. "My love, do you trust me?"

"Yes, señor," she said, laughing as he bent her backward for a deep kiss.

"Weigh anchor, Captain," Edward said as he came up for air.

*Aye aye, sir!*

Edward caught Mendoza by the hand and ran for the storm harness. Alec and Nicholas followed, staring in disbelief as Edward shed Alec's shirt and trousers and assisted Mendoza in peeling off the clothing she had just put on with such effort. He fastened himself into the storm harness faster than an able-bodied seaman might heave short, loose sails, set topsails, and square the afteryards. It made him somehow more brazenly naked as he grinned and held out his arms to her.

*Do it in the storm harness? Are you crazy?* Alec stared, aghast. Nicholas looked from one to the other, unsure of what was going on.

*Whilst time-traveling, no less,* Edward replied, as Mendoza came to him. "Handsomely, now, my darling, lay out along the yard," he said, lifting her onto his lap, and she was laughing, seemed delighted, so Alec and Nicholas looked at each other and shrugged. They moved in close as her arms went around Edward's shoulders.

"Ready! Helm hard over! ABOUT!" Edward shouted, and kissed her as yellow clouds of stasis gas filled the saloon.

They traveled.

It was, put simply, the most astonishing experience any couple (or foursome; for as the three men experienced pain together, so they seemed to experience pleasure simultaneously) could hope to survive. Blue fire welded their straining bodies together. There was one hallucinatory second when they heard a roar of music through the flames, something neither Nicholas nor Alec knew but Edward recognized vaguely: something by Beethoven? But he hadn't spent enough of his life in concert halls to be sure, and in any case he was too busy to give a damn.

## ONE MORNING IN 150,000 BCE

When it stopped at last, Nicholas and Alec were lying in a state of collapse on either side of Edward. Mendoza clung to him, gasping. They were drenched with sweat. There was sunlight flooding in, and the sound of the sea, and a vast creaking as the storm bottle retracted and the masts deployed. The anchor rattled away and dropped with a splash.

Edward opened his eyes and looked down at her.

"There now," he said, only a little unsteadily. "Wasn't that amusing, my dear?"

"Yes," she moaned. She opened her eyes and looked up at him. "We never did *that* before. I'd remember that."

"What's immortal life without a little variety now and then?" he said. He glanced out the porthole and saw cliffs rising sheer from an emerald sea, up out of sight. "And I believe we've reached our destination! Are we lying off Cape San Martin, Captain?"

*Aye, sir,* the Captain told him, with perhaps just a shade of uneasiness in his voice.

"I thought so. California, my love. Will you walk ashore?"

"Sleep first!" she pleaded, her head falling on his shoulder.

"Anything to oblige a lady," he said smugly, and unfastened the harness. Getting his hands under her he lurched to his feet, and after a tottery moment strode in triumph to Alec's stateroom, with Alec and Nicholas staggering after him, panting for breath.

They sank down on the coverlet and Mendoza was asleep almost at once. Edward found he wanted a cigar very much, and as the only place he could get one was in cyberspace he relinquished control to Nicholas, Alec having already passed out. Nicholas was too exhausted to do more than peer balefully at Edward as he took Mendoza in his arms, and then he too sank into unconsciousness.

*Cigar, please, Captain,* Edward ordered. He sprawled back into the pillows, taking a virtual Hoyo Du Monterrey from midair already lit. *Thank you.* He drew and exhaled sensuously, smiling at the ceiling.

**Right then, laddie, it's time we talked.**

*Talk away,* Edward said, blowing a smoke ring.

**What in thunder did you think you was bloody playing at?**

*I don't believe I care for your tone, sir,* said Edward blandly. *You're speaking to a commander in Her Majesty's Navy, remember?*

**You damned idiot, didn't you notice the Crome's radiation she was generating whilst ye was having yer fun?**

*Yes, thank you, I did notice.* Edward writhed in happy recollection. *Who'd have thought there were new pleasures to be discovered, at my advanced age?*

**Would it interest you to know that we nearly wound up off course on our beam-ends, thanks to yer little game?**

*What the hell do you mean?* Edward rose on his elbows, scowling.

**I mean that there was a second, there, when something pulled us a few points into the wind. Not that you'd have noticed, blazing away like a twelve-pound gun as you was, but we was yanked astern so's we was moving forward in time for a beat or two, d'ye see? It were all I could do to get us on course again so we didn't fetch up God only knows when.**

*Good Christ.* Edward sat up and took the cigar out of his mouth. *You think it was the Crome's radiation?*

*I reckon so, lad, since it happened when she was throwing it brightest.*

Edward narrowed his eyes, thinking.

*Now I wonder,* he said at last, *if this wasn't the same phenomenon that afflicted her in that canyon in Los Angeles? At the place with the quaint name.*

**Hollywood?**

*Hollywood, to be sure. She was taken forward then, as we were just now. Can it be possible the stuff exerts some kind of retrograde force? An energy of opposition, as it were? If that's the case, we really can travel to the future after all—since it seems we were being pulled with her. The trick is to get her to generate the radiation whilst we're in transit.*

**I don't like the odds. All the test records I've accessed show Crome's radiation ain't dependable for anything but blue lights. It ain't quantifiable, it ain't qualifiable. It never produces the same effect twice. Not under test conditions. I'll grant you it may manifest differently in yer lady than in mere mortals, but I'd want to run tests afore we tried anything.**

*But, look here. If she can go* forward *through time—what's to stop us sending her ahead to see what will happen after 2355?* Edward puffed out clouds of virtual cigar smoke in his excitement. *Good God, what a tactical advantage that'd give us!*

**Aye, maybe. But what if the Silence is caused by a cataclysm like a meteor hitting the planet? You might send her straight into an inferno. How'd we know, eh? We'd never get her back.**

Edward shuddered. *No. I won't imperil her like that, not for any advantage.*

**Besides, just because she done it once don't mean the lass can do it whenever we want her to, like a card trick. We don't know enough about Crome's.**

*One thing seems plain.* Edward looked down at Mendoza fondly. *It's passion strikes the spark.* He ran a hand along the curve of her thigh.

**It ain't plain at all! Could be a dozen different factors. I'd have said stress, more likely, maybe coupled with some sexual arousal. Don't you go planning on scudding along bare-poled through time with her again, until we know it ain't dangerous. I'll allow I can't think of a pleasanter way for a man to die, but them's my orders, laddie. See you follow 'em.**

*I beg your pardon?* said Edward, with a very unpleasant light in his eyes.

**By the powers, what's got you bridling so at a sensible command? My little Alec's always been one to do as he's told.**

And so was I, once, muttered Edward, having another drag on his cigar. *Until it got me eight bullets in my back.*

**Then all the more reason not to be a fool. If you'd had yer old Captain with you back then, you'd have lived to waltz away with yer lady here, and saved everybody a deal of sorrow and care.**

*And I maintain, Captain, that I did* live. *Look at me! My life force continues as strong as ever. We really ought to make plans to search for my own proper body, once Mendoza's herself again. I'm quite sure the Company's storing it somewhere, pending my revival.*

**There ain't nothing about it in the Project Adonai file, son.**

*Undoubtedly because it's been kept a secret. I know how these people think, you see, I was one of them! The right hand never tells the left what it's about.*

**And them autopsy pictures in the file?**

Edward grimaced. *Those might have been of surgery, not an autopsy.*

**Maybe. Whether or not you shuffled off yer own coil, I ain't letting Alec die. I'm for going after the silver tube you all come out of in the first place.**

Edward tipped virtual ash into a dish that materialized on the bedside table. He looked mulish a long moment before shrugging.

*As you like.* He patted Mendoza's derriere. *I dare say she'll be twice as happy with two husbands.*


LATER THAT SAME DAY


"Trees," Mendoza said like a prayer, clinging to the rail and pointing. They were making their way, without much sail on, along the primeval California coastline.

"Yeah," Alec said sleepily, "they're trees, all right." He put his arms around her and leaned, looking out at the forbidding country. It was all plunging gorges and soaring peaks of rock like black emerald, the land dropping steeply away into the sea. Here and there the cliff faces gleamed wet where falls descended, vaporing out to mist and rainbows before ever reaching the surf below. Trees marched in serrated ranks upward, making a dense green gloom in the canyons and striding like gods along the ridges, except where lightning or slides had cleared a few acres of mountain meadow, tiny patches of sunlight quiet and distant on the heights. His eyes widened as he took it all in. "Awesome."

"But the trees are bigger," Mendoza said. "And it's all *greener.*" She turned to look up at him. "When were we here before?"

Alec raced mentally through her journals. "Seventeen hundreds," he said. "The red Indians were here but the Europeans weren't much."

"Ah," she said, nodding. "Climate change. Look at all the streams! No walking miles and miles to find water now."

"Nope," Alec said. Nicholas, leaning on the rail beside them, wondered when she'd had to do that. He looked up at the somber wilderness and thought of her alone there in the long years, when he'd been . . . what? A sediment of ash in the bank of the Medway River? He reached out a hand to touch her face, but Alec was pulling her backward for a kiss.

"When can we make landfall, Captain?" he said.

*You see a likely spot, boy? Nothing here but avalanches and flumes. My charts say the coastline ain't so grim a few leagues southerly, so we'll try our luck there. I reckon you'll find plenty of room for a picnic then.*

"Okay." Alec kissed the top of Mendoza's head. A picnic, he reflected. I've got my ship, I've got *her,* I've got an undiscovered place, and we're going to go explore and have adventures together. Exactly what I always wanted. And I don't deserve any of it.

But Mendoza turned to smile at him, and he smiled back. He caught her hands and whirled her in a little impromptu swing dance along the deck. She followed awkwardly at first; but within a moment or two her body acquired the rhythms somehow, and she was matching him, step for step, effortless, anticipating his moves as no partner he'd ever been with had done. Nicholas and Edward paced them, looking on hungrily.

"Oh, this is marvelous," she said. "This is, this is—dancing! Isn't it?"

"That's my baby," Alec said. "I'll take you dancing—ballrooms, and clubs and—" He remembered a passage from her journal. "I know where we can go! The Avalon Ballroom on Catalina Island, you always wanted to go there."

"Did I? Okay," she said, twirling under his arm.

*Santa Catalina Island?* Edward frowned. *Are you mad? Dr. Zeus will infest that place, and I should know. I helped put them there.*

Alec ignored him, as the sheer elation of the physical movement caught him up in a way it hadn't in years. Mendoza swung back toward him, her face flushed with delight.

"Captain! Give us some music," he said, launching her with his hands, and as the music roared over the ship's speakers she came down light as a bird and sprang back, floating through the complicated steps as though she'd been dancing them all her life.

He gave a raw whoop of triumph and seized her, and they went together along the deck faster now, executing the figures in perfect time, moving as one body. Edward and Nicholas were pulled with them, running along helpless, too caught up in their arousal to notice when the deck began to crackle with blue fire.

The Captain noticed, and very nearly shut off the music; but after a moment's consideration he instead activated a whole battery of instruments to record, to measure and analyze the phenomenon occurring there on the deck.

And when the music drew to its close and the dancers stopped, panting, the blue light flickered out as though it had never been there. Nothing had happened, after all.

"My, this saves time," said Mendoza, watching as the cliff face as it dropped past them. "Did we do this before? All I remember is having to climb."

"Oh, we did that, too," lied Alec breezily, piloting the agboat over the lip of the cliff. Here a headland of broad meadows sloped back to the mountains. Immense redwoods spired up from the high places. Closer down to the meadowline there were oak trees, too, laurels and Monterey cypress.

Alec had brought them up on a long ragged point that projected out above the sea, open and sunny, perhaps a kilometer long and half as wide. On the north side of the meadow a dark cataract came roaring over green boulders before it plunged away, down the cliff to the sea a thousand feet below. Alec steered for it.

*Not back there,* Edward said. *Too close to the mountains! Best to put some open ground between ourselves and anything that might come out of those trees.*

*But it's shady and there's water,* Alec said. *Besides, if the Company tries any sneak attacks, we're armed.* He patted the disrupter in its holster meaningfully. *And it's too long ago for there to be any red Indians. I checked. Nothing here but us and Nature, okay?*

"Beautiful trees," said Mendoza dreamily, stretching out the new boots Bully Hayes had fabricated for her. Alec wore hiking boots, cargo pants, and an old shirt. Edward had ordered a suit of severely correct virtual Victorian field garb for the occasion; Nicholas, who felt hopelessly lost, simply wore his ordinary black clothing.

Alec took a deep breath as he pulled them up on the streambank.

"What a green place! Smell that air." He set the agboat down and jumped out, turning to her. Mendoza took his hand and stepped out on the alien shore, and for a moment looked startled.

"What a *big* place," she said. "I have so much to do."

"But we're on holiday now, remember?" Alec told her, shivering, for the shadow of the redwoods was ice-cold. He led her out into the sunlight. "No worries. Look at all the wildflowers!"

"Look at the *Datura meteloides,*" Mendoza said, then ran forward. "No, it isn't! *Calystegia macrostegia.* Look at the size!"

All Alec could see was a big white flower, but he came and made suitably astonished noises as she knelt over it, examining the leaves and following the vine back to its root as though it were a power lead. Edward was surveying the meadow, studying the treeline. Nicholas was watching Mendoza sadly.

"Variant of convolvulus, but the leaves are atypical—" she muttered, crawling along on hands and knees. "Sagitate, as all *macrostegia*—gigantiform, and—" She looked up, looked around. "Where's the—" Her gaze riveted with purpose on the picnic basket that Alec was just hauling from the agboat. "I need the—"

Her face became confused, and then went utterly blank. Alec, glancing over at her, felt the hair stand on the back of his neck.

*Why's she looking like that?* he cried silently.

**Blocked memory retrieval, I reckon,** the Captain told him. **The lassie**

*was programmed as a botanist, remember? It's hell going against yer*
*programming, believe me.*

Alec shuddered. Nicholas could bear it no longer and seized control.
He knelt down beside Mendoza, taking her hand.

"Quid rei est, mi amores?" he said gently. Her eyes focused and fixed on
him.

"Nescio—" she replied. "Quid faciam? Ubi sunt instrumenta mea?"
She halted, surprised, and then she laughed. "We're not speaking Cinema
Standard, are we? How strange."

"We have spoken in many tongues," he said, feeling his heart soar.
"And just so we used to speak long ago, when you worked in the Garden.
It was our way of speaking in secret. Do you remember when you were a
slave?"

"Yes, I remember that."

*What's he saying to her?* Alec asked. *What's that language?*

*Latin,* said Edward in disgust. *It seems Brother Nicholas has found means
to exploit his pointless skills. Well, never mind; it's proving useful in an awkward circumstance.*

"You worked in a garden and collected plants," Nicholas explained.
"You had a basket with tools. I think you must be remembering that. But,
my love, you are free now! There is nothing you must do any more, no
work other than to please yourself. Do you understand?"

"Oh!" Her cheeks were scarlet. "How embarrassing, to forget."

"No, no, my love," he said, unable to stop himself from leaning forward
and taking her by the shoulders. "It's sweet to speak with you in the old
way. It makes me remember when we were young, and lay together in that
garden."

"I remember this. We were supposed to be working; but we'd make
love all the time instead. And—they punished us?"

"Yes, beloved," Nicholas said, thinking that it was close enough to the
truth.

She was staring around at the solemn trees. "And this was a garden,
too. But . . ." She turned back to him, and her eyes were a little frightened.
"This is not a human place."

"No, beloved."

"Was I lost here?"

"Long years, my heart. Yet I have found you again," Nicholas told her, kissing her brow. "And I will bring your soul out of this darkness."

"But—" She looked up at him. "Who will do the work?"

*See what I mean? Programming.*

"You don't—" Nicholas struggled for words in frustration, and Alec stepped in.

"The Company's made some other slaves now, to do all that. You know what your work is? You've got this project going on, er, Indian maize! That was it. You remember that?"

*Smart lad.*

She blinked at his sudden return to English, but her face brightened with comprehension. "Yes! Must produce a variety with the vigor of ancient cultivars yet retaining the high yield of modern hybrids while increasing levels of tryptophan, lysine, and accessible niacin."

"Er—yeah," Alec said. "Except, er, of course, we lost everything you were working on, when the accident happened."

"Damn!"

"But it's okay! The Captain will help you start your work over and anyway, we've got all the time in the world now," Alec said. "Remember? So let's have our picnic, and then what do you say we go exploring?"

"Okay." She took his outstretched hand. He helped her up from her knees.


It was a nice picnic: smoked oysters on little crackers, soy protein sandwiches, and a big thermos bottle of iced fruit tea. They ate seated companionably on the gunwale of the agboat, and though Edward grumbled silently about the soy protein by and large they enjoyed their treat very much.

"It'll be even nicer when we can grow fresh stuff," remarked Mendoza.

"Yup," agreed Alec, not knowing what else to say.

Afterward they walked up the stream bank a few hundred meters, and Edward took the lead in their exploration. Nicholas peered up now and then at the mountainside, unable to shake the feeling that something immense and silent watched them as they clambered over the green boulders.

"If I didn't know better, I'd suspect this was jade," Edward said, stooping to examine a rock the size of his fist.

"It is," Mendoza said.

"I beg your pardon?"

"Spectrographic analysis?" She looked at him in surprise.

"Er—of course it is. By Jove, what a fortune this would be worth in Macao." He chuckled and tossed it away.

*Really?* Alec looked back at the rock. He stared around at the green pebbles scattered everywhere.

"Have we ever been there?" Mendoza said.

"Macao? No, my dear, I don't believe you have. I was there once, on some nasty business," Edward said. His face darkened a little. "Company business, as I know now."

"Oh," said Mendoza.

*Should we maybe take some of this stuff back to the ship?* Alec tried, without success in his virtual state, to pick up a glossy stone. *Might be worth something.*

*Hast thou not gold enough, boy?* Nicholas looked at him askance.

They reached the end of the box canyon and peered up at another waterfall; speculated on swimming in the freezing water and decided against it. They found gooseberries growing along the stream bank, but only Nicholas liked them. Mendoza cut a sprig and tucked it in her pocket. As they came back, Alec took control, bent and grabbed up a piece of jade at last.

"Let's collect some of this," he said.

"Oh. To trade with?" Mendoza looked around and picked up a piece obligingly.

"Yes indeed. I know places that'd pay serious cash for jade. Even if we don't trade it—big raw lumps of gemstone, what a cool kind of loot to have! Sheer barbaric splendor."

Mendoza nodded. "Okay. Let's have splendor."

"Great," Alec said, pacing ahead of her. "Come on, we can collect an emperor's ransom!"

There was a great deal of jade along the stream. Working together, in a few minutes they had filled all the bellows pockets in Alec's explorer pants and prized loose a boulder of considerable size, which Alec insisted on lugging up to the agboat, wet and slightly muddy.

"Whew!" he grunted, setting it inside and leaning away, bracing his hands into the small of his back.

*Alec, have you strained yerself?*

*No.*

"What will we do with it?" Mendoza said. "It's certainly a big one."

"Get Bully Hayes on it with some rock drills and have him carve something, maybe." Alec panted for breath. "Would you like that, huh? A statue? Or, hey, what about a jade throne? A jade bench anyway. And some jade drinking cups"—he began to giggle—"with *Souvenir of Prehistoric California* carved on 'em."

*Idiot boy,* said Edward loftily. Nicholas looked over his shoulder at the shadow under the trees. Somewhere far in, a coyote howled.

They wandered out across the meadow after that, holding hands as they ventured through the wildflowers to the cliff's edge, idyllic as could be, though Alec crunched rather as he walked from all the jade in his pockets, and found it difficult to bend his knees.

"It's pulling your pants down, too," Mendoza said affectionately, glancing around behind him. "Cheeky."

"Whoops." Alec hauled up on his waistband and unbuckled his belt to refasten it. Mendoza looked out over the wide sea and the *Captain Morgan* quiet at anchor below them.

"This is a beautiful place," she said. "But . . ."

"But what?"

"I think you become like a tree or a stone, if you get lost here," she said quietly. "Not human. That would be a good thing, if you were very sad."

"But you won't be sad anymore, ever," Alec assured her.

"I hope not." Her voice was older, quieter, thoughtful; not that of a young girl at the moment but very much the survivor Alec remembered from the agricultural station, the preternaturally calm woman who had ministered to him.

Now Mendoza frowned and turned her head to stare inland, just as the Captain transmitted:

*Alec! Heads up! Bloody big life form coming down that hill east northeast!*

"Oh, how tedious," Mendoza said, in tones of mild irritation. "That grizzly bear has noticed us."

"What?" Alec swung around to follow her gaze and beheld the biggest animal he'd ever seen in his life, an immense mass of yellow-silver fur shambling down toward the meadow, appallingly fast for all its clumsiness.

*"Ursus horribilis."* Mendoza shook her head. "Well, we'd better leave now."

"But—but—wild animals never bother you if you let them alone," Alec said.

"Yes, but that's a grizzly bear," Mendoza said, as though that would explain everything. "Shall we go?"

And then she wasn't there, she had just vanished from beside Alec, and the bear had come down off the hillside and was lolloping out across the meadow straight for him. It had cut off Alec from the agboat, where Mendoza was standing. Her expression of amazement was rapidly becoming one of consternation.

*ALEC!* the Captain roared. Alec stood rooted where he was in terror, aware of thirty pounds of jade where he'd never needed it less and a sheer drop at his back. Edward and Nicholas attempted to bolt and were pulled up sprawling by his immobility.

*Run, boy,* shouted Nicholas, desperately trying and failing to summon a virtual boar-spear. *What, art thou lame?*

*You bloody ass*—Edward said, and seizing control he drew the disrupter pistol.

*Stop! You can't shoot a wild animal!* Alec said, as the bear thundered ever closer and Mendoza reappeared near them screaming:

"What are you doing? Let's go!"

But Edward, his face cold and stern, was concentrating on the onrushing bear. He turned edge-on, stiffly upright in the stance of the nineteenth-century marksman, left arm down at his side, right arm extended at full length, taking careful aim.

"A moment, please, my dear," he said, and fired.

At precisely that same instant something bright came streaking in from the direction of the sea, having the general appearance of a badminton shuttlecock but being in reality the extremely small and precise guided missile the Captain had launched from a concealed port on the ship. It reached the grizzly bear's left eye just as the beam from Edward's disrupter did.

There wasn't as much noise as you'd think, but there was a lot more mess.

Edward lowered the pistol and looked at it appreciatively.

"My word," he said. He lurched slightly as Mendoza impacted with him, gibbering. He slid an arm around her.

"You could have—Why didn't—I thought you'd—" she said. Edward leaned down and kissed her, hard.

"Okay," she said in a faint little voice, when he'd lifted his mouth from hers at last.

"Now then," he said firmly, "there was never any danger, you see? But it would have been a trifle inconvenient to have had to sprint in these trousers. The jade, you know."

"Right," she said weakly.

*Alec, I'll—I'll keelhaul you when I get you home, so help me God.*

*Oh, shut up,* Alec transmitted, aware he'd virtually wet himself and hoping it hadn't carried over. Nicholas just stood there ashen-faced, staring at the creature that would have made short work of any pit bull in old London.

"Pity about the head," said Edward, crossing the (dreadfully short) distance between the spot where the vast corpse had come to rest and where he had been standing. He surveyed the body critically. "No way to mount what's left, I don't think! Though perhaps we can get the mechanicals up here to take the pelt, eh? Make a rather tasteful rug for the saloon, I dare say."

*Do you know the kind of penalties you'd have to pay if you killed an animal in my time?* Alec said. *Let alone made a trophy out of it?*

*You poor fool.* Edward looked up at the wild mountain, cold-eyed. *Nature loves her blood sacrifices. Be grateful she didn't take you instead.*

In the end he insisted on having his holo taken, one booted foot on the bear's foreleg, one hand displaying the disrupter pistol aimed at the sky in a casual sort of way, staring into the frontal camera lens with arrogantly glacial composure.

And after all, when they had returned to the ship the Captain pointed out that they could take neither bearskin nor jade forward through time with them, so it was just as well Edward had had the moment immortalized in a holoshot.

*You ain't taking up no big game hunting, neither,* he admonished Edward that evening, when Mendoza had fallen asleep and the gimbal light had been turned down.

*Oh, bugger off,* Edward said, producing a lit Cuban Punch. He was still unable to manipulate code to his satisfaction, but Alec had finally given up and written him a program he could use to make things like virtual cigars. Edward blew an indolent smoke ring now. *Out of all the kills I made in my life, do you think there were many I'd want to boast about? Shooting a bear seems positively virtuous by comparison.*

Alec glared at Edward. *So much for all your crap about two infants wandering in Paradise.*

*I never said weapons were unnecessary in Paradise. And our adventure today did serve to point up a lesson, didn't it?*

*Thou speakst respecting mortality,* Nicholas said to Edward.

*Precisely.* Edward angled his cigar like a pointer.

*Aye, and well you might. You see now, Alec, what near happened today? The girl come nigh to figuring out you ain't no immortal like her. You didn't know those rocks was jade, you couldn't spot that bear afore it became a threat, and you couldn't move at hyperspeed.*

*All too true, alas,* Edward said, looking at Alec severely.

*Like it was my lie!* Alec bristled. *I'm not the one who told her we were immortal.*

*A strategic necessity,* Edward replied.

*And you near got mauled by a bear, which would have given the game away pretty well, too,* the Captain continued. *As it was, you strained yer back.*

*I did not,* Alec said.

*Yes, you did,* Edward said, as Nicholas joined in with:

*Boy, thou liest.*

*I DID NOT!*

*Alec, you damned fool, I'm connected directly to yer nervous system, remember?*

*I told you about those little twinges,* said Edward smugly, *and if I recall correctly, whenever I invited a lady to assume the superior position it was generally because—*

**Belay that, Edward. Alec, son, here it is: you ain't never been sick a day in yer life, and I reckon if you lived quiet like a sensible man it'd take a couple of centuries to wear you down. But there's accidents, Alec, whether you go out of yer way to get killed like these two fine fellows done or just get hurt bad. And what's yer lady going to think, eh, the first time you sit down in the saloon careless and hit yer head on the booth lamp, as I've seen you do more times'n I can recall?**

*I don't do it all that often,* Alec said, sullen-faced, and Edward made a scornful noise. He flicked virtual ash from the tip of the Punch.

*Good God, I've seen you do it twice myself. And shall I tell you something else to which you may look forward, as the years advance? You may be a veritable Priapus just now, but—*

**Edward, stand to.**

*I don't even know what one of those is,* Alec snarled, and Edward was laughing in a superior kind of way when Nicholas said:

*Peace, thou. Boy, is it not plain? We can't lie to her forever.*

*I know,* said Alec, turning his head to look at Mendoza where she lay curled in Nicholas's arms. *And I know what I've got to do. So you can just shut up about it, Edward, yeah? I'll have the damn immortality operation, or whatever it is.*

**That's my little Alec.**

*After what she's been through, this is the least I can do for her. Especially if it's the only way we can keep her safe.*

*Good lad,* purred Edward. *A sensible choice and, moreover, a moral one.*

**Why, son, it ain't going to be no harder than getting yer tattoo. It'll just take a little longer. You might say this is Nature taking her right and proper course, aye.**

But Alec turned to Nicholas.

*Do you think it's the right thing to do?*

Nicholas looked down at Mendoza as she slept.

**Go on, Nick. You been studying religion; tell him it's right.**

*Ay,* Nicholas said. *Since it is done for love's sake. What other law is left?*

Alec nodded slowly.

*That's my good Nick! Now that we're all square, Alec, there's things we need to consider. I can start you on the Pineal Tribrantine Three straight off. The place we're stuck, I reckon, is that there crucible of prime DNA you were made from. I've already lifted the file for **Adonai** out of Dr. Zeus's archives. I even got biomechanicals designed what's better than the Company uses! Every one of 'em a molecular Philosopher's Stone. But I need that DNA for a genetic template. Think of it like a treasure map, Alec, what'll tell the little bastards where they got to go for the loot.*

Then obviously the next step is to locate the crucible, said Edward, and take it. Would it be a silver tube like the one in Mendoza's file?

*Aye, sir, likely, or a bit bigger. You were a lot more valuable, being an experimental prototype, so they'd have made a bucket of it.*

And where would they be likely to keep such a thing?

*Might be in a Company base in England, as that's closest to where the work was done; might be on Santa Catalina Island, that being a high-security location. The question is, when? Could be in either place or both places, different times.*

Can you narrow the search down? said Alec.

*Aye, lad, but there's a power of data to sift through, to be sure.*

And a good deal of preparation to make, Edward said. If we're to cruise through Time as though we were on the Grand Tour, we'll need suitable clothing for the various temporal ports of call. He stubbed out his cigar.

And coin, Nicholas added.

*Bless yer little hearts. See how well my boys can plan, when they leave off fighting amongst themselves? I'll get right on them questions as soon as yer all asleep. It's nigh seven bells, gentlemen, at the end of a busy day. Settle down now.*

There were murmurs of assent, and the gimbal lamp dimmed still further. The *Captain Morgan* cruised along under stars, smooth over the swell. After a while Alec's gentle snore filled the darkness, or it might have been Nicholas or Edward snoring.

As soon as the Captain registered that all three men slept soundly, there was a glint of moving steel from a corner of the room. Billy Bones crept forward to the bedside without a sound.

It drew down the coverlet and sheet, slowly, to expose Alec's bare thigh. One of its manipulative members came forward with a hypojet and took aim, preparing to deliver a charge of anesthetic and antiseptic to the target area on his leg. Ready to swing into place, after the hypojet deployed, was a tube tipped by a gleaming needle some six inches long.

But before it was able to deliver, there was a sudden movement in the bed. Mendoza, snarling at Billy, seized the hypojet and and bent it backward.

*Now then, dearie, now then!* whispered the Captain. *What a dutiful wife you are, to be sure, and such a light sleeper. But there's nothing amiss for you to worry yer sweet head over. Let go old Billy, there's a love!*

"What were you doing?" she demanded.

*Don't twist the frame like that, dearie, it hurts. Bloody hell, now I'll have to tell you. Poor Alec was so anxious you shouldn't find out what happened to him.*

"What happened to Alec?" Mendoza looked confused. She let go of the hypojet, and Billy Bones scuttled backward a few paces. "*What* happened to Alec? Tell me!"

*Well, Mrs. Checkerfield, we ain't been quite honest with you, to be sure; but it was all for yer own sake. That there accident, see, where you was hurt so bad? Our boy didn't like to tell you, but he was hurt bad, too,* the Captain improvised.

"He was?" Horrified, Mendoza turned to look at Alec where he slept.

*Aye, ma'am, he were, going back to save you. He weren't damaged so bad as you were, you may lay to that, but bad enough. You recollect what nanobots are, do you?*

"Biomechanicals?" she said, pulling away the blanket to examine Alec.

*Well, his were all destroyed when he was hit by a disrupter wave. You can scan him if you like*—the Captain said, observing that Mendoza was already doing so—*and I reckon you'll see how much he sacrificed to rescue you. Why, the poor lad's near as vulnerable as a mortal creature. He's got no little biomechanicals to repair his hurts.*

Seeing that this was indeed the case, Mendoza gave a wail of grief and threw her arms around Alec, who slept on unconcernedly. She kissed his sleeping face, dropping hot tears there. The Captain waited thoughtfully until she was a little calmer before sending Billy Bones forward to offer her a handkerchief.

"I *knew* something happened to him! I had dreams about—about blood, and fire," Mendoza said, wiping her eyes.

*Aye, ma'am. You must have known unconscious-like our Alec ain't quite himself yet.*

"His poor hurt back—" Fresh tears started as she reached out her hand to him.

*He were hiding his damage from you, so's you wouldn't be scared. But I reckon yer a brave girl, eh, and too smart to be fooled for long? And I reckon you've noticed he's, er, just a little scrambled? Sometimes—*

"The different speaking idioms he uses, yes," she said, her eyes widening in sudden comprehension. "I was beginning to be worried." She was silent a long moment.

"I, myself—am not completely recovered," she said at last.

*No, dearie, to be sure you ain't.*

"How can I protect him?" she said. "How can he be repaired, Sir Henry?"

*Well, now, I were just about to give him another treatment when you near broke old Billy's arm. If you'll allow him to get on with it—*

"Please!" Mendoza said. "I am so sorry, Sir Henry. The servomechanism is bent."

*Old Billy's seen worse, dearie, and he'll just take himself off to the shop for a new arm,* the Captain said, sending Billy in to inject Alec at last. *There now. Alec'll feel ever so much better come morning, Mrs. Checkerfield. But not a word to him that I've told you about this, mind.*

"No, of course not. His biomechanicals will rebuild themselves, now, yes?" Mendoza said, drawing up the coverlet around Alec and settling down to take him in her arms.

*Ah. Why, as to that—we've a bit of work to do yet. Got to plot a course for the storage facility where his genetic sample is kept. I reckon you'll recollect, ma'am, the DNA template the Company makes when they puts somebody through the immortality process? I want that afore I can make him what he ought to be. Again.*

She clung to Alec, looking as though she were going to weep afresh; but after a moment the fear was replaced by anger, and her black eyes went hard as stone.

"Dr. Zeus did this to us."

*Aye, girl, him and his lackeys.*

Mendoza was silent a long moment, watching Alec sleep. The Captain observed her keenly. He conjectured what broken recollections might be surfacing in her mind. Blood and fire and death, isolation and exile, lost hopes, unspeakable suffering?—and he wondered, with a certain amount of unease, what he should do if the amnesia lifted. But her voice was soft, when she spoke at last.

"How dare they?" was all she said.

*Damn right. Now, you be a good girl and go back to sleep, eh?*

She sighed and settled down again, closing her eyes. The Captain did the electronic equivalent of sighing, too, and sent Billy Bones limping off for repair. He was the most powerful machine in the world; he was clever and devious. Nevertheless, he spared no thought for the tiny sprig of gooseberry plant that Mendoza had set in a bud vase on the saloon table, in a spot where it might catch the morning sun.

*Alec!*

Alec grunted in annoyance. He rolled over and was jarred awake by the twinge in his lower back and a sharper twinge, lower still, that suggested an insect bite.

*Alec, we got a temporal anomaly!* The Captain, echoing in his head, sounded distinctly odd. Beside him, Edward sat bolt upright. Nicholas opened his eyes.

*A what?* Alec attempted to move his lower back into the warm proximity of Mendoza's bottom, but Edward took control, vaulting from the bed and dragging him along.

*In the saloon!*

*Is it dangerous?* Edward demanded, shrugging into Alec's bathrobe, which resulted in Nicholas being hauled unceremoniously out of bed as well.

*Well, it don't look dangerous—but—*

Edward strode away to the saloon, as Alec followed grumbling and Nicholas staggered after, looking dazed. Stepping over the door frame, they halted.

*Er,* said Alec.

"Good God," said Edward, so startled he slipped back, and Alec got control again.

There was a gooseberry bush on the table, reaching almost up to the gimbal lamp. The bud vase lay on its side near the bush; a lacy fanwork of roots had spread out over the tabletop, following the path of the spilled water.

*It didn't register on my sensors, not a damn one, and I ain't—*

"What's the matter?" said Mendoza, yawning as she came up behind them. She spotted the gooseberry bush and gave a little cry of delight.

"Oh, look how nice it grew!" she said, pushing past them. "Poor thing, it needs water. But, see? Now you can have fresh berries, anytime."

*You, er, made the bush grow yerself, did you, dearie?*

*God's Holy Wounds,* cried Nicholas.

"No, I just made it part of the ship's temporal continuum, like you said," she replied proudly. Standing there, naked, with a wilting gooseberry bush in her arms, she became aware of Alec's shocked expression. "Oh. Was I not supposed to do that?"

"No, no, it's fine—" stammered Alec, at the same moment the Captain boomed, **Well, ain't my girl clever, figuring that out all by herself! It were just a little unexpected, that's all, darlin'—**

"Oh, how stupid of me! We don't have anywhere to put it yet, do we?" said Mendoza, clouding up.

**We'll stick it in a bucket, so we will. Never you mind.** The Captain seemed to have developed a slight electronic tremor in his voice. **Old Flint's just fetching one along now.**

Edward shouted silently. *Her diary! Remember? This happened in her garden, and she didn't know why! She must have some unwitting power—and just now she doesn't know she can't, and therefore—*

**We ain't a-telling her she can't, neither,** said the Captain, privately. Aloud, he said:

*You leave that for Flint, darlin', and go get yerself some clothes on afore you catches cold. What about a nice hot burgoo for breakfast, eh?*

"Okay," said Mendoza. She set down the bush and took Alec's hand, leading him back into the bedroom. As he followed, he was uncomfortably aware that Edward was watching her with a look of hungry speculation.

# ANOTHER MORNING
## IN 500,000 BCE

David Reed woke to the alarm without surprise, quickly found his plug and connected himself. When he removed the sleep mask he was able to see that it was a bright summer day. Beyond the windows of his Flat the gardener was mowing the lawn in tidy green stripes.

Yawning, David got out of bed and went to the bathroom for a shower. Anyone watching as David pulled off his pajama top would get a good look at what a cut-rate job of cyborging looked like, as opposed to, say, the job that Alec Checkerfield had been able to afford. Alec's was a work of art, graceful spirals in an intricate pattern just under his skin; David Reed's was patternless, the raw straight lines of a hack job. And whereas Alec had merely to wear a contact connector that resembled a handsome piece of Bronze Age jewelry, David did need that plug stuck in its port just above his topmost cervical vertebra, and it did need to be removed and sterilized every night.

But David had no idea that he'd been made a cyborg on the cheap. Even if he'd known about the level of comfort and elegance he might have had if the Company had been willing to spend that kind of money on him, he probably wouldn't have complained.

Ancilla had laid out a clean towel and his clean clothes when he emerged from the shower. He thanked her briefly. She murmured something polite and went off to prepare his breakfast.

David didn't like speaking to Ancilla much, though she resembled a very attractive woman. She was an artificial intelligence, and he felt that artificial things were creepy, and much preferred conversations with real girls, like Sylvya and Leslie, even though they were in fact cyberprojections of real girls living half a million years in the future.

Moreover, Ancilla assisted him with his sexual health, and that was embarrassing.

He sat down at the table where, as always, she had everything ready: the cup of herbal tea steaming in its recess, the bowl of oatmeal in its recess, the soy protein strips arranged into a whimsical little face in their recess, the tiny cup containing his vitamins and medications. Ancilla had made the table lovely for him, with a bright assortment of holographic flowers. David accepted the thoughtfulness as his due, took his medication, ate his breakfast, and responded reluctantly to her attempts at small talk.

He emptied his teacup and got to his feet. "Well, I guess I'd better go to the Office now," he told Ancilla.

"All right, dear. Have a nice day," Ancilla said, from her corner by the window where she was engaged, as she generally was, in the appearance of crocheting an afghan.

David cheered up as he stepped out onto the yellow track. There was London all bright beyond his window, there was Sylvya meeting his eye in a way that suggested she had something she needed to discuss with him in private, and there was Leslie placidly eating a breakfast sandwich from the Third Floor Lunchroom.

David sat down at his console. He logged in, turning now and then to glance at Leslie's progress with the sandwich. Presently she finished and got up to go wash her hands, as they had known she must, for the Third Floor Lunchroom's breakfast sandwich was invariably wet and runny. David leaped to his feet and tiptoed out along the yellow track to her desk.

"What is it?"

Sylvya turned and leaned as close as she could, adjusting her optics. "The people from the Third Floor want to put on a baby shower for Leslie."

"They do?" David was mystified. "What's a baby shower?"

"It's a party for the baby before it's born," Sylvya said. "Everyone gives the mother presents. Baby clothes and bath things, you know."

"Oh," said David, thinking it sounded as though it were in rather poor taste. Sylvya seemed to know what he was thinking, because she added:

"It's very socially aware, really. Everybody helps, see? But *we're* her coworkers, and if anybody's going to organize a party for her, it should be us."

"Right," David said, with a vague sense of outrage.

"And we ought to have the party here, where she works, and not down on the Third Floor where you can't even go," said Sylvya, pouting.

"That's not fair!" David said.

"It's all that Brandi as usual, having her own way and bossing everybody," Sylvya said. Brandi was the Third Floor Supervisor.

But here came Leslie, still rubbing sanitizer on her hands, and David mouthed *we'll talk later* to Sylvya and followed the yellow track back to his desk.

Feeling brilliantly clever, he sent a message to Brandi on the Third Floor:

WE'RE ALL, YOU SHOULD HAVE LESLIES PARTY UP HERE SO I CAN COME TOO. THAT WOULD BE FAIR. WHAT DO YOU THINK? AND TELL ME ABOUT PRESENTS SO I CAN GET ONE FOR HER.

He sent it and leaned back at his console, feeling like the most subtle of diplomats. Then he settled down to evaluating the status of the contents of Recess Eighteen beyond the Portal.

By evening his feeling of cleverness had been replaced by a peculiar unease. He refused to think about why he might be uneasy.

Ancilla was sitting in her customary corner, looking out into the starlit garden, but she turned to him and smiled as he came in from the Office.

"How nice to see you, David! Did you have a nice day?"

"It was pretty good," he said brusquely, and went to the kitchen where his supper was waiting. Ancilla said:

"It's Savory Bounty tonight, with Lemon Herb Potatoes and Green Peas. That's one of your favorites, isn't it?"

"Sometimes," he said, filling his tumbler with distilled water. "I need you to order something in realtime."

"What is it, dear?"

"There's going to be this thing called a *baby shower* at the office," David said, lifting a spoonful of peas to his mouth. "I need you to order a present delivered so Leslie can get it at the party."

"How thoughtful!" said Ancilla. "What would you like me to get for her?"

"I don't know." David scowled at his Savory Bounty. The thought of Leslie was making him cross now.

"I see," Ancilla said. "Well, do you know if she's having a little girl or a little boy?"

"Little boy," David said.

"I can order some bath things and a blue bath towel, and have everything wrapped in blue," said Ancilla. "You really ought to send a card, too."

"All right," David said. "Do it."

She watched him as he ate.

"You seem a little unhappy this evening, David," she said. "Do you want to talk about it?"

"No!" he snapped.

"All right," she said, and sighed, and appeared to turn her attention to her crocheting again. He finished his supper hurriedly, leaving the dirty dishes where they were for Ancilla's servo to clear away. He was in some haste to get into bed, thinking that a good two hours of Totter Dan would drive away all those thoughts about Leslie.

Unfortunately, the game he chose tonight was Totter Dan in Microbe Land, which seemed to make the thoughts worse, especially as he was playing rather badly. Most of the time, instead of shooting the giant wobbling microbes and gaining Power Points, Totter Dan was missing and being engulfed by them, awful big round slimy things, absorbing him, swallowing him up . . .

Midway through his third game matters became acute. To David's dismay, Ancilla read his condition accurately and activated the sex glove, which came popping out of the bedside console the way air masks deployed on an aircraft in trouble, and it dangled there lewdly.

"Oh, dear, I *knew* you needed to talk," Ancilla said in a tone of gentle reproach, sitting on the chair beside his bed.

"I didn't want to," David said irritably. "Besides, it's only been six months since last time!"

"Well, but these things happen," Ancilla reminded him. "You have to expect them often at this time in your life. Someday they'll stop."

"I wish they'd stop now," David complained, adjusting his pajamas. "It's all that Leslie. Getting all big like that. She's making me do it. It's selfish."

"Can't be helped, David dear. Now, put on the glove. You want to be healthy, after all."

And it was good to be healthy, fundamentally morally good, so David put on the glove. Ancilla activated it, and stood and opened her robe to do the wonderful, frightening things she did for his excitement, that so fascinated and repelled him as he watched her.

It was over quickly. He groaned in relief, and the glove cleaned away all nastiness and retracted back into the console. Ancilla sat down again.

"There we are, David. Would you like to talk about it now?"

"No," David said, pulling up his blanket. "I want to go to sleep." He opened the drawer and took out his sleep mask hurriedly.

"Good night, then, David," Ancilla said. She retreated to her corner, and resumed looking out into the night.

"Good night," he said, after a brief conflicted silence.

# ONE EVENING IN 2318 AD

The Rogue Cyborg is doing serious Rogue Cyborg stuff. He's crouched before a data terminal as though it were an ancient altar, and from the look on his face what he's praying for is desperate and bloody revenge. The green light of the console throws his grim features into spooky relief. Of course, he's not really praying; he's stealing secrets, popping through locked files at a rate of speed that would be impossible for any mortal but Alec Checkerfield.

Only a Rogue, you see, could have possibly obtained certain codes, and only by having them downloaded to him directly from another Rogue. Otherwise he'd never have found them himself, not in a thousand years of hacking around. Since he only has thirty-seven years to play with, this is a good thing.

Now, abruptly, his whole body stiffens. He pulls back from the terminal like a diver rising into air from impossible depths, and gulps in breath with a cry. He shakes his head, clearing away superfluous concerns, focusing all his intention on a bright golden particular he has brought up out of the fathomless sea of general information.

It's a key, of sorts. He examines it in awe and disbelief.

Then he's on his feet, pelting down the corridor as fast as he can go. The giant in the vault opens pale eyes to watch his approach, though he is still unable to lift his head.

---

"Father," Joseph shouted hoarsely. "I've got it! I've got the goddam Holy Grail. Or a piece of it anyway. You know what I've just found? Part of the Temporal Concordance!"

What he was referring to, of course, was the—literally—ultimate goal of the quest for knowledge: the record of known history, from its beginning to the year 2355, that enabled Dr. Zeus to send its operatives to the exact times and places that might be best mined for things like winning lottery tickets, race results, and stock futures, to say nothing of more subtle objectives.

The Temporal Concordance resembled a map, in some ways; but those travelers who needed it most were shown no more than a bare inch at a time, by decree of All-Seeing Zeus, since otherwise he would not be exclusively All-Seeing, would he? And every Company immortal is taught, from earliest school days, that it is a wise decision to obscure the future, in greater or lesser degrees, from each operative, lest the griefs of immortal life become too terrible to contemplate.

Also, omniscience isn't the kind of thing you want to leave lying around.

"Is It A Fragment Of Code," Budu asked.

"Yeah! Looks like something interstitial." Joseph swarmed the ladder up the tank. "It's giving me surveillance reports from the years 2345 to 2353. Look at it and see if I'm not right."

He reached into the bioregenerant and downloaded his bright bit of key. Budu was silent a long moment, accessing, integrating, correlating, and then:

"It Is Part Of The Temporal Concordance," he said.

"Boy, oh, boy, nobody's gonna stop us now," Joseph chortled. "Look out, Dr. Zeus! And you're absolutely sure about this, Father?"

"Yes. It Corresponds To The Other Sections."

"So it—Excuse me?" Joseph blinked. "What other sections?"

By way of answer Budu reached out and downloaded to Joseph in return. He clung to the top of his ladder unsteadily, feeling like a struck bell.

"Oh," he said. "Oh, my gosh, that's a lot of information. How long have you had this?"

"Since The Fifteenth Century."

"Were you ever going to tell me?"

"I Never Told Labienus."

"Good point," Joseph said. He blinked again, still integrating. "I think I'll just . . . crawl off and lie down someplace quiet for a while, until I can defrag and rearrange this stuff in my memory. Is that okay?"

"Go, Son."

Joseph fell off the ladder, picked himself up, and walked into a wall. He righted himself and wandered away.

It was a week before Joseph opened his eyes wide in the darkness, and his bloodthirsty look was back with a vengeance. He lay there awhile, smiling unpleasantly to himself; then he got to his feet and trotted off to speak to Budu.

"I've found him, Father."

"Who Did You Find," said the giant in the vault.

"The guy who took Mendoza," said Joseph. "The mortal schmuck. Dr. Zeus has a dossier on him. Marco was totally wrong; he'll be no New Enforcer. Hell, he won't even be a mortal employed by the Company. All he'll really be is a weasely hacker who'll manage to get into some of the Company files, so they've got him under surveillance, there in the future. His name'll be Alec Checkerfield."

"If The Man Is No More Than That, How Does He Disable Marco." Budu stared at Joseph from beyond the glass.

"He'll use poison. Maybe the same stuff that Victor used to take you down. He'll probably steal it from Dr. Zeus! No wonder Marco was such a mess." Joseph paced back and forth.

"Why Is He Twin To The Mortal You Hate So Much?"

Joseph opened and shut his mouth.

"Sheer coincidence," he said. "He's not Nicholas Harpole or Edward Whoever at all. Just somebody who looks like them."

"Why Has He Taken Your Daughter," inquired Budu, marveling at Joseph's ability to lie to himself.

"He just, uh, accidentally captured Mendoza when he went to Options Research. Maybe he took her hostage or something."

"Why Would He Go To Options Research."

"That's a good question, and I'm confident I can answer it. He went to Options Research, uh, to, uh, hide out after he blew up Mars Two!"

"Would You Seek Refuge In That Place."

"Well, no, but—he left as soon as he saw what it was like! Okay?"

"Why Has He Taken Your Daughter."

Joseph gritted his teeth.

"This Man Is More Than You Want To Think He Is," Budu said.

"All right!" said Joseph, seizing his hair at the temples. "So what am I supposed to do? Go back to thinking he's Satan incarnate? That he comes back to life over and over and tracks Mendoza down and destroys her every time? To say nothing of Lewis. How much sense does that make?"

"No Sense Without More Information," Budu said. "Do You Still Want To Find Your Daughter."

"Yes!" Joseph said fiercely, looking up at Budu. "Because I don't care who he is, he's bad for her! If—if she's damaged, after Options Research—how can he repair her? He's a *mortal*! And he's the mortal who blows up Mars Two, so the police of three worlds will be looking for him. What the hell is he going to do, buy her a rose-covered cottage to settle down in? Raise a family? No, no, no. He can't have her this time."

"You Have Missed What Is Obvious, Son," Budu said. "The Botanist Mendoza Is The Only Operative Who Has Moved Against The Current Of Time. She Alone Might Be Able To Learn The Truth About The Year 2355. The Company Imprisoned Her To Prevent Any Enemy From Using Her For That Purpose. Your Enemy Has Now Captured Her."

Joseph's eyes went wide. *That's* why he took her. What if he's the one who brings on 2355? Oh, that's too gruesome. What do we do? What do I do? Help me, Father, we can't let that happen!"

"Then Take Back This Pawn Before He Can Promote Her To Queen. If You Can Recapture Her, She May Be Of Use To Us."

"But how do I find them, Father?" said Joseph, pacing nervously.

Budu bared his immense teeth.

"Know Your Enemy," he said. "Then Hunt Him Down."

————

Joseph began with the Hangar Twelve footage. He analyzed the images of Alec Checkerfield frame by frame, expanded them, sharpened them, filtered them; compared them with his visual transcript of the mortal he had known, Nicholas Harpole. He regretfully confirmed that he was looking at the same man, though the one wasn't even born yet and the other had died in 1555.

He had no idea how time and space as he understood them could accommodate that paradox. Worrying about it gave him a feeling as though wolves were tearing at his liver, though, so he didn't. He went after more information instead, searching for occurrences of the name Alec Checkerfield in the Temporal Concordance fragments.

There he found the transcript of the surveillance report from 2351. He was disconcerted to discover that Dr. Zeus seemed as though it would be watching Alec Checkerfield with an eye to employing him, rather than catching him in theft. He was further dismayed to learn that Alec would be, not some shifty hacker, but in fact a British peer with a considerable personal fortune and a very large yacht.

The surveillance image clinched it for Joseph.

It had been taken outdoors, against a background of some ancient city, and showed the mortal Alec Checkerfield striding along a processional way crowded with tourists. He was dressed badly, in a loud tropical-patterned shirt and bright orange shorts; he wore red canvas boating shoes without socks. Joseph very nearly felt embarrassed for him, until he studied the expression on his face.

Pale-eyed determination, sullen anger: this was a man who would let himself be chained to a stake and burned alive on a matter of religious dogma. This was a man who would risk his life to deliver weapons to political combatants, even if it destroyed both sides.

This was the enemy. This was the man himself.

And it was strange, but somehow this comforted Joseph, even as his sense of rage grew: for in all the shifting and terrifying world in which he now lived, here was one thing that had somehow remained the same. The big Englishman—whatever clothes he wore, whatever cause he fought in—would never change, could always be hated as the reliable symbol of everything Joseph opposed.

Of course, he still had to be killed.

# ANOTHER MORNING IN 300,000 BCE

There's been a lot of traffic to and from this weary island in this desolate sea in this lost epoch lately. The Temporal Fabric has thickened to such an extent as to make targeting the place in a time shuttle nearly impossible.

How many times does the murky dawn wash out the stars, how many bloody sunsets throw terrible shadows as the arms and legs on Marco's generator race mindlessly round? How many gray waves break on the shore? Nobody on the island could tell you. Time has long since ceased to have any meaning for them.

The only one with any sense of difference is the unfortunate Grigorii Efimovitch, who is still lying out on the steel table waiting for his disassembly to continue. He's not sure why it has stopped. He has no idea that he's even begun to grow back a little of what's been cut away from him over the centuries, but he wouldn't be surprised to learn it; he's an immortal, after all.

He lies there, unable to sleep, unable to rest, unable to stop repeating endlessly to himself the last sound he heard. It was an order. He was supposed to do something. He remembers perfectly, though he does not understand. He will obey, if he ever has the opportunity to do so, because he has learned that he must never, ever, *ever* disobey again.

So anyway, is it days or weeks before the still air of that island is displaced with a table-rattling *boom,* and roaring shadows streak across the sky? Who can say? Certainly not Grigorii Efimovitch, for reasons that would unduly stress the reader if related here.

But he feels the table rattling under him, he hears the shuttles screaming in, and he hears too the shouting after they've landed; brusque orders given, thundering running feet. He does not see the armed mortals come pouring through the doorway, or the unarmed immortals who accompany them.

Everyone sees Grigorii Efimovitch, however. Well trained as they are, some of the mortals stop in their tracks; and the ones whose stomachs aren't strong fail to keep their breakfasts down. For that matter, the immortals present are shocked.

Then Grigorii Efimovitch flaps and moves, screaming in silence, and is answered by half a dozen very loud screams from his audience.

A weeping mortal runs forward, pointing his disrupter rifle at Grigorii Efimovitch's head, to do what he thinks is the only humane thing. Faster than the eye can follow, an immortal is beside him, forcing the barrel of the rifle down.

"No," says Suleyman. "It won't kill him."

"But we can't leave him like this, lord," sobs the mortal.

"We won't," Suleyman says. Latif strides up to the table, reckless rage in his eyes, anger focused like a shield to keep the horror at bay.

"Secured. There are dozens of them here!" he shouts.

Suleyman by contrast is calm; his voice when he speaks is more quiet than his speaking voice normally is, more measured and slow in its cadence, almost devoid of emotion. "There'll be an inventory somewhere. Hard copy. Look for it. That file cabinet over there, probably." He points and Victor, who has been gazing around in silence, goes to the file cabinet and bends slightly to read the cards on its two drawers.

"Merchandise, A through M; Merchandise, N through Zed," he says in his clear cold baritone.

"Merchandise?" says Latif. "Oh, man. One of those bastards probably thought that was funny."

"I don't think they know enough history to be aware of the reference," says Suleyman carefully. "Gentlemen? Ladies? Let's begin the evacuation, please. All the coffins. I want the file cabinet, too."

"You heard the man. Move," Latif orders, and his voice breaks on the last word. Mortals and immortals stop milling about in horror and begin to clear the long steel shelves of their occupants, transferring the coffins one by one out to the fleet of waiting shuttles.

Nan comes walking from the dark interior, carrying herself preternaturally upright. "Kalugin isn't here," she says. "Nor Mendoza." Suleyman
simply puts out an arm and folds her against him. Victor paces close,
watching as she weeps in silence.

After a long moment, Victor clears his throat.

"There's no sign of Lewis, either, I'm afraid," he says.

"No?" Suleyman says. "Well, I suppose we ought to be grateful. Wherever they are, they haven't suffered this."

Victor nods slowly.

"There will be an accounting now," Suleyman says. "There'll have to
be, when the rest of them know. With a thousand voices all shouting the
same question, they won't dare silence any one voice. They'll have to answer."

"And pay," says Victor.

"Some of them," says Suleyman.

"They'd damn well better pray that none of these people are in any
shape to testify," snarls Latif.

"Oh, they'll testify," Suleyman says, a dark edge coming into his
voice at last. He turns to a mortal who is wandering about in a dazed
fashion, carrying a holocam. "Agaja, start with the generator outside.
Good shots of the arms and legs. Then this poor devil here, you see?
And perhaps after that we'll open some of the coffins, let the world see
what's in them. They'll speak for themselves, whether or not they have
tongues."


## LATER THAT SAME MORNING IN 2318 AD

Time might have long since lost its meaning on a weary island in a desolate sea in a lost epoch, but in the year 2318 it had a great deal of meaning, particularly in regard to tactics.

Within an hour of the return of the time-shuttles, holoimages were
abruptly being broadcast before the eyes of every Dr. Zeus board member,
Facilitator General, Sector Head, and Executive Facilitator on Earth. They
were also broadcast simultaneously in every Company HQ and safe
house, every research facility and base. As Suleyman had ordered, the

images began with Marco's generator and moved inside for a lengthy study of Grigorii Efimovitch on the disassembly table.

They dwelt awhile on the racks of instruments and Marco's living quarters; floated over to the steel shelves, where coffins were still being lifted down and carried out into the drear light; followed them outside and focused in tight as a weeping mortal activated the release on one coffin. With a spine-chilling hiss the seal broke, the lid rose and folded back on itself. The coffin's occupant flinched from the light and screamed its greeting to horrified immortals all over the world.

The mortal bent down and read the name engraved on the lid. "Baiton," she said, looking into the nearest holocam. "Its name was Baiton. Does anybody know this one?"

In an HQ in southern China, an immortal named Xiang Lan cried out in grief, for she had known Baiton very well indeed.

The scene was repeated several times during the broadcast. Finally, mercifully, the camera turned for a shot of Suleyman, standing in the doorway under the scrawled sign reading BUREAU OF PUNITIVE MEDI-CINE.

He stared into the foremost camera somberly.

"Suleyman, North African Sector Head. For the record, I state that on twenty-fourth July I received an encoded message purporting to be from Facilitator Grade One Joseph, with whom I have worked in the past but whom I have not seen in many years. The message gave me a set of temporal/spatial coordinates and claimed there were several operatives there in need of repair.

"Fully aware"—Suleyman cleared his throat—"that there have been rumors of certain operatives disappearing without trace for some centuries now, I judged it advisable to take a full security force with me when investigating Joseph's coordinates. This"—he gestured at the sign above the doorway—"is what we found when we arrived here. There are approximately two hundred and sixty-six individuals who have been, to a greater or lesser degree"—he cleared his throat again—"badly damaged."

He stepped forward and looked again into the camera. "By the time you view this record, all the operatives in question will have been evacuated to a repair facility at my headquarters in Morocco. These images are being simultaneously broadcast to operatives of all ranks in cities all over the world, to ensure my personal safety and the safety of the operatives and mortals under my command, due to the fact that no official investigation of the facts regarding this prison has yet taken place.

"I strongly urge you to make the content of this transmission widely known to all operatives. And if any operatives know of a fellow immortal who has disappeared, I urge you to come forward with his or her name and last known location. As soon as we have identified all the individuals involved in this incident, a list of names will be transmitted to all channels. More information will be broadcast as it becomes available."

He was interrupted by a mortal, pale and shaking, who emerged from the doorway behind him.

"Lord, we can't—we can't get that one on the table into his box—"

"I'll do it," Suleyman told him. He looked back into the camera. "We will do everything we can for these people. Whoever they are, for whatever reason they were sent here, *this is too much.* I conclude this transmission in the hope that I am perfectly understood. Suleyman out."


Did it cause a scandal? You could say that.

Suleyman's HQ was immediately deluged by inquiries from near-hysterical immortals worldwide. A list of the disappeared began to be compiled. It far exceeded two hundred and sixty-six names, however.

There was an immediate response from Dr. Zeus's main offices in the future, expressing dismay at the existence of the Bureau of Punitive Medicine, as it had come to be known after Suleyman's broadcast.

They claimed that they had learned of its existence from the Temporal Concordance, which stated that on 26 July 2318, Suleyman and his team would discover the location in the far past and liberate its prisoners. Of course, they had been unable to send a rescue mission prior to that date, since history cannot be changed, nor had they made its existence known, to avoid general panic. However, a committee was now being appointed for a full investigation of the incident, and a heartfelt commendation was extended to Suleyman for his heroic and timely action in aid of the victims.

Almost at once a second transmission came in from the future, but on a narrow channel accessible only to operatives above Executive Facilitator class, stating that their investigative committee had conclusively proven that the bureau was the work of a deranged Executive Facilitator identified as Marco.

It stated further that this individual, a Company operative since prehistory, had begun to show signs of emotional instability as long ago as 6000 BCE and had several times been called in for repair and upgrades, but had not responded satisfactorily to treatment. Before he could be hospitalized for further study, however, he had disappeared, and the Company had been searching for him ever since, though the APB had gone out on strictly classified levels to avoid alarming the rank and file.

Further, it reported that the investigative committee had been able to determine that Marco had apparently fled into the deep past and established a base for himself there, from which he had ventured only to capture other operatives, remove their tracking implants, and transport them back to his base, where he had obsessively conducted research with the aim of finding a way to reverse the immortality process, using his fellow immortals as experimental subjects.

The transmission concluded with the assurance that every effort was being made to locate Marco, and that appropriate disciplinary measures would be taken immediately upon his capture.

This was followed within an hour by a third transmission, sent only to Section Heads and Facilitators General above a certain security clearance. It stated that attempts to recover Marco were still ongoing, but that evidence had been uncovered to suggest that he might have other concealed bases at other locations in time, and might possibly have continued his experiments there after fleeing the Bureau of Punitive Medicine.

It added that if this was in fact the case, then the committee was forced to conclude that many unfortunate immortals who had dropped from sight over the years and whose whereabouts were still unrecorded might have become his victims, especially since further evidence suggested that Marco had used his Facilitator training to pose as a security technical. He was thought to have taken custody of operatives who were being transferred between bases for minor disciplinary hearings, and abducted them.

Still unresolved was the status of Facilitator Grade One Joseph, who had allegedly sent the coded transmission advising Suleyman of the existence of the bureau. Joseph, as far as the committee had been able to determine, had disappeared in 2276 under suspicious circumstances. He may or may not have been a member of the notorious Plague Cabal, most of whose members had been apprehended at that time. He may or may not have been guilty of collaborating with Marco. He may or may not have been responsible for the disappearance of another operative, Literature Specialist Grade Two Lewis. Further investigation was necessary before any conclusions could be drawn, and any operative with information that might assist the committee in its inquiries as to Joseph's whereabouts should contact it immediately.

This final transmission concluded with the Company's assurance that every effort was being made to locate the missing operatives and capture Marco, and with its expression of sorrow that this situation had occurred, though adding the observation that, given the complexities of Temporal Influence, such a terrible tragedy was perhaps inevitable, and might in fact have been worse.

# STILL ANOTHER MORNING
# IN 2318 AD

"Hey, Father?"

Budu opened his eyes and stared down through the glass. Joseph was peering up at him from the other side, a look of bright speculation on his face.

"Got a question for you. You remember way back, oh, it must have been fourteen thousand years ago, you and I were having a conversation about whether or not history could be changed? How all we had was the Company's word for it that it couldn't?"

"I Remember."

"So, what about it, really? Would it be possible, if you had enough warning? Like, if the Company had really wanted to, they might have stationed operatives to prevent Napoleon being born, or Hitler?" Joseph scratched behind his ear thoughtfully. "I was just thinking I might put it to the test. Give it the old college try, you know? For the sake of experiment. For Mendoza's sake, too."

He grinned up at Budu. "See, I found a few more details in the Temporal Concordance. About the guy. Alec Checkerfield. He's slouching someplace to be born already! Only not Bethlehem. The Concordance says he's going to be born on a boat near Jamaica on 12 January 2320. That's just two years from now. What if I was able to prevent that? Fix it so he's never even conceived. Wouldn't that be great? There'd be no Hangar Twelve Man, so no Mars Two Disaster. I know it's pretty radical, but what do you think?"

What Budu was thinking, regretfully, was that his son had gone mad in his loneliness and disconnection. It was not, however, the end of the world. Not for another thirty-seven years, at least. It was simply unfortunate, because Joseph's obsession with the mortal man was a distraction from the more important business of plotting a strategy to bring down Dr. Zeus. Though his desire to punish the mortal was praiseworthy, and the experiment in Temporal Physics probably worth the effort . . .

"Try," he told Joseph.


On 23 May 2318, at 11:45 AM, the alarm system at the San Francisco Mint went off by mistake.

It was obvious it was a mistake even as the first lights flashed, even as the bells rang. For one thing, it was broad daylight in the middle of business hours. The security officers were all standing alert at their posts; the Money Museum was full of tourists and tour docents. Within the vaulted plant, sterisuited technicians were all busy in the manufacture of new identification discs, extruding them, pressing them, cutting them, encoding them, sealing them, shipping them. Nowhere along the assembly line was anything out of place, no intruders seen anywhere.

All the same, the alarm had gone off, and this was the San Francisco Mint, so work clattered to a stop and all the entrances were sealed while a routine search was made. The tourists complained mightily about late luncheons. The authorities apologized. At last the glitch in the system was found and fixed. The technicians got on with their jobs. The tourists were released and given vouchers for free cable car rides.

When it was noticed that six disc blanks were missing from a tempering rack, the technicians conferred among themselves and simply made six more to fill the order. Why stir up trouble?

# ONE AFTERNOON IN 2319 AD

"Oh, wow!" said Keely the waitress, staring out through the window of the bar. The glass was small leaded panes, thick and very old, so she opened the window for a better view. "Check this out!"

"What?" Nelson the cop came and peered over her shoulder.

"He's all—he's all—" said Keely, pointing. Nelson stood gaping, with his cider mug half-raised.

"What is it, for Goddess's sake?" snapped Mavis, and pushed them aside to see. Just beyond the rose garden a sleek new BMW Zephyr had settled. Crossing the lawn, in obvious pride of ownership, was Joseph.

Not Joseph the shabby little holoset repairman: Joseph impeccably groomed, beard not just trimmed but pomaded, too. It made him look ten years younger. He wore a business suit of expensive cut, gleaming new shoes, had a thick coat draped casually over one arm. "Hi, folks," he said, seeing them assembled at the window.

Mavis was out of the bar and down the hall so fast she knocked an ancient framed photograph of Princess Diana off the wall.

"Well, hel-*lo*!" she said. "My, don't you look nice."

"Yes, I do, don't I?" Joseph smiled at her brilliantly. "You must be wondering at the change in my fortunes. Well, it's a long story, and I'd be delighted to tell you over a mug of your best persimmon cider. Shall we retire to a private room?"

"Why—yes," Mavis said. Keely was already running for the good glasses.

————

"... but then the CEO said wait, we can't let this man go! I'll make you a deal, Mr. Capra, he said. We'll retain your services at a hundred grand a year. Plus a fleet car. And I said, well, I don't know, could you throw in a health club membership?" Joseph paused to drain the last of his cider. Mavis listened, toying with the bright new emerald pendant he had given her.

"So we hammered out the little piddly details," Joseph continued, waving one hand dismissively. "And here I am. And why *am* I here, you ask, other than to deliver that little token of my esteem? I'll tell you. One of HumaliCorp's long-range goals is building up the potential of the North Coast here as a first-class vacation destination. I mean, sea, trees, scenery—we've got it all, right? The only thing that keeps ships from packing into this harbor like sardines is lack of recognition factor. But how do you get recognition?

"You get celebrities to visit! Then, word gets out and everyone else in the world will want to visit, too, see? So here's what HumaliCorp is doing: they're giving famous people all-expense-paid vacation packages at some of the local places, as a promotional gesture. They've already lined up Livilla Barrymore and Tommy Tournay at the Bay Breeze Lodge in Bodega! And Elton Molineux and Fifi Arrevalo just confirmed for two nights at Jack's Jenner Hideaway."

"Those people agreed to go up *there*?" Mavis said in disbelief.

"Ah, they're just show business," Joseph sneered. "Actors jump at the chance for anything free, honey, trust me. But we'd like a few classier people in on this too, the suborbital set, you know? Some British royalty or something? And I told the CEO: Say, I know an idyllic little place in Muir Harbor, and it's even got some English history attached to it. So he sent me here to cut the deal."

"You nice man," Mavis cried, rewarding him with an ardent embrace. Then she looked at him seriously. "But you did mean—your company is paying for it all?"

Joseph drew out his gleaming identification disc and held it up before her eyes.

"Every last cent and all possible surcharges, taxes, and extras, to the last thirty-percent gratuity," he said. "And we're going to need to send out an invitation to His Lordship and Her Ladyship. Got any classy fonts on your printer? Olde English or anything like that?"

No more than a week later, Keely came tearing up the stairs and pounded on the door of the room Joseph had taken.

"Mr. Capra," she screamed (she called him Mr. Capra now instead of You). "Ma'am says come real quick! She's got some mail from this earl or something."

Joseph emerged and ran straight down to where Mavis sat at her communications terminal, wringing her hands in excitement.

"Look," she said. "It's a letter! Isn't that one of those crest things rich people have on the sides of their cars? Doesn't that word there say EARL?"

"That's what it says, all right," Joseph said, grinning evilly. "Well, well. Mr. Malcolm Lewin, social secretary to Roger Checkerfield, sixth earl of Finsbury, begs to acknowledge His Lordship's receipt of our communication of Tuesday last and wishes to confirm that, as they are already conveniently visiting our Pacific Coast, the earl and Lady Finsbury will arrive on eleventh April to redeem his free reservation, though regrettably due to prior engagements his Lordship must depart on the twelfth."

"They can't stay both nights?" Keely pouted.

"Hey, that's okay." Joseph's eyes were glittering. "All I need is one night. His Lordship wishes to know whether mooring fees are included in the all-expense package."

"Are they?" Mavis dithered through her brochures.

"Sure they are," Joseph said, leaning past her to tap in a hasty response. "So they'll be arriving by yacht, huh? That's right, they hang out in the Caribbean a lot, don't they? Well, I'll just run right out to the pier and take care of everything this afternoon. Mustn't forget a single detail! I want this to be a trip they'll remember the rest of their lives."

Certainly the regulars at the Pelican would remember it, for the astonishing cleaning job that establishment underwent in the days preceding the grand occasion. Keys that hadn't been seen in years surfaced, as well as missing chair legs, candlesticks, framed prints on subjects no longer considered tasteful, and canceled permits from the Alcoholic Beverage Commission dating back three centuries.

Many of the quirky little safety hazards the regulars had long since learned to avoid were actually removed, or repaired, or filed down. The garden obliged by blooming. The family who owned the pier were even persuaded to haul three decades' worth of rusting marine junk away to a barn and brighten up the place with yachting flags. Everyone in Muir Harbor prepared for the earl of Finsbury's visit. Joseph especially.

Mavis was so grateful: well before daylight on the eleventh, Joseph was parked out on the pier in his BMW, which he had blazoned with a beautifully printed sign for the occasion that identified it as the Pelican shuttle. He sat at the wheel in a jaunty cap that looked vaguely service-related, scanning the horizon eagerly. Mavis brought him sandwiches and fruit tea at lunch, but his quarry hadn't appeared yet; nor had done so by teatime.

Just at the last possible moment anybody could stand the suspense, there was a cheery double beep from the car and Joseph drove in triumph up the green tunnel of pines from the beach, bringing Roger Jeremy St. James Alistair Checkerfield, sixth earl of Finsbury, and his lady wife Cecelia.

Immediately all hangers-on at the Pelican strained to assume the most nonchalant poses imaginable while pretending not to stare, as Joseph bustled in with a suitcase under either arm. The distinguished guests followed him. Mavis came forward, one hand uplifted in a graceful wave of acknowledgment.

"W-welcome to the Pelican," she chirped. "My Lord and Lady? I'm Mavis Breen, your hostess. I trust your sail was pleasant?"

"Yes, thank you," said Lady Finsbury.

Joseph scuttled up to the rooms with the luggage, leaving Mavis to stare at the titled couple as she struggled to think of something else to say. The earl took off his sunglasses and looked around. Lady Finsbury left hers on.

They were certainly aristocratic-looking, though dressed rather more casually than expected. Roger's face was a little puffy, and for that matter his chin wasn't quite what you'd hope for in a member of the House of Lords, but Cecelia was coldly beautiful. She was intelligent, too, to judge from the text plaquettes sticking out of the top of her bag.

"Oh, my goodness," said Mavis, "Are you a reader, Your Ladyship?"

"Yes, I am," Cecelia said.

"My gosh, that's such a lovely—uh, lovely—thing to do. I've always regretted I never learned, but—well, you know how it is out here." Mavis giggled shamefacedly. "We Californians. Wild and woolly. What are you reading, if you don't mind my asking?"

"The novels of Jane Austen," Cecelia said.

Before Mavis could confess that she had no idea who Jane Austen was, Joseph popped up at her elbow like a helpful devil and said, "Yeah! *Sense and Sensibility.* Great book, Your Ladyship."

"Oh!" Mavis's face lit up. "Why, I just loved that movie."

"Really." Cecelia's lips thinned. "How nice."

"Hey!" Roger had noticed the unmistakable smell of taps in the room beyond. "Is that a real bar in there?"

"It sure is, pal," Joseph said, stepping forward to take him by the arm. "With a great local selection of real ales and ciders you won't want to miss, trust me."

"Cool," said Roger, and let himself be towed into the inviting gloom. That left Mavis and Cecelia face to face again. Mavis bit her lower lip.

"Well—um—would you like to see your room?"

"Yes, please," said Cecelia, taking off her sunshades at last, and my, what chilly blue eyes she had. "And would it be possible to get two aspirins? I'm afraid I have rather a headache."


Roger bought everyone a round at the bar and instantly won the support of local law enforcement, who regaled him with their oldest and shaggiest tales of bootlegging, to which he listened openmouthed. Roger did most things with his mouth open.

He wasn't quite as stupid as he appeared to be. In fact, he was a teacher with a degree in marine biology at some institute or other, and spoke quite learnedly about coral reefs when encouraged, which the patrons in the bar did in hopes he'd buy another round. Somehow they failed to get that subtle signal across to him; but Joseph stepped in like a hero, flashing his identification disc to keep the drinks running free at HumaliCorp's expense.

So freely did they flow that Roger had to lean on Joseph, when it came time to navigate the narrow hall between the bar and dining room for the all-expenses-paid gourmet meal of local smoked salmon appetizer followed by local great white shark (clubbed at sea that very morning) grilled over local applewood with local vegetable medley.

But Joseph assured Roger he didn't mind at all if Roger leaned on him, and Roger thought that was really neat, and asked Cecelia if she didn't think that was really neat of Joseph? Cecelia just smiled tightly, though her smile faded somewhat when Roger invited Joseph to sit at table with them. Joseph demurred, but Roger pressed his invitation, so Joseph drew up a chair, after which Cecelia calmly took out *Persuasion* and read as she dined.

Joseph kept Roger entertained, with funny stories so well told the earl was helpless with laughter through the whole meal, unable to do much more than hold up his glass for refills, which Joseph supplied readily, especially after Roger spilled most of a pint of cider in the lap of his white yachting pants.

But that was okay, because, by a really amazing stroke of luck, cider wasn't made from grapes like port was, or it'd have stained astoundingly! At least, that seemed to be what Roger was trying to explain between giggling fits, and Joseph seemed to understand him perfectly. Perhaps the fact that Joseph was also helping himself to the cider improved their rapport.

He was near the end of a long story involving two corporate executives and a goat in a hotel room in Paris when Mavis brought in their blackberry crumble. She sniffed and noticed the spill.

"Oh, dear, should I send in Keely with the mop?" she said.

"N'sawright—" The earl waved at her. "Ol' Jolly Roger took it inna pants. B'they're whi' pants, see? So issokay. 'Cos c-cider's only yellow. Yeah?" He burst out laughing afresh.

"Gee, though, Your Lordship, that must be feeling pretty clammy about now," Joseph reminded him. "Your Ladyship, would you like me to escort His Lordship upstairs into dry pants?"

"Yes, thank you, that would probably be best," said Cecelia, not looking up from her book.

"Okey-doke," said Roger, and stood straight up, tottered, and promptly fell over with a crash. Mavis served out two helpings of blackberry crumble and tried to pretend that Joseph was not lifting an actual British peer over his shoulder and lugging him upstairs while laughing in a manner that certainly might have been more respectful. In fact, in her opinion Joseph oughtn't really be laughing at *all*, though at least Lady Finsbury didn't seem to take offense. She simply spooned up her dessert with remarkable sangfroid, and continued to read about Anne Elliot's visit to Lyme.

"Attaboy, Jolly Roger," Joseph said, "we're going around a corner, watch your head. Here's your nice room. Your fabulous room in the breathtakingly beautiful Pelican Inn, where pirates played in days of old. Or something."

"Yeah," Roger chortled. "Pirates . . . oof!" He made the mistake of sprawling across Joseph's back with his limbs extended, which resulted in his getting wedged in the upper part of the narrow little cut-corner hallway. Joseph lurched out from under Roger before jumping back to catch him as he slid down the wall.

"Whoopsy-daisy! Keep your arms and legs inside the conveyance, okay, Roger, old bean?" Joseph said in his best jolly-uncle voice, though his teeth were clenched. "If you weren't such a really tall guy, this'd be easier. But you are a really tall guy, aren't you?"

"Uh-huh," Roger said happily, allowing himself to be hoisted up again and carried head down another couple of meters along the hall.

"In fact—" At the door Joseph realized he didn't have a key, after patting all his pockets in turn. "In fact, how tall would you say you are, Roger, chum? Six foot five? Six-six?"

Roger made a gurgling noise suggesting he hadn't the slightest idea.

"Yeah. I'd bet if you ever had kids, they'd be inconveniently tall, too. Heredity can be a cruel thing, Rog baby." It was under the circumstances best that Roger was unable to see the expression on Joseph's face, which would have frightened him badly.

"Now, I've gotta set you down a second, okay? Gotta go get a key. Put your hands flat like you're gonna stand on your head, see? So you can brace yourself while I let you down? So that way you won't fall over?"

"Yeah," said Roger indistinctly.

"Okay, are you braced?"

"Yeah."

"Okay, here we go," Joseph told Roger, and let him down and stepped away from him. Roger promptly collapsed upon himself, subsiding in a boneless tangle with his ankles about his ears and his behind pointed at the ceiling.

Tugging his beard, Joseph stood briefly contemplating sweet England's pride. Roger seemed perfectly happy where he was, so Joseph sped back down the stairs and into the alcove behind the desk, where he found a room key and sped back with it.

Joseph unlocked the door with a flourish. When the door was thrown open, Roger sagged forward and uncoiled across the threshold, giggling feebly.

"Yeah, Your Lordship, isn't this fun? Pip-pip, cheerio and all that," Joseph said, taking Roger by the ankles and backing into the dark room with him. "You're such a mellow guy, Roger, I really almost feel bad about this, but—what if you had a kid who wasn't a nice easygoing chappie like his dad? What if all he got from you was ungodly height and a certain flair for complicated disasters, huh?"

He got Roger under the armpits and hauled him across the bed. Roger lay there blinking uncertainly up at the four-poster canopy in the shadows.

". . . Huh?" he said.

"Nice shoes," Joseph said, pulling them off. "Taylor and Sons', aren't they? But, Rog, I ask you, size sixteen? You must have to have these specially made. You don't really want to pass on genes like that to a kid, do you? Besides, you know what'd just be bound to happen? He'd inherit Her Ladyship's ramrod-up-the-ass personality. Those mean little eyes, too. I can tell. I've got an instinct for these things."

"Really," said Roger with his eyes closed, as though Joseph had just said something very profound.

"Trust me," Joseph said, unzipping Roger's fly. Roger opened his eyes and flailed around in vague alarm as he felt his trousers coming off.

"Hey—"

"No, no, s'okay, remember? We're just changing ourselves. We had a little beverage mishap. That's the ticket, you just relax and let your old pal take care of all your little problems . . ." Joseph said. "Oh, Roger, it's April eleventh, 2319, and do you know where your children are? Nowhere yet, my friend, but in nine months you'll be the unhappy recipient of a bundle from Hell if I don't help you."

Joseph's voice had taken on a beautifully soothing tone. It was the sort of voice to which you wanted to relax while it sang you away to dreamland. Roger found himself irresistibly overtaken by sleep, unable to open his eyes anymore. He was thereby spared seeing Joseph pulling on a pair of surgical gloves.

"How's about a standard lithotomy position for me, Your Lordship? There we go. You're having swell dreams, getting lots of rest, and you know why? No midnight feedings. No walking the floor with a squalling little seventh earl who'll grow up to be the latest edition of Nicholas Harpole and wreck my daughter's life again. Nope, Uncle Joseph is going to nip that tiny problem in the bud right now, old chap, old boy . . ."

There was a clatter nastily suggestive of metal implements of some kind being laid out. A faint hiss, a pleasant smell of cloves . . . and a strangled yell of outrage from Joseph.

After a full thirty seconds of burning silence, he straightened up beside the bed and fixed Roger with a glare of righteous accusation. Roger was snoring gently.

"All right," said Joseph. "You degenerate spawn of imperialist oppressors. What gives, here, mortal man?"

No reply from Roger. Joseph bent again and this time it was five whole minutes before he rose. With effort he controlled himself enough to speak clearly.

"Okay," he said. "So you've *already* had a vasectomy. Very responsible and decent of you, Roger. I want to sincerely thank you for your sense of public-spiritedness. At least he won't be *your* fault. So what this means . . . what this means is . . . Cecelia! That two-timing Jezebel!"

He worked swiftly as he thought aloud, closing and sealing, collecting his instruments, throwing a blanket over Roger.

"In fact, if the kid's born in nine months . . . and you're up here unconscious right now . . . and Her Ladyship is all alone downstairs—"

Joseph's eyes went wide with horror.

"What have I done?" he said, and then his words were echoing in the darkness with nobody to hear them.

Mavis, clearing away the dishes, started and nearly dropped them as Joseph came tearing down into the parlor.

"Where's Her Ladyship?" he demanded. "Who's she with?"

"She went out for a walk," Mavis said. "I think she was sort of put out, you know, with His Lordship getting so—"

"But is she alone?" Joseph shouted, grabbing her by both arms.

"Yes!" Mavis glared at him. "If you hadn't kept buying His Lordship all those drinks—"

But she was speaking to an empty room, and the door was swinging slowly back after having smacked wide open and banged the wall. Pursing her lips, she went and pulled it firmly shut against the perfumed night.

Joseph ran, keenly aware of what a romantic and very, very secluded spot Muir Harbor was at night. The impenetrable gloom and silence of the forest, the thickets of flowers along the bank of the dark stream, the faint crash of the pitiless sea, the white glint of the stars laughing down at him . . .

He emerged from the long aisle of pines and picked up Cecelia on infrared about fifty meters ahead of him, slender and upright, gazing out across the meadows above the lagoon. What was she watching so intently?

A man? No. It glimmered pale in the starlight. It seemed to be a wild horse, grazing in complete unconcern. So Her Ladyship liked wildlife? Great. As long as she confined herself to nature appreciation . . . Joseph decided not to take any chances, and advanced on her purposefully.

"Penny for your thoughts, Your Ladyship," he said in his friendliest manner.

Cecelia sighed, closed her eyes. After a moment she opened them and turned to look down at him.

"I beg your pardon?"

"Just a figure of speech, Your Ladyship," he said. "Say, I'm real sorry about His Lordship's slight overindulgence in spirits. Strong cider in these parts! Anyway I saw him all safely tucked into bed. He ought to be fine in the morning."

"How very kind of you," she said.

"Don't mention it. So, um . . . are you alone out here?"

"I was," she said, turning back to watch the white horse.

"Well, it's just as well I came along," he told her. "We don't usually get grizzly bears down here, but you never know, and wouldn't that be awful? With you and Roger so young and in love and all. Why, we had a couple go just like Pyramus and Thisbe out here, a couple of years ago. Terrible tragedy. Most people have no idea how dangerous bears are, but—"

"Pyramus and Thisbe?" Cecelia raised her eyebrows. "Aren't you the literary man, Mr. Capra!"

"Well—yes, I have a certain appreciation for the giants of literature," Joseph said. "And may I remark how nice it is to encounter a fellow enthusiast? How are you enjoying *Persuasion,* by the way? Is this your first time reading Austen?"

"No," Cecelia said, looking out across the meadow. The horse had wandered off. "I'm rereading the canon."

"Really? All Austen's stuff? Great," Joseph said genially, but he scanned the meadow for would-be rendezvous-keepers. There didn't seem to be any. "And do you find your appreciation of all those witty little observations has increased with time?"

"No," she said at last. "As a matter of fact, no, I don't. I loved those books as a girl. I read them now, and I grow impatient with Austen."

"Really?" Joseph stared at her in surprise.

"Yes." Cecelia's voice was remote and sad. "She saw human nature for what it is, with the miserable self-interest that motivates us, and the sordid bargains we make. All pettiness, weakness, inanity. How could she resolve every story with an improbable happy romance?"

"The literary convention of the time, I guess," Joseph said.

She gave him a look that acknowledged he was slightly more than a fencepost who had happened to overhear her soliloquy.

"Do you suppose she'd have had the courage to tell the truth, if she'd lived longer?" Cecelia wondered.

"What would you say is the truth, Your Ladyship?"

"That we can't possibly find perfect love in other people. Have you ever had a religious impulse, Mr. Capra?"

"I might have," Joseph said.

"Do you suppose it begins in a dissatisfaction with the inessential?" Cecelia looked up at the stars. "A desire for something more than human love?"

"Gee, I don't know," he said, realizing in terror that if any woman might give birth to his enemy, it would be this one.

"I don't know either," she said. "But I wish I'd begun thinking about this earlier in my life."

After a moment Joseph cleared his throat.

"I, ah, take it you and His Lordship are having problems, then?" he said. "Is there somebody else?"

She looked down at him scornfully. "Gracious, what concern is it of yours? Since you ask, however—I haven't the slightest interest in infidelity. Roger has his flaws, but he's never harmed anyone in his life."

"Really? That's nice," Joseph muttered, avoiding her eyes. "So maybe you'll be starting a family soon?"

"A family?" she said, as though that were the most absurd suggestion anyone could have possibly made. "Roger and I agree very nicely on a number of things, Mr. Capra, and one of them happens to be our utter disinclination to have children. Now or ever. I donated genetic material to the Kronos Biodiversity Project when I was a girl; as far as I'm concerned, that fulfilled my duty to posterity."

"Oh," Joseph said, feeling a metaphysical *splat*. He wiped imaginary custard and pie crust from his face, and glared in the direction of the grinning Fates.

He saw her back to the inn and watched the passageway all night, but no tall lover ever came sneaking along to her room. When they came down for breakfast, Roger was rather pale and sat carefully, but seemed to have no memory of anything untoward having happened.

After the Hearty North Coast Breakfast, the Checkerfields' butler came ashore to advise that they should depart. As compensation for not staying longer, however, the earl and Lady Finsbury posed smiling for a holoshot under the inn sign, and Roger had his butler write a dignified recommendation below which he made his mark. Mavis displayed it proudly over the bar for the rest of her life.

Joseph loaded up the Checkerfields' luggage and drove them down to the pier, where he saw them aboard their palatial yacht. Back ashore, he waved as they set sail, cursing himself for not managing to slip a bomb into one of their suitcases somehow.

Then he drove back, settled the charges, and told Mavis he was off to another business conference.

The first thing he did upon returning to the mountain was check the Temporal Concordance, to see if all references to Alec Checkerfield had been miraculously erased.

They hadn't been.

"So I guess that answers *that* big question in temporal physics, huh?" he told Budu gloomily, loosening his tie as he sagged down against the vault. "All that work for nothing! The little bastard—and he really is one—gets born anyway."

"You Could Try Again," Budu said.

"And do what? Swim up to their yacht in a subsuit and flippers to try to sneak aboard? Keep chasing after the miserable so-and-so in the hope I'll get a chance to do away with him?" Joseph growled. "Oh, yeah, I can just hear the laughs the gods of causality would have at my expense. '*Shark Attack in Normally Safe Waters!* Infant Unharmed. *Nanny Goes on Murderous Rampage!* Tot Saved by Chance Bystander. *Father Christmas Explodes in Harrods' Disaster!* Child Miraculously Escapes. *Classroom Taken Hostage by Macedonian Terrorists!* Our Interview with Lone Boy Who Was in the Lavatory at the Time!' No, thank you."

Budu bared his teeth in terrifying silent laughter.

"And You Have Forgotten Another Thing."

"Oh, yeah?" Joseph said, groping in his pocket for a granola bar. He peeled the wrapper off and took a bite, chewing forcefully.

"Dr. Zeus Would Protect The Boy. The Company Needs Him To Deliver The Bomb To Mars Two."

"Hell," said Joseph through a mouth of granola. "You're right. So even though Jolly Roger got a clip job and Lady Cecelia would rather be a nun, nothing is going to stop Dr. Zeus from producing that kid from somewhere. You know who ran the Kronos Biodoversity Project, don't you?"

"He Will Be Born. He Will Take His Place In History As The Hangar Twelve Man. Until He Has, You Will Be Unable To Touch Him," Budu said, and watched as Joseph drew the inference he had intended. Joseph stopped chewing.

"But *after*—!" he said. "After Mars Two he'll disappear. No more history to protect him. The son of a bitch'll have a time shuttle, he'll take it on the lam through the event shadows. Anything might happen to him there!" Joseph leaped to his feet and clenched both fists over his head. "Oh, he's mine, Father. He's dead meat. I'll track him down, punch his ticket to the afterlife one-way, rescue Mendoza, and still have time to relax with a cold one before Judgment Day! This is good."

"And Then I Will Have Real Work For You To Do," Budu said.

# ONE MORNING IN 1855 AD

San Francisco had come and gone.

Well, as far as anyone knew at the time. The boom had gone bust, the gold fields played out; devastating fires had repeatedly leveled the place. Nowadays the ready cash to rebuild just wasn't there, should another blaze sweep through. Once upon a time a merchant might have charged any price he wanted for a dozen eggs, or a loaf of bread, or a shovel. A month's wages hadn't been thought too high for a pair of socks, and as for a cigar—!

But nobody would discover the Comstock Lode for years yet, and just now men who had been briefly rich beyond dreams of avarice were creeping back into the City in hopes of getting jobs sweeping floors, emptying spittoons, anything to build up enough of a stake to allow them to drift back sadly eastward, or south to sordid early death in Los Angeles or Mexico.

But for the first time in California's history, there were abundant consumer goods available at low prices. You could get anything in San Francisco, and the sooner the better, because most of it was spoiling on the shelves. Of course, nobody had any money, so it didn't matter.

Mr. William Green owned a dry-goods establishment on Clay Street. That morning, in the cathedral-like silence at his counter, he had noticed an inordinate number of little brown moths flitting to and fro through the sunbeams. No customers having come in all morning, he had ample leisure to observe the moths, and discovered that they seemed to be congregating primarily around the sacks of flour stacked in the corner.

Closer examination proved that the moths were crawling out of and into the flour through the thousand pinprick holes they had chewed in the sacking. Mr. Green pulled a sack free and opened it, grimacing as he peered down into a cobwebby maggoty mess that should have been pie crusts and biscuits long ago.

*"Merde!"* Mr. Green had muttered, because his real name was Mr. Rambouillet. He had fled France owing somebody a great deal of money, and settled in San Francisco with the earnest hope of making more. That, however, is a story entirely unrelated to our present one, which continues:

Having resigned himself to the loss, Mr. Green spent the next hour dragging sacks of flour out to the four-foot-deep chasm the last good rain had cut down the center of Clay Street. One after another he pitched in the sacks, and each landed with a little *poof* of white dust, sad as a corpse flopping into quicklime. None of the few passersby remarked on what he was doing, as it was a fairly common sight lately.

Now Mr. Green stood in front of his dry-goods store, dusting his hands and thinking gloomily about getting into his stock of brandied peaches again. He had eaten his way through one case already. His was an addictive personality, which was one of the reasons he owed somebody in France a great deal of money. But:

" 'Dry goods and general merchandise.' Now, *this*," a voice said, "should suit us very well, my dear, wouldn't you think?"

"Maybe, señor," a voice replied, and Mr. Green turned to stare, and kept staring.

They were an odd-looking pair, who had made their way up Clay Street through the blowing sand. The young girl was dressed as a boy for some reason, not very convincingly given her figure. The man was extraordinarily tall and wore a curious twisted metal collar, though otherwise he was dressed in a nondescript enough way: white shirt and boots, timeless in their design, and a pair of blue *serge de Nimes* trousers very similar to the ones Mr. Levi Strauss had recently begun making over on Sacramento Street.

The man loomed over Mr. Green now.

"Is this your establishment, my good man?" he said, and it registered on Mr. Green that he was an Englishman. "And have you any ladies' garments ready-made?"

"You wish to make a purchase?" Mr. Green stammered, ready to scream because the only customers he'd seen in a week wanted something he didn't have.

"That is why I inquired, sir," said the Englishman frostily, looking down his long nose. "My wife has had an unfortunate accident with her trousseau, and desires to replace certain items of apparel."

"Well—well—I have got Chinese shawls," said Mr. Green, flinging open the door of his shop and waving frantically in the hopes he could get them to go inside. "Though no clothes for the ladies ready to wear, a thousand pardons, but I do have fine cottons, broadcloth or calico, linens, silks, bombazine, woolens—" He remembered the moths and bit his tongue, but the tall Englishman was nodding thoughtfully.

"That would suit," he said. "Yes, very well. And have you dressmakers' goods? Thread, buttons, whalebone?"

"Gardening tools?" the girl asked.

An hour later Mr. Green was standing on the wharf beside an empty wheelbarrow, smiling and waving at the couple as the man bent to the oars of a whaleboat. It bore the girl and all of Mr. Green's inventory in bolt cloth and notions out to their ship. The ship was strangely indistinct and blurred by distance, though it didn't seem to be anchored all that far out. It looked to be the size of a man-of-war at least, which was strange, too.

Mr. Green didn't care. He had a pocketful of twenty-dollar double eagles, bright and gleaming as though they'd been minted that morning (which in fact they had been, though they were all stamped with the date 1852).

Whistling, he turned and trundled his wheelbarrow back up Clay Street, avoiding the sinkholes and gullies. He was getting the hell out of San Francisco.

Returning to his shop, he paused in the act of removing his apron. His eyes widened. All across the bare plank floor, where trails of spilled flour had lain an hour since, lay fresh stalks of green wheat just silvering in the ear.

## LATER THAT AFTERNOON

Mendoza reclined on a cushion and watched as Alec fitted the steel skull-mask over the sensor mounting. He welded it in place with a few deft touches; stood back and surveyed the new servounit.

"Why do you give them all faces like that?" she said.

"Because they're my skeleton crew, get it? Ha ha." Alec leaned down and waggled a jointed limb to be certain there was adequate play. It was important that this unit's arms work smoothly, because it had no legs. Unlike the other four, it was built into a stationary console, with only limited motion along a rolling track. It had nine arms, however, fitted with all the tools necessary to enable it to measure, mark, cut, stitch, and sew, as well as a host of other functions related to the manufacture of accessories such as hats, gloves, and shoes.

Nicholas and Edward stood looking down at it in grudging admiration.

*It seems you've a talent for automata, boy,* Edward admitted. *Of course, we haven't seen it work yet.*

*You will,* Alec told him. "Captain, let's run a test, okay?"

***Aye aye! Activating new servounit now.***

With a gentle hum the unit rattled to blank life, all its arms flexing, shear blades clashing, needles pumping experimentally. It focused red and glowing eyes. It took a turn around its little track. Alec grinned at it.

"Cool. And your name is . . ." He leaned forward and tapped its skull. "Smee!"

***All systems shipshape. Shall I download costuming data?***

"Make it so," Alec said, and Smee halted as the Captain shot into its brain all the plundered costuming information Dr. Zeus had accumulated over the centuries, data on clothing from every nation on Earth in every year of recorded history, complete with patterns.

***That's done, by thunder! And programmed, too. Just let it have a look at ye for measurements, now.***

Alec stripped off all his clothes and stood naked in the center of the area circumscribed by Smee's track. It turned its head and fixed its red gaze on him; circled him slowly, scanning and measuring the topography of his body. When it had finished and filed the data away, Alec stepped free. Mendoza disrobed and took his place, whereupon

Smee repeated the process. The gentlemen watched with keen interest.

"I wonder if we could make more?" she said, as the red light played over her body. "They're so useful. What if they could swim?"

"What?" Alec pulled his attention back to what she'd said and replayed it in his mind. His eyes widened.

"Brilliant!" he cried. "Bloody hell, I could make, like, robot dolphins! Remember Long John, Captain? The little telemetry drone?"

*Mmmm. Submersible reconnaissance and defense units? That's my girl! Smart as paint!*

"Why, thank you," said Mendoza, looking pleased.

"I'd have to give 'em articulated spines, so they could swim like a dolphin does—all kinds of sensors in the head—and maybe a skin of bioprene—" Alec began pacing to and fro. "Maybe launch 'em like torpedoes when we arrive somewhere—or, no, say, four berths on the forward deck—"

*Do you know, that actually sounds useful?* Edward admitted.

"Come on, let's go play with some designs!" Alec seized Mendoza's hand and they made for the cabin door.

*Wait! Don't you want clothes?*

Edward took charge. "One complete set of women's morning wear suitable for the year 1855," he said impatiently. "One complete set of gentlemen's apparel, same. Is that sufficient?"

*For California, sir? Or England?*

Edward looked scornful. "Good God! England, what do you think?" he said.

They hurried away. Behind them, Smee processed the order and then turned, whirring along its track, scanning the bolts of cloth until it found a white silk it judged suitable for undergarments. Arms extended, pulled and measured material. Shears deployed and began to cut, as other arms selected thread from the available colors and bobbins wound at blinding speed.


THE FOLLOWING MORNING IN 1855 AD


Had Mr. Green been sober, or even conscious, he might have seen his very favorite customers returning in their whaleboat to the pier at the base of Clay Street. He might not have recognized them, however, since the only thing that presently distinguished them from any other couple was the man's extraordinary height, which was now emphasized by the fashionably tall hat he wore, in keeping with the rest of his unremarkable ensemble. His high stiff shirt collar and cravat concealed that odd bit of jewelry. The young lady with him was today properly clad in a hooped dress of pink sprigged calico. She wore a wide straw hat for the sun, decked with pink ribbons.

The gentleman carried a capacious leather satchel, which seemed to contain something rather heavy.

Having tied up their boat and proceeded ashore, they made their way up Clay Street. At the corner of Clay and Montgomery they paused, appearing to confer briefly; the young lady pointed and they turned down Montgomery.

Mr. Charles McWay, the clerk who happened to be on duty at a certain bank that morning, was a much busier man than Mr. Green had been. Mr. McWay's firm was weathering the current depression quite nicely, as in fact it would weather every banking crisis and recession for the next several centuries, which was why the lady and gentleman entered and looked about expectantly.

Mr. McWay was too preoccupied with the shopkeeper he was helping to notice their arrival, and after the customer departed he was busy completing paperwork; so when he looked up and beheld the very tall man who had appeared before him silently, he gave a slight start.

"Good morning, sir! How may I be of assistance?"

"Good morning," said the tall man, removing his hat. "I am advised that this is a reliable financial institution. I am presently obliged to travel abroad, and may not return for some years. Would it be possible to place a sum of money upon deposit here, against my return?"

He spoke with a well-bred London accent, and there was something so charming, so persuasive in his voice that Mr. McWay froze for a moment, staring in confusion into the man's pale blue eyes.

"Certainly, sir," he said at last.

"Splendid! Now, then," continued the Englishman. He lifted a leather satchel to the counter. "I have here the sum of five thousand dollars." Opening the satchel, he displayed a welter of bright coin, all twenty-dollar double eagles stamped with the date 1852. "I should like to deposit this at your best rate of interest."

"Yes, *sir!*" said Mr. McWay, producing a deposit form with alacrity. He dipped his pen in the inkwell and proceeded to fill it out. "And your name, sir?"

The Englishman's eyes narrowed in amusement. "William St. James Harpole," he said. The paperwork was done, the money counted, verified, and locked away in the vault, and a deposit book issued in the name he had given.

"Thank you so much, sir. You've been most helpful," said the Englishman, tucking the passbook away in an inner pocket of his coat. He donned his tall hat, took the empty satchel, and turned to the young lady. All this while she had been standing attentively at the front door, for all the world like a county marshal on guard, which seemed most odd to Mr. McWay.

"Mrs. Harpole? I believe our ship awaits."

She smiled and took his arm. To Mr. McWay's astonishment she actually skipped the few paces to the door beside her husband.

Then Mr. McWay's attention was diverted by another customer coming in, and when he glanced at the window once more the couple was gone. He never saw either of them again; but his firm was indeed a reliable financial institution, and the double eagles increased their number by compound interest over a considerable period of years . . .

And for a lark, Mr. and Mrs. Harpole immortalized their transitory persona in a holo taken on the deck of the *Captain Morgan,* posed against the rail with the sad little City in the background. Stern husband holding his tall hat in the crook of one arm, freezing the camera in his dignity, and on his other arm the wife, very young to look so haughty but with the suggestion of laughter at one corner of her slightly ironic mouth.

## LATER THAT DAY IN 1855 AD

"Given the amount of time it sat in that poor devil's shop, this is a surprisingly drinkable vintage," said Edward, pouring another glass of champagne.

He sprawled in a chair in the saloon, having removed his coat, waist-coat, and boots. Mendoza, reclining across his lap, had removed rather more of her clothing.

"At least we have ice," she said, yawning. "I don't think we used to be able to get cold drinks. Did we?"

"Not in California," he said, offering her a sip. She drank and sighed, leaning her head back.

The saloon had undergone a change in recent days. Fruit trees of various kinds stood here and there, lashed to bulkheads, growing in makeshift hydroponic containers. So did the gooseberry bush, which was now very nearly a thicket; so did several muscular grapevines, which had crawled up every available vertical surface, and looked capable of bursting out through a hatch and scaling the masts. They gave the place something of an exotic, hothouse air. All the plants had survived the jumps through time unscathed. The Captain had begun to have an idea why.

"Harpole," Mendoza said thoughtfully. "I remember that name. You used to be called that, didn't you? When we talked in the other language . . ."

Nicholas, who had been leaning invisible against her thigh, took control and smiled down at her.

*"Ecce, Corinna venit,"* he said, *"tunica velata recincta,*
*candida dividua colla tegente coma—*
*qualiter in thalamos famosa Semiramis isse*
*dicitur, et multis Lais amata viris."*

For a second or so Mendoza's gaze had a blank, machinelike quality that made Alec acutely uncomfortable; then she smiled and was human again, bright-eyed, happy.

*"Ergo Amor et modicum circa mea tempora vinum*
*mecum est et madidis lapsa corona comis,"* she said.

Laughter breaking on a sob, Nicholas kissed her, and she twined her arms about his neck.

*What are they saying?* Alec inquired.

*Lot of lewd love-play in Latin,* Edward said, irritable at having been thrust aside. *Ovid's* Amores, *I think. My Latin was never very good.*

*Why not? Nicholas knows a lot of languages.*

*Because I was sent to sea when I was fourteen,* said Edward. *If I'd been able to stay at school, I'd no doubt be able to rattle it off the way brother Nicholas does. Though my headmaster preferred to encourage more practical knowledge.* Edward's lip curled. *Hardly surprising, given that he was one of the Company's agents.*

*Your headmaster?* Alec said.

*Dr. Nennys,* Edward said. *I worshipped that man! Ever ready with fatherly advice and intimations that I was a boy destined for great deeds. As good as told me outright I was the bloody second coming of Christ. Hadn't aged a day when I met him again, fifteen years on. He got me into Redking's; sponsored my initiation into the Gentlemen's Speculative Society, too.*

*I had one like that,* Alec told him somberly. *Tilney Blaise. He was always cheering me on about what I was supposed to do with my life—like go to Mars, now that I think of it. He never aged, either. He tried to get me to go to work for the Company.*

He turned to look at Nicholas and Mendoza. *All our lives, we must have had the Company's agents around us, telling us what to do, pushing us to turn the way they wanted.* Alec winced at a realization. *Even Sarah must have been one of them.*

*Your nurse,* Edward said.

*She took care of me from the day I was born. I used to think she loved me.*

**Happen she did, lad,** the Captain transmitted in silence, **but she done what the Company told her all the same. The only one of 'em as ever disobeyed orders for you was Mendoza.**

*And look what they did to her,* Alec muttered. *And to us. What have we been but clay they've sculpted into men?*

*Dr. Zeus is going to discover I'm a good deal more than a golem,* said Edward darkly.

**To be sure they will, my lad. And I'd be pleased and proud to go over some of my little schemes with you, as you've the inclination?**

*No time like the present,* Edward said.

*What've you got, Captain sir?*

**Well now! It be a pleasant thing, to be sure, when a massively**

*powerful Company can engage the picked geniuses of a whole world to invent things for it; but I reckon ye lads've heard that a camel's a horse designed by committee? And so it is with Dr. Zeus. Too many committees and supervisory panels and executive boards, all second-guessing and hindering them geniuses. And there's a power of skulking bastards who's running things behind the scenes, and all fighting amongst themselves naturally, so there's more confusion. Big corporations is stupid.*

The better for our purposes, said Edward.

*Right you are, son. Well, that's one to us. Now, take them nanobots. Dr. Zeus has come up with the best anywhere, what does more things than anybody else's design. But they only been used for biological augmentation, see? They got a lot of other potential uses.*

Such as? Alec looked keenly interested.

*Oh, such as making robot drones what look just like dolphins. There ain't no Company accountants telling us we can't.*

I confess I can't understand one word in three of this talk, said Edward.

*I reckon you savvy more than you let on. Well, so: yer little dolphins is a right clever idea, Alec, and sure to be useful. But think about a mine, now, or any other infernal device, that looked like nothing more than a teaspoonful of gold paint! Nanobots in suspension, with a timed-release program alerting 'em to stir themselves, on a certain day in 2355, and become a weapon. Or a transmitter to send out a jamming signal, or get into targeted sites and rape and pillage until a certain bloody Doctor was begging for mercy. No quarter given, of course.*

*We builds our power base slow, laying down bank accounts and power caches all through time, just like Dr. Zeus has, so we can go anywhere to do what we need to do, until we're powerful enough. Then it'll be mayhem and black treachery, served up hot.*

Are you saying these weapons couldn't be detected if sought for, because they wouldn't actually exist until the moment they deployed? said Edward.

*Aye, sir. Until then they'd be no more than potential.*

Good God, that is brilliant, said Edward, with a chilly smile. My compliments, Captain. You really are quite the pirate.

*Just doing what I was programmed to do, lad, but thank'ee kindly anyhow.*

*Wait a minute! Mines?* Alec had gone pale. *Weapons? Infernal devices? You're talking about bombs!*

*Of course he is,* said Edward. *Weren't you listening to—*

**No, no, laddie, to be sure! I meant—**

*We can't go leaving bombs around!* Alec shouted. *Haven't I got enough innocent blood on my hands?*

**Son, that weren't what I meant at all. Figure of speech, see—**

*Of course that wasn't what he meant, you dolt,* said Edward quickly. *There needn't be any civilian casualties at all.*

**No human casualities, no indeed, son. Just an all-out attack on that bugger Zeus, what'd leave him so badly hurt he'll wish he'd never been activated. You'd not shed a tear for him, I'd wager, eh?**

*No—but—*

*And I imagine you'd like to see justice done,* said Edward. *Wouldn't you?*

Alec looked at him bleakly. *If justice was done, I'd be dead and rotting.*

**Aw, no, son—**

*As you like,* said Edward. *But you were only a dupe, Alec, remember that, a tool for wicked men. They'd like nothing better than to see you perish of remorse. In your place, I should think it my moral duty to bring the true guilty parties to an accounting for their deeds.*

**Truer words was never spoke, Commander Bell-Fairfax, sir!**

*And, after all, it may be that one or two of them deserve to die,* said Edward. *For example . . . what other sentence than death could possibly suffice, for the authority who consigned our lady to Options Research?*

Both Alec and Nicholas grimaced. Mendoza opened her eyes, and suddenly all her languor was gone; she was braced, wary.

"Darling, are you all right?" she said sharply.

"Perfectly well, my love," Nicholas told her, and kissed her to stop any other questions. Alec, staring at the floor, clenched his fists until the knuckles were white. Without warning he threw a punch at the bulkhead. His fist went through it harmlessly.

*I thought so,* Edward said, leaning back. *Call it execution, if you like; or even public service. One of the few tags I did learn was, let me see, "Qui parcit nocentibus innocentes punit"; which would be translated as, "Who spares the guilty punishes the innocent." There are cases where one is positively benefitting humanity by slaying judiciously.*

*Thou playst the boy like a lute,* said Nicholas, sadly.

*Well.* Edward sipped his virtual champagne. *Something to think about, in any case. And we really ought to begin planning an enlightened rule for Mankind, once we've toppled Zeus. Otherwise, some tyrant will undoubtedly club his way into power.*

Alec shivered. *I'm the last man on Earth to rule over other people.*

*That may well be the case,* said Edward.

# IN THE DARK NIGHT OF THE SOUL (YEAR INDETERMINATE)

The obscuring fog of causality rolls back, the lid of Schrödinger's box opens, and lo and behold! In nearly every century, on some coastline or other, a great ship has moored far out to sea and sent a little craft in to do business with the natives. Dolphins have coursed beside it, like an escort of sea-greyhounds.

The man and woman stepping ashore seldom draw attention to themselves, except insofar as people occasionally remark on the man's extreme height. Otherwise the couple are unremarkable in their appearance, their clothing perfectly appropriate for the season and year. Sometimes the man does all the talking; sometimes the woman alone speaks.

Now and then, as they make their way through exotic places, the man is distracted by a church or temple, and lingers a while to watch priests or rabbis or saffron-robed monks going about their businesses. Sometimes he will summon the courage to ask a question of one of them, in Latin, Greek, or Hebrew or, slowly and haltingly, in their own languages. Their answers are brief and to the point, or lengthy, with many digressions, but the result is always the same. He sighs and thanks them, looking rather like a dog that has lost its master. The woman takes his hand and they walk away together.

*Now then, Nick, wilt thou not sleep?*

Nicholas glanced up from the plaquette on which he had been studying the Pali canon of Buddha's teachings. He sighed and set it aside.

Mendoza slept peacefully; beside her, Alec and Edward sprawled at awkward angles, in unconscious competition for proximity to her. Outside, stars drifted down into a black ocean.

**You don't look like revelation has struck you, somehow.**

*No, Spirit.*

**This ain't any better than the Tao?**

*No.*

**Nor the Bhagavad Gita? Nor the Avesta, neither?**

*No.*

**I thought certain you'd like them Gnostic Gospels.**

*Nicholas shrugged.*

**And I reckon you ain't even looked at that nice book on Vodou.**

*Spirit, this is futility. What do the best of them but recapitulate the Ten Commandments, in one form or another? And I find no proof that men have obeyed strange gods any better than the God of the Israelites, or learned any more of the true nature of the Almighty. Shall I worship a cow? Shall I spin paper prayers on a wheel? I'd as lief go back to eating fish in Lent lest God smite me down, or pray to wooden Mary to take away the toothache.*

**Well, son, allowing for the foolishness, which I reckon depends on what port you hail from—ain't there any one seems better than the rest?**

*None, Spirit. That I must be kind and do no harm, I needed no prophets to tell me; but not one will open his dead mouth to say what kind and harmless Lord would create this dreadful world,* said Nicholas. *Nor permit abominations like Edward and me to walk in it.* He looked down at Mendoza broodingly. *Nor deliver a little frightened child into the Devil's hands. Nor let her lie forgotten a thousand years on the floor of the house of the dead.*

**Mm. Can't answer that one, lad.**

*I sought to build the New Jerusalem in my own heart, and my heart failed me. Shall I live like Edward, in my reason alone? But that is all ice and pride. Science will not grant me my soul again.*

**What do I tell my boy, then, if he gets the shakes about eternal life?**

*Set up no gods for thine Alec, Spirit.* Nicholas lay back and put his arms about Mendoza, pulling her close. *There is love, or there is nothing. The rest is vanity.*

———

When they purchase goods, they pay in hard cash. When they post letters, in those times and places with postal service, the correspondence is always addressed correctly, the postage exact, the paper and ink of the most ordinary for the time. Their occasional transactions with banking firms or attorneys are brief and discreet. Then the man and the woman put back out to sea, and are generally promptly forgotten, and never seen again.

They figure in few ledger entries and no history books at all.

But by the year 1863, in nearly every great coastal city on Earth—Venice, London, Amsterdam, Boston, New York—some old banking house or legal firm administers a long-maintained trust, now and then receiving directions from the present heirs or their legal representatives. Were all the dots connected, all the figures added up, Dr. Zeus Incorporated would be rather surprised to discover it has a rival in the very long-term investment game. The Company, however, is too busy taking care of its own considerable business to do such a thing, and anyway, why should it worry? Nobody else has the ability to travel through time.

So the names on the enduring fortunes ring no warning bells at Dr. Zeus: William St. James Harpole, Thorne Fairfax, Nicholas Mendoza, Alec Bell, Edward Checkerfield, Alton Finsbury . . .

And of course the Company doesn't think to check its own signals, bounced back through time to its operatives working in the past, to see if anyone has encrypted an interstitial signal in its own constant flow of messages. Thus the Captain continues to draw on his enormous twenty-fourth-century reservoir of memory caches, with scarcely a millisecond of time lag.

This is good, because the Captain now has a lot to coordinate: temporal itineraries, hidden funds, fiendishly clever nanobot weapons designs, the ongoing rejuvenation treatments for Alec, and the careful search of records to determine just where Alec's DNA vial might be stored . . . and research on the subject of Crome's radiation generators.

This last business goes ahead more easily for the Captain than for anyone else who has ever attempted to study the subject, for the reason that he is a tremendously powerful artificial intelligence and also because he has a Crome generator to observe, close at hand, around the clock, over a long period of time.

MIDMORNING ON 17 MARCH 1863 AD

On an empty stretch of the Pacific, lightning blazed down out of a clear blue sky. There was a wild roiling in the water, as though some great leviathan had been hit by the blast. Gradually the turmoil ceased. The *Captain Morgan's* storm bottle retracted, her masts and spars extended, and she clapped on sail. Tacking about, she steered for the South Seas, and white spray struck and ran from her bows like cream.

"*Caramba,*" sighed Mendoza, stretching sensually on Edward's lap. "We must try doing this while copulating again sometime."

"It has its points," said Edward, a little shakily. She looked up into his face at once, frowning.

"You're pale. Are you all right, Alec?"

He looked down at her and she saw his face change abruptly, eyes going wide and guileless. "I'm fine, baby," he protested, in what she was beginning to think of as his Beach Boy voice. He grinned and patted her behind. She uncoiled nimbly and stood up, and he unfastened the storm harness and stood to join her.

Alec, well along in his treatments with Pineal Tribrantine Three, appeared distinctly younger now. As a rule he tended to avoid looking in mirrors except to shave, so the fact that the planes of his face had tightened and smoothed discernibly went unnoticed. Some of the weathering of years' exposure to sea gales was disappearing also. What Alec did notice was that his back felt great these days, and his appetite was enormous. His nightmares, however, had not diminished.

But he went gladly enough with Mendoza to their stateroom, for they were suffering slightly from temporal lag. It had been close to midnight on the day they had embarked, though a bright midday sun was shining down now.

They clambered into bed and Mendoza fell asleep almost at once. Alec and Nicholas were also tremendously sleepy, but Edward couldn't close his eyes.

*What's wrong?* Alec said at last. *Oh. It's the date, isn't it? This is the day you . . . er . . . died.*

*It's the day I was shot,* said Edward in a strained voice. *Perhaps even now, miles from here, I'm in the very act of coming aboard the* J.M. Chapman.

*Why, man, it comes to nothing at last,* said Nicholas. He yawned. *For, see, here thou art, and here is she, happy after all.*

*I'm perfectly aware of that,* said Edward. *It's a deuced odd feeling, all the same. One can't help but wonder what would happen if—*

**If you tried to go there and stop yerself? You couldn't do it, lad. The Company's tried. History can't be changed and even if it could, there'd still be squalls. Two identical objects can occupy the same time, or space, but not the same time AND space,** the Captain said.

*I've no inclination to intervene on my own behalf, no; I deserved those bullets. But as I lie—apparently—dying, the poor child will be going mad. If only there were some way of letting her know we'd meet again . . .*

**Bless you, son, she believed that anyhow.**

*Just as well, I suppose,* Edward said, watching Mendoza as she slept. *You're quite certain it's necessary to be here?*

**Aye. This is the harbor bar, in a manner of speaking. If we're to go any farther, we got to get past this point in time. According to the laws of temporal physics, anything can go backward in time, and then forward again as far as its own place; but not past that point, d'y'see? That was why you had the annoyance of them clothes disappearing the other day.**

*But the plants remain with us.*

**As to that, sir, I got a theory. They're living organisms, what was grown right here, inside the time transcendence field. Zeus didn't never do no science experiments inside a T-field, see? Just crammed his operatives in them little cramped boxes and shuttled 'em back and forth. But this here ship, now, puts out the biggest T-field ever generated. And the plants belongs to the ship's time, so they can go anywhere it does.**

*That doesn't explain why the plants got so big so fast,* said Alec, rubbing his eyes.

**I'm still working on that one, son.**

*Yes, very well,* said Edward. *What about this "harbor bar"?*

**Why, we can travel anywhere afore January 2352, because that was our point of departure into the past. But yer lady there supposedly can't go no farther forward than 24 March 1863, because that's when she was sent back to Options Research.**

*And yet she seems to have gone into 1996, on that one occasion.*

*So it'd seem. Not only that,* **then** *she went with the clothes she was standing up in, and her horse, and that other poor bleeder and his horse, too. Plus their gear. So it ain't a hard and fast rule, whatever that lying bastard Zeus says.*

*Then we must learn more about her particular ability.*

**Aye. Now, we can stay here at the breakwater and just float forward a day at a time into the future, except that our Alec'd be dead of old age centuries afore we ever got back to 2352; or we can experiment with Crome's radiation and see if we can jump forward to 1996.**

*Is there any risk to her?*

**Them clothes popped back safe and sound once we went backward again, didn't they? But we ain't trying nothing until we know more. Now then: Alec and Nicholas has nodded off, and you were best to do the same.**

Edward was silent. He looked up sharply when the ship's bell pealed: eight bright little chimes.

*Noon,* he said.

**Aye, sir. Afternoon watch just commenced.**

*I wonder if I've been shot yet?*

**I wouldn't know that, son.**

Edward stared into space a moment, his eyes glittering. He leaned down, put his mouth close to Mendoza's ear and whispered something.


THE AFTERNOON OF 18 MARCH 1863


*Mrs. Checkerfield, ma'am, I wonder if I might have a word with you? Long as our Alec's busy with the servounits? Private-like, just you and me.*

"Of course, Sir Henry," Mendoza said, adjusting the mist element above the seedling tray. It had been tricky, setting up a hydroponics cabin aboard a sailing ship, but the Captain had done it. An ingenious system of spill catchments and ventilation permitted a garden to flourish without rotting a hole through the deck timbers. Roses bloomed in luxuriance, ivy and grapevines sprawled, waved aggressive green tendrils everywhere.

*Well, ma'am, I been accessing the data we lifted from Dr. Zeus, and I keep coming across references to that, er, Crome's radiation. Would you know anything about it firsthand, dearie, that you could tell old Captain Morgan? The better to batten down aforehand for any squalls we might hit?*

Mendoza stood absolutely still for a moment, her face immobile as a mask. The Captain did the electronic equivalent of holding his breath. Then she frowned.

"Crome's radiation?" she said. "I could download to you, but I don't seem to have the file. It appears to be the source of what mortals call *paranormal phenomena*. I don't think a lot is known about it. Crome's isn't a power, or an ability; it's simply a bioelectric effect produced by certain mortals. You can't *use* it for anything. It's like a birth defect."

*Ah! But it's a real phenomenon.*

Mendoza nodded, watching the bright water-beads forming on the little blades of corn. "Yes."

*Well now! That's interesting. I were afeared lest our Alec be such a one. From what I'm accessing, the Company seemed to think Crome's is dangerous.*

Mendoza nodded, biting her lower lip. She opened the maintenance panel on the desalinization unit and checked the filter; wandered along the kitchen-garden rows and through the miniature orchard, as though she had lost something. Finally she said:

"This is because he's still damaged, isn't it? Sometimes, you know, I think he must have a glitch in his language centers. You should run a diagnostic. It's as though he's not sure what temporal track we're going through, whether we're in the sixteenth century or the nineteenth or . . . I don't know. He *changes*. Sometimes when we're out among the mortals I pick up a stray emotion from a thief or a murderer, someone contemplating robbing us. I can laugh about it; but then I remember, and I could go mad like a dog, and kill them all, to think that he's vulnerable now.

"But he's not a Crome generator! He may be damaged, but he isn't a . . . a defective."

*Is that so, dearie? Well, what a comfort to have that settled, aye,* purred the Captain, observing her closely.

He continued to observe her over the next several days, and subtly administered a number of tests, far more devious and oblique than Rhine Institute flash cards but to the same ends.

When presented with a situation for immediate analysis where even subliminal data was available to provide a clue to the correct answer, Mendoza scored perfectly, as any cyborg would, to a degree that would seem supernatural to mortals. But when required to make a random guess, where no data, subliminal or otherwise, was available to suggest an answer, Mendoza showed no unusual talent for choosing correctly. Nor did she generate Crome's radiation at any time.

She had a cyborg's physical control and hyperfunction ability, enabling her to move, at need, too swiftly for the mortal eye to follow; but she was unable to move an object by any means other than extending her hand and picking it up. While she could scale a wall or go around a barrier so quickly as to appear to have moved through it, frame-by-frame analysis of her action proved she did not physically pass through the barrier. No Crome's was generated on these occasions, either.

On the other hand, Mendoza did generate Crome's fairly dependably under certain circumstances: extreme physical arousal, usually, though not always, strictly sexual; dancing with Alec invariably produced sheets of blue lightning. However, no paranormal activity occurred. Mendoza never seemed to notice the blazing lights at all. Alec and the others did, of course, but refrained from mentioning it at the Captain's request, and per-haps from a certain gentlemanly impulse.

Delving through Company files, the Captain found a detailed study of the phenomenon at Lookout Mountain Drive, where Mendoza had had her temporal mishap in 1862, complete with a record of anomalous mag-netic pulses in that area over a ninety-year period.

He read with interest the files the Company had kept before its exper-iments with Crome's had been discontinued. Its conclusions were: that Crome's radiation somehow caused an individual's electromagnetic field to bleed over into the temporal field, which *perhaps* caused what ap-peared to be precognition or déjà vu in certain mortals. Also, telekinesis could *perhaps* be explained by Crome's causing a disruption in the tempo-ral field, freezing objects briefly in time while space (following its normal orbital trajectory) swung out from under them. This *perhaps* accounted for documented cases of solid objects appearing to leap off shelves or float through midair, or even rain down out of a cloudless sky.

It might also account for the ongoing phenomena with the garden, wherein plants shot from seed to maturity in a night. Mendoza seldom generated Crome's on these occasions, but did seem to be able to produce the temporal distortion at will. Just *how* she did it remained a mystery. She had not volunteered any explanation, apparently under the impression that Alec also had the ability, and neither he nor the Captain had considered it wise to disabuse her of this idea yet.

The Captain made calculations, drew up tables. He analyzed his log for the time jump during which Edward and Mendoza had been making love, arranged all the data in new tables, cross-referenced everything . . . and began to form a theory.


## THE EVENING OF 25 MARCH 1863

*Well now, Mr. and Mrs. Checkerfield, what's yer pleasure tonight?* the Captain inquired jovially. Before anyone could reply, he went on: *You been working on that there maize all day, ma'am, and wouldn't you like to relax? I'd recommend a nice romantic holo.*

Alec, just stepping from the bathroom after a shower, made a face. Watching holos with Nicholas and Edward was tedious, when they weren't on drugs. He had to keep explaining the action for Nicholas, who could barely understand the dialogue, which so irritated Edward that fights invariably broke out.

But Mendoza set aside the sheaf of data printouts she'd been preparing to scan.

"A holo?" She looked intrigued. "Where we eat popcorn and watch plays in the air? I remember those! Yes, by all means!"

"Would you really like to see one?" Alec said, glancing at the others. Edward shrugged. Nicholas looked amenable.

"Could we? Do we have a—" Mendoza blanked, searching for words. "Projector?"

*Why, dearie, we got everything we need, including popcorn,* the

Captain said, just as Coxinga came crawling in bearing an enormous bowl of the stuff.

*That was rather convenient,* Edward said. *You've something in mind, haven't you?*

**Ask no questions and you'll be told no lies, me lad,** the Captain transmitted. He sorted through the hololibrary's several million entries and selected something entitled *Sins of the Flesh,* a twenty-second-century romance notorious for its use of subliminal cues to sexually arouse viewers. He angled a camera, studying his charges critically.

Mendoza sat up in bed and accepted the popcorn bowl from Coxinga. Alec, toweling his hair dry, sprawled beside her. Nicholas and Edward were left, as they usually were, to arrange themselves as best they could on either side. Looking over at Nicholas, Alec suddenly had what seemed to him to be a brilliant idea.

"I know what! Let's watch one of Mr. Shakespeare's plays."

"Shakespeare?" Mendoza looked vacant for a moment and then her eyes widened. "English playwright? Elizabethan era?"

"The same." Alec propped pillows behind them. "I used to talk with him, you know," he said, referring to the hologram at the Shakespeare Museum in Southwark.

"Really?" Mendoza seemed impressed.

*You needn't lay it on with a trowel,* Edward sneered.

*No, this'll be great. It'll all be in old English, yeah? Nick will be able to understand what everybody's saying, so I won't have to keep translating and driving you crazy.*

The Captain did the electronic equivalent of gnashing his teeth in vexation and scanned through his library for Shakespeare plays, subheading ROMANCE.

The first to pop up was *Romeo and Juliet,* which he hastily discarded after reading the synopsis. Briefly scanning *A Midsummer Night's Dream,* he decided it would do well enough, and scrolling through available versions settled on one from Warner Brothers circa 1935, as being produced in Elizabethan costume and therefore inflicting less culture shock on Nicholas.

"Did I ever meet Shakespeare?" Mendoza said.

"Er . . . no, I don't think you did. Nice guy, though."

*I knew no Shakespeares,* Nicholas informed Alec.

*Of course you didn't. You died nine years before he was born,* Edward said. *And Alec never really met him, either.*

*Then wherefore am I to—*

**Oh, shut up and enjoy this, you lot!** the Captain transmitted. **And see if we can't make this a nice romantic evening for the lady, eh?**

*Aha,* said Edward. *So that's the scheme. Aye aye, sir!*

Mendoza jumped a little when the panel in the ceiling irised open to reveal the holoprojector, which resembled a quartz crystal chandelier turned inside out. It descended into position.

"It's okay, baby," Alec said, sliding an arm around her. "You'll enjoy this."

"I'm sure I shall," she said uncertainly. The Captain dimmed the lights in the room. A big sphere of glowing smoke materialized in the air, just above the bed. The word OVERTURE appeared there, and some vague fairylike images; a symphonic arrangement of Mendelssohn's music came warbling from the room's speakers, and the show started at last.

Scholars are reasonably unanimous in their verdict that this particular film was not the most authentic Shakespearean production ever mounted, but certainly it had the most cobwebs and moonbeams, and it had remained popular with audiences right up to the time that Shakespeare's plays had been condemned as irredeemably politically offensive. As a result of its popularity, great pains had been taken in remastering it for holo, extrapolating the flat images out into three-dimensional ones. It had translated rather well, even in the black-and-white tones of the original film.

Mendoza snuggled against Alec, crunched popcorn, and watched the spectacle with evident enjoyment.

Nicholas sat watching with arms folded, determined to be polite for Alec's sake. As the play advanced, he found he had little trouble following the story, though it had been written forty years after his death and the actors' accents seemed strange and uncouth. But as the familiar cadences of language rolled on, he began to be drawn into the illusion, and found himself looking around involuntarily for a pie-seller or a bottled-ale vendor, of the sort that used to follow players' carts like flies.

Edward watched silent, absorbed, spellbound by the best that the Brothers Warner could lay before him, tinsel and glitter and all. His experience of staged Shakespeare, for whom he had a well-concealed passion, had been limited to one dusty performance of *Julius Caesar*. The rest his imagination had been obliged to provide from tiny print double-columned in a cheap edition read by blazing tropical sunlight, or by dim lamplight belowdecks, or in gaslit hotel rooms in dubious places.

Only Alec was lost, desperately reading the faces and body language of the shadows in his attempt to get some idea of what the play was supposed to be about. He turned to the others, hoping somebody would tell him; but they were following the action with such avidity he was embarrassed to ask.

So he stared, as fairies soared and flitted through his room. It had become the Wood Near Athens, a forest of dark silvertone. Ashen petals blew across his face as Puck bounded from a drift of leaves, and glittering cobwebs winked in phantom moonlight on the bedposts. As soon as he stopped trying to understand the words, the story began to tell itself to him: the two sets of ridiculous lovers, the troupe of clowns rehearsing in the darkness, the looming father and ice-pale mother locked in hostilities over the bewildered little mortal child. And such terrors! The wild boy with his crazy laugh, and the braying black-lipped donkey man in the night forest!

Having no significance, the words took on all possible significance. The story was a riddle, a message in a sealed bottle. What could it all mean?

So Alec watched in fascinated incomprehension, unable to look away as plaintive lovers struggled across his moonlit bedclothes and stumbled over his legs.

The Captain monitored the real lovers, their heartbeats and respiration rates. He saw a chance and acted on it.

Quietly he amped up the power to the holoprojector, and deployed his own projectors inset here and there in the stateroom's decorative molding. He fed subtle signals into Alec's nervous system through the subcutaneous port, and into Mendoza's as well through certain circuitry he had installed when he'd repaired her.

They were so absorbed in the action of the play that they scarcely noticed when the Wood Near Athens began to expand beyond the confines of their bed, indeed became more than illusory play of light over solid surfaces. That was a *real* moon blazing down from the star-spangles, wasn't it? And how had velvet moss and luscious woodbine replaced plain cotton percale? But it had, and first Edward and then the others noticed they were reclining on a virtual bank where wild thyme grew, and sweet musk-roses canopied overhead, stars winking through. Only Alec was startled. The others, having no way of knowing that this was a little beyond even twenty-fourth-century remastering capabilities, accepted it as part of the show.

Just to their left, Titania slumbered beside Bottom, as Oberon looked down with a sardonic smile. Over there the lovers had fallen together, muddy and bedraggled but properly paired off at last. The perfume of nodding violet and eglantine was strangely intoxicating, as well it might be since it was laced with pheromones, jetting from the stateroom's air vents.

So the king of shadows summoned his host to follow into the haunted virtual night, and the slow passionate strains of Mendelssohn's *Nocturne* came yearning from the speakers. Over at the other end of the clearing a moth-fairy was engaged in a sensual ballet with a muscular black shade, fluttering ineffectually her powdery wings while he possessed her inexorably. This was about the point where Mendoza noticed that she too had been endowed with spangles and a certain silvery light, and that not one but *three* black-winged shadows had turned and were regarding her with identical hot-eyed stares.

"Oh!" she said, applauding. "How very—"

Clever? Inventive? Whatever praise she had been about to bestow on advances in entertainment technology, Nicholas had fastened his mouth over hers before she could make another coherent sound. She squeaked happily, struggled insincerely as Alec and Edward seized her. What followed on that mossy couch, under the astonished moon, was so extreme, so erotically complicated, and so pleasurable that poor old Mr. Shakespeare's phantom holographic self, away in 2352 London apologizing to a group of Ephesian tourists for writing *Taming of the Shrew,* found himself smiling without knowing why.

On the *Captain Morgan,* the Captain observed carefully as the act progressed, and noted when Mendoza began to sparkle with the blue fire of the Crome effect. At precisely the moment when it was at its most intense, he generated a subsonic tone that set the quartz crystal structure of the holoprojector vibrating.

Nothing happened. Or . . . not quite nothing. He modulated the frequency. This direction? No . . . That way?

The very air trembled, the silver illusions flickered for a moment, though the lovers didn't notice. A spontaneous temporal transcendence field had begun to build inside the stateroom. The Captain watched as its whirling lightnings sent a tentacle toward the bed, where a blue thread of fire extended from Mendoza's ecstatic body and arched to meet it—

The Captain silenced the tone immediately. It didn't stop; the crystals in the holoprojector were still resonating. In panic he retracted the holoprojector up into its recess, and that did the trick, though the room was plunged into darkness relieved only by the spectral flame of Crome's radiation, playing over Alec and Mendoza where they embraced.

Hastily the Captain dropped the projector again and resumed the program. On the level of his thought that was not piling up and evaluating data—for the Captain had many levels of thought—he observed Mendoza's naked body, and congratulated himself once again on the job he had done rebuilding her. Who'd have thought that lissom little thing making his boy happy had ever been the pitable fragment he'd salvaged? Why, he must have regenerated at least eighty percent of her organic mass—

And he'd done it right here, within himself—

*Within the largest temporal field ever created.*

The Captain did the electronic equivalent of gasping and smacking his forehead.

In the virtual Wood Near Athens, three powerful incubi shared between them a spirit of no common rate: so thoroughly that nobody was able to pay any attention to the action of the play, though the Lord woke his Lady, the fiendish kid removed the donkey-head from bully Bottom. Not until Peter Quince came timidly forward to speak his prologue did they lie there, all four, giggling in exhaustion at Pyramus and Thisbe.

"I liked that," Mendoza said, as the stateroom returned to normal and the lights came up. "I don't remember movies being that much fun at all!"

"Yeah," was all Alec was able to say, collapsing onto his back.

"That thing we were doing, was that—" She groped through the ruin of her memory. "Was that *going into cyberspace*?"

"Sort of."

"*Caramba.*" Her eyes were wide. She leaned up on her elbow and looked at him inquiringly. "There were three of you. I didn't know that could happen in cyberspace."

"That was just—er—the special effects," Alec temporized.

"Really?" Mendoza lay down again. "Impressive!"

Nicholas gave a wicked chuckle and nudged her. She jumped and looked over her shoulder, startling everybody.

"I could have sworn you just—" she said, staring through Nicholas. Alec reached up and pulled her down.

Nicholas and Edward looked at each other in wild surmise.

Unnoticed on the floor beside the bed, the popcorn bowl had filled with green sprouted shoots of maize.


## THE MORNING OF 26 MARCH 1863

*Seven bells in the morning watch, Mr. and Mrs. Checkerfield, and a grand good morning to ye! Fair skies, wind's out of the south-southwest, temperature twenty-three degrees Celsius, swells at one meter!* The Captain's voice rang with strange triumph.

Alec opened his eyes to a breakfast tray heaped with oyster savory, fresh strawberries in zabaglione, and vitamin-fortified orange juice. Beside him, Mendoza yawned and stretched.

"Coffee," she implored.

*To be sure, dearie, Jamaica Blue Mountain with cream.* Coxinga extended one of its arms with a mug freshly poured. *And there's yers, Alec lad. Now then! We been here in 1863 long enough. I reckon it's time to move on.*

"Okay," said Alec sleepily, rolling over. Edward, in the act of shaking out his virtual napkin, looked up sharply.

*We're to make a time jump? Ha. Then all that moonshine last night was intended to accomplish something! What have you found out, Captain?*

*What I needed to know,* the Captain told him silently. *Are you up to another ride this morning, boyo? Yer old Captain's solved the wench's riddle at last. With her at the figurehead, we can cut through to the future easy as climbin' through the lubber-hole!*

"Huh?" Alec and Nicholas sat bolt upright, obliging Mendoza to clutch at her coffee.

"What is it?" she asked, looking worriedly at Alec.

"Nothing!" Alec said, reaching for the oyster savory. "Just feeling bouncy this morning. So, er, Captain sir—what do you reckon, shall we lay in a course for the twentieth century? Say, 1996?" *You're absolutely sure about this? No way you could be mistaken at all?* He sipped his coffee and almost gagged. It was liberally laced with time travel cocktail.

*Aye, lad,* the Captain said aloud. ***And you may rest easy on the calculations, by thunder. I been running a program all night to check my figures.***

"Is it particularly hard to get to 1996?" Mendoza said, reaching for the toast.

***No, ma'am. But the further you go past the year 1950, the more crowded things is, so it's as well to be certain sure where you make landfall, lest you capsize some swab what ain't watching out. As you'll remember, I'm sure?***

"Oh," said Mendoza, who didn't remember anything of the kind but didn't want to say so.

"Yeah," said Alec, as confidently as he could. "Because that's the era we need to start turning over some of those bank accounts to electronic transfer, isn't it, Captain?" He popped an oyster patty in his mouth and chewed, looking sincere.

***I reckon our lawyers will have done that already, lad, but there ain't no harm making sure, now, is there?*** the Captain said. ***What's more, we could do with a spot of provisioning. They had them supermarket things back then, see.***

*What on earth is a supermarket?* Edward spooned down virtual zabaglione.

***What it sounds like, what d'y'think?*** the Captain replied silently. ***All the beef chops and brandy yer little heart desires, me bucko. But no cigars! Understand? You can do what you like in cyberspace, but Alec's got to use them lungs.***

*Fair enough,* said Edward. He set aside his empty dessert glass and looked hungrily at Mendoza. *Try not to dawdle, Alec.*

Alec glared at him and Nicholas just shook his head.

All the same, by the time the breakfast dishes had been cleared away they found themselves desperately ready as well, in spite of nervousness about what they were about to undertake. Mendoza, lingering over a second cup of coffee and a new-printed sheaf of data on the tryptophan content of her maize cultivars, found herself scooped up and carried from the bed.

"Hello?" she said.

"I was just thinking," said Alec. "What could possibly top last night? Let's find out, what do you say?"

"Okay," Mendoza said, dazed but happy. She gulped down the last of her coffee while Alec fastened himself into the storm harness, and then went obligingly into his arms. Without, the four dolphin servos rose on the crest of a wave and leaped on deck. Flint and Bully Hayes loaded them into their torpedo-berths and scuttled into the wheelhouse, as the sails furled, the spars retracted. The great storm-bottle closed down.

As the air filled with golden gas, with blue fire, a discreet and unfamiliar humming filled the air. Its source was the battery of quartz crystal resonators the Captain had installed that morning, while Alec and Mendoza slept. And now, as the lovers rode to bliss, the charge built and the humming grew louder. The time drive powered up.

Distracted by the noise, Mendoza opened her eyes and saw Alec's face, white and tense. She opened her mouth to ask him what the matter was—

There was a quiet, though dreadfully audible CLICK—

There was a blue flash—


SOME OTHER MORNING

And then there was a roaring darkness as they plunged into deep water and rose upward again, turning as they came, bobbing out into sunlight.

The yellow gas vented, the storm canopy opened, the dolphin servos shot out into a new sea. Alec clutched Mendoza close and kissed her, hard, as tears of relief streamed down his face. The eerie silence was broken by the Captain's thundering laughter, and by Mendoza saying worriedly:

"Alec, darling?"

"I'm fine," he said, rocking her in his arms. "And you're fine, and—and everything's all right."

*Aye, son, to be sure!* gloated the Captain. ***Thirty leagues due west of San Francisco and it's 30 June 1996. All artifacts from 1855 present and accounted for. Zeus's brass arse be damned! How's that for a neat bit of navigation?***

They sailed for the City that night, through seas liberally strewn with floating trash and oil slicks. As they came slowly in through the Golden Gate under power, sails reefed, Alec and Mendoza went up on deck and leaned on the rail, staring in fascination at the lights. So did Nicholas and Edward, who were rendered nearly speechless by the size of the Golden Gate Bridge alone. Not so Mendoza, however.

"Oh, this is so changed from 1855," she said. "Look, look, Ghirardelli Square!" She fairly jumped up and down, pointing at the luminous sign.

"Can we go there? I've never been here in this time, I can't have been, I'd remember this! I always had the impression that the earthquake destroyed everything but it can't have, can it? Oh, isn't it beautiful?" She paused for breath and coughed, making a face. "Phew! What a smell, though. Is that internal combustion engines?"

"Old-style automobiles," said Alec, pointing at the hundreds of tiny lights moving on the bridge and along the steep streets. "Serious pollution."

"And look at the twentieth-century ships." She leaned forward, peering through the night. "And that must be Fisherman's Wharf . . . look, there are people sitting in the restaurants having cocktails. Oh, how civilized!"

*Where?* Edward stared vainly. Alec and Nicholas looked, too, but could see no more than minuscule rows of lit windows along the pierside.

". . . Though I can't say I care for the clothes," Mendoza added with a judicious frown.

"We'll find something you like," Alec promised, putting his arms around her. "Go shopping, yeah?"

She leaned back and looked up at him, a little sadly.

"We haven't . . . had this kind of thing a lot, have we? The things that mortals take for granted. Shopping, and sightseeing, and picnics and . . . just being man and wife?"

"No," Alec said, burying his face in her hair. She looked out at the lights.

"I can almost remember," she said quietly, "talking with you about the things we'd do, if we could ever have lives of our own. That must have been before the accident, yes?"

Edward took control, shoving Alec aside.

"Yes, my dear," he said. "We had that conversation a long, long while ago."

She sighed.

"Do you think they'll ever leave us alone?"

Edward smiled. His eyes had a disconcertingly icy sparkle; though it might simply have been the reflection of the lights on Telegraph Hill.

"Why, my dear, that's a dead issue," he said. "We've taken the offensive, now. And we'll see if that god they've made has any power to help them, when we run them down at last."

And Mendoza smiled, too, and settled back in his arms, and they regarded the glowing City spread out before them.


## THE FOLLOWING MORNING

The first day of July 1996 fell on a Monday, so there were few people loitering on Marina Green to remark on the whaleboat that appeared out of the fog, working its slow way across the water and in among the yachts, tying up at the boat dock.

The couple who came ashore drew even less attention, though some passersby noticed the man's remarkable height, and the way the couple stood staring in disbelief at the traffic roaring by on Marina Boulevard. But nobody heard the girl saying uncertainly:

"I think those lights are a signal, aren't they? The colors mean something, surely."

She started toward the intersection, and the man seized her and pulled her back.

"Christ Jesu, love!" he shouted. She turned to stare at him, and he stammered: "Er . . . we have to be really careful of the automobiles, okay? They used to kill a lot of people."

"I'm sorry." She took his hand. "But, see how that light over there just changed? I think this one's about to go, too, and—there! They're all stopping for us."

So they crossed the street, the girl smiling a bright artificial smile at the zombie drivers of the sleek cars and pulling along the man, who regarded them with the wild-eyed stare of a thoroughly alarmed horse, especially as they passed a vehicle broadcasting music loudly enough to hurt his ears, a thudding beat counterpointed by a staccato recitative. He seemed to compose himself, however, when they reached the comparative safety of the corner of Marina and Buchanan, and looked around with hard determined eyes.

"Very well," he said. "No worse than London, really. That's the market, is it? Rather small for our purposes."

"That's just a flower stall," the girl said. "I think the market's inside that big dome. See through the glass?"

"Oh," said the man. "I believe you're correct. And, according to that sign, there's a banking agent on the premises. How very convenient."

So they advanced across the parking lot toward it, located a door, and leaped back in astonishment when it opened automatically for them. The man recovered first.

"Come on. All doors do that nowadays, okay?" he muttered to himself, and grabbing the girl by the hand he hurried in with her.

Once inside, they stopped, staring.

"Oohhh," murmured the girl. "This will be . . ."

"This was the last big . . ." the man attempted.

". . . era of mass consumer goods before the General Prohibition laws will be enacted," the girl finished. She turned to look at the man. He turned to look at her. There was a moment of sizzling silence before he whooped:

"We can get *anything* here!" A couple of aproned clerks and customers turned to stare at them, and he lowered his voice immediately. "We'll just, er, pretend we buy groceries like this every day. Come on. See those carts? You're supposed to take one and push it around in front of you. You just go up and down the aisles, putting things you want in it. Okay?"

Which is what they did, as soon as they'd figured out how to get through the turnstile. Each took a cart and the man turned immediately to the right, into the meat department, and the girl followed. Here they prowled along the open butcher's bin, exclaiming to each other in hushed tones at how tidily it was all presented, every cut individually packaged in its own little white tray and wrapped in transparent film. The man seemed surprised that there was no mutton or goose to be had, and precious little veal; but he loaded huge bleeding clods of beef roast into his cart with both hands, and the girl concentrated on the beautifully plucked and dressed chickens. Neither of them touched the ground meats.

Reining themselves in with visible effort, they pushed on. The man was astonished by the selection of cheeses, took whole wheels. The nonedible items fascinated them, too; they stared and whispered, or giggled together until they were red-faced. They seemed greatly impressed by the canned goods, and selected the ones with the brightest labels. The jars of preserves and jellies captivated them; they took at least one of every color, and several jars of honey. They loaded up on coffees and teas.

They didn't quite seem to know what to make of the frozen foods aisle, until the girl gave a stifled shriek and made straight for the ice cream. The man remained staring at the frozen dinners in perplexity; opened a freezer case door at last, and stood gazing in a long while, as frosty air rolled around him in clouds. At last he took out a Salisbury steak dinner and opened it, and held the compartmented tray and the printed box side by side and looked from one to the other, knitting his brows, until a clerk advanced on him like an annoyed wasp.

They took several sacks of refined sugar. The cookie and cracker aisle delighted them, as did the gourmet foods. Into the cart were swept all the tins of paté and sardines, and all the jars of chutney and pickled gherkins. The girl went nearly mad in the candy aisle, dumping into her cart Toblerones, Lindt and Hershey bars, to say nothing of every Ghirardelli product available. They came around the corner into the aisle featuring alcoholic beverages and stood dumbstruck for a moment before deciding that they needed another cart, so the girl waited while the man went to fetch another. Thereafter he steered them along expertly, one hand to each, and the few other customers in the store at that hour began to stare at them.

They didn't notice. They filled the third cart entirely with liquors and mi-crobrewery ales. The man pulled down a bottle of Captain Morgan Spiced Rum and stood smiling at it, misty-eyed, while the girl loaded in José Cuervo. At the baked goods section their carts began to be difficult to man-age; and when they turned the very last corner and saw the fresh produce section opening out before them, there was a moment of stunned silence before the girl, without a word, went running back to get a fourth cart.

At last, trundling two carts each, they conferred briefly and then wheeled their purchases up to the nearest checkout counter. The clerk stared at the tower-piled carts in disbelief and said at last, "So . . . you're having a party?"

"That is correct," said the tall man. He smiled nastily and added: "In fact, my good man, we are celebrating your Independence Day."

The girl cleared her throat and said, "And, ah, we will be paying for this with electronic transfer of funds, okay, señor?"

"You mean your ATM card?"

"Of course!" The girl smacked her forehead with the palm of her hand. "You'll have to excuse us. We're new here."

"So these are all together," the clerk said, leaning forward to look at all four carts. "O-kay. He's buying all the liquor, right?" He looked sternly at the girl. "Because I know you're not twenty-one yet, honey."

She looked guilty. "He's buying," she said.

The clerk sighed and pulled out a microphone. "Mikhail, I need a box boy at station six, please, station six." He shut it off, then thumbed the button again and added: "Make that two box boys please, repeat, two." He began the exhaustive task of ringing up the contents of the first cart. The man and the girl watched in fascination, and whispered to each other as he pulled items across the bar-code scanner.

"So, you folks are new to San Francisco?" the clerk said. "Where are you from?"

"The sea," said the man automatically, and then grimaced.

"Spain," said the girl, at the same moment the man said: "London."

They looked furtively at each other.

"Originally," the girl explained. "But . . . actually we're from Jamaica. Now."

"Yes," said the man.

"Okay," the clerk said stolidly, plowing ahead through the groceries. "I sort of guessed *you* were from England, sweetie."

"Well, yes, yes he is," the girl said, wringing her hands. "He's . . . um . . ." She looked at the man, who was dressed in a very loud tropical-print shirt, blue jeans, and red canvas boating shoes. A late-twentieth-century concept popped into her head. "He's a British rock and roll star!"

"Really?" The clerk looked up, staring at the man.

"And I'm his groupie," she added desperately.

"Okay," sighed the clerk, and went on checking out their purchases.

The amount due was astronomical, and there was an extremely tense moment for all parties involved when the man, after seeming to listen to an interior voice, clumsily ran a new-looking ATM card through the little push-button device and keyed in a code. What sighs of relief when it went through without a hitch!

They had a moment or two to wait, however, as the two box boys, now assisted by the checkout clerk, were still laboring away at bagging their groceries. The man ventured over to the automated teller and studied it bemusedly, before withdrawing a certain amount in cash. The girl picked up a copy of the *Weekly World News* and flipped through it, raising her eyebrows now and then.

"You'd like some help out with this, huh?" said Mikhail the box boy, as the man came strolling back, tucking away his wallet.

"No, thank you, I believe we can manage quite nicely," he said. "Shall we, my dear?"

"Okay," said the girl, putting back the *News*. She gripped a cart handle with either hand, pushed, and her two carts rolled easily if ponderously out through the nearest self-opening exit. The man followed her. He was saying "Really quite an ingenious device, when one is laden with parcels—" when in an entirely different tone of voice he interrupted himself to exclaim: "Oh, my God, that guy's selling cappuccino." And then, in an undertone: "Right out in public, too!"

Mikhail went to the door and watched their uneven progress through the parking lot and across the street.

"Americans buy so many groceries," he said in awe.

The clerk just shrugged and said, "Takes all kinds to make a world, sugar."

Another commemorative holo, on the deck of the *Captain Morgan,* and in the background the immense dirty vivid pulsing sharp-towered City. The young man, with his wild hair and loud shirt, is holding up two gallon jugs of Captain Morgan Spiced Rum like trophies. The girl, in simple Levis and a Giants T-shirt, is brandishing a box of Rice-a-Roni in one hand and a box of gloriously Technicolor breakfast cereal in the other. They are both, the boy and the girl, grinning like loons.

## LATER THAT AFTERNOON

"Wow, we're going to be purging preservatives and toxins out of our systems for weeks," said Mendoza happily, tossing the last of the canned peaches to Alec, who stacked them neatly away. They had already filled the bar to capacity. "I can make tamales at last. And all that Theobromos! Though I'd really like to go to Ghirardelli's. We can buy more cloth at the woolen mill."

*The mill ain't there in this time period, begging yer pardon, but no matter. There's plenty of other wholesalers here.*

"Good," said Edward, taking control and dusting Alec's hands. "We'll need at least as much as we got from that poor fellow in 1855. And I believe ready-mades are rather more available in this era?"

*Indeed they are, sir. I diddled the automated tellers; you can withdraw all you need by this afternoon, so you'll be well provided for. Bit of shopping, eh, Mrs. Checkerfield, dearie, what d'y'say? And a lovely romantic supper for two someplace, aye.*

"Of course, we've the raw materials to see to, as well," said Edward, buttoning the top button of Alec's shirt. Alec promptly took control back and unbuttoned it again.

*I already done the deals. There's consignments awaiting us at the warehouses south of Market. Nothing to do tomorrow but go ashore to a place on Lombard Street, pick up the internal combustion wagon*

*I rented for you, and go collect the merchandise. Neat, eh? Three boat-*
*loads and we'll be set up nicely. So just relax this afternoon, me dears.*
*Old Captain Morgan's got things well in hand.*

They did go ashore and have the romantic afternoon he'd encouraged them to have. They moored the whaleboat at the municipal pier and walked up to Ghirardelli Square, where Alec took Mendoza into some of the finer shops. Three hours later she had a completely new wardrobe, pearls and peach satin, soft things in summer sherbet colors. Edward, moreover, had taken control long enough to select some dignified new clothes for Alec.

So they were unlikely to draw mortal attention, when, laden with shopping bags, they strolled hand in hand into Ghirardelli's. Nevertheless, the counter girl seemed in a distinctly agitated condition as she greeted them.

"I'm sorry, I'll have to ask you to wait a moment before we can seat you," she said. "We've got a little cleanup going on." And in fact they could see a couple of busboys, mopping and moving tables around beyond the frosted glass partition.

"Has there been a disturbance of some kind?" Edward inquired, frowning.

"We just had to pour two drunks into a taxi." The girl shook her head. "It takes all kinds, I guess. Would you like to see a menu?"

After a shared hot fudge sundae Mendoza got a little giggly, so they left Ghirardelli's and wandered down to the bottom of Hyde Street, where they stood looking out at the bay and the green hills beyond. Alec put his arm around Mendoza. She put her arm around him. After a while he leaned down to kiss her.

"Hey! You people want some music? Serenade or something?" yelled a black man with a trumpet. "Support the artists, you know?"

Alec raised his eyes, without lifting his mouth from Mendoza's, and groped in his pocket. He thrust a bill at the man, who ran forward and caught it, and examined it briefly.

"Holy cow! I'll play you twenty serenades, for that kind of money. What you want to hear? You want some jazz? No! I know what you want," he said, and lifting his trumpet to his lips he began to play *La Paloma*. He stopped after a few bars to ask: "You like that one? That okay?"

Alec signed okay and made a come-on gesture, as Mendoza sighed and leaned into the kiss. Unnoticed, green blades of grass began to emerge from the edges of the pavement, waving up toward the sun. The man began again, *La Paloma* strong and slow and passionate. It echoed across the quiet water, and all along the waterfront.

You could hear it on the *Captain Morgan* where she lay at anchor in her obscuring fog bank, and the Captain was in fact listening, monitoring Alec and Mendoza's progress through the dolphins' telemetry system. You could almost hear it out at Alcatraz, where a young British conspirator named Alfred Rubery had been interrogated about a plot to invade California, and let slip the name of Edward Alton Bell-Fairfax. You could hear it up at Ghirardelli Square, where Joseph and his friend Lewis had gotten so stoned that very afternoon, never knowing that Alec, and Edward, and Nicholas, were draping a strand of pearls about Mendoza's throat within shouting distance of them.


They stayed a few days in 1996, because the business of loading on raw materials took longer than they had anticipated. Mendoza was the only one who knew how to operate a truck, and that only in theory: and even the limitless ability of an immortal being is insufficient for the experience of driving in San Francisco.

But after a few minor misadventures, they had successfully loaded the *Captain Morgan*'s cargo holds with the contents of several chemical supply, metal, and fabric warehouses, most of a lumber yard, and $417 worth of assorted seed packets from a garden center. By the evening of the Fourth of July they had wrapped up their affairs and were able to cruise out beyond the Golden Gate Bridge, where they dined on deck while watching the fireworks celebrating American Independence. Then they sailed away, bound for other places, other times.

# ANOTHER MORNING IN 500,000 BCE

"So what are you getting Leslie?" Sylvya said, lingering just at the edge of the yellow track.

"Some bath things and a towel," David said. "And a card. All in blue. It's been ordered and it'll come to your house."

"Great!" Sylvya looked excited. "And now the Third Floor isn't being so selfish, we'll all have a lovely time."

"We will, won't we?" David looked smug. "Anyway, there's lots of room on this floor."

Actually he had done more than force the Third Floor to agree to change the location of the shower: they had to admit Sylvya into the planning committee, and she promptly found a less expensive place to get decorations. There had been some bitter grumbles that the more expensive decorations were nicer, but thrift was after all morally correct. Sylvya arrived that morning in triumph with a mysterious package she sent down to the Third Floor for safekeeping.

"Do you know what the others are getting her?" David asked.

"Darla's getting her nappy service and Mirlene got her a pram," Sylvya said. "Jenna got clothes and Cyntia found a TotMinder that has over six hundred songs in its memory."

"Well, that's Cyntia, isn't it?" David threw up his hands in exasperation. "Spending more to make the rest of us look bad."

"Oh, no, she took up a collection in her subdepartment," Sylvya said. "So they all shared the expense."

"Ah." David nodded, satisfied. Cooperation within a group was *much* more morally correct. "What about the party treats?"

"Sharona's committee's doing them," Sylvya said. "Sandwiches, I expect, and fruit punch. And Aerocrisps."

"Well, good," said David. "Everybody can eat those."

Sylvya shuddered, remembering the disaster two years ago when there'd been a potluck luncheon and somebody had brought in lentil cakes, forgetting that one of the girls in Brandi's department had a legume allergy. She'd had a reaction. There'd been tears and recriminations that had gone on for weeks.

"So it's all planned, then," said David. He glanced over at Leslie's desk and it occurred to him that she'd been away at the lavatory for a strangely long time. "Er—I wonder if Leslie's all right in there. Do you think you should go see?"

"No!" said Leslie, from a completely unexpected direction. David turned in astonishment to see her standing there, smiling, bearing in her arms a big bouquet of flowers, and behind her Mr. Chandra the Departmental Manager stood smiling, too.

"SURPRISE," they all said. There was a little tootling fanfare from his console and David turned back to see the words HAPPY BIRTHDAY shimmering on his screen, behind a scatter of bright electronic confetti.

"You didn't really think we'd forget, did you?" said Sylvya gleefully.

"Do we ever forget?" Leslie said, bringing the flowers forward and setting them in a vase just beside David's window. "There! Now you can look at them while you work. You see? Delphiniums and white roses. Your favorites."

"As always, David, it's very nice having you work for us," murmured Mr. Chandra.

David reflected that he really was a terribly lucky man, to be employed by Dr. Zeus Incorporated. He knew that lots of big corporations weren't nearly so thoughtful as regarded their employees' happiness. This hadn't exactly been a surprise—they remembered his birthday every year, year in, year out—but that only made it all the nicer, something to be anticipated shiveringly all day from the moment he removed his sleep mask.

"And you'll find a little something downloaded to your entertainment console when you go back to your Flat this evening," Mr. Chandra said.

David looked up sharply at Sylvya and Leslie. "No! *Not* Totter Dan's Mountain Rescue? You didn't!"

They giggled wildly.

"Wait and see," said Leslie.

"Oh, you didn't," David said, hugging himself.

"And you can all go early to lunch," Mr. Chandra told them, bestowing the final beneficence of the day. "Back at two. Shoo now. Go have fun."

Well! What a happy man was David Reed.

# ONE MORNING IN FEZ, MOROCCO, 2319 AD

Suleyman was working at the credenza in his study. It was a lovely room, elegant in a spare way: high bare walls set with Moorish tile, fine old carpets on the floor, tiny latticed windows far up the walls that would have made it difficult for an assassin to shoot an arrow through them, once upon a time, or for any unidentified person to lob an explosive device through them now.

Not that Suleyman expected anything so trivial or half-hearted from his enemies. A bomb would be merely a warning gesture, after all, and the opposing side in this game never gave warnings. Besides, on this particular day in 2319, many on the opposing side weren't even born yet.

Then, too, there were more than two sides, and the degrees of opposition varied depending on which side was considered in relation to which other side. All very confusing. One would need to be a fairly old immortal, with a calm and not easily distracted mind capable of appreciating extreme subtleties, to keep track of it all; and Suleyman had days when he felt neither so calm nor so good at geometry as he ought to be.

He became aware that he had a guest long before he could hear the voices approaching his study, so he logged off and closed up the inlaid rosewood cabinet that housed his credenza. By the time the double knock sounded on his door he had already risen, and was crossing the room with his unhurried stride to open it.

He regarded Latif and his visitor, a formidable-looking lady who would once have been described as Nubian.

"Nefer," Suleyman said with genuine pleasure, holding out his hands to her. She rushed into his arms and embraced him, murmuring an exclamation of relief.

"This is the Nefer who used to be one of your wives?" said Latif, leaning in the doorway and grinning.

"Oh, yes," Suleyman said. "Back in 1699, wasn't it, Nef?"

"God, that was a long time ago," said Nef, still holding tight to him. "You don't mind if I just cling here a minute, do you? You smell like safety."

Suleyman raised his eyebrows at that. "Latif? Tea, please? And—you haven't dined, have you?" he said, frowning as he pulled back to look at her. "You haven't slept, either."

"I've been running since I found out," she said, in an exhausted voice.

"Tea, brunch, and a guest room," predicted Latif, turning on his heel and going off to arrange matters.

"Come on," Suleyman coaxed, leading her to the divan. Nef still wore field clothing, dusty and travel-stained, and carried her field pack by one dangling strap. She collapsed into the pillows and stared at him with haunted eyes.

"I know this is going to sound incredibly stupid, but I only just found out about—*that place*," she said.

"The Bureau of Punitive Medicine," Suleyman said, his smile fading.

"And I know what you're thinking. Where's she been, in a cave?" babbled Nef. "Well, as a matter of fact I have been living in a cave, I've been on Gradual Retirement because there's not a lot for me to do nowadays, and so I'd just sort of taken an extended vacation in the Serengeti, and you know how it is when you're really having a good time, you just lose track of the years, and one day I noticed I was out of discs for my field unit so I thought I'd just hike into the nearest base and Kwame took one look at me and said Father Damballah, where've *you* been, I was about to report you as disappeared, too, and I said, What? And he told me about everything that happened back in July, and he told me all the rumors, and I thought—oh, shit, I'd better find someplace safe. And this was the only safe place I could think of," she finished. "Sanctuary!"

"Are you formally asking for my protection?" Suleyman said.

"Oh, yes." She nodded, closing her eyes wearily. "Please, Suleyman.

I'm not in trouble, I haven't done a damned thing wrong, but I'm just the kind of nobody that's becoming superfluous nowadays. And some of these rumors I've heard . . ."

"You know you're welcome here, Nef." Suleyman took her hand again. "But I'd like to know what you've been hearing."

"Well, Kwame played me back your broadcast," Nef said, wincing at the memory. "And of course everybody says it's just the tip of the iceberg, that there are actually hundreds of us that can't be accounted for. Everybody seems to be talking about some Literature Specialist named Lewis, because he's supposed to have been sold out by the Facilitator Joseph, who's supposed to be one of the suspects. Him and somebody named Marco. Suleyman, I used to work with Joseph. He was a Company man to the bottom of his slimy little heart, but I can't believe he'd be mixed up in something like this."

"I don't believe he is, myself," Suleyman said. "But, since nobody's been able to locate Joseph, he can't wash away any of the filth that's settling on his name either. Very convenient."

"That's what I heard," Nef said. "And that the whole Gradual Retirement plan is just a way to make us lose track of each other, so the Company can dispose of immortals as we get closer to 2355. People whose work is done." She shivered. "God knows mine is. I haven't had a posting in ages."

Suleyman shrugged. "Maybe. We can't learn much from the people we rescued. It appears that a lot of them were there for disciplinary reasons. No innocents, like Lewis.

"But there are, yes, hundreds of people still missing. Maybe the bureau was simply where the real offenders were imprisoned, and the rest are at some other location we've yet to find."

"How hard is the Company searching?" Nef said.

"Not very," Suleyman said. "There was quite a splash when we dragged the bureau before their eyes, but the ripples are dying away now. A formal inquiry, a committee to look into the question. And a few of the disappeared have miraculously turned up in unlikely places, with no memory of where they've been for the past few centuries.

"I know that some of the elite Executive Facilitators I've always suspected of really running the Company were horrified at what we found, horrified and angry as hell. I wouldn't be surprised to learn that some of the mortal masters have met with untimely ends, up there at their end of time. I may have precipitated 2355 by bringing this out into the open," he added grimly.

"Now I really want sanctuary," said Nef. "I don't suppose you'd like to get married again? Though Latif's a little old to need a mother."

"He'd appreciate one anyway." Suleyman smiled again. "For the time being, at least, things are going to be better. I don't think any more of us will vanish, in the immediate future. We accomplished that much."

Nef sighed. "Nothing ever turns out the way we think it will, does it? Even when history cannot be changed."

"Even then," agreed Suleyman.

# SANTA CATALINA ISLAND, 1923 AD

*Alec!*

Alec opened his eyes, and so did Edward and Nicholas. The Captain had called them silently, so Mendoza slept on in Nicholas's arms. Calm early morning, the ship rocking on a mild swell, the cabin full of reflected summer light.

*We're lying off the leeward side of the island, son. Arrow Point. You'd recognize the place, Edward. I been scanning for Company structures. They got a transmitter array concealed in one of the mountains, and a couple of manned stations. There's an underground storage facility, too, that ye'll want to be looting, I shouldn't wonder.*

*How well defended?* Edward asked, sitting up.

*Nothing but electronics, and I can send 'em a fireship. The stations have a three-cyborg complement each. We won't trouble with 'em. Near as I can tell, they're just collecting and shipping loot other operatives have acquired.*

Edward stared out the window at the looming island, at the dry hills and sea-facing cliffs. As they cruised slowly past, a particular outline of cove tugged at his memory. He grimaced and turned away, but all he said was: *It looks a good deal less green than I remembered.*

*Well, now, lad, it's been sixty years since you seen it.*

*What's the plan, Captain?* said Alec, watching Edward's face.

*Why, son, what'd be more natural for a innocent young couple of tourists than to wander about and have themselves a good look at the pretty scenery? Aye, but you'll be laying a few mines under the Company's keel. Metaphorically speakin', of course.*

*And our silver vial?* Nicholas said. *Is it here, Spirit?*

**Something's here, by thunder. There's a storage unit with yer file designation on it, according to the records.**

*Then we'll take it,* said Edward.

**To be sure, bucko, but not with blazing cannons nor drawn cutlasses, eh? Quiet-like, leaving no traces, just like they taught you when you signed on to be a Political.**

Edward's eyes glinted. Nicholas and Alec exchanged glances.

*What of our lady?* said Nicholas. *This was her prison a long weary while. Will she not remember, and grieve?*

**Why, son, why should she, with you at her side? And it's changed a good deal, remember.**

*And we can take her dancing, yeah?* said Alec. *At that ballroom she wrote about?*

**That ain't built yet, but we can jump ahead later. Get yerselves up and dressed.**

*Splendid,* said Edward, and taking control from Nicholas he leaned down and woke Mendoza with a long, hard kiss.

"I know I remember this place," Mendoza said, looking around at Avalon as Alec dragged the whaleboat up on the shingle beach. "Did we live here?"

"Yeah," Alec said, panting. "A long time ago." He tied the painter to a pier piling.

"It must have been, because I don't remember the town . . ." Mendoza found a dry rock and sat to pull on her stockings and shoes. "Though it seems a nice little town. Perhaps we could have a cocktail somewhere, later?"

"Okay," Alec said. "The First Prohibition is going on in this time, though, so we'll have to find what they called a speakeasy."

"What fun." She looked around, frowning slightly. "Weren't there more . . . trees?"

"Things change," he said apologetically, handing her up over the seawall and onto Crescent Avenue. She pulled him up beside her.

They wandered along the street, a young man in a white linen suit and a young girl in a summer frock of peach-colored silk, with a strand of pearls about her throat. He wore a Panama hat; her white summer hat kept coming off in the wind, until they stepped into a shop and he bought her a hatpin. He fastened on her hat for her and they walked off, holding hands.

On a street running back from the beach they found what had been a tent city, and was now rapidly being converted to a residential neighborhood. It was an odd process to watch: in some places the owners of the tents were simply slapping board and batten walls over canvas ones, or putting up modest Yankee clapboard cabins with names like Conch Cottage or Kilcare. Bougainvillea bloomed beside the finished ones, that were painted white or pink or green. The homes in progress stood like hopeful skeletons, bright new wood bleeding out amber pitch under a hot blue sky.

"Why are we here?" Mendoza murmured.

"I'm looking for a certain address," said Edward, who had taken control. He smiled and tipped his hat to an elderly lady. "According to the Captain, this particular house, which is in the process of being built on this particular day in history, will still be standing in the year 2355. Ah! And here it is."

They stopped and regarded a house three-quarters finished. Workmen were hammering away.

"What a charming residence this will be," said Edward, loudly enough to be noticed.

"And such a lovely location," said Mendoza, clasping her hands.

The foreman looked up and saw them.

"I wonder, sir, whether the property is for sale?" said Edward, taking off his hat and smiling pleasantly.

"This place is already sold, I'm afraid," the foreman said. "But Mr. Glidden's building more. You could inquire at his offices, up on Maiden Lane."

"Yes, I might at that." Edward nodded.

"Do you suppose, if we were very careful, we might walk through this one?" Mendoza said. "Just to see what the others will be like?"

"Well—since you're interested—well, sure," said the foreman, doffing his own hat and coming forward to offer her a hand up over the foundation. Edward followed smoothly.

"We won't be a moment," he told the foreman.

"Yes, sir, you go right ahead," the foreman replied, and stood back to watch them as they picked their way through, peering desultorily into rooms and exclaiming over this or that architectural feature.

"Jesus, ain't they polite?" grunted a carpenter, watching from his ladder.

"Real well-spoken," the foreman agreed. "He's English, huh?"

"Sounded that way."

"Tall, too," added the foreman. He was unable to better express exactly what he found so striking about the couple. The girl moved with a grace and self-control not often seen in people so young. And there was something eerie about the tall man's eyes, in the way they focused on you and just . . . persuaded you, in the nicest possible way, to tell him what he wanted.

Closely as they were watched, somehow no one noticed Edward slipping his hand into his pocket to bring out a little bottle, nor did they see him lean down to slide it between the laths near the baseboard of a wall.

It dropped into the darkness with a soft thump and settled into the position it would occupy for the next four centuries, until the morning in 2355 when its contents would awaken and, snatching molecules from their surroundings, arrange themselves into a fairly dire weapon.

"Oh, this must be the kitchen!" Mendoza said. "Look, darling, how modern and up-to-date."

"And yet preserving a certain quaintness," Edward added. He took her arm. "Yes, I think we really must make inquiries. But we've detained these good men long enough! Let's be on our way, my love."

They made their exit, thanking the foreman profusely, and walked away down the quiet street. At the corner Edward stopped, took Mendoza's face firmly in both hands and bent down to kiss her.

"Well done," he growled. "Oh, we were made for each other!"

"Of course," she said. "Where now?"

They continued their stroll up the canyon, climbing the steep bluff to the first hole of the golf course. There they sat for a few moments, on a conveniently placed bench, and anyone watching them would have assumed they were admiring the view. Edward withdrew some postcards from his coat pocket and passed them to Mendoza, who sorted through them thoughtfully.

Edward then took out what appeared to be a fountain pen, something small and cylindrical anyway, and removing the cap held it out over the lawn a moment. Anyone watching would have assumed he was attempting to shake ink down into the nib. In reality he had just activated a small laser, burning a vitrified tube to a depth of one meter in the earth under the beautifully manicured lawn. He passed the laser to Mendoza, who did not write on the postcards with it, though anyone watching them would have gotten the impression she was doing so.

Edward, meanwhile, took out a roll of Lifesavers, loot from their raid on 1996. He opened it, in the process dropping a spiral of silver paper on the lawn. He leaned down to pick it up at once, and in the same movement, with flawless sleight of hand, dropped a tiny vial down the shaft he had burned in the lawn. The sporting party just arriving to tee off did not notice.

He put a Lifesaver in his mouth and offered one to Mendoza, who accepted it. They sat on the bench and watched, apparently fascinated, as four middle-aged gentlemen who had clearly already located a speakeasy launched unsteady shots in varying trajectories. As the caddies were hoisting bags for the long trek down to the second hole, Edward rose and approached the nearest golfer, crushing in the top of the vitrified tube with his bootheel as he came.

"Pardon me, sir," he said, removing his hat once again. "Would you happen to know the location of a reliable source of refreshment?"

"Huh?" The old duffer focused on Edward with difficulty. He met Edward's gaze and his face lit with sudden comprehension. "Oh! Yeah." He glanced about furtively. "Hotel Saint Catherine. Fine place. You ask for Johnny."

"You've been most kind," Edward said, bowing slightly. The golfer stared past him a moment, goggling at Mendoza, who had bent over to adjust her stocking and in the process was further obliterating any trace of the tube.

"You're welcome," he said, and lurched away. Edward replaced his hat, put his hands in his pockets, and walked back to Mendoza, who stood up flushed but smiling.

They wandered farther up the canyon, along an aisle between spindly little palm trees, and noted the presence of a riding stable to their left. Farther still and the recent extension of the golf course opened out, irregularly green yet but determined. Alec, staring up at the looming mountains, recognized them.

*This was where the time shuttle crashed. This used to be her cornfield.*

*Doth she remember it?* Nicholas peered at Mendoza worriedly.

But Mendoza seemed quite unperturbed by memory, pleasant or otherwise, as they rounded a foothill and regarded a wide canyon opening out to the left.

*Her little house is gone,* mourned Alec.

*Oh, really!* said Edward. *Did you honestly think it would still be here, after a hundred and fifty thousand years?* And in fact there wasn't a trace, not of Mendoza's house, not of her garden. Even the verdant forests that had covered the hills were gone like phantoms, having given way to chaparral and sagebrush.

**You got the girl, laddie. She belongs to the sea now, like us. Don't grieve yer heart for no house nor a few trees,** the Captain transmitted.

*But if I'd stayed here with her,* said Alec, *if I hadn't gone on to Mars like an idiot . . . all those people would still be alive.*

**Aw, son, just now they ain't even been born yet.**

*So you're watching us, are you, Captain?* Edward paused and looked about. *Well then, where's the next target?*

The spot was quite deserted, and so there was no need to obscure their movements as they concealed the third bottle.

"A fine morning's work," said Edward. He reached out to Mendoza, who was gazing up at the mountains. "And now, I think, we've earned a pleasant luncheon at the Hotel Saint Catherine. Wouldn't you say so?" He turned her face to his. She started a little, but smiled for him.

"Oh, yes," she said. "By all means."

They walked away together down the canyon. Behind them, there was a queer disturbance in the dust; its surface roiled like seafoam, alive with green and springing blades of corn.


A tunnel through the cliffs at Sugar Loaf Point brought them out upon Descanso Bay. The sea was clear as glass, full of waving purple and amber weed, where fire-colored fish swam slowly. Above the water's edge, a hard-packed road ran along to a broad green lawn.

"Well!" Mendoza stopped, staring across landscaped grounds at the queenly white hotel. "How elegant."

"Indeed it is," said Edward, his gaze coming to rest on a beachside pavilion where a white-jacketed waiter was polishing the counter. "And that, unless I'm much mistaken, is a bar."

They made their way to it through flowering hibiscus and bougainvillea; but when Edward politely inquired if Johnny was to be found, the waiter glanced over his shoulder before leaning forward to suggest that Johnny might be on duty in the main restaurant. So they walked up across the lawn, in through the lobby, and were promptly shown to a table by the terrace doors.

"Has Johnny reported for duty today?" said Edward. Their waiter, without batting an eyelash, replied:

"He certainly has. He just waited on those people—" He nodded meaningfully at a table farther in, where a party in tennis togs was chatting happily over what were obviously glasses of white wine. "He's busy at the bar just now, serving ginger ale to all those golfers, but I can get his attention for you."

"That would be splendid," Edward said, placing a perfectly counterfeited bill of large denomination on the table. "Of course, I understand that American laws quite prohibit the sale of, for example, two glasses of a good La Tour Blanche, but if Johnny might be persuaded to bring us the same lemon squash he just served that party—?"

"I'll see what I can do," the waiter said, bowing and vanishing. Mendoza sank back in her chair.

"This is insane," she said. "Why would mortals make it so difficult to get two little glasses of white wine?"

"Human nature, my love." Edward grinned and set his knee against hers under the tablecloth. "The desire of a few to dictate morality to the whole. And why do the masses submit willingly? Apathy. Or, perhaps, the opportunity to experience the thrill of the forbidden! To be obliged to resort to code words and secrecy. Appropriate for our business, wouldn't you say?"

"Our deadly and desperate business," she intoned theatrically.

"Sinister and subtle," he agreed, taking her left hand in both his own. "And, best of all, *our* business alone. Never again to be posted on some fool's errand."

Mendoza shook her head. "I remember being sent to the ends of the Earth . . . I wanted so badly to get back to you, and I couldn't."

*Careful, man,* said Alec.

"Don't think of those times, my dear," Edward said. He kissed her hand.

"They tried to separate us, didn't they?" she said.

"And very foolish of them it was, too," said Edward. "Considering how well we work together. They'll have all of time to rue their mistake. Either that or a very short space of time indeed." He looked up. "Ah. I believe Johnny is about to make his appearance."

"Your lemon squash, sir," said the waiter, putting down two napkins followed by two nicely chilled goblets of wine.

"Thank you," Edward said, watching narrowly as the waiter slipped the bill into his apron pocket and vanished again. "I daresay we've seen the last of that banknote. Oh, well." He lifted his wine. "A toast, my love? To our continued—nay, rather our eternal—partnership!"

They clinked glasses and drank.

"Pleasant," admitted Edward. "Though hardly a La Tour Blanche."

*It's a California white,* Alec informed him. *I smuggled enough of the stuff to know.*

"Lovely," sighed Mendoza, leaning back in her chair and gazing out through the terrace windows at the sea. "What happens next?"

"A brief journey back to the *Captain Morgan* to change into suitable riding attire, and then we assail the mountain," Edward said. "I believe we may acquire a souvenir or two. Luncheon first, however." He glanced in annoyance at the crowd around the bar. "I do hope one needn't rely on Johnny for a *carte du jour* as well." He had found of late that he was finding the taste of virtual food insipid.

"I don't mind," Mendoza said, lifting her glass for another sip of wine. "I could sit here, just like this, for years and years."

Little parrots chattered in the garden. The crowd at the bar parted for a moment, and a man could be heard saying:

". . . trust me on this, pal. Private bungalow on the back lot with your own valet, chauffeured private car, room service—and I don't mean a box lunch sent over from the commissary, either, I'm talking about—"

Nicholas, who had been gazing at Mendoza, looked around sharply. He seized control from Edward.

"God's wounds! *Doctor Ruy.*"

Alec and Edward turned to stare at the bar, where the speaker had faltered into silence and was, to their horror, staring back at them. His personal appearance was nondescript, save for the loud Argyle pattern of his golfing sweater. He was stockily built, of somewhat less than average height, olive-skinned, with bright black eyes that were presently wide with disbelief.

"Who?" Mendoza had gone paper-white, wouldn't look.

*Who is it, man, for Christ's sake?* said Alec.

*Her damned father,* Nicholas snarled, and to their consternation he began to rise, apparently with every intention of assaulting the man at the bar.

*Are you crazy?* Alec grabbed at his arm, without effect.

*Bloody Hell!* Edward wrested control back from Nicholas and turned to Mendoza. "Go, my love. Through the terrace door. Now," he said, very quietly. He glanced over and saw that the black-eyed man was trying to push his way through the crowd to them. Edward got up swiftly, taking Mendoza's trembling hand. She came suddenly to life and they fled together, out onto the terrace and across the lawn.

Her hand began to twist in Edward's, and he realized that she was about to shift into hyperfunction. Just as suddenly she was solidly *there* again, staring at him, for she'd remembered his limitations. Neither of them said anything, though, as they ran on.

As they sprinted along the road back into Avalon, Edward raged: *Where are you, you damned machine? Why didn't you warn us?*

**He ain't one of the operatives assigned to the island,** the Captain transmitted. **I been keeping watch on them. I didn't know that one was here!**

*Well, you know now,* panted Alec. *Is he following us?*

**No. He's still in the bar. He ain't sent any broadcasts to alert anybody about you, neither. Don't worry! If he tries to come after you I'll lob a missile his way. If the cliff above the road collapses, I reckon it'll take him a while to dig himself out.**

*Oh, that* will *be inconspicuous,* Edward shouted in exasperation.

**Well? You got any better ideas, Commander Bell-Fairfax, yer worship?**

*STOP FIGHTING!* said Alec. *That was the guy who recruited her, wasn't it? That was Joseph!*

*That same devil, aye,* raved Nicholas. *That same smiling liar and son of a mongrel bitch, that same thieving rogue I swore I'd kill with these two hands!*

*He's an immortal, you bloody fool,* Edward said, as they emerged from the tunnel and plunged on toward Crescent Avenue, past staring vacationers.

*Is he so? Can he suffer, as my love suffered? Let him lie an eternity in darkness, too, and I'd grant him his eternal life,* Nicholas retorted. *He made her a slave! Wilt thou let him chain her again? That subtle dart that poisoned her keeper, Spirit, canst thou not make one to sicken the likes of Doctor Ruy?*

*Now, there's an idea,* said Edward, after a heart-pounding moment. *I wonder if—*

*Let's just keep our heads about this, all right?* Alec said. *We don't want to get close enough to him to find out, do we?*

Mendoza had reached the whaleboat and was frantically pushing it down the beach into the lapping water, looking back over her shoulder. They vaulted the seawall, landing with a scatter of shingle, and Alec took the prow.

"In," he said. She needed no second urging but tumbled over the gunwale, and crouched shivering in the stern as Alec launched the boat and leaped in. A second later they had put about and he was rowing at his best speed. Red-eyed dolphins followed in his wake, scanning as they went, ready to turn and ram any pursuit.

"Who was it?" Mendoza asked, giving in to tears at last as they hurried aboard the *Captain Morgan.*

"You didn't see?" Alec took her hands, staring at her.

"Only your face!" she said. "I was afraid to look at what you were seeing. I can't ever remember you looking so angry, except—except when—"

Alec put his arms around her and held tight. "Don't remember. Don't think about it. It was somebody we don't want to run into again, that's all. And I'm not going to do anything stupid, baby, I promise you." He glared at Nicholas.

"But what are we going to do?"

"We're going to time jump right now." Alec looked down at her. "And nobody's going to get hurt."

*Coordinates set, lad,* the Captain announced, as Coxinga crawled up to them with a tray and a glass. *Stirrup cup for good luck, eh?*

Alec gulped it down, gagging. Mendoza tugged at Alec's hand, pulling him toward the storm harness.

"Please, let's get out of here," she said, wiping away her tears. "Let's go somewhere safe."

*If only there was somewhere safe,* thought Alec, as he held her tightly. Yellow gas came roiling into the cabin.


## EARLY ONE AFTERNOON IN 1435 AD

But the waters off Lord Howe Island proved quiet and relatively deserted. The *Captain Morgan* extended masts, spars, and rigging and dropped anchor. Though the dolphins deployed and patrolled for any Company shuttles that might have followed them, none put in an appearance. The ship's laser cannons remained silent and invisible behind their gun ports.


## THE FOLLOWING MORNING

*Wakey-wakey, me dears. Breakfast! All yer favorites,* the Captain crooned. Coxinga edged close to the bed, offering a laden tray cautiously. It was set with the best service and bore all the delicacies Coxinga's galley had to offer.

Alec and Mendoza both sat bolt upright, staring.

"I had the worst nightmare," Mendoza said.

"Me too," Alec said. Shakily he reached out to pull her close, assuring himself that she was really there. "Let's forget 'em, okay?"

"Okay," she said.

*Now I'd call that a right clever plan, especially as things is looking a little more cheerful than you might expect,* said the Captain ingratiatingly.

"Oh, really?" snapped Edward, taking control to reach for the tray. "Given yesterday's debacle, I should estimate our chances of looting that storage site are nil. They'll undoubtedly be watching for us."

*Well now, lad, I'd have thought so, too; but it seems we had a stroke of luck. The, er, operative in question never reported seeing ye.*

"I beg your pardon?" Edward halted in the act of pouring coffee for Mendoza.

*Hey, what?* Alec looked astonished.

*Wherefore?* Nicholas demanded.

*I been scrolling through Company records hell-bent-for-leather whilst ye was sleeping, particularly that one immortal lubber's personnel file. Interesting reading! And I found out a power of useful things about that there Facilitator, but the long and the short of it, Mr. and Mrs. Checkerfield, is: the Company don't know! Not even his visual transcript tipped 'em off, since it were just a glimpse of ye for a second or two. The clerk monitoring his datafeed didn't notice.*

*Wherefore?* said Nicholas more loudly. Mendoza lifted her head and looked around, frowning.

*And as to why he didn't tell nobody—why, that's another stroke of luck,* the Captain said. *It seems that particular operative'll get hisself in trouble with his superiors. The last few centuries of his file is annotated all to hell and gone with speculations about his loyalty. Finally they'll transfer him to a numbered site, and he'll disappear from the records. File closed, matter dropped.*

"You mean they'll send him to—" Alec blurted, appalled, before Edward silenced him and the Captain said quickly:

*Coventry, aye, that's what it seems like. So no further trouble from* **him.**

"My compliments, Captain, you're quite correct," said Edward with iron composure, adding cream to Mendoza's coffee and presenting her with the cup. "That is a stroke of luck. Have you any suggestions on how to proceed next?"

*There ain't nothing to stop us going ahead with the plan, is there? We'll just rest up, let the generators recharge, and skip ahead a little. Say ten years, this time. Then for that storage locker!*

"I rather think you're right," Edward said. He shook out Mendoza's napkin and offered it to her. "What do you think, my dear? Are you game?"

She accepted the napkin, but did not smile. "I don't know that I am. I don't want you taking risks. I dreamed—awful things. I wish I could convince myself they were only dreams." She looked somberly into his eyes. "I think you must have been reckless, in your time. I think I must have killed mortals, once. I'd do it again, if anyone hurt you. Please, don't let it come to that, señor."

Edward, meeting her gaze, controlled his emotions.

"Never again," he said. "We will never be parted again."

They regarded each other a long moment, before Mendoza sighed and looked down.

"Perhaps we can try a raid," she conceded. "As long as Sir Henry says it's safe."

*Wherefore art thou whey-faced, boy?* demanded Nicholas of Alec, who was sitting with his hands pressed over his mouth in horror. He stared at Nicholas.

*Didn't you hear what they did to Joseph? You've* seen *Options Research. Would you want your worst enemy sent there?*

*And so he hath been,* said Nicholas. *The devil's in Hell, where he doth rightly belong.*

*But he could have reported us, and he didn't! He didn't betray Mendoza. And, even if she hated him for it—if he hadn't taken her out of that prison when she was a kid, she'd have died there,* Alec said.

*He took her to suit his own purposes,* Nicholas muttered. *Belike he kept silent for his own reasons, too. But he hath worked evil in this world and if he suffereth therefor, it is no more than justice.*

*Justice doesn't exist! We* did *worse things. Nobody deserves to go to that place,* Alec said. *Anyway, weren't you Christian types supposed to forgive everybody?*

*I will shed no tears for that bastard's damnation,* said Nicholas stonily.

*No wonder nobody's left that believes in your stupid religion,* said Alec.

*Gentlemen, please.* Edward sipped his coffee and looked at them askance. *I would prefer to dine in a tranquil atmosphere.*

AVALON, 1933 AD

The pier pilings and the seawall looked a little more weathered than they had the week before (or ten years before, depending on whose relativity one applied). The quaint old church with its statue of Saint Catherine of Alexandria, hand raised in blessing over her ship's wheel, still perched on its steep hill. Sugar Loaf Rock was gone, and so was the tunnel; both of them had been blasted away to make a foundation for the grand Casino, which towered in the sunlight like a sea-king's palace. But the water was just as clear, and the same red fishes still moved slowly to and fro.

They tied up their boat and splashed ashore, the young couple in smartly cut riding clothes. The tall man was carrying a saddlebag. They walked directly up Sumner Avenue in a businesslike way, without sight-seeing, and up Avalon Canyon, along an aisle of palm trees somewhat taller and more respectable-looking than when they had gone that way last. At the stable they rented a fine pair of trail horses. The man fastened his saddlebag into place. They rode away into the mountains.

*What a lucky chance! The Company's shifted their manned bases. They're all over on the windward side of the island now.*

*That's good, is it?* Edward peered uneasily through the bright morning. They had been making their way along the spine of the island, well below the rimrock on the leeward side. He had control again. Alec and Nicholas paced alongside at either stirrup.

*Aye! It means there ain't a Company operative within five kilometers. No posted base personnel nor no unexpected visitors, neither. The way's open, free and clear. If you watch the trail to the right, you ought to see what looks like a track to an old mine adit.*

*Very well,* said Edward, looking down into a sharp-dropping valley. The interior was fairly rugged, with plunging gorges and steep yellow meadows overflown by ravens. Of the forests that had once towered there, not a shadow remained but scrub oaks on the lower hills. All else was bare and broken rock.

"I'm sure I don't remember this," said Mendoza, frowning. She looked across at Edward. "But I rode somewhere with you. Didn't we, before the accident?"

"So we did," Edward said. He reached across and took her hand. "We were trying to get across to this island, then. Now, you see? We've reached our destination at last, and they've been unable to stop us."

She brightened at that. Then she leaned past him, staring at something. "Is that what we're looking for?" she asked, pointing.

He turned. Some twenty feet below the trail grew a band of sage and artemisia, lower, more uniform than the surrounding brush. It was evenly three meters wide, and curved along the hillside a good distance before ending abruptly in a tumbled mass of rock and spurge laurel.

"That was a road once," said Mendoza.

"So it was," Edward said. *Well, Captain?*

***That's it, laddie. Bull's-eye.***

"And it's been a long time since it was used," said Mendoza, urging her mount over the edge of the trail for a closer look. "To judge from the growth. See there? Those are all older plants, with a lot of hardwood."

"I'm no botanist, my love, so I'll trust your word," said Edward, following her. "How long since it's been used, would you say?"

"Sixty years?" Mendoza turned her head to one side, considering. "Sixty, I think."

"Well then," said Edward. He smiled and rode forward.

Once they were actually on it, there was no question that the place had been a road, though it was gently crumbling now. In the clarity of full sunlight, Edward was able to perceive a faint wavering on the air before the rockfall.

"This is some sort of deliberate illusion," he said. "Isn't it?"

"Of course," said Mendoza, looking at him sidelong.

***Aye, lad, and if you'll stand to a second***—The Captain paused. Suddenly the tumbled rocks vanished, revealing a featureless bronze door in their place. An unseen mechanism clanked within. ***Haar! Security's off-line. At 'em, me hearties!***

They dismounted, tying their reins to a non-illusory laurel. Edward crouched before the door, studying it for brute force traps. Satisfied that there were none he could perceive, he tugged gently at the recessed knob. The door swung open, revealing a smooth-walled passage beyond. There were no cobwebs, no hanging roots, no pools of water; only a clean dry corridor with rows of drawers set flush in its walls, stretching away as far as they could see into darkness.

Edward narrowed his eyes, considering it. He reached down and tossed in a pebble. It bounced and fell without incident.

***It's safe, laddie. But you'd best be quick, all the same. Yer looking for a drawer labeled BTM 417.***

"BTM 417," Edward said aloud.

"Is that what we want?" Mendoza stepped across the threshold. She scanned the walls. "Tsk! They're in no order, are they? Let's search."

The drawers were of all different sizes and shapes, labeled according to no discernible system. Some had little file cards of yellowed pasteboard, with names or numbers neatly written in copperplate script. Some had pasted tags of an odd silvery tissue, with legends in curiously blurred type. A few others had engraved brass plates, of a disturbingly familiar design.

Though it did not seem to disturb Mendoza, who paced along the corridor, scanning as she went. She stopped before one drawer. The somber brass plate on its front was engraved: BTM 417.

"Here it is," she said, turning to Edward, who had followed cautiously. "Shall I open it?"

***No,*** transmitted the Captain in a panicky sort of way. He had just scanned the drawer and its contents. ***Don't let her see, son.***

"Let me," Edward said swiftly, putting his hand on her wrist. She looked up into his eyes, startled. In his smoothest voice, with his nicest smile, he said: "I'd be very much obliged, my love, if you'd stand guard at the entrance."

"Are we in danger?" she demanded, and he could see the change in her, as though she were a self-drawn sword, white-edged steel tensing to launch itself.

"Unlikely," he replied. "But it's best to take no chances, wouldn't you agree?"

"I would, señor," she said, and went back to the daylight, where she stood obediently scanning the trail.

***Brace yerself, son.***

*Oh, really!* said Edward. *How bad can it be?*

He opened the drawer.

It opened out a long way, being perhaps seven feet deep. Long before it had extended in full, Edward had let go and drawn back; but the rolling mechanism was so nicely balanced the drawer just kept opening on its own, as though a ghost were pulling it.

Though not the ghost of the occupant of the drawer.

It was a skeleton, cleanly laid out on a metal tray in the pattern of its original articulation. All the bones were present, though some of the ribs and two thoracic vertebrae had been shattered and wired back in place, as had one lumbar vertebra. There was no sign of healing, indicating that these injuries had occurred at the time of death. It was the skeleton of a male in his late thirties.

He had apparently been in very good health up to the time of his sudden death. The teeth were all present and in splendid condition. The skeleton itself was very large, with massive femurs. There was something peculiar about the articulation of the arms and neck. There was also something peculiar about the skull, quite apart from the fact that the top of the cranium had been sawn off and then reattached with wire after the brain had been removed.

Alec gulped, as it dawned on him whose skeleton this was. Edward, still in control—though he was losing it—had backed against the opposite wall and was staring, white-faced, into the drawer.

*What, man, art thou faint?* said Nicholas. Edward looked up at him.

*I'm dead,* he said quietly. *I am a dead man. There's proof, there are my damned bones.*

*Is this all?* Nicholas made an impatient gesture. *Wherefore art thou amazed? Thou wert born mortal, as I was, and lived certain years, as I did, and died and came to this.*

Edward was shaking his head.

*I didn't think—*

*Ah.* Nicholas leaned close, looking him in the eye. *Then, think! How many didst thou send to this same charnel state? Wilt thou tremble that it befell thee, too, at last? Is it not justice, Homicide?*

*Shut up,* Edward cried.

*Please,* Alec said. *Leave him alone! It's awful enough as it is, do you have to make him feel worse?* He turned to Edward. *So what if they didn't preserve your body? You're not completely dead. We're talking, and you've been riding a horse, and—and drinking, and eating, and having great sex—*

*You have!* Edward said. *You're alive, and I'm that thing lying there. I thought they had the science to—I had been promised a resurrection. Damn them! They never had any intention of bringing me back. I was unmade and mounted like a bloody museum specimen! But I'll live again, by God.* Edward pushed himself upright and surveyed the old bones. *We'll take them away with us. Captain! You can repair them, clothe them with new flesh—and I'll go into my own body, and—*

**Son! Son, I can't do that.**

*You repaired Mendoza!* Edward's voice rose in a howl. *You can repair me!*

**Edward, lad—she never died. There weren't much of her, but what there was, was still alive. This thing's dead. I can't even take DNA from it, because you was almost forty when you died. D'y'see? Too many replication errors by that time. You ain't a machine, to be repaired. You were a mortal man.**

*And what am I now?* Edward demanded.

*Thou art a spirit, that never believed in spirits,* Nicholas informed him. *There's irony for thee.*

**Stand to, both of you! We're wasting time. There's more there than the bones, ain't there? Some electronics, should be. There's got to be something to give us a clue where yer DNA vial is.**

Nicholas took control and reached in past the skeleton, to a steel box at the back of the drawer. He pulled it out and opened it.

There was a man's hat, of the stovepipe style worn in the middle of the nineteenth century. It had been Edward's. So had the pair of riding boots.

There was a package of clothing, sealed in some transparent material. It appeared to be a complete suit from the same historical period, and was in fact what Edward was wearing when he died. It was covered in dried blood. There were at least seven bullet holes visible, and the right lapel of the coat was torn. The tear had not occurred during Edward's lifetime. The coat had been torn when five security techs pulled Mendoza screaming from his body.

There was a battered leather saddlebag, smaller but otherwise not very dissimilar to the one they had brought with them. It contained Edward's personal effects. Nicholas sorted through them:

A man's watch on a chain with a seal, engraved with Edward's initials; a Spanish-English phrasebook, printed in 1860; a clasp knife; a canteen; a pair of field glasses; a small pistol, in a leather holster cracked with age; a wooden case containing ammunition and cleaning supplies for the pistol; three knives in strapped sheaths. A garrote. Three tiny glass vials containing a white powder. A small tin case of picklocks. A box of matches. A white linen handkerchief. A folded telegram, yellow and crumbling. A ring of assorted keys. A silver pen with a steel nib and cap. A set of cufflinks, plain brass with a fouled anchor design. A wallet containing banknotes and other currency from several nations. A letter of mark issued to Edward Alton Bell-Fairfax, authorized representative of Imperial Export & Company. A silver card case, containing about fifteen pasteboard embossed cards reading:

*Edward Alton Bell-Fairfax*

*Redking's Club* *Mayfair*

The last item in the box was a case containing a number of small, odd-looking plaquettes. Each framed a pair of transparent slides pressing between them a slice of what resembled human tissue. Below them was a readout screen, speaker, and connector port. Nicholas held one up to the light, staring without comprehension.

**That's good,** said the Captain. **There'll be data encoded in that. Leave the rest of it. Take the box and get back to Mendoza.**

*No,* said Edward, grabbing without effect at the saddlebag. *I want my things!*

*Wherefore, fool?* Nicholas fended off his frantic attempts to seize control. *What need hast thou of vanities anymore?*

*I WANT THEM!*

*Oh, let him take 'em,* pleaded Alec. *If we don't shift it, Mendoza's going to come see what's taking us so long, and if she sees this—*

*She must not.* Moving fast, Nicholas removed the plaquette case and the saddlebag from the box. He slid the long drawer shut, and grabbing up their finds ran for the entrance, where Mendoza was ceaselessly scanning.

"We're safe," she said. "Was it in there, your loot?"

"No, love," Nicholas said, stuffing the case and smaller bag inside the saddlebag they'd brought. "Naught but time's trash." He turned and pulled the door shut. Unlooping the reins, he bent to give her a hand up into the saddle; swung up easily on his own mount. She cantered ahead of him up the old road, and he waited only for Alec and Edward to catch his stirrups before following her.

They rode along in nervous silence a while. Mendoza was wondering why he had switched his speaking idiom again.

"What was in there?" she asked at last.

"Ghosts," Nicholas told her.


They returned to the ship, where Billy Bones accepted the saddlebag and hurried off with it. Mendoza watched this, but said nothing. Nor did she remark when they lifted anchor and sailed away at once for Panama.


Edward was finally able to wrest control from Nicholas as they emerged from the bathroom, after showering away the dust of their ride. Without a word he pulled Mendoza to the bed, where he made violent love to her in silence. Though he sank down exhausted at last, the mute agony did not leave Edward's eyes.

Mendoza asked no questions. Edward lay his head on her breasts. She put her arms around him and sang, some wordless and soothingly monotonous little tune. Gradually the despair went out of his body, and Edward slept.

Alec, who had been waiting patiently with Nicholas, said:

*Council of war, Captain sir?*

**I'm still analyzing, lad. Them tissue samples—**

But at that moment Mendoza, who had been stroking back Edward's hair, spoke quietly.

"Sir Henry."

**—Aye, Mrs. Checkerfield!** the Captain said aloud.

"What was it, in that place? What did he see to upset him like this?"

**—Well, now, dearie, I'm sure it ain't nothing for you to worry over—**

"To Hell with that," she said, and both Alec and Nicholas jumped. "Tell me the truth."

**Er—aye, ma'am, to be sure. It was more evidence of Dr. Zeus's perfidy, d'y'see? Something nasty the Company did a long while back. He**

*wouldn't talk about it, good lad that he is, lest it rake up old sorrows for you, but it bothered him powerful.*

"Obviously. What did he bring back, that he took such pains I might not see?" Mendoza said.

*Just something as might be useful—as a matter of fact I was just starting to analyze it, as is me duty, when you called, ma'am, and I'll be happy to get back to it when we're done chatting—*

"Then get back to your duty," she said wearily. "I remember this, I remember when he'd come to bed like this. Hard as steel, heartsick, and nothing I could do comforted him. Something bad always happened, then, didn't it? Fire and blood. What will take that look out of his eyes?"

*Missus, you mustn't be afeared. Nothing's going to hurt my boy, nor you neither, ever again. Not with the plans old Captain Morgan's laid. But yer tired, dearie; that was a long ride and a rough wooing. Shut yer eyes and sleep, eh?*

Mendoza nodded, looking down at Edward. She drew the blankets up over his shoulders. He started, wild-eyed, clutching at her, but she stroked his face and murmured to him, and he lay his head down again without really waking. She leaned into the pillows and gazed up at the improbable pirate carvings, wondering for the twentieth time why on earth Alec had decorated their bedroom in Early Captain Blood.

The Captain did the electronic equivalent of wiping sweat from his brow, but he wasn't off the hook yet.

*She's starting to remember everything, isn't she?* said Alec. *She'll know we've lied to her, and worse—what if she remembers Options Research?*

*Now, lad, there ain't no danger of that.*

*Yes, there is! She's remembering the way you changed, when she lost you in England.* Alec glared at Nicholas. *Stiff-necked Puritan bastard.*

Nicholas was outraged. *He took her sulking rude, and lieth there now sprawling on her! Not I.*

*He can't cope, man. I don't think I could either, if I saw my own corpse laid out in a drawer,* Alec said.

*A few old bones,* Nicholas said impatiently. *And look, boy, here is the lesson: He and all his Age of Reason were so proud, and so haught, in their science and their power, they held themselves very gods on Earth. Now, see! His worldly Empire's perished and so hath his vain flesh. He is confounded by mortality's blind emblem in his own face.*

*It's still not fair to be cruel to him about it,* Alec insisted. *If you hadn't been burned at the stake the Company'd have a drawer like that for you, someplace. And what are you both? You're just ghosts.*

*Ay,* said Nicholas. *But there was no place for spirits in all his philosophy, boy. I died, I know it well; he will not know, though the truth lie stark before his eyes, and so he lechers with his ghostly prick to deny it. Yet he's a spirit still.*

*So what's he supposed to do now?* Alec snapped. *Are you so happy being dead? But maybe you are. You went out of your way to get yourself burned alive. You wanted her to burn with you!*

Nicholas grimaced. *I knew not what she was. I*—He brought his fist up close to his chest and struck, painfully. *Nor I knew not myself, neither. I lived in lies no less than Edward did. But the truth—*

*That is one dark house your God lives in, man.* Alec shook his head. *You can keep your Age of Faith. Whyn't you find somebody to worship who isn't a shracking psychopath?*

**Let it alone, now, Alec. Yer lady ain't going to remember Options Research. Her brain'll fit together enough pieces of the jigsaw puzzle to give her a nice picture she can live with, and lock away the rest. I reckon there's some memories you'd be glad to be rid of, yerselves.**

*And that's true, too,* said Nicholas, shuddering.

Yeah. Alec thought of Mars.

**Right. Now, about that council of war.**

*What were those things in the pluquettes?* Alec asked reluctantly

**Pieces of Edward, what d'y'think? And I'll thank you not to tell him. No end of data in them little files, too, which is lucky; forensic analysis reports with references to another location. See, they left the skeleton and these bits here, once they'd done with 'em, but the jewel of the lot's at their storage facilities in England.**

*What jewel?* Nicholas frowned.

**The brain,** the Captain said, **which was the same as yer own little anomalous beauty of a brain what set me free, Alec, and yers, too, I reckon, Nicholas, but unlike any others as ever was. It weren't dissected, but sent back to Stratford.**

*Stratford-on-Avon?* Alec said in disbelief. *Where Mr. Shakespeare lived?*

*Aye. There's a Company storage facility hid in a place what ain't never going to be bombed, nor demolished, nor catch fire. I've already checked its manifest. Another unit with yer file designation is there.*

*That's way inland, though, isn't it, Captain sir?* Alec said. *How are we going to manage?*

## ONE MORNING IN WARWICKSHIRE, 1600 AD

It does stop raining in England, occasionally. In the month of August, it even stops raining long enough for the roads to become disagreeably dusty, or at least it did in the year 1600, when few roads were paved.

So the dust lay in a fine powder on the starched linen ruff about the throat of the tall gallant who trudged along in the bright morning, and on the brim of his copatain hat, and on his thigh-high boots, and on all the bright brass buttons on his well-cut doublet. It powdered the velvet hat of his lady friend, too, and her ruff, and her bodice and brocade overskirt; which was perhaps why she was looking a little sourly on the green paradise of Warwickshire.

They had been walking along that road since before sunrise, when they had hidden their conveyance in a ruined barn and set off on foot for Stratford. They had passed only three travelers: a respectable spinster, riding back from London with a basket of hornbooks for the pupils of her dame school; an adolescent boy with vomit on his doublet and torn hose, looking sick and furtive as he slunk along the narrow lane; and a sturdy beggar with a crutch, a purported veteran of the Armada battle twelve years previous, who eyed the couple thoughtfully before deciding that the man was too big, and too well armed, to attack.

Had he decided to attempt to rob the couple, he would have noticed the winged shape floating directly above them, to all appearances a common hovering hawk. He wouldn't have noticed it for very long, however, because it would have blown off his head with a small guided missile within seconds of his making any threatening moves toward his intended victims.

But since he passed by them with no more than a nod and a cheerful good morrow, he lived to eventually father offspring, one of whose distant descendants did a very large favor for a corrupt prime minister, and was rewarded by being made first earl of Finsbury. The pattern of history sighed in relief, took another loop around itself, and continued on its way unchanged.

When the beggar was well out of earshot, Mendoza said:

"That mortal wasn't really a cripple."

"Like enough, ay," said Nicholas grimly, putting his hand on the hilt of his sword and turning to stare after him. "Well, we'll hire us horses at the first good inn we pass. Less danger from low rogues, and less dust."

"Good," said Mendoza, sneezing.

The first good inn was just beyond the next spinney, as it turned out, so they were able to continue their journey in comparative comfort in a gratifyingly short space of time.

*Where are we now?* said Alec.

*A greener place than I knew,* said Edward in wonder. *No railway. No canals. No factories. No coal smoke. And, somewhere under this curiously cloudless sky, the Swan of Avon stretching his wings.*

*The what?*

*Shakespeare, you imbecile!*

**Now then, lads, don't spoil things with a fight.**

*Mightn't we at least ride by his house?* fretted Edward.

**We ain't sightseeing, bucko. We got a storage facility to find.**

*And anyway, he won't be here,* Alec informed Edward. *He spent all his time in London until he quit show business. He told me so himself, when I used to visit his museum.*

*That was an actor portraying Shakespeare, Alec,* Edward said with barely controlled contempt.

*No, it wasn't! He was a computer-generated hologram.* Alec glared at Edward. *And he was as real as they could make him, too. Somebody dug up his lead coffin from where it was buried, and scanned the body. They did a forensic reconstruction and then they programmed in every word he ever wrote and did an extrapola-whatever so he was just the way he would have been really, see?*

*Then he was no more real than your Captain Morgan,* Edward said.

**I'll show you real, you lubber!**

*Peace, thou, for Christ's sake.* Nicholas looked around impatiently.

"Here we are," said Mendoza, as they rode into Henley Street.

And Nicholas stared, more struck than Alec or Edward, at the world he'd missed: a small town quiet and prosperous, secure from Spanish invaders or Papist oppressors, untouched by fire or sword. Comfortably bourgeois, with dungheaps that reeked no worse than in any other little town, and a great many oak-timbered and impressive homes of the well-to-do. A fine guildhall, where traveling companies of players might perform. A respectably solid stone bridge over the river.

And in Henley Street, and Sheep Street, and Ely Street, ducks sauntering boldly; through the windows of the splendid modern school, sullen resentful children droning out their recitation; by the Market House, two goodwives listening breathlessly to the hot gossip a third was dishing out; down the green aisle of elm trees, a self-important alderman in grand clothes cantering along on a self-important horse.

Beyond the bright town, green dreaming hills and blackberry bramble where the fairies were supposed to haunt, and fields where Robin Goodfellow was thought to dance circles in the green corn, when townfolk shut their windows against the night.

Nicholas stared at it all and tried to tell himself that his death had weighed in the scale, that this England might not have existed had he not gone willingly into the fire.

Then he saw an ancient making his way along Bridge Street, hobbling on a stick, clutching a fur-trimmed gown about him with one gnarled hand. Nicholas realized with a shock that he would be just so old, now, if he'd lived, and all this pleasant mundane place would still be here.

It hadn't mattered at all that he'd lived or died, not to England. She went on without him, self-sufficient. Even God had shrugged off his sacrifice. The knot of misery about his heart tightened once more, and as it did he felt another surge of anger toward Joseph.

He found himself reaching out desperately, and feeling Mendoza take his hand he gripped it tight. They rode on, through Stratford-upon-Avon.

Beyond the outskirts of the town they followed the Captain's directions to a certain high wood, dark with rooks and less palpable shadows, not an inviting place. No paths led there. They rode in under its gloom all the same, and careful searching disclosed the wavering trick in the air obscuring a grove darker still. The steel-winged hawk circled once over the forest. As the panicked rooks flapped out in all directions the illusion vanished, to reveal another bronze door.

*This is it, lads,* the Captain said. *BTM 417, same as afore. Quick now.*

"Wait here with the horses, love," said Nicholas, dismounting and handing Mendoza the reins. "I'll not be long."

"All right," she said, looking uneasily out through the black trunks to the sunlit world beyond that wood.

He kissed her hand and went to the door, which opened easily at his touch.

Nicholas found himself looking down a stone corridor much like the one on Santa Catalina Island, clean and dry, lined with drawers. Not far in was one drawer with his file designation on it. Holding his breath, he opened it.

*Whew.* Alec relaxed. *No skeleton, anyway. What are those things?*

*Don't touch 'em, lads!* The Captain was referring to a pair of containers of roughly four-liter size, of ceramic or opaque glass. *They're tissue specimen jars. They'll go transparent for viewing, if they're handled.*

*Ugh!* Alec yelled silently, as comprehension hit him. *One of those must have Edward's—*

*Shut your damned mouth,* Edward said.

*But, then, what's in the other—*

*You don't need to see it. Let's just say that things don't burn down to a nice anonymous pile of ashes in a country where the wood's always wet.*

Nicholas shuddered.

*Not so easy to be objective about your own mortal remains, is it?* said Edward tightly. *No psalm for the occasion, brother Nicholas? No heartening words about the sea giving up her dead on the Last Day? Do you suppose what's in those jars will be made incorruptible? But I daresay the Company's already made certain it's well preserved.*

*That'll do, Edward.*

*I merely point out—hello, what's this?* said Edward, taking control to reach deeper into the drawer. He pulled out a third and smaller jar.

A little chime sounded and a quiet unhuman voice announced: "PRO-JECT *ADONAI*, THIRD SEQUENCE ORGANIC RESIDUE." The opaque sides of the jar cleared, to reveal several small objects floating in transparent preservative.

They appeared to be a clump of dun-colored hair, one whole tooth and broken pieces of at least three others, and an ear.

Alec gasped.

*Here now! Don't go all green, laddie, it's only cloned stuff. When you was in the infirmary after yer accident, I made some bits and pieces to scatter about in the shuttle afore I sunk it in forty fathoms. These scraps fooled 'em into thinking you was killed in the crash, until we could raid them lubbers in Albany Crescent.*

*But what's it doing back here in 1600?* Alec asked.

*Standard Company procedure, son. The more secret Secret Material is, the further back in the past they hides it.*

*You . . . cloned this? Cloned, is that the word?* Edward peered into the jar. *You made an ear? Might you make a whole body as easily?*

*No, and we ain't got time to go into why now. Look. Be there more of them plaquettes?*

*Just a couple,* Alec said doubtfully. *Do we take 'em?*

*If that's all there is, aye. Maybe there'll be clues in them like there was in the others.*

They stashed the plaquettes, which framed rather nasty-looking bits of things nobody wanted to examine particularly, in Nicholas's belt pouch, and hurried out to where Mendoza waited with the horses.

"Any luck?" she said, waiting to hear whether he'd slip back over to Victorian or Transatlantic idiom again.

"Small luck, but belike we'll have better," Nicholas told her, swinging up into the saddle. He leaned over to kiss her. "Let's to sea again, love."

They rode back the way they'd come, into Stratford. Edward craned his neck longingly, peering into Chapel Lane.

*There's New Place!* he said. *Good God, that's the Bard of Avon's own house. Mightn't we at least ride close to see it?*

*Can't we, Captain sir?* Alec asked. *It means a lot to him.*

Edward glared at Alec in embarrassment. Nicholas shrugged and urged his horse into the lane.

"This house would be his that wrote the fairy play?" Nicholas asked, pointing. "Shakespeare, was it not?"

"Is it?" Mendoza looked up, interested. "Nice garden."

The property in question took up most of a long deep lot, with the splendid brick-and-timber house away at the end of it, fronting Chapel Street. Over the wall that enclosed the yard, they could see orchards and a couple of barns. Roses climbed the walls of the distant house, waving toward its plentiful chimneys. Espaliered fruit trees could be glimpsed against the far walls. Vines arched over a long pergola, shading the central walk. There was a strong fragrance of honeysuckle, and sweet herbs, and flowering privet.

*Here's flowers for you,* quoted Edward reverently, *hot lavender, mints, savory, marjoram, The marigold, that goes to bed wi' th' sun, And with him rises, weeping—*

Alec and Nicholas looked at him in disbelief.

"Look at that formal knotwork," said Mendoza in awe, urging her horse closer. "Look at the *Lavandula spica!*"

*Mightn't we ask to see the garden?* Edward implored. *There might be a servant home, and if we paid—*

"Beautiful box hedges, too," Mendoza added, leaning on the top of the wall to see better.

"I thank you kindly, madam," said someone, standing up more or less under her nose. He had apparently been kneeling on the walk just the other side of the wall, weeding.

"Oh," said Mendoza, abashed.

*Hey!* Alec exclaimed in delight. Edward gasped, peering over the wall.

Nicholas, seeing Mendoza's discomfiture, rode close and looked down at the man who stood there, regarding Mendoza with an expression of mild annoyance as he rubbed dirt from his hands. He was a neatly made fellow of average height, with a receding hairline and a trim beard, and handsome regular features. The only thing remarkable about him was his eyes, which had an unnervingly piercing stare. Altogether he looked like nothing so much as the lead singer for Jethro Tull.

"I cry thee mercy, goodman," said Nicholas politely. "Art thou the gardener here?"

*No, you idiot!* groaned Edward.

*That's, er, him actually—*Alec said.

"—Or are you the master of the house and a gentleman, as clearly your bearing and countenance do proclaim?" Nicholas revised in haste.

"This is my house, sir, and my garden," Shakespeare said with some asperity.

"It is a marvelous garden, sir, truly," Mendoza said. "The lavender knots, particularly. And the, er, roses."

"Mm," said Shakespeare.

"I, myself, have had but ill luck with my lavender in all this English rain," Mendoza temporized, blushing. "I do protest, sir, I have never seen any so fine as this of yours. I pray you excuse the rudeness of our too-open regard! We meant no unmannerly behavior."

"Well," said Shakespeare, looking a little mollified.

"But as for the lavender, kind sir, I must ask! How have you such abundance to make knots wherewith, and in this shrewd air?" Mendoza babbled. "You never grew them from seed? Hell itself may freeze over before the knavish things will sprout, and yet I can get no cuttings of mine to live."

*Wow, she's good at lying,* Alec said in awe. *Company training, huh?*

Shakespeare, meanwhile, was looking smug.

"I pray you, lady, did you root them in sand?"

"Certes, as who would not?" Mendoza said. "Grow cuttings in clay or loam? It is impossible."

"Ay, ay, so it is, lady," said Shakespeare, stroking his beard craftily. "Pray, took you cuts from the wood of the said lavender?"

Mendoza hesitated a moment. "Well—" she said, wondering why she'd blurted out spontaneous prevarication.

*Good God,* Edward said in anguish, *this is the foremost poet of the English tongue, and is she going to spend the whole damned time talking about lavender?*

"Ah!" said Shakespeare. "There your error lies. They must be little and new shoots, lady, not old wood that hath lost the vigor of youth."

"Is it even so?" said Mendoza, smiting her forehead with the palm of her hand. "And I have been cutting the old wood all this weary time! Truly, sir, you are master over me."

Shakespeare arched one eyebrow at that, as Nicholas put out a hand.

"Peace, wife," he said, trying not to giggle. "I would inquire, patient sir, whether you are not Shakespeare the poet?"

Shakespeare threw him an oddly furtive look. "I am that he, sir," he admitted.

"Oh, sir, your *Rape of Lucrece!*" Mendoza said, attempting to make a good impression. "We bought us two copies i'Paul's churchyard and read them to tatters, did we not, husband? And your *Venus and Adonis,* too."

"So we did," Nicholas agreed cautiously. Shakespeare looked rather gratified at that.

"Why, I am glad they pleased," he said. "I have another in hand, to speak truth. More matter of Ovid: Actaeon his outrage 'gainst the goddess Diana, lewdly observed in her bath, and his transformation thereafter to a hart."

Edward muttered an oath of surprise. Nicholas looked intrigued.

"Diana in her bath?" he said. "Naked-pale as the watery moon? Now, there's matter that will speed, surely."

"Ay, with the gallants at Court," Shakespeare said, grinning. "You see how it will be, sir, much Rhyme Royal treating of fair wet bub—well!" He broke off, looking sidelong at Mendoza. "But peradventure you shall read, sir, an you apply to Master Field again, a year hence."

"H'm! Peradventure I shall," said Nicholas. "Well, then, Master Shakespeare, for your forbearance I do thank you humbly. Truly the garden is a poem, and each poem severally a garden of divers delights. Let us on, wife, and use no more of this fair gentleman's time."

*NOOO,* screamed Edward in silence. *For God's sake, can't we even get a photograph?*

*Captain, can you take an image with the remote cam?* Alec said, watching Edward in uneasy concern.

**Oh, bloody Hell. Nicholas, turn and point out the hawk.**

And the hawk-remote swept in low, as Nicholas pointed to it and said:

"Marry, she stoops! I hope you have no chickens at hazard, sir."

"Oh, fie," said Shakespeare, frowning up at the camera, and so his image was captured: prosperous gentleman with slightly muddy knees, staring up indignantly from his side of the garden wall, with the Elizabethan gallant and his lady staring up, too, posing for the camera on their side of the wall.

"Whose should that be but one of Greville's again?" Shakespeare muttered. "I'll get me a fowling-piece, and see how he liketh hawk pie."

"Truly it is a shame, the way folk will let their birds range unmewed," said Nicholas sympathetically. "Well, we must away. Bid Master Shakespeare good-day, wife."

"Good-day, Master Shakespeare," said Mendoza.

"And to you, little madam," Shakespeare said, smiling at her. His remarkable eyes widened as an idea occurred to him, and he held up a hand. "But stay you, now. Here's an herb for you, lady, this same sweet lavender." He scooped up one of several small clay pots containing live cuttings and handed it over the wall. "An it live it'll be a goodly bush in a year's time; and, remember you, it is the young wood that hath the life in it."

Mendoza accepted it, wide-eyed. "I do thank you, gentle sir."

"Y'are most welcome, lady," he said, and returned to his weeding as they rode away.

"God, that was embarrassing," said Mendoza. "What possessed me to come up with all that plausible incidental detail? Was that something we used to do for the Company?"

"Ay," said Nicholas, with just a trace of smugness. "Thou wert a most complete, excellent, and perfect liar."

*You damned fool,* said Edward as he ran along at Nicholas's stirrup. *Do you know how many generations yet unborn would pay fortunes even to have a glimpse of that man, let alone five minutes' conversation, and you wasted my chance to ask even one question about his plays?*

*Tush! We'd vexed him enough, spying into his garden without his leave,* Nicholas told him. *Should I have insulted the fellow further by reminding him he'd been a common player?*


THAT EVENING, OFF SKEGNESS, 1600 AD

*At least we've the damned lavender bush for a souvenir, even if the rest of the job was an utter failure,* Edward said dully, watching from across the saloon as Mendoza fastened the repotted slip into a newly installed solarium window. Nicholas, who had control and was using it to read *Venus and Adonis,* ignored him.

**Now, that ain't rightly true, begging yer pardon. It looks like there's a power of data in them new plaquettes.**

*Well, bravo,* said Edward. *Perhaps they'll send us racing off on yet another chase across Time, for a few more pathetic fragments. What a prize.*

**Belay the sarcasm, swabbie.**

*We could go on another supermarket expedition,* said Alec. *More beef chops and brandy? That'd be fun, wouldn't it?*

*Endless jollity,* drawled Edward. He cocked an eye at the nearest of the Captain's cameras. *And yet, I must admit I was intrigued by something. Those scraps of Alec you made, Captain; explain to me, if you please, why it was within your power to make an ear but not a whole body.*

**Why, lad, a tooth or an ear ain't got to think, do they? And those bits didn't even have to live. All they had to do was look real. It didn't matter that they was cloned from Alec's thirty-year-old DNA with its chain errors. But if I tried to clone a whole body from Alec now, hell! Even if it could be managed, and I ain't saying it could, all you'd get would be a baby. A sick one, at that, as wouldn't live more'n ten years or so.**

*But we're never sick,* said Edward. He watched Mendoza, who was humming to herself as she added a shot of plant food to the lavender.

**No, see, because you were made from pure new-minted stuff. Not the DNA of another adult whose replication code had begun to deteriorate. Recollect what that Shakespeare gent told yer lady, about not cutting slips from old wood? He had it exactly so: the new wood's the stuff with the life in it.**

Alec grimaced. *I remember this now,* he said, *I saw a program on holo about clones. Little bald kids getting old when they were only five. Progeria, it's called.*

**Aye. Premature aging, because of being cloned from adults. You see now, Edward? You hated the thought of getting old bad enough. Would you want to be trapped in a body that was decrepit afore it'd hit puberty?**

Edward shuddered. Nicholas looked up from the text plaquette.

*Why wilt thou still deny death?* he said, sighing.

*Because my life went for nothing!* Edward said fiercely. *I was created to save mankind from its misery, and my makers wasted me on petty politics and murder. I had a purpose, almost a divine one, and I never fulfilled it!*

*What vanity.* Nicholas chuckled. *Thou wert no Lamb of God, to take away the sins of the world.*

*On England's pleasant pastures, etcetera,* said Alec scornfully.

Edward ignored them, staring up at the camera.

*Look here, Captain. Granting that another body couldn't be made from the one Alec's got—we're after our original phial of life-stuff, aren't we? With which you intend to inform the little nanobots that will make Alec immortal. Very well; why couldn't you make whole new bodies from the pure substance, also? Three of us were made, but there might just as easily have been six, or nine! Why not a new body for me, and for Nicholas too, for that matter?*

Nicholas lifted his head, startled. Alec opened his mouth to speak but stopped, struck by the possibility. Mendoza, oblivious, was tying back tendrils of the grapevine that had begun to scale the aft companionway.

**I'll tell you why not,** said the Captain firmly. **Say I did it, which I could, say I got a nice blastocyst started and on its way to being a baby. It'd be genetically identical to you, but it'd only be a baby at the end of nine months. And even if I made it a baby cyborg, which I might, and downloaded yer program into its little brain—there you'd be, trapped in a child's body until you grew up.**

Edward looked nonplussed, but he said defiantly: *Only a score of years, after all. And mightn't there be a way to bring the body to manhood, before I entered into it?*

**Only by shutting it in a regeneration tank once it was born, and keeping its consciousness turned off until it was man-sized. You'd be cheating it of any life or personality of its own,** the Captain told him. **A ghost possessing an idiot.**

Edward sneered. *And pray, tell me how that would differ from my present predicament?*

Alec clenched his fists and half rose, but the Captain barked out:

**Stand to! No brawling on this ship, d'y'hear? Now you listen, Commander Edward Alton Bell-Fairfax. Even if I was to clone a new body for you—which I ain't—there'd still be the problem of where the little bugger'd live for the first nine months. When Dr. Zeus was growing you lot from a spitwad o' cells into babies, he had to get you human host mothers. The trick can only be done in a woman's womb. Which we ain't got.**

Edward turned slowly to look at Mendoza, who was singing to herself as she picked clusters of grapes.

*Haven't we?* said Edward. *I rather think we have.*

The Captain said something unprintable. There followed a moment of stupefied silence before Alec gasped:

*You shracking bastard!*

Edward looked scornful. *Ah, but I know your difficulty. Your future's ruled by those Ephesian termagants, isn't it? You've been persuaded childbed is some sort of horrific ordeal. Would I entertain the idea for a moment, if that were really the case?*

*Thou lov'st her not,* growled Nicholas, shaking his head. *My poor mother died of me, so young she was, so monstrous was I in her little body. She went cold to her grave as I mewled in the nurse's arms.*

*But our lady's immortal, man,* Edward protested. *She wouldn't die.*

*It would hurt her!* Alec said.

*No more than any woman out of the uncounted millions who have borne children safely,* Edward countered, *and perhaps less. Good God, the maternal instinct is the foundation of the female soul! What could be more natural than to give her a child, in the only way possible for us?*

*And what more unnatural than his desire?* Nicholas said in disgust. *Filthy incest, when the cold-eyed boy was tall enough to demand her favor.*

*That's* wrong, Alec said.

*Is it? Stop frightening him, you pious fool! Alec, don't you see there'd be no actual blood relation at all? We're so far beyond the pale of humanity that his damned Bible and its prohibitions don't apply to us. We have no fathers. We have no mothers. We are ourselves alone, and the only family we have is that one woman!* Edward thrust out his arm at Mendoza. She glanced up from the basket of grapes and smiled.

"We've got nearly enough to make a little wine," she said. "Wouldn't that be nice? Chateau de Morgan."

"Ay, sweetheart," Nicholas said, smiling back. As she turned to hand off the basket to Coxinga, he glowered at the others. *And she that hath suffered the fires of Hell for our sakes, thou lusteth to use like a breeding beast,* he retorted. *But thou hast forgot—*

*No, damn you,* Edward said. *Mightn't it be a delight for her, as well? Why shouldn't we merge with her in every possible intimacy? Wouldn't we be restoring a natural right the Company took from her?* Edward leaned forward and stared into Alec's eyes. His voice became enticing, eerily gentle.

*Motherhood, Alec, is a sacred word, not an obscenity. Human mothers love their children. We're not human, more's the pity, so we can't blame the women who bore us if they never regarded us with affection; but it hurt you to the soul, I know. What if you were to relinquish this older body to Nicholas or I, for a fresh young one? Think of finding that sacred love at last in her arms, Alec! And do you imagine for a moment that she wouldn't yield herself up to that purpose, if we asked? She who has suffered, as brother Nicholas so eloquently put it, the fires of Hell for your sake?*

Alec gulped for breath like a man trying to keep from drowning. *No!* he howled, launching himself across the table at Edward. *I swear I'll kill you first—*

*I see the idea appeals to you.* Edward sidestepped him and pushed him back, slapping his face, but he surged up again and landed a sound right hook on Edward's jaw, sending Edward reeling, and both Alec and Nicholas were jerked after him as he fell. Mendoza was still singing quietly as she tidied up the vines, the same little tune with which she'd lulled Edward to sleep.

**Stand to! Stand to now!** *Nobody's killing anybody, I say! And nobody's having no babies neither, d'y'hear me? You can wheedle all you like, Edward bucko, but you ain't getting yer way this time, not whilst I'm Captain. You leave off scaring our Alec or you'll be sorry, and you may lay to that.*

Edward snarled, rising with a dangerous look in his eyes; but Alec, panting, stared him down. As they faced off, Mendoza slipped into the booth beside them.

*Peace,* said Nicholas wearily. *It's all one, Alec. She'll bear no children. Remember her book, how that she hath a device in her womb?*

*Oh!* Alec turned in surprise. *That's right. She said she had a contraceptive, er—*

*Symbiont,* Edward finished for him, and then turned suspicious eyes toward the Captain's nearest camera. *Does she? But then, why were you so adamant about—*

*She's still got that, hasn't she, Captain?* Now Alec looked suspicious, too.
**Of course she does, laddie—**
*He's lying,* said Edward in triumph.

*You disabled it? When you rebuilt her?* Alec was aghast. *What did you go do that for?*

**Now, Alec, son—**

*He's got his own plans for her, the old devil!* Edward said.

**It ain't my fault I'm programmed to see you get everything you need to make you happy, is it, Alec? And you, er, did use to think you might like being a daddy someday, with a little lad or lass running about the ship, eh? So I thought, well, never hurts to keep them options open—**

*That was before I knew I was a shracking monster,* said Alec, slumping into his seat.

**Granted, I'd have to do some fancy genetic work, but . . .**

*I can't believe you did that!* Alec shouted.

*Someone's to have a new immortal body, but not ME, is that it, Machine?* demanded Edward, and his smile was worse than his expression of rage. *I see what you're after, even if your boy can't. She's the chalice for your—*

*Enough, in God's name,* said Nicholas, aghast. *Who shall protect her from us?*

"So how is *Venus and Adonis*?" Mendoza inquired, peering at the screen of the plaquette. Nicholas turned without a word and put his arms around her.

"That good?" she said.

"The story's well enough; but cruel to the lady, with no care for her poor heart," Nicholas said, stroking her hair back from her face. She looked up into his eyes.

"You're worrying about something again," she said sadly.

The lavender bush, across the room, had shot up to waist height and opened purple florets.

# ONE EVENING IN 2320 AD

In the dark hall under the mountain, a single brilliant illumination brought a steel table and its occupant into sharp relief against the blue gloom. The figure stretched on the table was massive, bulky with muscle, not nearly so human in appearance as Frankenstein's monster though decidedly healthier-looking, with fair skin a fashion model might envy. She wouldn't envy him his face, though, with his flat forehead sloping straight back and his newly-shaven jaw that looked like it could wrench a steel plate off a tank. Wide eyes pale as glass stared off into the darkness, without expression.

He lay there naked, but for a folded sheet draped across his midsection, and his head was turned sharply to one side. A surgical incision had been made to peel back the skin of his neck and throat, exposing the muscles beneath. These too had been cut and opened out here and there, bleeding only slightly as the surgeon picked and prodded at them with his tools.

"Boy, no wonder you haven't regained full mobility," said Joseph, shaking his head as he reached for a hemostim. "None of these muscle groups have reattached. That virus sure did a number on your biomechanicals, Father. So, where was I? . . ."

He began to giggle as the absurdity of the moment struck him. Leaning over to catch Budu's eye, he flapped his wrist. "Well, anyway! My stars, honey, who gave you this *dreadful* perm? You go on soaking your nails while I just take a second to go see how that *in*-teresting little old lady in Chair Six is doing!" He staggered backward, whooping in merriment.

Budu's eyes swiveled sideways to regard him. He bared his huge mouthful of quite sharp-looking teeth in what might have been a smile. His instinct was to knock Joseph across the room, but he summoned patience and forbore, remembering that his son's hold on sanity was a little precarious nowadays.

"Oh, boy," Joseph wheezed, wiping his eyes on the back of his sleeve. "Golly, it doesn't take much to break me up, does it? Oh, well. So! Alec Checkerfield. Really *in*-teresting life story. The big smoking gun, see, is that it turns out Jolly Roger is a junior exec with Jovian Integrated Systems."

Budu growled in comment.

"Yeah! One of the Company's DBAs. And on twelve January of this year, all of a sudden there's a news release from His Lordship announcing the birth of a son and heir. It'd probably be quite a surprise for the surgeon who gave Roger his vasectomy, except that the doctor dies in a skiing accident the same day, and isn't *that* a suspicious little coincidence?" Joseph sneered.

"Dr. Zeus probably farms the little monster out to Roger and Cecelia because they resemble him and they can be controlled, since Roger's owned by the Company, even if he is the earl of Finsbury."

Budu made a noise that meant agreement.

"But!" Joseph brandished a scalpel in the air. "Even the plans of an all-powerful cabal of scientists and investors can fail. And the reason is, and I've said this like a million times now, *we overestimate our ability to control mortals.* Because, you know what I've learned from the Temporal Concordance? Cecelia will divorce Roger and take off to join the Ephesians, and why the Facilitator in charge of the project didn't see *that* coming I don't know. Roger dumps the kid at the family manse in London and goes back to get drunk on his boat, until he's killed. Poor old Roger."

Joseph's mouth tightened, and Budu saw the light of obsession glaring in his eyes again.

"Poor Cecelia, too, even if she was a snooty bitch. See, there's two more of his victims! They had a happy enough marriage, for what they were, and *he* comes along and what happens? Misery. Even as a baby, he's gonna be wrecking lives. This is the kind of trail he leaves wherever he goes—"

Budu growled again, indicating his neck with one impatient hand.

"Okay, okay. Sorry. Wow, I don't know how I missed this thyrohyoid when I put your head back on but I sure missed it, didn't I?" Joseph bent and paid close attention to his task for a moment before going on. "What was I saying? The kid.

"Alec Checkerfield. He grows up. When he comes of age—shortly after poor Jolly Roger takes the deep six, under distinctly fishy circumstances—he gets himself cyborged!"

Budu growled thoughtfully.

"Yeah, not a complete cyborg like one of us but something like a port junkie? Which procedure no ethical doctor would perform if they knew His Satanic Lordship's little secret. He's got some kind of inhuman powers. He's a mutation the Company's experimenting with, I'm positive. There've always been rumors about genetic engineering . . ."

Budu wondered wearily whether he ought to tell Joseph the truth. It wouldn't comfort his son, but it would certainly bring matters to a head. And then, alive or dead, Alec Checkerfield would no longer take up valuable time.

"So here's our boy, mean as Nicholas Harpole and dangerous as that other guy, Edward Whosis-Hyphen," Joseph continued. "Does his thing on Mars and in his usual fashion makes things worse for mortals everywhere. Gets away with it, too, first stopping at Options Research in his time shuttle to abduct Mendoza, for whatever reason."

Budu gave him an impatient look.

"But we'll get him." Joseph's voice hardened. "We'll get the son of a bitch. If he's even anything that natural!

"I think I've got a chance. You said I should get to know my enemy, Father, and you were so right! Because I've discovered his weakness," Joseph said, beginning to giggle again and waving the hemostim around wildly. Budu put up one hand and clenched it on Joseph's wrist, glaring at him out of the corner of his eye.

"Ow! Sorry. It's funny, that's all. Alec Checkerfield, unlike his previous selves, is a kid of the twenty-fourth century, and guess what? Like all his generation, he's a self-indulgent moron. Get this: the big goofball is obsessed with pirates. He buys himself a yacht the size of the *Titanic*, all fixed up like a pirate ship. You wouldn't believe what he'll spend on it!"

Budu blinked, struck by the similarities between the life of Alec Checkerfield and another Company foundling, of sorts, whose life he'd been investigating shortly before the 1906 earthquake had buried him under several tons of Chinatown.

"He likes his pleasures," said Joseph. "It's easy to set a trap for somebody like that. All I have to do is find him. Maybe there's a way of tracking the shuttle's energy signature. It works in the movies. Maybe I can lie in wait for him somewhere, and when he least expects it—wham! Strike three and you're out, Nicholas, for keeps this time."

Joseph fell silent, sealing up the edges of the wound. Budu swallowed experimentally, finding it suddenly much easier to inhale.

"The only problem," continued Joseph, "is finding him. Even with him being such a big ugly needle, the haystack of time is so freaking huge. And he's—hey!" he said, for Budu had braced his good arm on the table and levered himself up into a sitting position. A moment's concentration, and he had shakily raised his head to stare down at Joseph. He worked his mouth experimentally, drew a deep shuddering breath and spoke.

"You're missing the obvious again, son," he said, in a pleasant tenor that was nonetheless oddly flat and without intonation.

"Yaay!" Joseph threw up both arms in a gesture of triumph. He scrambled up on the table and knelt there, hugging Budu. "Oh, Father, you wouldn't believe how I've missed the sound of your voice."

"There is something you need to know."

"Oh, this is so swell, this is what I've needed you to do all along, plan a war for me, because there's nobody as good at it as you, you were always the best, and I mean that sincerely, Father—" Joseph said, tears in his eyes. Budu went on staring at him implacably. "And—something I need to know?"

"The boy *is* some kind of Enforcer," said Budu. "Marco guessed correctly. You should have seen this long ago. His face. His size."

Joseph screwed up his features, looked away. "I never noticed any resemblance."

"You're lying," said Budu. "And he has our skills. He has the Persuasion."

"You mean he's persuasive? Yeah, but—"

"No. He bends the will of others," Budu said. "As we did. When he commands, he is obeyed."

"Now, *that's* nuts," said Joseph desperately.

"Nicholas Harpole was executed the first of April 1555, before four hundred and nineteen witnesses," said Budu. "He preached a sermon. You remember what he said; you were there."

"He . . . tried to make the audience rise up in rebellion against Bloody Mary," said Joseph. "Or die at the stake with him."

"Twenty-two of his audience followed him to the stake within three months," said Budu. "Most of the others either rose in rebellion or committed suicide within the next five years. Of the two immortals who watched him burn, one destroyed herself. The other became a rebel, after years of servile and unquestioning service to the Company."

Joseph gaped at him a moment, and then shouted: "No! That's not true, damn it, that's—that's total coincidence! You can't tell me that son of a bitch got inside *my* head!"

"He did," said Budu.

"And you never lie, do you?" Pounding his temples with both fists, Joseph began to pace in a circle. "Of course you don't. Of course he's got hellish powers. That's what I've been saying all along, haven't I? Help me find him, Father, help me stop him!"

"If he can travel through time, where will the boy go? Think," ordered Budu.

"Okay, right, think. Where will Alec Checkerfield go?"

"You've told me," said Budu, "that this boy is obsessed with pirates. There are no pirates in his time. He is given a time shuttle."

"He goes back in time to see some *real* pirates," Joseph yelled. "Of course! Gee, I really have to apologize, Father, I just don't seem to be thinking clearly today—so obviously he goes back in time to the golden age of piracy, which he must know was at the end of the seventeenth century, and he probably goes to Madagascar—or wait, no, what am I thinking? He's born in the Caribbean. He names his ship the *Captain Morgan.* He goes to old Jamaica! In fact, he goes, he's bound to go, sooner or later he *has* to go to the wickedest pirate city on Earth—"

"Port Royal," said Budu.

# OTHER TIMES, OTHER PLACES

At a cemetery on the outskirts of London, on a bright chilly October afternoon in 1888, a funeral cortege pulls up. The casket is taken from the splendid hearse, and carried with pomp to the graveside by pallbearers in black-ribboned top hats. Mourners file in respectfully through the iron gates, making their way across the grass between the obelisks and statuary, like so many black chess pieces moving between white ones.

The deceased was well known, his mourners are many, and the young couple in elegantly cut black go quite unnoticed where they stand to the rear of the crowd, though in his high silk hat the young man is quite the tallest person there.

The Reverend Mr. Gideon, glancing up in the midst of reading the office for the burial of the dead, does wonder for a second at the expression of icy triumph in the face of the young man, who is contemplating a group of wheezing elderly gentlemen; but the Reverend Mr. Gideon has been at his business long enough to know that a lot of bizarre emotions break loose at funerals, and he goes right on reading without missing a beat.

The deceased is laid to rest, and one by one the mourners file by the grave, some of them stooping to toss in a handful of earth as they pass. The young couple are the last to observe this ritual, and the waiting sexton and his assistant fail to notice that, while the young lady tosses in her handful of earth, the young gentleman tosses in what appears to be a small bottle of gold paint, which falls between the casket and the grave wall, out of sight. It isn't gold paint. It is about a teaspoon's worth of nanobots designed to unleash extreme vengeance on Dr. Zeus Incorporated, on that distant day in 2355 when the world ends. Just now, however, it is completely harmless.

On their way to the gate, the young couple draw abreast of one of the elderly gentlemen, who is making his laborious way along with a cane. He trips on a marble urn, stumbles, is about to fall when the young man catches his elbow and sets him upright. The old gentleman peers up into his face, scowling in an attempt to make it out. His jaw drops.

"Good God," he says hoarsely. "Bell-Fairfax!"

"I regret to inform you that you are mistaken, sir," says the young gentleman, smiling with formidable teeth. Eyes brightening as an afterthought occurs to him, he adds: "Merely his bastard. Good afternoon!" He tips his silk hat, turns on his heel, and walks away swiftly to rejoin his young lady.

The old man gasps, his eyes roll back in his head, he pitches forward into somebody else's memorial wreath; and the daughters and elderly wife who come running back to his assistance, crying out "Papa!" and "Ambrose!" wonder, in their consternation, why the tall man is laughing as he strides on.


In a dance club in a cellar in swinging London of the 1960s, one young couple seems to be having less fun than their peer group. Perhaps they find their polyester and vinyl clothes ugly and uncomfortable. Perhaps the very tall youth objects to having to duck continually to avoid hitting his head on the beams of the low ceiling. Perhaps the girl is mortified by her appearance in the makeup of the era. Perhaps they find the atmosphere of packed mortal bodies, also wearing polyester clothing in the stifling heat, oppressive; and perhaps they find the popular dances clumsy and graceless. The music is sublime, however, and so presently they retire from the dance floor and find a quiet uncrowded corner, where they sit and listen appreciatively.

The reason their particular corner is uncrowded is because the wall behind it is broken out for some sort of electrical work in progress, and plasterboard, earth, and trailing wires are only carelessly fenced off with a sawhorse. And as the music throbs, as the dancers bounce and twist and shake their heads, as the colored lights whirl in blobby patterns, the youth leans back casually and pokes something small into a dark recess between two bricks. Even in the pandemonium, he can hear something rattling down inside the wall, and smiles at the girl.

As he leans back, however, something trailing a thin curl of smoke is thrust under his nose. He looks up, startled, at a person of uncertain gender in beaded and fringed clothes, who murmurs something inaudible, but whose expression of all-embracing affection makes it clear an invitation is being offered. He signs confusion. The person tucks the little twisted cigarette between his lips. Not wishing to be impolite, he takes it between his thumb and forefinger and inhales deeply.

The girl is distracted from her wistful contemplation of the bar by his snorting coughs, and though she turns instantly the purveyor of peace and love has drifted off to offer it to others, and the youth's pupils have expanded to alarming size. In response to her frantically signed question he mouths the word *ganja*, and she rolls her eyes. Getting one arm around him, she helps him to his feet and they leave. He hits his head on the beams four times before they manage to reach the exit.

Venice, bride of the sea! And though the Bridge of Sighs, the golden Rialto, and St. Mark's glimmer in the ripple-reflections as enticingly as they ever have in this year of 1797, and though the pigeons flutter in clouds and cast their shadows as beautifully as ever on the paving stones of the square, the tourist trade is down, thanks to that annoying little man from Corsica zooming about being the wonder of the martial world, and the fact that he has bestowed on the Venetians a brand-new constitution of their very own doesn't quite make up for it.

There are practically no British tourists there at all. This suits the hoteliers and cooks just fine, *grazie*, because the British complain ceaselessly about Venetian cuisine and notions of plumbing; but the *gondolieri* are feeling the pinch, because Britons love gondola rides. So Vittorio murmurs a prayer of thanks as the tall Englishman and the young lady engage his services, and poles out enthusiastically along the rank canals between the houses, and into the wider places where it isn't quite so obvious that people have been emptying their chamberpots into the canal, or indeed simply thrusting their bottoms out the windows for convenience. In his energetic haste he scarcely notices the Englishman dropping a small object over the side of the gondola. People drop so many things into the waters of Venice.

And the fresh wind off the lagoon does the trick, because the Englishman and his lady are clearly not put off by the sights, sounds, or smells. Indeed, they grow quite actively romantic as the gondola rocks along, and Vittorio watches with one appreciative eye as he bawls out a love ballad in the time-honored *gondolier* tradition. So amorous do they become, in fact, that Vittorio begins calling attention to their activity in a particularly amusing way he has devised: improvising new ballad lyrics in idiomatic Venetian for the benefit of his fellow *gondolieri* and shouting them loud enough to be heard across the water. He doesn't look back at his passengers as he describes the lady's attributes and the gentleman's amazing flexibility. Poling along, he begins to notice that his fellow *gondolieri* are giggling and making cautionary signs to him.

He turns on a downstroke and goes cold all over to observe the expression with which the Englishman and his lady, now sitting up, are regarding him.

Meekly he poles back to the landing and ties up his gondola. Glaring at him, the Englishman steps out and extends his hand to the lady, who leaps up gracefully despite her billowing skirts; and as she passes Vittorio she advises him, in flawless idiomatic Venetian and no uncertain terms, just exactly what he can do with his pole.

They don't tip.


Egypt in 2213 is just beginning to recover from a nasty war and horrifying air pollution. It needs tourist income as badly as it ever has, and the bright animated brochures put out by the Tourism Bureau contrast the eternal pyramids, lit as though from within by their own ancient red light, towering above the modern metropolis of West Bank Cairo, where little electric cars in every color of the rainbow zip through the wide clean streets. In fact the pyramids are shown from every possible angle except any likely to feature the Sphinx, which for the last sixty years has had no head, due to an embarrassing incident involving a miscommunication between the presidential palace and the Egyptian Air Force.

But the resourceful itinerants who make their living from the romance of Egypt have worked around this problem: they have simply programmed their cameras to provide the missing features in any shot taken of the unfortunate monument, which fact they scream helpfully at all persons arriving at the river taxi dock in front of the Cairo Sheraton.

They're not sure what to make of the young couple in tailored white linen who arrive from Alexandria via some sort of hovercraft, but they do their best to sell them portraits taken with the Sphinx in the background, portraits taken with the pyramids in the background, portraits taken with donkeys, portraits taken with camels, portraits taken with cutout figures of world leaders. The tall man strides through them, towing the fascinated young lady after him, and he waves them away with a firm and practiced hand. He glances up occasionally at the hawk that circles above him, far against the blazing sun. He will not buy beads, he will not buy carpets, he will not buy brass or copper; he will not even buy tequila, which is going at bargain rates since the Greenest-of-the-Green Party cut the subsidies to Upper Nile farmers of blue agave in their continuing efforts to impose Prohibition.

All the young couple wish to buy, it seems, is a Pyramid Pizza. They make for the nearest branch of the nationwide chain, spotting from afar its giant winged pizza-disc logo, and after ordering at the window they take seats on the outdoor terrace overlooking the Nile. It's a pleasant place to sit. The terrace is shaded at present by a photoreactive transparent canopy, and will one day be shaded in a rather more natural way, for it is in the process of being landscaped. Palm trees are being planted along the edge of the terrace even as the young couple are brought their iced tea. While they wait for their pizza, the young lady strikes up a conversation with the elderly gardener, who is setting a baby tree in the deep hole that has been dug for it.

He's astonished to discover how well she speaks the dialect of his village, and how much she knows on the subject of date palms. They engage in a lengthy conversation that ends only when the project foreman stalks up, demanding impatiently that the gardener finish planting the damned palm.

The young couple excuse themselves and finish their pizza. The old gardener goes back to shoveling earth around the roots of the little palm.

He does not note the flash of gold in the bottom of the hole, visible there for a split-second before his next shovelful buries it. He finishes planting the palm and says a quiet prayer, hoping the new tree will thrive, as the young couple tidy up their table and leave.

His prayer will in fact be answered. The palm he has just planted will thrive, will grow to gigantic size and venerable age, to such an extent that tourists in the year 2355 AD will still be pointing it out as a city landmark . . .


Portland, Oregon, its gray heart beating forever along two great river arteries running to the North Pacific. Its Old Town is gritty and civilized in the midst of improbable forest. Autumn is already as cold as death when the river fog rolls in, and drifts of oak leaves bury the sidewalks, bright as fire, red as blood.

Along the waterfront, not far from the Maritime Museum, there is a fine restored business block with a view of the Willamette, and there a certain legal firm has its offices. In this year of 2023, the name is Dowling, Dowling and Spratt. Over the decades its name will change, but not its location or its purpose. It is and will always be an unadventurous, reliable establishment.

So the elder Mr. Dowling doesn't think much of the business laid out before him by the cold-eyed young Briton in the impeccably cut three-piece suit. It's the sort of silly idea that inevitably leads to problems for estate claimants years down the line. The young man, however, seems grimly serious about it. He is willing to pay the hefty fee Mr. Dowling quotes him for the service he has requested. After all, no funds are involved: merely the delivery of a certain item to a certain address on a certain date in the future.

Mr. Dowling would feel better about it, all the same, if he knew what the item was, without necessarily knowing all the particulars. His client decides this request is reasonable. Has Mr. Dowling two envelopes of differing sizes?

Mr. Dowling has. He reaches into a desk drawer and produces a plain white letter envelope and a larger manila one. He watches as his client withdraws an antique silver card case from an inner breast pocket, and extracts what appears to be an ordinary ivory-colored business card. Has Mr. Dowling a pen?

Mr. Dowling offers his own Montblanc. The young man takes it and writes on the card: "I will be with you on your wedding night. With the compliments of Edward Acton Bell-Fairfax." As he writes, Mr. Dowling notes the antique brass cufflinks he wears: very nice fouled anchor design, with a matching pin worn in his fine silk tie. The Englishman places the card in the white envelope and seals it. He writes a name on the white envelope, places it inside the manila one, and seals that. Finally he writes a date on the manila envelope. He offers it to Mr. Dowling, who takes it and looks at the date. *9 July, 2355.* Beautiful copperplate hand, at least. He shakes his head, but when the young man returns the card case to his pocket and pulls out a debit card, Mr. Dowling is all respectful attention.

A considerable amount of money is transferred into the account of Dowling, Dowling and Spratt. As soon as the transaction has cleared, the young man stands, towering over him, and leans forward to shake Mr. Dowling's hand. With mutual cordialities they go to the door, beyond which the young man's lady friend is patiently waiting, sipping a café latte. She rises with a smile. They depart.

Mr. Dowling returns to his desk and, staring down at the envelope, shakes his head again. What an absurdly easy way to earn a month's income! But a client is a client, and Mr. Dowling has every intention of seeing to it that this particular client's wishes are honored, so far as it is in his power. He and both his associates, as well as every person in his employ, will be long dead by the delivery date specified on the manila envelope. Nevertheless, he pulls out his keyboard and sets up a file with detailed and specific instructions. He scans the exterior of the envelope, and enters its image in the file. He saves and closes.

Having done that, he takes the envelope itself and locks it in his firm's safe.

On his way back to his desk, he pauses at his window. The young couple are still out on the waterfront promenade, walking arm in arm. They are smiling, laughing at some private joke. Watching them, Mr. Dowling cannot say why he feels a shiver of apprehension, cold as death; but he does, and as they walk away together a gust of wind sends oak leaves dancing eerily about them, bright as fire, red as blood.

———

As a rule, if one walked along the beach at Monterey in autumn, one would have splendid views. Emerald green sea breaking white on dark rocks and shading to a deep and powerful blue farther out; to the south the serpentine forest of cypress and pine rising on a peak, aromatic and haunted in the noonday sun. To the north, dazzling bright sand hills, stretching away to a windy sunlit glimpse of Santa Cruz.

Unfortunately there's been an El Niño condition in this year of 1879, and the summer fogs have lasted well into autumn, so all one would see on this particular day is a grayed-out closed-down perspective, like a Victorian photograph of a landscape. Sea the color of ashes, sand the color of ashes, wet fog hanging in wreaths through the tops of the twisted and spectral cypresses, all the jewel colors lost. Naturally enough, the frail man, himself more than half wraith as he picks his way among the tide-pools, is depressed. But then, he depresses easily.

He cheers up easily, too. His moods could best be described as hysterically mercurial, which is only one of the reasons the motherly lady he's courting hasn't quite made up her mind about him. He perches now on a prominence of rock and rolls his trouser legs up again, for they have become soaked. He can roll them up quite a distance on his pipestem legs. It isn't just that he's emaciated from illness; his whole graceful body, slender feet and long expressive hands, is weirdly attenuated. That, and his enormous eyes—too wide, too bright, in his thin face—contribute to his otherworldly appearance.

He notices the whaleboat appearing out of the fog. From whence has it come? A shadowy something on the obscured horizon suggests an immense ship, big as a clipper at least but phantomlike. Why is it standing on and off so far out in the bay? And why are there only two persons in the whaleboat, which is of considerable size to be rowed by only one man? He begins to tell himself a story about the occupants of the whaleboat.

To his delight, they are rowing straight for the cove where he sits. They near him and his imaginings go from crime to romance, for he observes that one of the two is a lady. He leans his chin in his palm and stares at them, fascinated, as they approach his rock. The lady has bright hair, is simply dressed in brown calico and a shawl. It is impossible to tell her age, for though her face is rounded and young, her gaze is mature, assessing.

The man is striking in appearance, too, wearing sea boots and rough serviceable clothes cut well. How effortlessly he bends to the oars and sends the boat flying along! Too homely really to be a hero, but a character and no mistake. What kind of character?

They pass their observer, as dolphins play in their bow wake, and a moment later they make landfall. As the man leaps out to pull their boat up on the sand, splashing through the surf foaming about his boots, it becomes evident that he is remarkably strong. And quite tall, towering above the young lady! The frail man rises and hurries across the rocks to get a better look at the couple, trying to make it appear as though he is just sauntering in a casual sort of way.

He is in luck, for the pair stand there several moments beside the boat, discussing something. They seem irresolute. Are they worried about leaving their boat? Why are they going into the old Spanish capital? Her long braid and golden earrings suggest that the lady is Iberian, despite her pallor. The daughter of an exiled Spanish don, returning in secret to claim some birthright? She reaches up to stroke back the sailor's lank hair in an unmistakable gesture of intimacy. Are they lovers? Must be!

The frail man halts, for he is out of breath. He stoops to pretend to examine a clump of sea-wrack. Unfortunately this brings on a coughing fit, which is the end of his unobtrusive scrutiny. The young lady turns and fixes her black stare on him and it connects like a blow, not hostile but terrifyingly intense. She advances and asks him a question, in beautifully aristocratic Castilian. He knows enough Spanish to understand that she is asking him if he'd like to earn a few dollars watching the boat while they go ashore, but he isn't proficient enough in that tongue to reply gracefully, and so he stammers:

"*Perdon yo, por favor, Señorita, pero—parlez-vous français?*"

"*Mais oui, certainement,*" she says, in the perfect accents of a native Parisienne. Then she puts her head on one side, frowning at him. "*Etes-vous ecossais, Monsieur?*"

"*Oui, mademoiselle,*" he admits, thinking peevishly that his accent can't be that pronounced.

"Well then, we can talk in English!" she concludes, in flat American. At that moment the sailor gasps as though he's seen a ghost, and he cries:

"Robert Louis Stevenson!"

And to Louis's astonishment the sailor strides forward and seizes him by both fragile shoulders, and stares down into his eyes with burning adoration.

"Er—" says Louis, as the woman looks swiftly from him to the tall sailor and back again.

"Ah! Of course. You must be the author of"—she appears to be thinking rapidly—"*An Inland Journey*. Are you not? That very entertaining travel narrative, Alec."

"Man, oh, man, I love your stories," says the sailor hoarsely, with tears standing in his eyes. He seems to be English, and though his voice is pleasant his accent is strange and uncouth.

"Yes, he does," affirms the lady in a nervous sort of way. She thinks again and rattles off: "We've read *A Lodging for the Night, Will o' the Mill, The Sire de Maletroit's Mousetrap, The Latter-Day Arabian Nights,* and *Providence and the Guitar;* and that's all we've read, of course, because that's all that's been published *at this time,* Alec," she adds with what might be a warning in her voice. "But we enjoyed them very much and do hope you'll write more."

"Oh, we do," says the man, letting go Louis's shoulders and grabbing his hand to pump it vigorously. "You—er—you won't mind if I shake your hand?"

"No," Louis says, for the extraordinary warmth of the man's skin seems to go right through his own thin chilled fingers, and anyway he wouldn't care if the fellow had the clammy grip of death, because he's read Louis's stories! "Actually I've a number of new pieces drafted, you know. I'm, er, gathering material from life."

"Brilliant." The man shudders pleasurably. He can't seem to take his eyes off Louis. Suddenly he turns his head a little to one side, just as the girl had done. His nostrils dilate, he inhales, and a puzzled look comes into his eyes. "Oh—you're diff—" he begins, and then stops himself.

"Well, rather obviously we can't ask you to watch our boat for an hour or so," says the girl quickly.

"Oh, I wouldn't mind—er, ma'am—" Louis says, and she throws out her hands in a gesture of slightly theatrical chagrin.

"And how remiss of us! We haven't introduced ourselves. This is my husband, Alec—Harpole, and I am—Mrs. Harpole."

It is too obviously an alias, and Louis's eyes gleam with understanding.

"Very pleased to meet you, Mrs. Harpole," he says in a conspiratorial sort of way. She looks at him consideringly, for a long moment.

"Mr. Stevenson," she says, "may we rely on your discretion? We are here under something of a cloud. We had hoped to run ashore swiftly and accomplish, ah—what we had hoped to accomplish, and get away again to our ship before—" Her eyes glaze over slightly in rapid thought. "—Before my father's enemies could come to know of our presence here. I trust I need say nothing further, other to assure you that our intentions are completely honorable?"

"Nothing at all," Louis cries, thrilled to the marrow of his bones. "Look here, I'll be delighted to stay with the boat."

"Oh, sir, how gallant," she replies, with a charming smile. She puts her hand on her husband's arm. "We are very much obliged to you. Let us haste, then, Alec dear. We won't be more than an hour or so, Mr. Stevenson, I promise you."

And the tall man lets go Louis's hand only reluctantly, with more protestations of high regard, and Louis watches as the two of them run away in the general direction of the Customs House. When they are gone, he clambers a little self-consciously over the gunwale of their boat and sits at the oars, gazing out at the gray sea-phantom in wildest speculation. Some sort of Flying Dutchman, perhaps? The dolphins have remained, circling in the near water, almost as though they were waiting.

Louis tries the oars once, utterly failing to move them, and marvels at the strength of the oarsman. He can't define to himself just what is so striking about the man, other than a peculiar quality of being not quite human.

Which is a little ironic, in light of the fact that Alec has been thinking exactly the same thing about him.

In just over an hour the couple return, flushed and gleeful, and they have brought him a present: a bottle of the best brandy Sanchez's Tavern has to offer. The tall man presents it to Louis shyly, as a hawk comes swooping low out of the fog above them and vanishes again. Louis makes a valiant pretense of helping the man push the boat off into the surf. He stands waving from the shore as they cut away through the gray water, dolphins leaping after, until at last the fog obscures them.

Louis returns to his bare corner room in the French Hotel, clutching the brandy bottle to his skinny chest, and curls up on the floor in his blanket in the gathering dusk. He does not notice, now or ever, the tiny dab of new plaster on the adobe wall above his head, and even if he did it's unlikely he would examine it closely enough to learn that it conceals a vitrified tube containing a tiny bottle of something resembling gold paint.

He warms himself with the brandy and with working out, in a dozen different ways, the imaginary adventures of the couple from the phantom ship. His last thought, before he drifts off to sleep, is a question: Will their story have a happy ending?


THAT SAME EVENING OFF THE BAY OF MONTEREY, 1879 AD

"This is *so* cool," Alec said, as he admired the holoshot. "There we are, and there he is, and he looks just like his pictures!"

"What a stroke of luck, eh?" Mendoza said, kissing his ear as she leaned past him to set down a dish of green corn tamales. "And how neatly it solved the problem! No chance of his walking in on intruders in his room, when he's guarding their boat."

*It could only have been more unfair if you'd gotten his autograph,* groused Edward.

*I already have his autograph,* Alec said smugly. *Bought it at auction, years ago.*

*Puppy!*

*Creep!*

**Belay that, both of you,** the Captain ordered.

"And Mr. Stevenson will go off and write *Treasure Island,* which will inspire you to build this ship and go cruising around the Spanish Main," said Mendoza, slipping into the booth beside him and shaking out her napkin. "I think? That's why all the pirate things in here?"

"You could say that," said Alec. "He was always one of my heroes. When I was six, I'd have given anything to have had a chance to talk to him about pirates." He scowled at his place setting. "My father wasn't around, so . . . stories meant a lot to me. *Treasure Island* especially."

Mendoza, just reaching out to help herself to grilled fish, halted.

"Your father?" She blinked. "When you were—we must have been children, once. Mustn't we?"

*Thou fool!* Nicholas groaned.

"Yes," said Alec, mentally kicking himself. "But . . ."

"I can't remember anything about being a child," said Mendoza. Her eyes were wide and distant. "Why can't I remember? We must have had— mothers, and fathers—"

"Er—we were orphans," said Alec, taking her hand.

"Was it . . . unpleasant, when we were children?" she asked cautiously.

"At first," Alec improvised. "But, er, the Captain came along to look af ter us. It was great, because he told us stories, and taught us about stars and navigation and everything. And then later he, he helped us escape from the Company!"

"It must have been a nice childhood, then," said Mendoza, relaxing a little.

"Oh, that part of it was brilliant!" said Alec with enthusiasm. He looked at her sidelong. "We'd, er, sail around to different islands, and have adventures. Build sand castles. Pretend we were digging for buried treasure. We learned all about the real pirates, too. Like, the way the Brotherhood of the Coast's ships would pass each other, and when they weren't sure if they were pirates, too, one of the ship's crews would call out, 'Where do you hail from?' and the other ship's crew would call back—"

" 'From the sea!' " said Mendoza with him, as she held out her wineglass for Coxinga to fill. "Yes. Oh, it sounds lovely. I wish I could remember."

As he clinked glasses with her, Alec thought sadly: *No you don't, baby.* He looked over into Nicholas's somber gaze, and thought of the dungeons of the Inquisition. He found himself with an irrational desire to buy her dolls, sweets, games, anything to give her the idyllic childhood he'd just been inventing for them.

The idea came out of nowhere, bright as lightning, and seemed the best he'd ever had in his life.

"I can't believe I've never thought of this before," he said. "Why couldn't we go see some *real* pirates?"

"Because they were filthy, sadistic, and murderous mortals and it would be terribly hazardous," said Mendoza, sipping her wine.

*Aye, dearie, I'm afraid that's just so.*

"Well, but we wouldn't invite them on board," said Alec. "We could just go back to the Spanish Main and watch them!"

*Seek out thieves and murderers for sport?* Nicholas frowned in bewilderment.

*You young idiot, do you have any idea of the risk you'd be running?* said Edward wearily, pushing away his untasted virtual dinner. *You've never associated with any real criminals, have you?*

*I have so,* said Alec, incensed.

*Alec, smugglers of Cadbury's cocoa and double-cream brie hardly qualify as authentic felons—*

**Well**—began the Captain, in a considering kind of voice. Edward and Mendoza looked up at the camera with identical expressions of amazement and disapproval.

**Happen there's this plan I been revolving, see,** said the Captain. **It seems that Dr. Zeus has a satellite in geosynchronous orbit stationed smack above Jamaica. It's one in a series he's got linking his bloody communications network. I was afeared he was using it to spy on you, Alec, so I had a good look at it.**

**Now, this here Jamaica satellite is the master, see? Everything in the system comes and goes through it. The bloody thing's only protected by a distortion field to hide it, and a little ring of orbiting laser cannon to take out any space debris that might blunder towards it.**

"Don't be stupid," said Edward, seizing control. "If it's that vital, it's sure to be better protected than that."

**Haar! Aye, says you; but yer not taking into account the way the big fat fool's mind works. He don't need to protect it any better, thinks he, and why? Because his Temporal Concordance says it'll never be attacked, at any time in recorded history. Mind you, the Temporal Concordance don't go past 2355; and besides, a lot of history's recorded wrong, ain't it? So . . .**

"So if we planted something to activate then, that would take out this satellite—" Mendoza squinted thoughtfully as she unwrapped a tamale. "Or better still, override its signal and replace it with a false signal of our own—"

*Bless yer little heart, dearie, that was just what I were about to say. A nice deadly bolus for the Jamaicasat. Antigravity to take it up there, RAT transmitter to lie to the lasers so they'll think it's a maintenance servo and let it past them, where it'll eat through the hull; and then our own little satellite, what clamps on the Jamaicasat and unfolds like a steel daisy, see, and picks up broadcasting without a second's interruption once the Jamaicasat's killed! Dr. Zeus will never know anything's happened, but from that moment on I'll be controlling every signal that's sent.*

"Captain, I must apologize," said Edward, lifting his wineglass to the camera. "You have once again demonstrated your brilliance at treachery, and I stand in awe." Mendoza looked across at him, one eyebrow raised. "But I fail to see how this has anything to do with pirates, other than being itself an act of piracy."

*We got to lay the trap, don't we? And it's best laid right under her keel, which is to say somewhere on Jamaica itself. Ah, says you, but where? Mighty unstable place, Jamaica; deforestation and reforestation and the ground all dug up for plantations, so's you'd be hard put to find an acre of land that ain't going to be disturbed one way or the other afore 2355. Worse still, there'll be earthquakes.*

"So there shall," said Edward, who didn't get the point. Alec shoved him aside and took control again.

*A powerful lot of earthquakes.*

"Well, an earthquake wouldn't damage our mine, but it might uncover it from wherever we'd concealed it—" said Mendoza.

*One bloody BIG earthquake.*

"Port Royal," yelled Alec, jumping up at his place. Bang, his head collided with the lamp and he sat down abruptly.

"Darling!" Mendoza reached out to him in concern but he caught her hand and kissed it, grinning.

# ONE AFTERNOON IN
# SPANISH TOWN, JAMAICA,
# 1682 AD

Her name wasn't Mavis Breen, but it might just as well have been.

She kept an inn in Spanish Town, the Goat and Compasses, which bore an uncanny resemblance to the Pelican in Muir Harbor, and she was a compact muscular lady of opulent attributes running just slightly to plumpness as she gravitated toward middle age. She kept a husband, too, which was why she was Mrs. Dolly Ansolabehere instead of Miss Dolly Venables.

She hadn't particularly wanted a husband—Dolly was a strong-willed lady and preferred to call the shots in her life and her business—but like a stray dog he had somehow made himself useful, and the less formal relationship she would have preferred to establish with him was impossible, thanks to the nosiness of the Reverend Mr. Carrowes. All the clergy in Jamaica tended to zealotry in their moral crusades, overcompensation no doubt for their complete inability to do anything about that teeming cesspit of immorality across the bay: Port Royal.

Jamaica, like Dolly Venables, had had to compromise.

The British had captured Jamaica from the Spanish in 1655, eager to please Oliver Cromwell, but realized they had little chance of holding on to it should the Spanish make any determined attempt to get it back. Indeed, there was only one armed force of ruthless and effective fighters ready to hand, capable of driving off any Spanish, French, or Dutch incursion, and it wasn't the British Navy.

No, it was the Brotherhood of the Coast, that loosely organized multi-national gang of privateers and pirates. The privateers had licenses and investors backing what they did, the pirates hadn't, and that was about all there was to distinguish between them. Moreover, a treaty or a fit of pique on the part of an ambassador could shift a man's professional status in an hour. It was the veneer of respectability on privateering, however, that legally enabled the British holding Jamaica to, as it were, invite the big chicken-killing dog into the yard to protect its sheep.

A fortress was built on a wide sandy hook of land that projected into the bay opposite the future site of Kingston. A crude and violent little city grew up around it, full of all things necessary to attract vicious clientele and make them happy repeat customers. Taverns and brothels without number, gaming houses, lodging houses, merchants eager to convert plundered goods into cash, purveyors and providers of every item the discriminating cutthroat might need when going on the account, warehouses in which to store it all, and churches for the salvation of any souls that might crawl in between drinking binges. It was Port Royal, and it was deemed the wickedest and most impudent place since Sodom or Gomorrah.

It was also a fantastic commercial success. So the deal with the Devil stood, and though the rest of Jamaica—which had been settled by God-fearing Puritans, mind!—wrung its hands in shame, it was also able to farm its sugar cane without fear of foreign invasion, and pocket the profits.

Mrs. Ansolabehere's situation was far less morally painful. Dr. Ansolabehere was of a most agreeable, not to say docile nature, as husbands went. He had appeared in the common room of the Goat and Compasses one night in 1660 with no belongings other than a small sea chest and the clothes on his back. After a meal, a warming glass of rum, and an hour's charming conversation, he had somehow taken up the position in Miss Venables's life that he had occupied, with few interruptions, ever since.

And really she could not, in any way, admit that she regretted the nuptial arrangement. In addition to his considerable proficiency in the arts of love, Dr. Ansolabehere was quiet and clean, and never attempted to exert control over the household although he was, as she discovered, an excellent financial advisor. He was a capable surgeon (which even the most genteel of taverns required now and then), did not drink to excess, and tolerated her occasional infidelities with the greatest amiability. Best of all, he had an absolutely reliable remedy for the Pox.

There were only two peculiarities about the man: his obstinate refusal to market the remedy, which Mrs. Ansolabehere found most vexing, for it might have earned them more than six sugar plantations if sold freely in Port Royal; and his sea chest.

The sea chest was quite small, quite heavy, and never opened. Indeed, as far as Mrs. Ansolabehere knew its lock had no key. This need not present any difficulty for a determined woman with the proper hairpin, but Dr. Ansolabehere seldom let it out of his sight. Moreover, he had informed her that its contents were private; and Mrs. Ansolabehere had heard enough folk tales, and after all had seen into enough sea chests at her age, to respect his wishes utterly in this regard.

However, he had made one curious request. If at any time during his temporary absence from the house the sea chest should begin to *whistle*, she was to let him know immediately, regardless of where he might be or what he might be doing. So firmly had he insisted upon this, and with such an unpleasant and unaccustomed light of adamance in his black eyes, that Mrs. Ansolabehere had been quite unsettled for some hours afterward.

Judge, then, with what vexation Mrs. Ansolabehere received the news from Caroline, her maid, that there was an odd sound coming from Dr. Ansolabehere's room; especially since this news was conveyed whilst Mrs. Ansolabehere was greeting none other than the Lieutenant Governor himself, Captain Sir Henry Morgan, who had arrived with a party of friends and was intent on aggravating his dropsy with a few hours' determined application of Mrs. Ansolabehere's best rum.

"What?" she hissed over her shoulder at Caroline.

"It be squealing, ma'am," repeated Caroline.

"Why then, go—go poke under the bed with a broom, sure," Mrs. Ansolabehere said. "Away! My apologies, Sir Henry. Here is my best table, with a cool breeze from the door, and here is John to serve. Will you dine, too? For I assure you I have an excellent hotpot on the fire."

"No damn'd soup," growled Sir Henry, lifting his haggard face. "I've enough water in me as it is." He did not resemble the dumpy self-satisfied fellow depicted in Exquemelin's notorious *Buccaneers of America* (a careful examination of its illustrations will reveal that all the pirates in that lurid compendium seem to be drawn from one model) but rather the other attributed likeness, the shadowy three-quarter portrait of the dark saturnine man in red, smiling enigmatically as the Mona Lisa. "Rum, madam! And ginger biscuits if you've got 'em."

"To be sure," Mrs. Ansolabehere said. "Sent hot to the table, sir, within the hour!"

She and Annie, the cook, were frantically getting a pan of ginger biscuits into the oven when Caroline reappeared in the doorway of the kitchen, clutching a broom.

"It be still squealing, ma'am," she said, close to tears. "And it ain't under the doctor's bed, ma'am. It be the little chest what's squealing, ma'am."

Upon hearing this, Mrs. Ansolabehere swore an oath, gathered up her skirts, and ran upstairs to see for herself.

There could be no doubt: the little sea chest *was* whistling where it sat in its accustomed place against the wall on the other side of the bed. Not a live whistling, as though a tiny man or demon were in there, but a shrill mindless noise like an ungreased axle on an oxcart. Mrs. Ansolabehere poked the chest with her foot a few times, experimentally, but the sound changed not in pitch nor stopped; so Mrs. Ansolabehere sensibly shut the door on it and went back downstairs, where she bid Abraham the ostler ride to find Dr. Ansolabehere and give him the news.

Joseph was rather enjoying lying in wait for dreadful and bloody revenge. He had a nice dry place to sleep, decent food, pleasant enough mortal company, and an adequate sex life. All he had to do was stitch up a cutlass wound every now and then and keep a good supply of penicillin on hand.

He had found a reasonably dry limestone cave and fitted it up as a primitive laboratory, which was where he was, preparing another batch of his miracle cure, at the moment the alarm in his sea chest went off.

Probably he was subconsciously aware it had gone off, for he found himself unaccountably restless. Why should he be uneasy? Budu certainly wasn't in any danger. He was recovered enough now to deal with the situation if intruders entered the bunker under Mount Tamalpais in Joseph's absence. Moreover Joseph had gotten the impression that his father was looking forward to a little peace and quiet in which to continue his relentless perusal of classified Company files.

Nor was there any likelihood the time-transcendence container would be discovered, not where Joseph had concealed it. No, his edginess probably came from a pessimistic sense that sooner or later, according to Murphy's Law, the damned alarm would go off when he was here in his secret cave, the one place nobody would be able to find him.

And, of course, this was precisely what had occurred.

What was in the sea chest was equipment that constantly monitored the signals being broadcast through the geosynchronous Company satellite immediately overhead. Budu had identified for him the telltale resonance that would indicate Alec Checkerfield's AI was piggybacking its signal through that satellite, interstitially hidden. The equipment in the chest was programmed to sound an alarm the moment it detected that resonance. The alarm would mean that Alec had come at last to Port Royal, as Budu had predicted he must, sooner or later.

But the Pox was in full flower at the moment, and Joseph had a lot of penicillin to prepare. What with one thing and another it was tropical dusk, full of fireflies and perfume, before Joseph came trudging back to the Goat and Compasses.

"Doctor." Abraham came running out to meet him. "Oh, sir, we been searching for you these four hours! Ma'am says you must come straightaway."

"What's the matter?" asked Joseph, instantly alert.

Before Abraham could make reply, however, a snarling figure lurched into the doorway and fixed Joseph with an unwavering stare, which must have been difficult given that he was seeing at least four of Joseph.

"You. Doctor! I wan' bleeding, d'y'hear?" croaked Captain Sir Henry Morgan.

"Well, of course, Sir Henry," Joseph said cheerily, assuming that a drunken and belligerent Lieutenant Governor was the emergency for which he had been summoned. "At once. Shall we retire to a private room?"

"But, Doctor—" said Abraham.

"Naaah," said Sir Henry, staggering out into the yard in his shirtsleeves.

He waved an arm at the tavern dismissively. "Too bloody hot innere. Le's do it here." He collapsed on a bench.

"A wise choice, Sir Henry," said Joseph, opening his bag and rummaging through it. "The evening air is blessedly refreshing, do you not find it so? And, I'm sure, will speedily revive one, should one grow faint in the course of the operation. Abraham, fetch me a bowl from the kitchen."

"But, Doctor—" said Abraham.

"Not gonna fucking *faint!*" said Sir Henry, outraged. "Good God! Good God, what d'y'take me for, man? Y'know what I done at Panama? Eh? Y'think I'm a man to swound at the sighta li'l blood?"

"No indeed, Sir Henry," Joseph said, rolling up the Lieutenant Governor's sleeve and swabbing down his inner arm with a handkerchief soaked in spirits. He glanced up as Abraham came hurrying out with the bowl, followed by Mrs. Ansolabehere, who remained near the door, making impatient faces at him. "I meant rather my poor man here might faint. Here, Abraham, hold it close. Wife, I have come, what more can I do?" he snapped at Mrs. Ansolabehere, who straightened up in annoyance and decided she'd done all that spousal obedience required of her. She turned on her heel and went back inside.

Joseph deftly opened a vein and listened for a while as Sir Henry expounded ramblingly on his personal theories for the cure of dropsy, which seemed to consist principally of restricting his diet to warming substances that might drive out all his watery humors by their fiery and subtle operation on the blood. Highly spiced food was therefore certain to do him good, as was rum, being a flammable spirit, so if he could just manage to drink enough of it . . .

By the time Joseph had Sir Henry's arm bandaged and escorted him back to his party, night had fallen. It wasn't until he was trudging through the hall on his way to the staircase that Mrs. Ansolabehere was able to lean out of the kitchen door and inform him:

"Your sea chest is whistling, husband."

What a look of consternation on his face! With a piercing yelp of dismay he was gone, and she heard his thundering footsteps as he sped up the stairs and across the hall to his room. A second or so later the footsteps came thundering back down, accompanied by the high-pitched whistling, which was now a little louder and more insistent. Mrs. Ansolabehere stepped out in the hall to explain that she had *tried* to tell him, but she never had that satisfaction: for Joseph, bearing the sea chest in his arms like a crying child, was across the common room and out the door before she could utter a word. There was a clatter of hoofbeats starting up suddenly and fading out as someone galloped away.

"Ma'am." Abraham ran in, eyes wide. He was carrying Joseph's long wig in his hands, having been hit in the face by it as Joseph cast it off. He came close to her and said in an undertone, "Doctor's just rode off on Captain Marley's horse without a by-y'leave!"

Mrs. Ansolabehere uttered another oath, rather worse than the one she had uttered earlier in the day. Putting on her most inviting smile, she grabbed up an onion bottle of the cheaper sort of rum and advanced on the table where Sir Henry and his guests (including Captain Marley) were still carousing.

"Now, my fine gentlemen, what about a dish of turtle stew with peppers, hotter than Hell and sweeter than Heaven? And more rum all round? Come, it is a black day when I cannot treat such heroes in my poor establishment!"

Those present who were still capable of understanding what she had just said raised a hoarse cheer. She thumped down the bottle on their table and hurried back to the kitchen for a tureen of stew, hoping to God her husband brought back Captain Marley's horse before he sobered up enough to notice it was gone.

## THAT SAME EVENING IN PORT ROYAL, 1682 AD

***There it is,*** the Captain said. ***What d'you think?***

Mendoza, in a gown of emerald silk and lace that left her shoulders bare as the heroine of any pirate film, sought in the ruin of her memory for comparison. It told her only that Port Royal looked like any other little waterfront city she had seen. It had brick houses, crowded along narrow lanes and alleys. It stank badly, too.

Alec gaped and wondered. It didn't look anything like New Port Royal, which was largely an enormous outdoor shopping mall built out on pilings over the archaeological site. "It looks so old," he said.

*Well, it ain't. It ain't even been here thirty year, and it's only got another ten to go afore the earthquake sinks it. Mighty short space of time to get the reputation it has, aye; but if you wanted to catch yerself a disease or lose a few thousand doubloons in an hour, I reckon this here's the place you'd come. Now, you ain't staying no longer than it takes to do the deed, matey, understand?*

"We'll be back by twenty-three-hundred hours," Mendoza promised, watching Alec as he went to the davits and vaulted into the the boat. He was dressed for the occasion in knee breeches and seaboots and a full white shirt, and over all a long coat of brocade edged in gold, in which she thought he was desperately handsome.

Under this dashing ensemble Edward had insisted that Alec wear his full complement of stealth weapons, so there were at least three knives, a garrote, and a mid-nineteenth-century pistol on which to rely in the event of trouble, to say nothing of the brace of flintlock pistols and cutlass that Alec wore openly. All the same, Mendoza and the Captain had agreed between them that any mortal threatening Alec would be rendered harmless, one way or another, before the need for weapons arose.

*And where's the toy, now, lass?*

Mendoza placed a demure hand in her bosom and withdrew something that looked like a rock, roughly the size and shape of an egg. There was absolutely no indication, looking at it, that it was full of what resembled gold paint; or that on a certain day in 2355 it would fulfill its potential and build itself into an antigravity missile. No marine archaeologist encountering it in the sunken ruins beforehand would bother to bring an ordinary lump of stone to the surface. With a smile she tucked it back out of sight and accepted Alec's hand as he helped her over the side. The dolphins cruised to and fro in an inconspicuous sort of way, scanning the waters.

Alec rowed out into the harbor, under the hot sky of Jamaica that he had known all his life, over the familiar waters of Kingston Bay that he'd crossed a hundred times: but there before him in the pink evening light lay the utterly alien place of his dreams, enchanting and deadly.

He stared around as they began to pass between the ships. He knew most of them had to be merchant vessels really, and none of them flew black flags in port. All the same, some had seen fighting, bore the scars of powder and ball. They were stripped-down and sleek, lines taut, every-thing businesslike and efficient. Though the black mouths of their guns were hollow and silent, they exhaled menace. It was terrifying to pass them.

They tied up at the Queen Street dock and walked ashore. Edward brusquely took control as they neared their first group of obvious bucca-neers, picturesque, filthy, and very drunk, happily looking for trouble. One glance into Edward's cold eyes, though, and they crossed to the other side of the lane.

There were pretty black women selling food: roasted yams, bullas and fried cakes, cut coconuts ready to be sipped and nibbled from, star-apples and plantains. There were respectable shops with wares displayed in their respectable windows: blue willow china, porcelain dogs, Dutch faience ware to catch the eye of the idling shopper for an impulse purchase. Banal and ordinary, until one reflected that some ship had been assailed in blood and screaming and fire for these consumer goods.

There were houses three and even four stories high, that had clearly grown in segments as the fortunes of their owners had leapt unsteadily upward. At their windows, bawds and strumpets watched the passers be-low in languid boredom, or leaned down their long curls and the occa-sional badly-secured tit and called enticements into the street. Mendoza sneered at them, clinging firmly to Edward's arm.

The churches looked as rawly new, as badly planned, as grubbily busy as the rest of the place. Nicholas regarded them in wonder. He was not so much amazed by the fact that prostitutes and thieves were flocking in to evening prayer (who could be more in need of salvation, after all?), but there was a Roman Catholic church within blocks of a Protestant one and both were doing about equal business, coexisting peacefully.

Alec gasped at the stench, and then at the displayed carcasses, as they came upon the meat market. Edward was amused at his reaction and Nicholas bewildered, for it was no worse than any meat market *he* had ever seen. The reek of raw sewage and unwashed bodies was fairly pal-pable, too, but the pleasant smells were also formidable: perfumes strong enough to knock you down breathing out of the apothecaries' shops, sup-pers cooking in the taverns and bakehouses, tobacco smoke, cloves, san-dalwood, spilled rum.

As the night purpled and lamps began to flare, they found themselves looking into a goldsmith's window, admiring the rings and rough-cut jewels in settings.

"Did we ever have wedding rings?" Mendoza wondered suddenly, looking up at Alec, who happened to have control at that moment.

Alec looked down at her, feeling at tug at his heart. "We never had a chance to get any," he said at last. "Come on." He pulled her into the goldsmith's shop with him, and a while later they emerged, with a small box containing a pair of rings that had been cast from one Spanish doubloon.

A few streets farther on, in an area that history would record as never being fully excavated by marine archaeologists, they found an inn of the nicer sort: half-timbered brick, three stories, leaded glass windows without even a glimpse of prostitutes at them.

There were ladies of questionable profession, it is true, sitting inside the dark paneled common room, with heavily-wigged gentlemen in long waistcoats, and the air was blue with smoke from churchwarden pipes. There were one or two scarred and evil-looking men seated at a game of cards in the lamplight. It was a quiet place all the same, just what the Captain had told them to look for. Edward found the publican and ordered dinner for two, to be served in a private room upstairs.

They waited on a settle while their order was got ready. Alec sat staring around, drinking in every detail: the pewter tankards and leather drinking-jacks, the onion bottles, the herringbone-brick floor. It was just like his dreams, only dirtier.

Mendoza was thinking that it wasn't so bad, really. Vaguely she could remember a worse place, and thought it might have been called *Los Angeles*, just as dangerous and less fun overall. She did not relax her guard, however, remaining prepared to break mortal necks if there was any danger to Alec.

Edward watched tensely, no less on edge than she, sizing up the ugliest of the card players. Nicholas waited beside him, and of all of them he felt perhaps most lost: for the room was like a room in Tudor London, and yet just enough was unfamiliar to bewilder him. He sighed and perched on an edge of the settle beside Mendoza, reflecting that he might have carried her away with him to some such place as this . . . if it hadn't been raining, that last day. If the roads hadn't been muddy. If it hadn't been a

bitter cold night. If . . . Nicholas sighed and attempted, with his usual lack
of success, to provide himself with a virtual pot of ale.

The publican appeared out of the smoke to tell them their room was
ready. He showed them up to it, bowing them in with a flourish (Edward
had paid in gold) and departed discreetly. There they stood, staring. In addition to the candlelit supper for two they had ordered, there was a
canopied bed in the room. Alec nearly pushed Edward over in his haste to
grab control back.

"How very romantic, señor," said Mendoza.

They looked at each other and then, uttering identical whoops of delight, leaped on the bed, with its fine tapestry counterpane and its bol-
sters. Mendoza had to lay aside two flintlock pistols and a cutlass and
Alec had to plow through yards and yards of ruffling silk before they
could obtain their objective, but obtain it at last they did. Passersby in the
street below stared up at the open window in envy, at the wild laughter
and wilder moans issuing from up there.

Therefore it was a little while before any attention was paid to supper:
turtle soup and smoked pork loin, peas, rice, and yams, and a bottle each
of sherry and rum. Mendoza looked at Alec's face above the waving candle
flames, and suddenly the laughter went out of her eyes.

"Wait. We did this before," she said nervously, "Once. Didn't we?
Weren't we in a room like this, and we ate supper at a little table, and
you . . . you were angry about something?"

Nicholas seized control and reached out—across how many centuries
of lost time? —to take her hand. "I was a fool," he said. "And would to
God we'd run away then, and not waited for morning!"

"But what happened?"

"I had a chance, and I wasted it," he told her, blinking back tears. Groping in his pocket with his free hand, he found the box from the goldsmith's shop.

"Here!" Nicholas pulled her to the window, to the vista of blue night
with its million stars, over doomed Port Royal that echoed with drunken
singing. "Here. Without are dogs and enchanters, whoremongers and
murderers; but let them bear witness." He took out the smaller of the two
rings and raised her left hand, slipping it on her finger.

"So. I will cleave to thee and be thy husband, and never forsake thee again, but share thy fortunes through the world. And wilt thou have me, love?" he pleaded, taking her two hands in his own.

"But I've always been your wife," Mendoza said. Taking up the other ring she put it on his finger, and folded his hand closed. "There."

He caught her up and kissed her, and they swayed together in the candlelight before the window. Down in the street, weaving between the shadows cast by the flickering torches, a staggering wanderer applauded them.

Nicholas half-thought he might die then, dissolve into a memory in Alec's blood, finally granted absolution; but nothing happened except that Alec, who had sworn he'd never marry again, kissed Mendoza. Edward, who had sworn he'd never marry at all, kissed her, too.

So they sat down to their wedding supper at last, a hundred and twenty-seven years late, and drank to their future.

Long afterward they descended to the common room. Mendoza waited in a corridor while Edward found his way to the jakes, which were quite the most noisome he'd ever encountered, and under pretext of pissing used the opportunity to drop the mine down a hole in the floor. He emerged gratefully, and they went out again into the fevered night.

The mine stayed where it had been dropped, through earthquake and flood and terrifying numbers of years, until the afternoon in 2355 when it woke to its programmed destiny. But Mendoza and her husbands walked back to Queen Street without incident and rowed out to the *Captain Morgan*, where they came aboard quietly and went to bed in peace.

Joseph had had an eventful, and terribly slow, ride to Port Royal.

Galloping through the dark and the fireflies, he had three times been halted by thieves demanding his purse. He had stopped only long enough to kill them like cockroaches and ride on; but the third one had shot his horse, after which he was compelled to run. Hyperfunction, it should be noted here, is easy enough for an immortal but cannot be sustained indefinitely, particularly when the immortal in question is attempting to carry a heavy sea chest. In any event, it was four o'clock in the morning before Joseph, limping and panting, staggered into Port Royal and made his way to the waterfront adjacent to Lime Street, carrying the sea chest swathed in his coat to muffle its squealing.

Spotting a likely boat tied at the dock, he jumped down into it and cast off, rowing swiftly out into the harbor. When he was far enough from shore to be unobserved he shipped the oars and sat still a moment, catching his breath. At last he reached forward and depressed an unseen catch. He opened the lid of the sea chest.

The squealing was immediately louder, and the colored lights inside blinked frantically until he reached in and turned a knob. At once the shrill noise stopped, the red lights went out; but the green and yellow ones continued to blink at him.

He considered them, tilting his head as though listening to the night, as his boat rocked on the tide.

It was blessedly quiet, with the alarm shut off at last. Across the black water he could hear the sounds of Port Royal in its fitful sleep: a single dog barking at two drunks reeling home, glass breaking in an alley somewhere. A rooster called attention to the fading stars, for it was by now nearly five o'clock. Joseph listened, still turning his head this way and that, but seemed unsatisfied. At last he turned away from the harbor, out toward the Caribbean.

Almost at once he stiffened and leaned forward. There! His attention focused on an immense and indistinct something moored well off Lime Cay. His eyes narrowed, his lips drew back from his teeth in a grimace of concentration.

Then he began to chuckle, most unpleasantly.

"You son of a bitch," he told the big ship. And how swiftly and neatly he dipped the oars in the water again, and how quickly he rowed out across the night ocean, making for his prey; and how surprised would have been anyone who knew the obliging little doctor from the Goat and Compasses, if they'd seen the expression of animal ferocity on his face in that dark morning.

The closer he got to the big ship, the blurrier and more confusing its outline became. The only constants were its two running lights and a faint amber glow toward its stern. When he had crossed three-quarters of the

distance he paused, shipping the oars again, and reached into the seach-
est. He cast an involuntary glance upward in the direction of the satellite.

Thirty meters away, something surfaced and regarded him with unfor-
giving red eyes. It cut smoothly through the dark water toward him. From
three other directions, dorsal fins rose into sight and sped forward, con-
verging on Joseph's boat.

Joseph was too preoccupied with what he was doing to notice them.
He turned two knobs at once, in opposite directions.

All the lights on the big ship went out. Suddenly it stood exposed, out-
lined black against the pale gleam of morning with no blurring, no confusion whatever: unmistakably one of the vast pleasure yachts of the
twenty-fourth century. Joseph had broadcast a signal to jam the Captain's
interface, cutting him off from the satellite and from Alec as effectively as
though he didn't exist. It was only a matter of time, of course, before an AI
that powerful and resourceful remodulated its signal around the jamming; but it doesn't take long to kill a mortal man.

Something hit the hull of Joseph's boat, throwing him backward where
he sat. Heart pounding, he scrambled up again, on the defensive. No further blows came; but there in the water beside him was the smooth
finned menace, motionless, its momentum lost. Shark? He grabbed an
oar and jabbed at the thing.

The oar hit with an unexpected *clunk* and the object bobbed gently.
Joseph eyed it, suspicious. Some kind of torpedo? He pulled the oar back
in haste, but whatever it was just continued to float there, harmless.
Harmless *now*. Scanning, Joseph noted the circuitry, the electronic confusion and paralysis.

"Son of a bitch," he said. "Robot Flipper."

His unsettling grin returning, Joseph dipped the oars again. He pulled
smoothly forward to close the last of the distance to the big ship. Drawing
alongside, he tied up to its anchor-hawse and then, hand over hand,
moved silently up the wet cable and so came aboard her.


Alec opened his eyes and looked around. Edward and Nicholas, just
opening their eyes on either side of him, scowled. Underneath him Mendoza slept on, sprawled in yards of white silk trimmed with lace.

There she was, truly his wife now, and here he was still half dressed in his pirate clothes, and he had just had the most wonderful night of his life, with everything he had ever wanted at last. Whether he deserved it or not.

So why did he have the overpowering sense that something was horribly wrong?

*Captain?*

There was no answer.

*Look at the machine,* cried Edward, sitting bolt upright. Alec turned and saw Flint, immobile, frozen in the act of picking up his brocaded coat from where he'd thrown it the night before.

That was when he heard the faint but unmistakable sound of footsteps on the deck.

He slid out of bed and sat on the edge, hastily pulling on his boots. Mendoza curled on her side, murmuring something nonsensical, still fast asleep. Alec bound on his cutlass and stuck one of the flintlock pistols into his belt.

He closed the stateroom door behind him and cautiously made his way through the saloon to the deck, with Edward and Nicholas stalking alongside. As he stepped out to the pale morning, he reached into the ship's security system with his mind and ordered an emergency lockdown. All over the ship, then, he heard bolts shooting into place, locks ringing shut.

Someone else heard it, too. Someone who had been standing half hidden by the foremast turned, stared along the length of the deck and met Alec's stare.

Joseph smiled, an ironic and mirthless smile that twisted into his beard.

"Hello there, *pendejo,*" he said, and without haste he began to walk toward Alec.

Neither of them was prepared for what happened next, however.

*"Doctor Ruy!"* howled Nicholas, seizing control. He drew the cutlass and charged Joseph, who stopped smiling and halted in his advance.

"Wait a minute," he said, and winked out. Nicholas skidded to a stop and swung about, snarling.

"Where art thou," he shouted, hoarse with rage, "devil from Hell?"

*"Who* did you call me?" inquired a voice from the foretop. They

looked up, Nicholas and Edward and Alec, and beheld Joseph staring down in consternation.

"Devil," Nicholas said through his teeth. "Come down, thou coward, and be cut to pieces an I cannot kill thee."

"No," said Joseph. "The other thing you called me! What did you say my name was?"

"Doctor Ruy Anzolabejar," said Nicholas, sheathing the cutlass and starting up the fore shrouds after him. "Or it may be Lucifer, or it may be Legion. Wilt thou live still with thy head off?"

*Nicholas, wait,* said Alec. *He's an immortal! Do you want to get us killed? We have to explain—*

"How the hell do you know that name?" Joseph said. "And why are you speaking Tudor English?"

Nicholas laughed, pausing in his climb up the shrouds to stare at him. His pupils were black and enormous.

"Oh, Doctor Ruy," he said, shaking his head. "Hast thou forgotten *my* name?"

"Well, it can't be Nicholas Harpole," said Joseph, backing rapidly into the upper shrouds. "Because he's dead!"

"Ay, and haunting thee," Nicholas said, pulling himself nimbly over the futtock shrouds and seating himself on the foretop. Withdrawing the flintlock pistol from his belt, he took careful aim and fired at Joseph, who winked out and promptly reappeared across from him on the main top.

"Say, you don't seem to have brought your powder horn with you, Nicholas," remarked Joseph, grinning. "And you can only fire those old babies once without reloading, you know."

Nicholas shrugged and thrust it back into his belt. He turned and began to work his way out along the yard, footing it carefully across the stirrups.

*Stop him!* cried Alec, pulled stumbling along.

*You damned lunatic!* Edward fought for control, without success.

"So anyway," Joseph continued, "I need to get this cleared up before I kill you. Who are you really? If you actually are Nicholas Harpole, you're looking pretty good for a pile of cinders."

Nicholas didn't deign to answer, edging out to the end of the yard. At this moment they heard a crash from below, and a desperate pounding, but neither man dared take his eyes off the other.

"Of course, it wasn't really the fire did you in," Joseph said. "It was the kegs of gunpowder. Remember that? Tied around your chest, a little friendly push to send you off to Hell? And I thought it did. I mean, it really blew, I watched your liver and probably half your spinal column go flying—SHIT!"

This remark was occasioned by the fact that Nicholas, clinging to the yard, had managed at last to exert his physical will on the ship's rigging system. With a low metallic scream the whole spar was turning ponderously, a half-rotation as though to catch the wind, enabling him to ride it around to the point of the main yard, to which he leaped and clung, glaring in triumph at Joseph.

"Nice jumping, Quasimodo," Joseph said, scrambling to his feet and edging out along the opposite arm. "So you've been cyborged, or you wouldn't have been able to control the rigging like that. And that would mean you're really Alec Checkerfield, AKA his lordship the seventh earl of Finsbury, right? So, why are you claiming to be the guy who wrecked my daughter's life, back in 1555?"

"Thou liest," Nicholas said, coming rapidly after him. "Thou art Father of Lies, but never her father."

"No, only the guy who gave her eternal life, okay?" Joseph shouted. "And with immortals, that counts for something. Not that I was a very good father, I have to admit. I didn't see what was coming when she fell for you!"

"Thou whoreson pander, *thou* madest the match," Nicholas said, coming faster now. "Bid a little virgin girl beguile thine enemy, so thou mightst work thy treasons unobserved!"

*You fool, what does that matter now?* Edward fought again for control and was cast off with a force that made him see stars.

Joseph came to the end of the yard and paused there, looking around, squinting in the growing light from the east. Winking out was beginning to be difficult, tired as he was. Cursing, he hung by his hands a moment and then launched himself at the main shrouds, where he caught hold and began to scramble his way down.

"You got any more of those pistols, Nicholas or Alec or whoever you are?" he called out, as Nicholas came after him hand-over-hand. "I'll bet if I can get to one before you do, I can blow you right back to wherever you've been all this time. Only problem is, could I be sure you'd stay there?"

*Nick, let's be reasonable about this, man! It's not his fault you died, after all*— said Alec, but he might have been pleading with a stone wall.

The pounding from within the ship was louder now, frenzied as they both neared the deck. Abruptly it fell silent.

"Was that her?" Joseph turned an outraged face up to Nicholas. "Have you got her locked up in there? Has she finally had enough of you? You never loved her. You're using her to find out about the Silence, aren't you? That's really why you took her from Options Research, isn't it? It's *your* fault she wound up in that place! Did you like seeing what you'd done to her?"

Nicholas halted at that, looked down into Joseph's eyes with an expression so like Budu's that all Joseph's fury evaporated in panic terror. Just as Nicholas thrust out an arm, grabbing for his throat, Joseph let go the ratlines and jumped the rest of the way, landing on the deck with a hollow *boom.*

Then he had to run, for Nicholas leaped down after him, and he sprinted for the quarterdeck with Nicholas in hot pursuit. He had just time to rattle futilely at the door of the saloon before he had to dart away again, around the mizzenmast and back along the deck toward the bow, barely ahead of Nicholas. Nicholas had drawn the cutlass as he chased him and raised it for a head-cut, slashing it through the air so that on two occasions it actually did come uncomfortably close to Joseph's neck gimbal, and this plus the very real horror he felt at the idea of a New Enforcer on the loose now decided Joseph that the game had gone on long enough.

He was as close to collapse from exhaustion as an immortal can be, after the night he'd had, but he summoned a last burst of speed and sprang up on the foredeck, and from there over the starboard rail into the bowsprit netting.

Nicholas vaulted after him and came to the rail, glaring down, for he had heard no splash; but Joseph was not there under the bowsprit, where he had expected to see him. Joseph was behind him, having scrambled back around on the port side. He grabbed up one of the decorative belaying pins upon which Alec had insisted when the ship had been designed. Joseph had to spring into the air to club Nicholas with it, but he managed to connect with a crack that echoed across the water. Nicholas toppled forward, unconscious. So, unfortunately, did Alec and Edward, obliged to share Nicholas's concussion.

"Damn," gasped Joseph, clutching his side with one hand. He staggered and sat down heavily.

"Now, the only reason I haven't killed you yet," a voice was saying as Alec opened his eyes and groaned, "is because I want some answers first."

The sense of something-being-horribly-wrong was a lot stronger now than it had been the last time he had awakened, with very good reason. His hands were tightly bound behind his back and secured to his belt; moreover he was hanging upside down, having been trussed around the ankles with a clewline and hauled up to dangle in midair. Joseph was sitting on the deck with the other end of the clewline in his hand, watching him.

"How's it going, big boy?" he said. "Actually that's a rhetorical question, because I don't give a rat's ass. Here come the real questions, okay? Number one: Where's Mendoza?"

"Piss off!" said Alec, and Joseph grinned.

"Wrong answer," he said, and let go the clewline so that Alec plummeted toward the deck. He caught it again, just before Alec's head hit wood.

"Next time I won't grab it so fast," Joseph said. "It's okay if you don't want to tell me where she is. I'll find her if I have to take this ship apart. So, let's move on to question number two: Just exactly what are you, Nicholas? Give me the specs on the New Enforcer."

"I'd be happy to explain at some length," said his prisoner, "in any other position. If I lose consciousness, threats shan't avail you much, I'm afraid."

Joseph sighed.

"Okay, who the hell is *that*? How many of you are in there?" His face darkened. "Have you developed a multiple personality disorder or something? Oh my God, you have, haven't you? You've figured out yet another way to make my baby miserable, you son of a bitch!" And he bared his teeth and gave the clewline a jerk, so that Edward felt as though his shoulders would dislocate, but he endured it and said:

"No, no, nothing like that at all! You're quite correct: the Company had a hand in my making. Our making, I should say. I wonder if you can guess the rest of it?"

"I wonder how hard your head is in relation to that deck?" growled Joseph. "But okay. Some kind of serial immortality? The Company maybe experimenting, with memory transferred from body to body? Huh." He looked impressed in spite of himself. "Well, it obviously works. So you must be some kind of clone, then, right? Produced from Nicholas? But—"

"You'll have to excuse him, I'm afraid," said Edward with his most temporizing smile, though the effect was slightly lessened by the fact that he was hanging upside down. "He really does hate you with quite an irrational passion. And poor Nicholas is, after all, the product of an ignorant and superstitious age, with an accordingly limited capacity for any understanding of science—"

He grimaced and shut his eyes for a moment, fighting back Nicholas's attempt to break free, but Alec more or less sat on Nicholas for him. Joseph watched closely. Edward drew breath, opened his eyes, and continued: "I beg your pardon. The vertigo does make it difficult to give you the answers you need. And in any case, sir, neither you nor I have any reason to be at odds with each other. If you'd just let me down—"

"Like hell I will," Joseph said, scowling as he stepped close to stare at him. "I know who you are, now. You're that Brit secret agent who got himself shot to death in Los Angeles, aren't you? Edward something?"

"Commander Edward Alton Bell-Fairfax, late of Her Majesty's Royal Navy, at your service, sir," Edward said, politely enough under the circumstances. "And not quite as dead as you'd think."

"Too bad," said Joseph tightly. "Mendoza went nuts and killed six mortals because of you. And, you know what else? You got my best friend killed."

"I should be sorry to think so, sir, but I don't recall—"

"No, you don't recall! You were able to do it from your goddam grave, okay? Lewis found your daguerreotype portrait. He realized you were something weird. He became obsessed with you." Joseph gulped for breath. "The Company found out he knew too much, and they screwed him. He's someplace as bad as Options Research, if he's even still alive. That's your fault!"

"Then allow me to make amends, sir," said Edward in a reasonable voice. He was beginning to realize in horror that his captor hadn't quite got both oars in the water, and negotiation might be futile. "If you were to release me, I might be able to rescue the fellow. After all, I rescued my wife from a similar—"

"She's not your wife!" Joseph said, yanking on the line nearly hard enough to dislocate Edward's ankles, too. In his momentary agony and chagrin at having picked the wrong thing to say, Edward lost control and Nicholas surged to the fore.

"Ay, devil, my bride and my flesh," Nicholas said, grinning. "Sealed to me of her own will in despite of all thou couldst do, in a holy bond—"

"In an unholy bond," Joseph snarled. "What's she known from the day she met you but grief? It wasn't enough you broke her heart getting yourself burned, no. You had to come back and drive her crazy! And you taught her to kill mortals, which is something you're really good at, too, isn't it? It's what you were made for, huh, Mr. New Enforcer? Only the Company designed *you* to kill innocents. Like in Mars Two!"

But Nicholas had stopped listening to him and was laughing in his throat, teeth clenched as he concentrated with a glittering stare on the main yard immediately above Joseph. As Joseph ranted on, he got it to release. With a clinking *whoosh* it came plummeting down, and Joseph had just time to register what was happening before he leaped clear, letting go the clewline as he did so.

Nicholas was able to writhe as he fell and land on one shoulder, with a grunt of pain. As he lay there gasping, Alec grabbed control.

"Look, man, I never wanted to kill anybody," he yelled. "Nobody told me what I was! I didn't find out the Company'd been running my life until a couple of years ago."

"Ha. Alec Checkerfield, I presume? You know, pal, I believe you," wheezed Joseph, tottering over to the cutlass and picking it up. He sighted along its blade at Alec. "The way the Company jerks its people around. But you're pure poison and you never should have existed in the first place, and I'll be doing everybody, and I mean everybody, a favor by running you through with your very own authentic pirate cutlass. Jesus, Alec, why pirates?"

"No! Please, not now, not like this, my life will have been for nothing!" Alec cried from his heart, squirming backward. "How am I ever going to make up for what I did?"

"You can die and leave Mendoza in peace, how about that?" Joseph offered, making an experimental lunge with the blade.

"You don't understand!" Alec said. "I know I'm a shracking monster, but I love her. I've been taking care of her, she's been happy! Doesn't that mean anything to you, if you love her, too? For the first time in her life, she's not a slave! And she loves me."

"Says you," Joseph told him wearily, pacing toward him with the cutlass. "The really awful part is, no matter how many times I kill you, the Company'll just bring you back again, won't they? But you won't get *her* again, punk. Think about that while you're regrowing in your jar—"

At this moment the forward hatch exploded upward in a mass of fragments and splinters, glinting in the first light of the sun. Mendoza rose through it, eyes ablaze with fury. Her white silk was torn and trailing after her journey through the emergency access crawlspace in the bulkheads, and she was armed with the first weapon that had come to hand in Alec's weapons locker, which happened to be a double-barreled speargun. From the hatchway after her came snaking grapevines, waving and crawling toward the morning light.

Joseph, regaining his feet after leaping back from the explosion, stared at her. Then he drew a long breath, and exhaled.

"Mendoza," he said pleasantly. "Baby. Nice to see you again, kid. You know, and I mean this sincerely, you look great—"

She leveled the speargun at him and fired.

"Okay, so you're a little sore at me," he said from the foretop, as the head of a spear plunked into the rail immediately behind where he'd been standing a split second earlier. Looking up and fixing him with a black glare, she backed toward Alec. She knelt to unpinion him with one hand, keeping the speargun trained on Joseph. The vines began to scale the foremast in an aggressive kind of way.

"So I was about to kill the boyfriend. I'm sorry, okay? But I've been kind of worried. I thought maybe you were hurt, or something. I mean, you never called. You never wrote."

"Why the hell should I?" she said. "I haven't the slightest idea who you are."

"What?" Joseph peered down at her, as she freed Alec's hands and moved to untie his ankles. "What do you mean, you don't know who I am?" He leaned forward to scan her, so far he nearly fell from his perch on the foretop. "You've known me since you were four years old!"

"Stay up there," she ordered, keeping the gun trained on him. "I've never seen you before in my life, but I'd be delighted to pin you to that mast."

But Joseph was still scanning, looking distressed.

"You've been damaged!" he said. "Somebody's rebuilt you, and they didn't do it to specs—and there's some kind of block on your memory."

Mendoza ignored Joseph, lifting Alec into a sitting position, and as he hissed in pain and clutched at his left arm she scanned him. Then she looked up at Joseph with a murderous expression.

"You've broken his shoulder! Severe concussion, scalp laceration, multiple sprains and contusions . . . little man, I'll kill you."

She aimed the speargun and fired again, just as the first green tendril groped at Joseph's ankle. Joseph avoided the spear by throwing himself sideways, which carried him off the foretop into midair. He twisted to land on his feet and fell and rolled, springing up again in a crouch.

"Nice shot, but you don't have any other spears in that gun, do you?"

"No, but I can club you with it," she said, rotating it swiftly in her hand. "And if you come any closer to him, I will."

"Mendoza, honey, you wouldn't do that," he said coaxingly, stepping over the sprawling vines. "And anyway, I'm not after that big loser now. Trust me! All I want to do is have a look at that block on your memory, okay? I can fix it. You'll be good as new, little girl. Come on, you can't be comfortable like that—"

He was advancing on her steadily, one hand stretched out in a placatory gesture, and she was trembling as she gripped the speargun.

"What are you, crazy?" Alec said hoarsely, struggling to get between them. "Stop it! You know where she was. You know what happened there! *Do you want her to remember that?*"

Joseph stopped, staring at Alec. He was just opening his mouth to speak when earsplitting Klaxons sounded, causing sleepers across the bay in Port Royal to sit up in their beds and wonder if Judgment Day had come. It was still ten years away, however. The Klaxons, warbling down into a sort of electronic growl of rage, were merely the Captain signaling that he had at last remodulated around the jammed signal and was very much back online.

From all parts of the ship came the sound of locks snapping, drives powering up, and a clashing noise that grew louder, resolving into the scuttling approach of Billy Bones, Flint, Coxinga, and Bully Hayes. The servounits emerged from the saloon and advanced on Joseph menacingly, chattering like so many giant steel crabs.

"Whoops," said Joseph, and turned and ran. He vaulted over the rail with all four of them still in hot pursuit. Landing neatly in his stolen boat, he cast off, bent to the oars, and rowed away like mad.

Before he had got well clear, however, he saw with horror that gunports were opening out in the formidable side of the *Captain Morgan,* and the mouths of what could only be laser cannon were emerging. They swiveled to aim, and fired in unison, but he had already plunged into the water and was diving down for dear life. The laser broadside vaporized both his boat and the sea chest containing his signal monitor.

Peering up from below, Joseph saw four black shapes diving toward him. They nipped at his desperately kicking heels all the way back to Port Royal, and squealed insults at him as he waded ashore.


THE EVENING OF THAT SAME DAY, 1682 AD

Mrs. Ansolabehere was not disposed to be charitable when Dr. Ansolabehere finally returned. This in spite of the fact that his face was gray with fatigue, his clothing ruined, his hat lost, his beady little eyes sunk back in his head. Smiling and curtseying to a departing customer, she swept down on him where he stood swaying in the doorway and frogmarched him back to the kitchen, where she boxed his ears soundly.

"Where hast thou been, sir?" she hissed. "Art thou drunk? Art thou mad? And wherever is Captain Marley's horse?"

He stood there in stupefaction a moment, clutching his ears. Then he began to glare resentfully, and without a word he strode over to the bar and helped himself to an onion bottle of rum. As she looked on unbelieving he extracted the cork with his teeth, spat it across the room, and drank half the rum as though it were water.

"What, husband!" she said.

"I'll tell you what, wife," he said, wiping his chin. "The horse is dead. I'm mad, all right, and I'm going to be drunk pretty damned fast, for all the good it'll do me. What else? Oh, where've I been? Well, that's a long story, and I don't feel like telling it right now."

She just stared at him. He scowled at her and drank down the rest of the rum. Then he helped himself to two more bottles and marched out the back door.

She never set eyes on him again.

## MOUNT TAMALPAIS, 2322 AD

The giant under the mountain was aware when the outer threshold was crossed. He withdrew his attention from the Company files through which he had been cruising, relentlessly as a shark, and focused on the tunnel. After a millisecond's analysis of the approaching footsteps' rhythm he relaxed. He rose from the console, looming in a shapeless robe made from blankets, and watched as Joseph came tottering down the aisle between the vaults.

"Son," he said.

"I'm back," Joseph replied. "How's it going, Father?"

They considered each other. It had been nearly twenty years since Joseph had seen Budu, though of course from Budu's point of view it had been no more than a few days. Joseph thought Budu looked great. Budu thought Joseph looked as though he'd been through a wringer.

"You failed to recapture your daughter," Budu stated.

"Yeah," Joseph agreed. He sank down and stretched out on the stone floor, folding his hands on his chest.

"It doesn't matter. She might have been useful, but we won't need her for victory. While she's with that boy, the Company can't use her either. I've been finding out a lot about him. Interesting."

"Uh-huh." Joseph closed his eyes. Budu inhaled the scent of rank exhaustion and alcohol, and grimaced, but kept annoyance out of his voice as he said:

"You look tired, son. You'll need to rest for a few days. Restore yourself to optimum physical status. I have work for you to do."

"Okay."

"You'll begin by completing the corrective surgery on my right arm."

"Okay."

"Then you'll go out again. I have a list of things to be stolen. It may take you years to get everything. You must also seek out a certain man and speak to him. You'll need to prepare carefully for this, and exert your powers of influence. He's necessary to our plan."

"Okay. How's the plan going?" Joseph opened his eyes again.

"Completed." Budu smiled in a fashion that would have terrified anybody but Joseph. The blue light glinted on his teeth, his eyes. "All potential elements in place. We'll bring the masters down with one strike. I know the hour and the location. You have only to wind the clock, son."

"Sure. Sure, I can do that." Joseph yawned. "So what about this guy I'm supposed to talk to?"

"A unique case, son. A living riddle. Immortal, but not one of us. A Company stockholder, but not one of them. Lord and master in his own place, and yet Dr. Zeus has his name on the list for removal in the last hour."

"Why's that?"

"He's been a necessary compromise. They required his existence, and yet he should never have been born."

"Huh! Like Nicholas Edward Alec Harpole Finsbury whatever . . ." Joseph's eyes were closing.

"You didn't kill him," Budu said, watching Joseph. Joseph opened his eyes and looked up at the towering blue-lit figure that studied him.

"Uh . . . no, as a matter of fact. I didn't."

"Why had he taken your daughter?" said Budu, in the tone of one who is about to announce a checkmate.

"Because . . . he loves her. Her really does love her, after all." Joseph's eyes were exhausted, bewildered. "Can you beat that?"

"No," Budu said, "you can't. And now you've got that through your head, maybe I can trust you to pay attention to something else."

## AT THE PELICAN INN, 2333 AD

"Oh, wow," said Keely, pausing at the window. She shifted little Nelson to her other hip and leaned closer for a better look.

"What is it now?" said Mavis irritably, not looking up from her accounts plaquette. She had just been informed that, due to recent increases in the cost of living, the bribe necessary to obtain hotel permits was going to increase by eight percent.

"It's Mr. Capra," Keely said, and Mavis's ears pricked up. She bustled to the window and stared out.

Yes. A *new* BMW Zephyr, a brand-new suit, too, and wasn't Joseph looking trim? She put her hands to her temples and smoothed back the gray, hoping it wasn't too obvious, before she hurried to the door.

"Well, hello, stranger," she said coyly, flinging the door wide. Joseph stopped on the walk, put down his briefcase, and held out his arms, smiling.

"Gee, Mavis, you're looking great," he said as they embraced. "I mean that sincerely. Long time no see, huh?"

"Ages," she murmured in his ear, wondering if he still had that expense account with HumaliCorp.

"Yeah. Yeah, it's been ages. Say, are you still making that swell persimmon cider?"

"Kee-LY," she yelled through the door. "Two persimmon ciders in the Snug, now!"

"Yes, ma'am," Keely said, scrambling obligingly.

"And will you stay for dinner, too?" Mavis inquired, leading him into the house.

"Of course. In fact, honey, I'm staying the night as an actual paying guest. I've got a long drive ahead of me tomorrow, and I'd like to have a nice relaxing evening first," Joseph said, gazing around the familiar rooms and inhaling deeply.

"Well, we'll just have to see that all your stress melts away, somehow," Mavis promised, sweeping little Nelson's blocks and rag dolly out of the Snug without even looking at them as she bowed Joseph to a seat. "Though I have to tell you, dear, you just seem to get younger all the time!"

"Uh—well—" Joseph glanced swiftly at the gray in her hair and felt a pang. He put on an embarrassed expression and indicated his neat little jet-black beard. "I keep this dyed, if you want the truth. I have to, for my clients, see. Business."

"Really? I'd never have known," Mavis said, wide-eyed.

"Yeah," Joseph said. He began to giggle. "Sort of a Grecian formula."

Keely brought their cider and hurriedly picked up the blocks and dolly, giving Joseph the opportunity to note that she was considerably more bosomy nowadays. He sighed in contentment and raised his glass to Mavis.

"Here's to love," he said.

"Okay," Mavis said, her heart beating fast. They drank. She reached across the table and took his hand.

"How are you doing these days? Are you still with HumaliCorp?"

"Who? Oh. Yeah, as a matter of fact, they've been keeping me pretty busy," Joseph said.

"How far do you have to go tomorrow?" she said.

"Way down the coast," he said, having another taste of his cider. He swirled the glass, breathing in the fragrance. "Below Monterey. San Luis Obispo Protectorate, as a matter of fact."

"Oh, my, that's a long way," Mavis said, looking worried. "Are you sure it's safe?"

"It's not that wild any more," Joseph assured her. "I hear they haven't had any trouble with bandits in years. The guy who runs the place laid out a lot of money on patrols to keep the Salinas open for produce freighters."

"How exciting."

"In fact," Joseph said, taking another sip, "that's the guy I've got to go talk to."

Mavis looked astonished. "The man with the big castle?"

"Yeah," said Joseph, and she noted a certain uneasiness in his black eyes.

"Oh, my, that really is exciting," she said. "I knew somebody who went there once and saw all the statues and things. And you're going to talk to him? The Protector? I can never remember his name—"

"Hearst," Joseph said, lifting his glass to gulp down the last of his cider. He set the glass down. "William Randolph Hearst. The, uh, tenth."

# LONDON, 2352 AD

They had been following the Facilitator Sarai since she'd left Jamaica, but she didn't care.

Sarai no longer cared about much. She had one loose end in the skein of her very long life, one unresolved question; once she had her answer, they could come to take her away and do whatever it was they did to operatives who disappeared. It wouldn't matter.

She didn't have her answer yet, though, which was why she'd taken the trouble to evade them this far.

Sarai stood now outside the office block in Gray's Inn Road, scanning. They were still following her; in fact they were closer now than they'd been during the while she'd walked up and down before the sad silent house in John Street. Probably she would let them take her this afternoon. Sarai was tired. She felt old.

She didn't look old. She had all the lithe grace she had perfected over centuries, and only the too-sharp eyes in her smooth and elegant face were any indication she had worn chains on a slave ship, carried an axe in Saint-Domingue against the colonials, dodged Tontons Macoutes in Port-au-Prince.

She exhaled now, and her breath puffed out steaming in the chilly air. The drenching rain had stopped at last, though thunder was still rumbling overhead. The sun was streaming through a rift in the clouds, lighting up dark London with heartbreaking beauty.

Yes, *heartbreaking* was the word for it.

And look: there was a rainbow; a good sign, maybe a blessing on her finality. Sarai craned her head to follow its arc. Where did it come down? Just over there in front of that empty shopfront . . . where the young man stood staring at her. No, not a young man. An immortal.

*Why hadn't she noticed him?* Shocked, Sarai turned and fled into the building. The aglift was just arriving and she leaped in, surveying buttons one through six before hitting five. The door took forever to close but no grim-faced stranger shouldered his way through, and as the lift zoomed silently upward Sarai murmured her thanks. All she needed was a little more time, all she wanted was her answer.

The lift let her out into a tiled lobby, very posh. The door with gold lettering read: CANTWELL AND CANTWELL, SOLICITORS GENERAL. Sarai strode forward and let herself in.

The mortal girl at the console looked up in surprise.

"Yes?"

"I hope you can help me," said Sarai. "I have a message for one of the gentlemen's clients. They represent the earl of Finsbury, don't they, girl?"

The receptionist's eyes widened. Her hand moved on the console— below Sarai's sightline, but Sarai had seen the muscle twitch in her shoulder and knew perfectly well what she was doing. There; abruptly the surveillance cameras had fixed on her, and she was aware that someone in the room beyond was listening intently.

"The seventh earl, yes," murmured the receptionist.

"There is no other," said Sarai impatiently. "You listen to me, now. I want to get a message to his lordship, and he's not at home in John Street. Where might he be, please?"

Much emotional excitement in the room beyond, and the mortal girl's wariness increased. But she smiled, ever so politely, as she said:

"His lordship is on extended holiday in the South Seas. I'm afraid he left instructions that he's not to be disturbed under any circumstances."

"Well, does he ever call for his mail, girl?"

A long pause.

"If you'd like to leave a message—" said the receptionist at last. "Or perhaps tell me your name—"

"Wouldn't mean a thing to you. My auntie was his lordship's nanny, a long time ago, you see? She's getting old now, soon to die, wanted to see him before she goes. Maybe there's a little bequest. When do you reckon his lordship will get the message?"

"Er—" the receptionist looked panicked, glanced at the closed door behind which someone listened. "Generally they're forwarded every twenty-four hours—"

Sarai knew that the mortal was telling the truth, as far as she knew it; but she didn't know much, and there was no end of worry and uncertainty emanating from the person listening out of sight. Probably one of the Cantwells. She bared her teeth.

"All right then," she said. "You give a message to his lordship, eh? Tell him old Sarah needs to see him now. She can't die happy till she does. I'll be back in touch."

She turned on her heel and left. She wouldn't be in touch, actually, but it would have been impossible to have left any contact information. In any case, she doubted whether Alec Checkerfield was really going to get her message.

He was probably dead after all, she concluded, as she stepped into the lift. The mortals had seemed to think he was, to judge from their fear and confusion. Little boy lost and gone, no point to this long chase after all. She slumped against the wall as the lift hurtled downward with her, closing her eyes against hot tears.

If her eyes hadn't been closed, she might not have noticed that it took twice as long for the lift to drop between the fifth and fourth floors as it did between any of the others. She did notice, though, and when the lift stopped she opened her eyes again, and peered upward suspiciously.

"What the bloody hell?" she said aloud, welcoming any chance to think about something besides death. She stepped out when the doors opened and marched straight off into the street, not pausing until she was across it and had turned back to stare up at the building.

They were very close now, at most no farther away than Theobalds Road. They had picked up her signal again. She didn't care. Wasn't this funny, to have uncovered a little mystery in her last moments of freedom? Why did this building have more floors in it than showed on the lift buttons?

For there could be no doubt: there was a floor concealed between the fourth and what was officially the fifth floor. Not concealed very much, because it had windows looking out on the river, and she could detect two mortals moving around inside. All the same, it couldn't be reached by the public lift, and probably not one in a million mortals walking the streets of London would ever notice the discrepancy. She, herself, had nearly missed it. Suddenly she heard a click, just barely audible, and felt a chill.

"Did you get in?" said a voice at her side. She turned, staring, too astonished to wink out.

"Who the hell are you?" she demanded of the immortal who had watched her from the rainbow's end.

He looked impatient. "Latif, Executive Facilitator Grade One, Second-in-Command North African Sector. Do you want to go with me, or let the techs arrest you?"

"I don't give a damn, boy," she informed him. Now he looked annoyed.

"Well, I do, okay?" he said, and taking her arm he pulled her away with him, around the corner to where a sleek agcar was hovering. There was a mortal at the wheel. They got into the car and it zoomed away from the curb at once, making for the A10. There was a faint distant outcry from the techs; Sarai heard clearly the words *she's done it again* before they dropped out of range.

She leaned back in her seat and looked around. Nice upholstery. Very posh car.

"So you're from Suleyman, are you?" she inquired, wondering if she was going to be able to keep from crying again. Latif, who had not taken his eyes off her, just nodded.

"Did you get in?" he repeated.

"You might offer a lady a drink, you know," she said.

Without expression, he opened a cabinet and revealed a nice little minibar complete with hors d'oeuvres. He said nothing more as he fixed her a dry martini and several little crackers decorated with bright savory pastes. She watched him drop the olive in, hugely amused, and decided she wasn't quite ready to give up yet.

"All right?" said Latif, presenting her with the martini. She accepted it, smiling at him graciously.

"What a nice fellow you are," she said. "Suleyman's child Latif, eh? He has obviously taught you manners." She sipped her drink and reached for a cracker. "What was it you wanted to know, now?"

"Whether you got inside," he said.

"To be sure, that was it. To the invisible fifth floor? No, dearie, not I; I'd only just noticed the bloody thing when you so kindly came to my rescue. I was there on quite another matter. Seeing a solicitor, you know."

"Cantwell and Cantwell?" Latif arched his eyebrows. "You were seeing them about Alec Checkerfield."

That broke her composure.

"How—"

"You worked under Nennius," Latif stated. "He sent you out to the Caribbean with a mortal baby in 2321."

She nodded, staring at him. She had another sip of her martini.

"You were on that project," Latif continued, "until 2326. Then you drew some Gradual Retirement time and went to Haiti. You were there until 2345. When did you go back to work for Nennius?"

Sarai drained her martini in a gulp and held it out to him. "I didn't. I hate his guts, sonny boy, if you want the truth. No rum in that bar, is there?"

Latif shook his head. "Just gin and vermouth. Sorry. Why do you hate Nennius?"

"He's a nasty man, that's why." She set the glass down on the tray when he didn't take it from her.

"Why do you think he's nasty, Sarai?" he asked.

She drew a deep breath, expecting to be able to reply calmly, but the grief ambushed her. Latif looked disconcerted at her pent-up scream. After a moment he produced a starched white handkerchief from his coat pocket and offered it to her. He watched as she sobbed and rocked in place, struggled to control her pain, mopped her streaming eyes.

"My Alec," she gasped. "My good little winji boy. Innocent as a lamb once. They got to him. Twisted him up inside, you know, hurt him, I guess so he'd do the thing they wanted him to do. That was Nennius's ordering. He had a purpose for that baby, and I never knew what it was until too late."

"You mean what Checkerfield did at Mars Two?"

Sarai winced, but nodded and blew her nose. She had control again. "He wasn't a mean boy," she said, in a thick voice. "You believe that?"

Latif just turned his palms out. "I didn't know him," he said.

"I went up there to see if they could tell me where he was," she went on. "They don't even know. Company got him, that'd be my guess. Slipped him out of this world as deft as they slipped him into it."

Latif fixed her another drink.

"You've been running awhile, haven't you?" he observed.

"Since New Year's," she replied. "And what a tired old lady I am, boy. But your secret fifth floor? No idea what it is. The lift doesn't stop on it, you see. Something the mortals want secret for themselves. Must go up by the stairs, or there's a separate lift from some other floor maybe."

"That was what we thought, too," Latif said. "Did you see any sign in there with, maybe, the words ALPHA-OMEGA on it? Like Alpha-Omega Trust Funds, or Mutual Assurance or anything like that?"

"Alpha-Omega?" Sarai looked dubious. "Sorry, no."

Latif seemed annoyed, but he shrugged. "Too bad. Anyway—I've been authorized to offer you sanctuary, if you want it." He held out the fresh martini.

"Have you indeed?" she said slowly. She took the drink and tasted it before she went on. "For the last few years of the world? Well, that would be like old times. I used to be in Suleyman's harem, boy, you know that? Long long ago."

Latif smiled briefly, the warmth crossing his face like a bar of sunlight.

"I know. With Nefer and Nan."

She nodded, feeling her taut-wire nerves begin to slacken. The release was delicious, irresistible, but she reminded herself that there was undoubtedly a price tag on the rescue.

"So he wants everything I know about Nennius's operation, I reckon?" she inquired.

"Of course," said Latif, with no trace of irony.

"He's got himself a deal, then." Sarai told him. "Nennius! I'd love the chance to grind his proud face in the mud for that baby's sake, so help me God."

Latif nodded and leaned back in his seat. Sarai leaned back, too, having another sip of her martini. The car sped on toward Tottenham Airpark through slanting bars of sunlight, though rain was falling again now and the sky to the west was purple as a bruise with massed cloud. The rainbow followed them, faithful.

# LAYING LOW, MONTEGO BAY, JAMAICA, 1950 AD

Bogue House was a splendid new hotel of absolutely modern design, all straight lines, diamonds, and rectangles, flat planes painted white and olive green. No superfluous ornamentation at all. It was laid out in a series of courtyards around palm trees. It had one blue kidney-shaped pool, a restaurant, and a bar where dry martinis were served any hour of the day or night, just opposite the lobby. There were Matisse lithographs in the rooms. There were sports cars in the white gravel car park, MGs, Austins, and Jaguars, a Bentley or two. Bogue House was intended for smart young clientele with fast lives.

One day a big elegant yacht moored out in the bay, and a poky little rental car, stalling and backfiring, came up the long driveway that led to Bogue House. The young lady who was driving the car fought it into reverse and parked, cursing volubly at it in a curious Spanish dialect. When it had surrendered at last she leaped out and went around to the boot, from which she pulled a wheelchair. This she opened and set up deftly for the car's passenger, a battered-looking young man with a bandaged head, one arm in a sling, and both ankles in brace bandages. She was seen to very nearly lift him bodily into the chair.

Were it not for this slight oddness, they would have been nicely anonymous, for there was otherwise nothing to distinguish them from the other smart young clientele. The girl wore correct summer white, the young man correct white trousers and a blue sports blazer. Moreover, being in a wheelchair, his unusual height was not apparent to the observer.

She pushed him briskly into the severe modern lobby and signed them in as Commander and Mrs. James Hawkins, and was rather high-handed with the staff, and managed somehow to give the impression that Commander Hawkins had been heroically injured in a helicopter accident. Commander Hawkins sat there looking pale, uncomfortable, and very heroic indeed. He did not remove his black sunglasses. His wife did not remove hers. She paid in cash. They departed immediately to their room. They called for room service.

They stayed there six weeks.

At first they seldom ventured from their room, and looked warily around when they did emerge, and spoke to no one. Later they dined in the hotel restaurant and Commander Hawkins tottered about their courtyard with a cane, leaning on his wife, who if she was sharp-tongued with waiters seemed to adore him unreservedly. Once when a gardener (a stocky, olive-complected man) rose suddenly from the hedge he was clipping and startled Commander Hawkins so that he staggered and almost fell, she nearly attacked the man.

During this time a pair of petty thieves, noting the young couple's prolonged absence from their yacht, took it upon themselves to row out to the big vessel by night to see what loot might be had. They were never seen again, though their sunken boat was spotted by a diver some months later. It appeared to have had multiple holes burned in it by a large hot poker.

But there were no further unpleasant incidents ashore. Soon the commander was steady on his feet, and he and his wife seemed brave enough to go down to the beach, where they sat at first in beach chairs under the tall palms and later, after the commander's arm was out of its sling, swam together in the bright blue water amid sporting dolphins, or lay on mats under the bright blue sky. They were seen to laugh. At last they checked out of Bogue House and returned to their big elegant yacht, though they came back for a week or two to sun themselves on the beach in front of the hotel.

"Just another anonymous couple in Paradise," Mendoza crooned to Alec, pressing with all her weight as she massaged a photoradiation-blocking oil into his lower back. He moaned an incoherent but ecstatic reply. "Except for your amazing tattoo, Commander Hawkins. You must have had that done by Maori tribesmen, yes?"

Alec giggled sleepily.

"Yes, I can see it now," Mendoza said, working her way up his back. "It was during the war. Valiant young Commander Hawkins was ship-wrecked in the South Seas. His enemies torpedoed his battleship. Everyone escaped in the lifeboats except Commander Hawkins. *He* bravely swam in his lifejacket through miles of deadly shark-infested waters until he crawled up half-dead on a tropical shore. The islanders rescued him, and so impressed were they by his bravery that they made him an honorary member of their tribe, and gave him a splendid tattoo for the occasion."

"Mmm," said Alec.

"Yes. This particular tribe was ruled by a queen, and she took one look at this dishy Englishman in his tattered commander's uniform and said, 'Oh, baby! Come to my private hammock, you gorgeous British sailor boy, and I'll give you a swell tattoo.' She was particularly infatuated with his legs." Mendoza felt cautiously along the tendons of his ankles, smoothing in oil. The painful red marks from the clewline had disappeared fairly quickly.

"What'd she look like?" Alec said, only hanging on to consciousness because it was so pleasant to be ministered to.

"Oh, you know. Red sarong. Hibiscus flower stuck behind her left ear. Dorothy Lamour in *The Hurricane*," Mendoza said, working oil into the soles of his feet.

"Uh-uh. She has to be you," said Alec indistinctly.

"Ah. Okay; this island was peopled by the rare Spanish Maoris," speculated Mendoza. "A unique culture dating from the sixteenth century, when a storm blew a Spanish galleon off course and the survivors intermarried with the islanders. And so . . . the islanders practiced many unique customs, like . . . oh, I don't know, maybe they had bullfights or cooked with olive oil or something. What do you think?"

Alec didn't answer. Lulled by sheer pleasure, he was having a blissful dream about tropical islands, and so for that matter was Nicholas, who was already snoring beside them.

Mendoza patted Alec fondly on the seat of his bathing trunks. She was preparing to stretch out beside him when Edward opened a bright wakeful eye and regarded her.

"My dear, I wonder if I mightn't ask you to anoint one last spot?" he inquired.

"Of course," she said, observing that he had switched over into his Victorian idiom again, and wondering why. Rising to her knees, she picked up the jar of oil. "Where, señor?"

"Here at the back of my neck," Edward told her, indicating with a gesture. "Under the collar, you see? It would be most uncomfortable to sunburn just there. One's dress shirts do tend to chafe."

She drew breath, remembering she mustn't touch that spot lest she inadvertently download from him, and was about to mention this when he rose on his elbows and worked the torque's fastening.

"Here we are," he said triumphantly, slipping it off. "Now you needn't fear."

"But—is that safe?" she asked. "Didn't that just break the connection between us and Sir Henry?"

"Only temporarily," Edward assured her. "For I can put the collar on again at a moment's notice." He waved a dismissive hand at the horizon, where the *Captain Morgan* was anchored. "If that mad little fellow comes back, our good Captain will pick him off with a broadside, I promise you."

"Sir Henry won't worry?" Mendoza looked out at the horizon uncertainly.

"The Captain, my dear, is a machine," Edward said. "And tends on our pleasure, and not the other way around. In any case, I shouldn't think it's entirely healthy to wear the collar continually, should you?"

"Maybe not," she said, and bent to rub oil into his neck. He arched his back and made an appreciative noise.

Meanwhile, the Captain had gone immediately on the alert the moment his connection with Alec was broken. Fixing on Alec's last known position, a powerful long-range camera rose from its concealed housing on the deck and telescoped outward, scanning the beach. It found Edward and Mendoza, spotted the torque lying on a corner of the beach mat, assured itself that Joseph was not lurking in the immediate vicinity, and extended to observe at closer focus just what might be going on.

"My dear, any more and my spine will positively melt," Edward growled sensually. "Or stiffen to a degree inconvenient in such a public place." He reached up a hand and pulled her down beside him.

"We could always go back through the past and find a time when there weren't any mortals here," Mendoza said, smiling. "Make love in the surf, eh, like in *From Here to Eternity*? Of course, we'd have to bring our own martinis."

Edward shrugged, never having seen *From Here to Eternity*. "And sufficient weaponry for whatever antediluvian creatures might be haunting the place. I'm afraid, my dear, that caution is still called for until I'm restored to my proper state of permanence."

She nodded sadly and put her hand on his. Following Joseph's attack it had been necessary to clear the air on certain matters. Alec had admitted he wasn't quite as immortal as he ought to be, and Mendoza had admitted she'd known, and there were tears and embraces, and she had been rabidly defensive of him ever since.

Edward gazed down at their two hands now, each with its wedding ring. He sighed, smiled a little ruefully, and looked up with a wide-eyed and frank expression.

"I've been meaning to speak to you about something, my dear, and I hope you won't take it amiss," he said.

Unfortunately for Edward, he had never seen *2001: A Space Odyssey* either. The Captain's telescope zoomed in to focus on his moving lips.

"What is it?" Mendoza asked.

"One gets the oddest notions when one's been convalescing; perhaps it comes of so nearly losing you, when Joseph had me at his mercy, but . . . I find myself with the strangest desire to . . ." Edward paused as if searching for words. "To establish our union in a more palpable outward form."

Mendoza looked at him blankly, wondering what on earth he was talking about.

"In short, my love," Edward said, squeezing her hand, "I wonder whether we mightn't consider having a child?"

Mendoza was so utterly surprised it took her a moment to answer. He watched her face closely.

"You mean . . . reproduce?" she said incredulously.

"That is exactly what I mean," Edward said, smiling.

"Like *mortals*?"

"Not exactly as they do," Edward admitted.

"But . . ." Mendoza blinked. "I'm not sure we can do that, can we? We're not—I mean, I—"

"There would be certain technical difficulties, to be sure," Edward said, "which could be easily overcome by the Captain, if he could be persuaded how necessary an infant was to our happiness. And wouldn't you like to experience Motherhood at last, my dear?"

"I've never thought about it," Mendoza said truthfully. "I just always assumed it was one of those things mortals do and we don't. Are you sure it wouldn't be impossible? I don't think I have all the parts, for one thing."

"You have everything I need, my dearest," Edward said. "It may, in fact, be impossible to produce a child of our combined genetic heritage. But I did a great deal of reading on the subject, you see, during those long evenings when pain prevented me from sleeping—"

Mendoza remembered waking once in the night at Bogue House to find him staring tensely into a text plaquette, his pale eyes flickering over the words at high speed.

"Oh, my love, I'm sorry—"

"Don't distress yourself. One ought always welcome the opportunity to improve one's mind, don't you think?" Edward leaned closer. "And I'd not have awakened you for the world, my dear, after you'd cared for me so devotedly all day. But to continue: there is, I find, a procedure wherein the bare beginnings of life can be artificially initiated elsewhere, and then implanted into the receptive womb of the mother-to-be, there to grow to fruition over nine brief months. This procedure requires no surgery and may involve only the slightest discomfort, if indeed any."

"Really?" said Mendoza, watching his face as he spoke so earnestly, and knowing already that she couldn't deny him what he wanted.

"Yes. It would appear that this was not only possible, but quite commonly done in the late twentieth and twenty-first centuries, before certain 'Zero Population Growth' laws were enacted," Edward said. "Need I mention that the results were, unfailingly, happy mothers with bonny babes? Only the mortals' need to curtail their own numbers caused the practice to be discontinued, and, naturally enough, such mortal laws do not apply to us, any more than their absurd prohibitions on coffee and tea!" He waved a contemptuous hand.

"But—" he continued, avoiding her gaze and drawing a deep breath, "the question is, my dear—do I dare ask you to make this sacrifice for my happiness? Any inconvenience, however minor, would be yours alone. I have proceeded on the assumption that you would be grateful for the restoration of a prospect the Company had so cruelly taken from you—I mean the sacrament of maternity—but perhaps . . ."

"I would be cut to pieces for you, señor," she said, and she meant it, and he knew it. He shivered, but did not falter in his intent. "Of course I wouldn't mind having a baby, if you want one. Though it might be better to wait until you've dealt with the Company, don't you think? And until we've recaptured your DNA vial."

"Oh, certainly not until then," he said. "Indeed, we'd require the vial to produce our boy."

Mendoza noted that he wanted a son, and shrugged mentally. She didn't mind.

"We might design him all of a piece, with the accompanying nanobots to render him impervious to harm. And then, my love, we'd be doing something new in this world," Edward said gleefully. "Producing a child *born* to immortality, with eternal life as his birthright! All those clever tiny mechanisms transmuting him from his first heartbeat, all those tedious and painful years of surgery unnecessary. Every mortal flaw tempered out in your—what was that apt phrase of Shakespeare's?—your nest of spicery." With an expression indescribably rapacious and yet reverent, he set his hand under her heart. "Good God, how I'd envy the little fellow, nestled safe and warm in there! Rocked to sleep by your dear body, berthed in the water of life itself. And only imagine what he might do, as a man! He might be the hero to bring the world back to a Golden Age, at last."

Mendoza gazed into his eyes. His pupils had become enormous. "If this is what you want, señor, we'll try. I promise. As soon as it's safe," she said.

"Not a moment before," he vowed, taking her in his arms. They sank back down and she looked up at him with a wry smile.

"Of course, we'd have no fun at all in bed for a while," she said. "Though I don't suppose you'd be much interested in me."

"My love, I'd want you desperately," Edward said. "How else, when you became the vessel of my immortality?" He kissed her chin, her throat, her cheek, and murmured into her ear in a soft pleading growl she'd never heard him use before: "Oh, give me *life!*"

"All the life I have," she promised him, a little frightened by his passion. She put her arms about his bared neck and kissed him back. "I think it's time to go back to the ship."

"My thought exactly," he said, releasing her, and sat up. With swift hands he slipped the torque around his neck again.

*So it's Edward, is it?* said the Captain in his inner ear.

*Yes. My apologies; but I only took it off a little while. I was having Alec's neck massaged,* Edward explained, nudging Alec and Nicholas awake. Their snores broke off in unison as they sat up, bewildered.

The Captain did not respond.

*What's the matter?* Alec demanded.

*Nothing's the matter,* Edward told him, laughing. *But if we don't go back to the ship and blessed privacy soon, we'll shock the good citizens of Montego Bay.*

As it happened, they set the boat to rocking wildly before Alec sat up and took hold of the oars again. Mendoza leaned back in the prow and trailed her hand in the water languidly. As they came alongside the *Captain Morgan,* she laughed out loud. When Alec looked at her inquiringly, she said:

"I was just thinking it's a good thing we can't reproduce just like mortals. Otherwise we'd be up to our ears in babies!"

"Wouldn't we, though?" chuckled Alec. Edward just looked smug. He was still looking smug, in fact he was positively swaggering as they paced along the deck to the saloon; until he disappeared.

Alec, walking ahead after Mendoza, heard Nicholas's cry of surprise. He turned and stared into Nicholas's shocked face, and looked around for Edward, who was nowhere to be seen.

*Where'd he go?*

*I know not! He vanished away like—like a candle blown out.*

*Captain!* Alec cried in silence, running absurdly to the rail to look over. Mendoza turned.

"Alec?"

**Stand by, Alec.**

*Captain, Edward's gone!*

"Alec, sweetheart, what is it?" Mendoza was beside him in an instant, taking his hands and staring into his face.

"I—" Alec gulped painfully for breath. "I just thought I saw him again. Joseph."

"Where?" she asked, her eyes going flinty at the mention of his name.

"But he's not really there," Alec said. "It was just shadows."

"Darling, you're white as a sheet," she said. "Post-traumatic stress. Come on. We're quite safe; the Captain's here, and any miserable little dog-men the Company sends after us will be sorry they tried again. Am I correct, Captain?"

**Aye, ma'am,** said the Captain tersely.

"Let's go inside, now," she coaxed. "Would you like to shower first? Nice relaxing hot water? And supper afterward, and then perhaps we'll weigh anchor and cruise off for a change of scene. I think we've been here long enough."

"Right," he said shakily. He and Nicholas followed her into the saloon, watching each other in terror.

Edward found himself, abruptly, in darkness and utter silence. Worse: he had no sense of feeling in any limb. He was nothing but a point of consciousness in a vacuum. He screamed and heard nothing, not even the sound of his own pounding heart.

Did he have a pounding heart? But he was dead, wasn't he? A skeleton in a drawer, a few corpse parts preserved in formaldehyde?

"NO!" he raged, and heard himself. There! And he could hear his heart, now, yes, and his own breath coming raggedly, yes, and he *had* eyes, by God, he just couldn't see with them at the moment but that was because he was sitting in the utter darkness somewhere, and it was somewhere familiar, too, and any minute now he'd remember where it was.

Sitting. Sitting, not standing, he was certainly crouched, he could feel the cramping in his muscles and an unpleasant splintery surface under his buttocks, because he was naked. Or, no, not completely naked: there was something cold and heavy around his wrists, about his ankles. He moved, and heard clanking. Metal? Shackles.

He'd been in a place like this, once. This must be a ship's brig, like the one on the *Zagreus*, where he'd awaited trial after assaulting Captain Southbey. He turned his head, half-expecting to see the remembered pattern of light through the hatch cover in long stripes. Behold, there it was! And he could see himself. So his eyes had simply been getting used to the darkness, that was all.

Edward had all his senses back, now, he could smell the salt tang in the air, and the heavy tarry reek of the ship. He could taste his own salt sweat on his upper lip. It was stifling in here. He looked down and saw in sharp detail his chains and what secured them: a great eyebolt sunk in the timber of the bulkhead. Gritting his teeth, he pulled on it with all his strength. There was an audible creak, but it held him.

*Bloody hell. How'd you come back on, boy?*

"Captain!" He looked around desperately. "Something's happened. Find a way to get me out of here."

*You've turned yerself on, and you've built yerself a site to boot.* There was a disgruntled tone to the Captain's voice. *How'd the likes of you manage that, I wonder?*

"Captain, can you hear me?" Edward said. "Captain!"

*Oh, I hear you right enough, Edward.*

Edward's eyes narrowed. "Ah. Ah, I see now. I removed the collar. I broke your hold over Alec for a moment, and you didn't like that, and so you're punishing me."

*No. I ain't punishing you, Edward. Mind you, I'm going to, but I was too busy to deal with you proper-like just now. I was going to leave you off for a while, to give the others a little peace whilst I made up my mind what to do with you. Yet here you be, and here's this place, and it's damned inconvenient, says I.*

"Inconvenient—" Edward's mouth was dry. There was no water in his prison, not even the cracked wooden tankard there should have been.

*Well, let's see if I can't shut you down again.*

A wave of darkness and cold rolled over him, with a paralyzing numbness, and he howled and fought for all the sensations that had been so noisome and uncomfortable a moment before. He held on to his thirst and the stink of the ship, the close foul heat, the raw pain in his wrists and ankles.

*By thunder, you don't want to go down, do you? Yer a strong little bugger, Edward, I'll give you that.*

"What are you doing?" Edward shouted. "What are you doing to me? I won't die, do you hear me?"

*I thought it'd be enough to shut you off. Ah, it's a damn shame, too. Look how useful you was at Options Research! I were thinking you'd come in right handy once we'd got the DNA.*

Edward began to shake with anger.

"Useful, am I? Handy, am I? Damn your insolence! I have better things to do than wait on that boy."

*No, Edward, you don't.*

"I tell you I do! Is this your plan for me, Machine? I'm to have no life of my own, I'm to serve merely as some sort of *useful* proxy for your boy? Do you think you can pull me out like a pair of gloves for him, when he faces something difficult?" said Edward, wrenching at his chains until he felt them cutting into his wrists.

*Aye, that were the plan. I were hoping you'd integrate with him, by and by. But you won't behave, and I don't know what to do about it, afore God I don't. I can't let you out; you'd only pull another such trick as you just done, putting my boy in danger to see if you could get away with something. And what's poor Mendoza to do, now? You been leading her on to think Alec wants a baby, and you know damned well that ain't true. Yer a liar, boy, and to the lady what loves you best in all the world.*

"*I'm* a liar? As though you haven't got your own plans for her! You restored her ability to bear children, didn't you?"

*That ain't your business, Edward.*

"You truly think Alec will fight immortality, is that it? Is her womb an insurance policy for you? You think she'll bear you a new body for him, if he insists on wrecking the one he's got?" said Edward furiously.

*Ain't you a clever lad! Too clever by half, aye.*

"You think your boy *deserves* eternal life? The idiot seventh earl of Finsbury?" Edward raved. "Look at the hash he made of his one attempt to better mankind! You think he deserves Dolores? I'll never forget the look on his face, when he realized what she was. *Thing,* he called her!"

*My little Alec may not suit you, but he's my boy, and what's more important, he's alive. All you are is a program, Edward. A recording of a dead man's memory what can't be shut off. I'll figure out a way, all the same, though, bucko.*

"No," Edward said, lunging upward. He broke the chain and beat his bleeding fists against the door of the cell. "You can't do this to me. I'll have my life back, do you understand? I have work to do! I *will* walk the Earth again, in spite of you, or Alec, or Nicholas, or the Society! I WILL NOT BE SILENCED!"

*Please, Captain sir, can you talk to us now?* said Alec, shivering with Nicholas under the jets of the shower.

*I'm busy, son.*

*But Edward's gone,* Nicholas said.

*I know.*

*But we've got to get him back!* Alec said.

*I've got him, Alec.*

Alec and Nicholas looked at each other, bewildered.

*Thou hast rescued him, then,* said Nicholas.

*Not exactly, lad. I've had to give him a bit of discipline.*

Nicholas frowned. *Punishment?*

*Aye.*

*But how'd you make him disappear?* Alec demanded.

*I shut down his program.*

*WHAT?*

*Aye. I've known how to shut it down for a few months now, but there didn't seem to be no need, did there? Ye'd all been getting along well enough.*

*You just—just switched him off?* Alec looked as though he was going to be sick. *Would you do that to me? Or to Nicholas?*

*Not to you, lad. I could shut our Nicholas down, aye, but he behaves himself most of the time. He only went berserk the once.*

*But that's* horrible! *You can't just shut people off like they were lights or something,* said Alec.

*Nor can he. Spirit, thou liest!* Nicholas said firmly. *We are no shadows of thy casting, nor canst thou kill us. Thou hast but hidden Edward away.*

*Well, lad, you may be right at that; for he won't stay off, it seems. I don't know how he's still able to do what you can do without him having an actual physical brain anymore, Alec, but he done it, and he's throwing himself quite a tantrum at the moment.*

*Let him go, Captain sir, please!* Alec said.

*Ought I, now? And don't you want to know what he was shut up for doing? Whilst you two was asleep, he talked yer lady into letting him grow himself a new body in her womb.*

There was a moment of shocked silence. Nicholas began to pound his right fist into his left palm. *That smiling whoreson bastard,* he muttered.

*That was why she was talking about babies!* Alec realized.

Unfortunately, it was at this precise moment that Edward managed to break free of his prison and popped into existence there in the shower with them, naked and bleeding.

*HA,* he said. *I told you you wouldn't—*

He was unable to finish his sentence, however, because Nicholas punched him right in the mouth, and followed with two more blows in rapid succession before Edward collected his wits enough to start hitting him back. Alec, uncertain whether to dodge blows or hit Edward too, slipped and fell backward against the shower door, which opened abruptly and they fell, all three, on the bathroom floor in a cursing, struggling mass.

Hearing the crash, Mendoza was instantly beside Alec, who was gasping and convulsing as the others strove for control.

"Sir Henry," she screamed, taking Alec in her arms. "He's having a seizure!"

It was a full hour before she could be calmed down enough to be assured that Alec had not developed a short-circuit as a result of his concussion, but had merely slipped on the soap and been too out of breath to explain this when she'd found him. An hour of her heartbroken crying was enough to make even Edward feel miserably remorseful, and a general truce was agreed upon all around. The Captain administered mild tranquilizers, put everybody to bed, and weighed anchor for Maui.

## ONE MORNING IN LAHAINA, 2281 AD

They strolled through the old village between Front Street and the highway, debating endlessly about where to have breakfast.

"Hey, this place is still here," said Alec, stopping in front of a bright-painted eatery. "I mean—it's here already. I used to come to this place all the time . . . or I guess I will. It looks so *new* now."

"The 'WHALER GETS HIS' café," Mendoza read aloud, craning her head back to look up at the sign, which showed a mortal in nineteenth-century foul weather gear regarding, with an expression of annoyance, the harpoon protruding from his chest. In the background, whales leaped up on their tails with big cartoony grins. "Well, it is new, darling."

"Great food," Alec said, looking down hopefully at his two tiny reflections in the optics of her sunglasses. She had awakened shortly before dawn with a screaming nightmare, and wept uncontrollably after while he held her. Though he had assured her that she looked fine now, she was still worried that her eyes were red, and wouldn't take the glasses off.

"Is it good?" She peered through the window.

"Really good." He took both her hands in his and leaned down to kiss her. "Pretty lady, can I buy you breakfast? Hawaiian-style omelet? You'd like it a lot."

She smiled at last. "Okay, señor."

They went in and Alec found that it was even brighter and newer inside, though the menu was not substantially different. A Hawaiian omelet turned out to be soyfluff with bananas and caramelized onions, bizarre but delicious with an iced glass of unbelievably pungent local ginger ale. The lightheartedness of the fare was counterbalanced by the antiwhaling artwork printed all down the sides of the menu and on the paper placemats, perhaps a bit unnecessary given that nobody had intentionally killed a whale in two centuries.

"Why are they so down on whaling so long after the fact?" Mendoza said, slipping off her sunglasses at last. She squinted up at a poster depicting Moby Dick triumphantly devastating the crew of the *Pequod*. Her eyes were still a little red.

"I don't know," Alec said, reaching across the table to squeeze her hand. "Maybe because the Royals over here are all members of the Beast Liberation Party."

*Ridiculous,* muttered Edward, polishing off virtual kippers. *Conservation's all very well, but turning on one's own kind?*

*Thou art no more kin to man than to the whale, monster,* Nicholas said gloomily, watching Mendoza's pale tense face as she stared at a harpoon gun mounted above the door.

*Monstrousness is in the eye of the beholder,* Edward retorted.

"I wish we could be sure about that—Joseph person," said Mendoza at last. She lifted her ginger ale and held the cold glass against her cheek.

"Baby, I promise you, it's okay," Alec said. "The Captain checked it out. He's just a rogue on his own. He'll never find us again without a signal transmitter, and who knows? Maybe the Company'll get him first."

Her mouth tightened, but she didn't say anything.

"Come on," Alec said, waving his credit disc at the waiter. "Let's go find a botanical garden or something, yeah? Buy some souvenirs?"

As it happened, there was a pushcart not a block away, full of ti logs and splendidly phallic looking plumeria cuttings. Alec insisted on selecting the very largest of the latter for her, with such broad mugging and double-entendres Mendoza was in stitches, her unhappiness seemingly dispelled at last. They sauntered on hand in hand, Mendoza clutching the bagged cutting, and looked for a place to buy Hawaiian shirts.

Three shopfronts on, however, they encountered the roaring mouth of an amusement arcade. Alec stopped, staring into the lurid gloom.

"Look at the old games!" he said.

They all seemed madly futuristic to Mendoza, but she looked politely and followed as he tugged her into the pandemonium. They wandered down an aisle between booths that pulsed with garish light, that shrieked and boomed, threatened and challenged. In every direction were holographic globes full of things exploding, or crashing, or going to lightspeed. Nicholas had his hands over his ears, looking pained. Edward's nostrils flared in disgust at the smell, a combination of mildewed carpet, shaved-ice syrup, hot popcorn, and machine oil.

Alec, however, was enchanted.

"COOL," he shouted over the noise, pointing to a particular holographic game. "LOOK AT THAT! IT'S ONE OF THE ORIGINAL DEATH-DEALING DANS."

"WHAT'S AN ORIGINAL DEATH-DEALING DAN?" Mendoza screamed.

"THEY'RE ILLEGAL NOW! I MEAN, IN THE FUTURE. BUT THEY WERE SUPPOSED TO BE ONE OF THE BEST GAMES EVER DESIGNED," Alec said. "I NEVER IN A MILLION YEARS THOUGHT I'D EVER GET TO PLAY ONE."

"ISN'T TIME TRAVEL GREAT?" Mendoza screamed back. "WHY ARE THEY ILLEGAL, ALEC?"

"OH, BECAUSE . . ." Alec waved a hand vaguely. "THEY JUST WEREN'T VERY NICE, THAT'S ALL."

In fact, Death-Dealing Dan had been prohibited due to the fairly graphic and straightforward object of the game, which was to kill as many assailants as bloodily as possible in the shortest possible time. As they stared at it, the game played itself in display mode. A succession of horrifying-looking thugs appeared within the holographic globe and brandished weapons of every description at them.

"I HAVE TO TRY," Alec said, and pulling out a credit disc he paid for five games. Mendoza watched as he stepped up on the dais. She couldn't help but shiver as the body frame closed into place around him, a steel exoskeleton, and the pointpistol came up into his hand. Suddenly Alec seemed very young, very vulnerable, within the machine. She fought back an irrational urge to throw herself snarling at the first opponent who materialized, a decidedly subhuman creature with a low forehead and a club.

"BANG," yelled Alec, and its chest exploded outward in a bloody mass. At the top of the globe appeared the glowing words: 10 POINTS!

*This is Abomination!* said Nicholas, aghast.

*It's not real,* Alec explained distractedly, as another figure began to materialize out of the mess of the previous one. *It's just pictures!*

"BANG," he yelled at a black-clad figure who attempted to karate-kick him, and its head blew off and blood fountained from its neck stump. 20 POINTS!

*Thou slaughterest for sport?* demanded Nicholas. He was furious. The blood-mist within the globe thinned and a soldier in uniform leaped upward, spraying out bullets from an automatic weapon. Alec dodged within the body frame, crying "BANG," and his opponent's right arm blew off, but a siren wailed and a brilliant spot of red light appeared on Alec's left arm. Mendoza's hands flew to her mouth.

*Nick, shut up!* Alec snapped. *See what you made me do? I only got ten points on that one and the game scored ten.*

*Oh, don't be stupid,* Edward said. *The game's cheating for you, can't you tell? You're not even pulling the trigger.*

*Uh uh, man, it's a brain game. The gun isn't real. It's just to focus you,* Alec growled, dropping within the frame to fire at his next assailant, some sort of costumed supervillain with a bow and arrow. "BANG." The supervillain's lower torso blew open. Intestines poured out. Mendoza flinched and Nicholas wrapped his unseen arms around her, glaring at Alec. 40 POINTS! *The body frame reads your reflexes, see? And you sort of think your shots into the game's computer.*

Edward watched closely. The groaning supervillain faded and a shaven-headed Punk, massively muscled like no real Punk that had ever lived, came roaring toward Alec with a broken bottle.

"BANG," shouted Alec in triumph, taking off the top of the shaven head, and the Punk blinked comically through streaming blood before it dropped. 50 POINTS!

*Then, this is like pulling meals and clothing from thin air?* Edward speculated. *And cigars. Creating "virtual" things?*

*Right,* said Alec. *The old games really made you work for it—* He gasped as his next assailant emerged.

It was a naked girl, voluptuously endowed, smiling as she rose and lifted her hand in what might have been a beckoning gesture—

"Oh," said Alec, and saw her gun just too late, for even as he dropped into a crouch and yelled "BANG," the siren went off again and a red spot of light appeared between his eyes. GAME OVER! YOU DIE! GAME OVER! YOU DIE!

"Damn," Alec complained. Nicholas was shocked into silence. Mendoza, pale and shaking in his arms, said very quietly:

"Alec—please—"

He turned and looked at her, with red holographic blood moving slowly down his face until the game reset. "It's okay," he said, surprised by her reaction. "It's just a game."

And then she saw his face undergo that change as it often did, without altering a single feature and yet becoming another man's: eyes cold and hooded, smile infinitely too experienced and a little weary.

"I simply hadn't the measure yet, my dear," he said. "I won't die again, I assure you."

He turned back within the steel exoskeleton, and took a firm grip on the pistol.

Here they came again, the garish and absurd parade of enemies, and he methodically blew their heads off as they appeared. He was no longer crying out "Bang" when he fired, and he was firing quickly.

10 POINTS! 20 POINTS! 30 POINTS! 40 POINTS! BONUS! BONUS! 100 POINTS!

He did not hesitate when the naked girl appeared, but shot her, too, and coolly blasted away the next eight opponents that followed her, two of whom were also female. His score rose dramatically, until:

GAME OVER! YOU WIN! REPLAY! GAME OVER! YOU WIN! REPLAY!

*You're* good, admitted Alec, from where he had been thrust to the sidelines.

*Small wonder if he is,* said Nicholas tightly.

Edward did not reply. He was tensed, breathing hard, focused on the ball of light. As the game resumed, something strange happened.

The opponents began to go down, exploding in blood, even before they were quite in place; certainly before they had time to raise their assorted weapons. No sooner had the game begun than it was over, with the glowing letters announcing:

GAME OVER! EXPERT! REPLAY! GAME OVER! EXPERT! REPLAY!

None of the others spoke, watching in amazement. Edward had scored over a thousand points. He merely settled his feet more securely on the dais and fixed his attention on his target. The game began again.

It was as though a deck of cards were being riffled in midair, if cards could bleed and scream, so swiftly did the opponents appear, so swiftly did each die and vanish into the next one. So swiftly, too, did the glowing numbers climb, as Edward's score reached 5000.

A fanfare sounded and the letters above the globe flashed purple:

YOU HAVE REACHED THE SECOND LEVEL! HAIL, DEATH-DEALER! HAIL, DEATH-DEALER! HAIL, DEATH-DEALER!

And a new legion of enemies sped toward him out of the bloody ball, every human monster imaginable, guilty of all possible crimes and ugly as the crimes themselves, glimpsed for no more than a fleeting second before shredding to pieces. The game went on longer this time, but only because there were twice as many opponents. Edward was playing faster still.

The console housing the game began to hum faintly.

Edward scored 100,000 and the game began again without preamble. They were demons, now, hurling themselves at him and dissolving in blood-bursts of all colors, grotesques, and they came apart and surged back as the others had not, so that he was sometimes facing more than one opponent at a time. Though he was shifting now slightly from side to side within the body frame, his speed of kill diminished not one iota and his score rose inexorably toward 1,000,000. He wasn't even sweating, though his face was pale and set.

The console, however, was now whining distinctly.

New game! Or so the others guessed, because bright letters appeared for a split second announcing something above Edward's score as it passed one million and went on upward, and you couldn't even see what he was shooting at now, it was nothing but a howling miasma of blood, and the score counters were flickering too fast to be read—

Everything in the arcade was flickering—

Blackout!

And for a second there was darkness and deafening silence, before disgruntled yells rose from other customers within the arcade. As the cloudy sunlight filtered in from the street door, Mendoza looked up at a towering backlit shadow and felt herself seized and thrust into a holocabinet. Edward's laughing mouth was on hers, Edward's hands were violent, tearing at her clothes, writhing out of his own, and she was lifted and forced back against a console. She surrendered and loved him, whatever he was, there in the dark.

In their passion they did further damage to the arcade's property, tearing a steering wheel and seat from the booth they were in. It was only with tremendous effort that they kept themselves silent in the last moments of their paroxysm, as angry voices came past their refuge in the half-dark, and lights were beamed on the Death-Dealing Dan unit. Smoke was rising from its console, thin acrid vapor full of floating ash. There were muttered exclamations and a clank as something dropped from the ceiling: then very rude noises, as chemical foam spurted everywhere.

Mendoza shook with suppressed laughter and felt Edward shaking, too, before he hoisted her for one last nearly painful ecstasy. They hid there in the cabinet, gasping for breath while somebody stalked past threatening:

"Okay, who the hell did this? Who's been fucking with Death-Dealing Dan, huh?"


Adjusting their clothes, they escaped into the alley behind the arcade before power could be restored and the surveillance cameras consulted.

"I've got it," said Edward in triumph, grabbing Mendoza again and waltzing her round and round in the alley. "My love, my bride, my heart, I'VE GOT IT."

"What?" she wanted to know, just as lightning cracked blue overhead. It began to rain, big hot drops spattering down through slanting sunlight and cloud, with the smell of wet concrete and tropical flowers rising all around. There was a dull *boom* from the arcade behind them, and a piece of console flew out through the doorway.

"Er—we'd better go now," said Alec, asserting control. Mendoza grabbed his hand and they ran for their lives, but Edward laughed still.

Mendoza was falling out of her torn blouse before they had gone two blocks. Luckily the rain was dropping in blinding sheets by then, so Alec pulled off his shirt and she was able to wrap it around herself before anybody saw. They ducked into a shop. Alec was just paying for a new pair of Hawaiian shirts when the Captain sounded in his ear, louder than the summer thunder:

**Bloody Hell, Alec, get back aboard straightaway. That damned arcade's on fire!**

*Okay,* Alec said. *Was anybody hurt?*

**No,** the Captain said grimly, **but somebody's likely to be.**

Edward, smiling, said nothing. They splashed across Front Street and made their way to where the agboat was moored.

*How did you do all that?* Alec asked Edward, as they cast off and headed back out to the ship. *You never played a brain game before, did you? They didn't have anything even like 'em, when you were alive.*

*I am* alive, Edward told him gleefully. *Occidero, ergo sum!*

*Canst thou wonder, boy?* said Nicholas in disgust. *Murder was all his trade, when he lived; he is a murderer still.*

*I beg your pardon.* Edward leaned forward, a glint in his eyes. *Were you under the impression I was using the skills I learned in Her Majesty's service? Not at all, I assure you. No wonder you've been able to do it so easily all these years, Alec!*

At this point Mendoza, sitting up in the bow and peering back at Lahaina, noticed the black smoke gushing up from the arcade, and heard the sirens screaming through the downpour.

"Oh, my God, we set it on fire," she said in awe. "How can anything burn in all this rain?"

Edward took control again and grinned at her, lounging at the tiller.

"The heat, my dear, was prodigious in there," he drawled.

She giggled nervously, watching the smoke. Her face was pale.


They weighed anchor and sailed away from Maui, setting a course for Tahiti. Away from the islands, they passed well out of the storm and sailed on blue water, and it was easy to pretend the incident had never happened, in the sunlight and stiff breeze of a Pacific afternoon. Mendoza planted the jaunty little plumeria cutting and gave it a prominent location in the botany cabin, where it promptly shot up and opened in clouds of bloom. The Hawaiian shirts were hung up in the wardrobe, the torn clothes consigned to Smee's care. The incident receded behind them like Maui itself, sinking into the horizon.

For a while.

Gray early morning on the open sea, just at the hour when survivors of a sleepless night begin to be able to make out the shapes of the furniture and realize, despairing, that the stars have faded. Alec, however, was sound asleep and dreaming, in his vast bed, with its gilded skull-and-crossbone carvings.

. . . *They had closed his body in the jade framework, and he couldn't run, but that was all right because this was his chance to atone at last. So he nodded courteously at the skeletal host standing all around, the charred victims of Mars Two whose blood was still unavenged.* His *victims. Hanging here at Execution Dock was the least he could do for them. He was already rotting away. One leg was gone, and the rest of him was a tangle of wires and chips. His skull was golden. No human thing at all, really.*

. . . *And then it wasn't Execution Dock, it was the arcade, and the dead of Mars were waiting to see him play. There was a dog at his feet, leaping back and forth. "Go for it!" it barked, in Joseph's voice. There were other spectators, too: big men, all his lost fathers, glaring with cold pale righteous eyes.*

*And the game was starting, and the globe of light materialized in front of him, and there was the monster! Guilty Alec Checkerfield, in his loud shirt, the Hangar Twelve Man . . .*

. . . A deck below, Smee the servounit hummed and shook in a kind of electronic palsy. It flailed its arms. It raced twice around its track. Halting before a bolt of cotton, it gripped one end and yanked.

The cloth spilled out and Smee went through the motions of measuring it, but at frenzied speed. The cloth caught, bound in the joint of one of his manipulative members. It began to wad up, bunching, tight and tighter.

. . . A deck above, Alec was wadding the sheet between his fingers, sweating as he slept.

. . . *He looked disdainfully at the pointpistol. "This thing's no use," he informed the crowd. "No silver bullets." But Alec knew he had what it took to set things right. He had an amazing brain. He took off his head, hefted his golden skull, and bowled it straight and true at his image.*

*BANG! Yes, he blew himself away, watched with satisfaction as his liver and maybe half his spinal column went flying. And everyone was cheering except Mendoza, who was weeping within her blue-lit tank. "Hey," he told her regretfully, "this thing's bigger than both of us. What was I supposed to do?" . . .*

. . . A deck below, the snagged and crumpled cloth was piling high. A thin curl of smoke had begun to rise from Smee's stuck arm, as its servo-motor keened.

A sensor in the room noted the heat, and suddenly a ceiling-mounted camera opened a red eye and swiveled. Ten seconds later the door opened, and Flint and Billy Bones scuttled in. Billy Bones reared back, swung a weighted blade, and sheared off Smee's arm. Flint caught it before it could drop burning plastic on the dry cotton, and hurried off to dispose of it safely. Billy Bones stalked to Smee's control panel, reached in and shut it down, and pulled away the torn cloth. Then it moved close, running a scan of Smee's systems. It noted that no oil dripped from the lubrication housing . . .

. . . "No, really, it's not you. It's me," he was explaining, but she just kept crying. "You're a wonderful person, and you deserve somebody much better . . ."

**Wake up, Alec.**

Alec woke to find the room crackling with blue flames. Mendoza struggled beside him, in a nightmare she couldn't seem to escape. He reached for her at once.

**Leave her be! Best she sleep.**

But—holy shit, the bed's on fire, said Alec dazedly. Edward and Nicholas sat up on either side of him, staring.

**On fire, says you? This ain't nothing to what it might have been. Why the bloody Hell ain't you been doing routine maintenance on the costume servounit?**

What? Alec rubbed his face. What did you—oh. Smee? But I have been, Captain. What's going on?

**No, you ain't. I played back the surveillance data, and you didn't refill Lubrication Reservoir Six last time you worked on him. Why, Alec?**

Well—then, I must have forgotten! Okay? Alec turned distractedly to Mendoza, but Nicholas was holding her close and frowning at him. Captain, have you crashed or something? It's, what, two bells, morning watch?

**Aye, and a damn good thing I were standing watch, too.**

Have we narrowly avoided some calamity? Edward inquired, looking hard at Alec.

Ignoring him, the Captain fed the surveillance data from Smee's cabin straight into Alec's brain. Alec received it and went pale. "Shrack," he muttered aloud.

*Shrack, is it? Is that all you got to say for yerself, boy? Remember that little talk we had, about what'd happen if I ever caught you trying to scuttle yerself again?*

*Captain, I swear, this was an accident!* Alec said.

Unwilling to show Alec the other surveillance footage—that of Alec's fingers working on the sheet in eerie unison with Smee's gripping members—the Captain attempted to get his rage under control. The red lights on his cameras flickered. Edward looked from Alec to the cameras. He leaned back, folding his arms, watching in silence.

*Accident. Aye. Well, afore we has any more accidents, I reckon it's time to get down to business. There's been enough shore leave! We're going after prizes, now.*

*Okay, Captain,* said Alec, in the most reasonable voice he could summon. He looked worriedly at Mendoza, who had grown quieter; though blue lightnings still shimmered across the coverlet.

*I been finding references in other Company files to a place designated as Alpha-Omega. It's about the farthest point back in the past the Company's got a facility: 500,000 years BCE. I reckon I mentioned that the more valuable things is, the farther back in time Dr. Zeus seems to stow 'em? So this should be the richest cache yet. And what's in it, near as I can tell, is biological material.*

*Which would be DNA, I guess,* Alec said.

*Aye, most likely. Genetic components, from every race what's ever evolved and a lot of 'em what went extinct. I reckon this is where the Company got the stuff they mixed you from in the first place, so it makes sense they'd keep the rest of the batch here, too. It looks likely enough to plan an expedition, leastways.*

*Yeah,* said Alec after a long pause. Nicholas looked at him.

*Thou art afeared,* he said. *Come, boy, thou shalt be made free of sickness and death. Wherefore then wilt thou fear?*

*Because I killed all those people in Mars Two,* Alec said miserably. *And then I crawled away and hid, when I should have stood trial before the whole world.* He turned to Nicholas. *That's one thing I have to respect you for, man. You weren't a coward. You had your moment when you stood up and confronted your accusers, you know? You faced the fire. I'd give anything for the chance to do that.*

Nicholas looked horrified.

*No, boy! That was vain pride. God, God, wilt thou not learn from my error?* **You listen to him, Alec, that's bloody good advice.**

*You don't think it's—sinful, or unnatural, or something? Me becoming immortal, too? With all that Bible stuff you used to read?* Alec said.

Nicholas grabbed him by his shoulders. *What did I learn therefrom? I accomplished nothing in my time, save only comforting a frightened girl; and then I betrayed her, in the name of my own salvation. Who am I, to have eternal life? Yet it may be granted to thee, boy. Take it!*

*I can't even imagine Eternity,* said Alec.

*Then wilt thou send her to walk there alone? I left her in darkness, at the mercy of time. Thou must not!* cried Nicholas.

Alec looked around the room and knew they were still there in their hundreds, the dead of Mars, unseen, and knew they would never go away as long as he lived. Despairing, he reached out and stroked back Mendoza's hair.

*Oh, baby . . . if only we'd met some other time.* But Nicholas shook his head.

*All time is one. What thou art, thou art in any age of the world,* said Nicholas. *Edward and I bear witness to that. Redeem our sins, boy, for we cannot.*

*He hasn't the courage,* said Edward quietly.

*You go to Hell,* Alec raged, turning on him. *You've never been sorry a day in your life for anything you've done, have you?*

*I took my punishment like a man when my hour came round,* Edward replied. *If there is a God who cares about anything you've done, He'll strike with retribution soon enough; you needn't go crawling to Him begging for it in the meanwhile. Set your course for Alpha-Omega, Captain, make a way and a means. Alec's outrun the clock long enough.*

Mendoza gave a little cry and clutched at Alec. They bent to comfort her at once, all three; but she sighed and relaxed again, sleeping on.

# FEZ, 2352 AD

Nefer was busy. It wasn't the most dignified work in the world, for an august lady with several millennia under her belt—shoveling horse manure into a fusion hopper, going back and forth across the courtyard from the stable to the utility area—but it kept her happy.

She set aside the shovel, hosed down the stable floor, and washed her hands. Then she hoisted a great sack of feed mix and filled the manger. Her charges whickered and moved in for their breakfast at once. She leaned against the stall, watching them with a tender smile.

They were not, as you might expect, purebred Arabians. They were rather odd-looking little horses, actually, at least to anyone unfamiliar with cave paintings. They had been extinct for thirty thousand years, as far as the mortal world knew. What three mares and a stallion were doing in Fez, in a walled garden secure from casual observers, is a long story that needn't be gone into here.

"You'll like this stuff, Hippie," Nefer told the stallion. "This is Oatie Delight. Mortals eat it for breakfast food. It costs a lot, but what else have I got to spend money on, huh?"

The little horse nodded wisely, pulling away and going to the fountain-trough for a drink.

"I hope it's not too salty," said Nefer. She looked out across the courtyard as Nan emerged from the guest compound, still wearing her dressing gown, carrying a cup of coffee. Nefer waved. Nan waved back rather listlessly and after a moment walked across to join her.

"So, how are things in Paris?" inquired Nefer.

"A little colder than I care to endure just now," Nan replied, sipping her coffee. "But the work goes very well."

"And . . ."

"No change," said Nan, too quietly, and Nefer put an arm around her and kissed her.

"I'm so sorry," she said, and cleared her throat. "I heard your museum got the Da Vinci horse."

Nan nodded. "I'm advising and Shemaiah is doing the actual hands-on restoration. It ought to be magnificent when it's finished."

"I can't wait to see," said Nefer. "At least . . . I guess I'll get to see a holo or something on it."

She sighed. Nan shook her head.

"Nef, dear . . . you know it would probably be safe to travel. You might get Latif to escort you."

"It isn't just paranoia keeping me here," Nefer replied. "Not completely, anyway. We're conducting a sort of experiment. Will anybody in the Company notice I've dropped completely out of sight the last few decades? I haven't set a foot outside the gate since I got here. Is anybody monitoring my data transcript any more? How hard is it to disappear?"

Nan stared into her coffee. The stallion wandered up to the edge of the stall and studied her. She reached out to stroke its nose. "I suppose it would be easier if one had agoraphobia," she remarked.

"I wish!" Nefer said, reaching for a brush and leaning over to stroke tangles from the stallion's spiky mane. "If it wasn't for my little babies keeping me busy . . . I always hated layovers. Sometimes at night, I dream I'm out on the Serengeti, or even in the desert. I can see for miles, just miles of open yellow plain. So much air and light! And there are herds going down to the green places where water is and I can see every detail, all the calves and foals just perfect, so tiny. Wildebeest, zebra, gazelle. Every creature I ever saved is there. I can almost reach out and touch them. Sometimes I wake up and I'll have walked in my sleep, for crying out loud, I'll be standing at the casement window with my face pressed against the blinds."

"That's your programming," observed Nan.

"A conditioning nightmare? Maybe. But it'd be a good dream, Nan, if

I didn't have to wake up," said Nefer. One of the little mares noticed the attention the stallion was getting and came pushing up to the wall, too. "Oh, sweetie, you're just Miss Envious, aren't you? Look at you, look how nice your mane is. I must have spent an hour brushing it last night." Nefer chuckled sadly. "See the kind of time I've got on my hands?"

Nan made a sympathetic noise over her coffee. Nefer tilted her head back to look at the sky, hot and blue above the high wall.

"I guess that's how they'll get me, in the end," she mused. "One of these nights I'll dream that dream again, and I won't be able to stand it anymore. I'll just get my field kit and walk out of the house, leave the walls behind me, walk into that yellow landscape. Follow the coast down through the western Sahara or go back through the mountains and strike out inland, make for the Blue Nile and follow it up. Actually?" She turned her head to look at Nan. "Actually, if I'm still around when 2355 comes? That is what I'll do. I've promised myself. Let the Silence find me out there, with the herds."

There had been a time when Nan would have hastened to say something dissuasive and morale-boosting. Now, however, she simply nodded.

"Good for you," was all she said.

They stood there, watching the little horses for a while in silence, and then Nefer said:

"How in the world did it ever come to this?"


They went back into the great house through a side door—Nefer remembered to step out of her gumboots before she came in, this time—and walked together as far as the library. There at the door they paused, looking in at Suleyman and Latif, who had just arrived with a guest—

"Sarai!" Nefer screamed at the top of her lungs, closely echoed by Nan, and they hurled themselves across the room at Sarai, who screamed, too, and there was a very loud moment of tears and sirenlike mutual greeting. Latif stood back, wide-eyed, and Suleyman just laughed.

"Can we assume from this you're all still friends?" he inquired.

"Omigod," Nefer gasped, "I thought you were one of the Disappeared!"

"I've been working in Hell, I'll tell you," Sarai replied, grabbing a hand-kerchief out of Latif's breast pocket and wiping her eyes. "But I reckon this close to the end of time, Suleyman wants all three wives under one roof again."

"The Three Graces," said Nan, striking a pose. Suleyman came close and put his arms around them, pulling them together.

"Family reunion," he said. "For as long as we have, ladies."

The mortal servants came crowding into the doorway to stare. Latif cleared his throat and caught their attention.

"Tea," he ordered. "And pastries. Lots of them." They hurried to obey and he turned back to the other immortals. "I also brought in the mail," he informed Suleyman, gesturing to a package on the table.

"We got a delivery?" said Nefer hopefully, letting go her hold on the others and stepping over to see what the package was. "Is it that collec-tion of *National Geographic Presents* holoes I ordered?"

"Nope," Latif replied. "It's from London HQ."

"Darn," said Nef. "Would anybody like to tell me why, in this day and age, it still takes four to six business hours to ship something to Africa?"

Suleyman joined her at the table and opened the shipping printout. The others watched his face as he read it.

"What is it, Suleyman?" Nan asked him.

He paused a moment. Then he cleared his throat.

"Next year is the Company's thirty-fifth official anniversary," he said. "In celebration of this fact, the Board of Directors has a little token of its esteem for its immortal personnel! A special way to say thank you for our millennia of faithful service. I'm to distribute these throughout the North African Sector. All cyborg operatives are to receive one, and wear it proudly in the future."

Nobody said anything. They stared at the package. At last Latif reached out and struck the foam casing in the appropriate spot. It cracked and fell away to reveal a brightly-printed gift box. Suleyman removed its lid.

The box was full of round cloisonné badges, each about an inch in di-ameter. There were hundreds of them in the box, all identical.

Latif swore and turned away. Nan remained where she was, clutching her coffee cup. Sarai scowled at the box. Nefer moved forward in disbelief and scooped up a handful of the little pins. Looking down at them, she let them fall through her fingers; then raised her shocked eyes to Suleyman's tired ones.

The badges represented an old-fashioned dial face, of the kind still to be seen on historic clocks like Big Ben, simple white enamel with black Roman numerals. No time was represented, however, for the clock had no hands.

"It's starting," whispered Nef. "After all these years."

"Welcome to the future," Suleyman told her.

*Alec? Mrs. Checkerfield? I've got some news.*

"What is it?" Mendoza said, adjusting the spray valve over her maize plants. They had grown none the worse for time travel on the high seas, and good-sized ears stuck out at angles on each stalk. Alec, crouching over a thermostat he was repairing for her, looked up sharply.

*We're making landfall for some looting and pillaging, me dears. It's a place goes by the designation Alpha-Omega.*

"Alpha-Omega?" said Mendoza. "The beginning and the end? Where in time would you put a place with a name like that?"

*A long ways back, dearie. Farther than we ever gone, though we can manage it right enough. I'm still evaluating data, but it's looking like Dr. Zeus ain't secured it too well! Maybe they reckon it's so far in the past it don't need defending. Seems there's only one maintenance tech in the place, and a mortal one at that.*

"A mortal?" Mendoza was incredulous. "Surely not."

"Captain sir, that's nuts," Alec said. "Why would they leave an ordinary person in charge of something that important?"

*Haar! Well, he ain't ordinary, Alec,* the Captain said slyly. *Turns out this mortal's been cyborged. Can you imagine that, matey? And he's there because Alpha-Omega is something the mortal masters of the Company don't want to entrust to their immortal slaves. Now why would that be, I wonder, unless there was something special kept there? Like maybe the slaves' DNA templates?*

Mendoza turned bright eyes to Alec. He put his arms around her and clung tight.

"Well, then, Captain," he said in as firm a voice as he could muster. "Lay in a course. Let's have a look at the place."

# STILL ANOTHER MORNING
## IN 500,000 BCE

David Reed tried to focus his attention on his console, wishing he could help in the baby shower preparations.

Mr. Chandra had called Leslie down to his office, ostensibly to discuss changes in Lunchroom decor (they were both members of the redecoration committee, so it was perfectly plausible) but in reality to get her out of the way.

As soon as she had gone, Brandi and most of the Third Floor staff, as well as three caterers, began arriving in the secret lift bearing the decorations. This included great crowding bunches of blue balloons they'd spent most of the morning blowing up. As a consequence they were all rather giddy and breathless, and everybody was giggling as they climbed on chairs to fasten up baby-blue streamers and blow up more balloons. It seemed like great fun.

But somebody had to monitor the Recesses beyond the Portal, because it was terribly important work. What if one of the refrigeration units failed? What if one of those rows of gleaming tubes was unable to maintain optimum temperature? The thought was enough to make David shudder. In fact, sometimes he woke with nightmares about it, and had to plug himself in for a midnight visit to the Office, just to make certain nothing of the sort had happened.

And of course nothing ever had, because the Company had installed all possible backup systems, in addition to maintaining rigorous servicing schedules. Still—

If the stuff in the gleaming tubes was to spoil, it wouldn't be stored medicine or experiments that would be lost; oh, no. It would be whole races of humanity.

As it had been explained to David long ago, genetic diversity was very, very important. The more diverse the human gene pool was, the better were humanity's chances of adapting to any new and unexpected conditions it might encounter, now that it was beginning to push outward into Space, to say nothing of surviving any unexpected natural disasters such as polar shifts or meteor strikes on Earth.

Unfortunately, humanity had been both unlucky and foolish. Out of the dozens of races that had once lived in the world, only a handful had survived into modern times. Some ancient races had been rendered extinct by war. Some had been simply crowded out, retreating into remote regions and forced to breed amongst themselves, which killed them off with lethal recessives.

That had been the bad luck. The foolishness had come when people began to form theories about the process of Evolution. They got it all wrong: most people interpreted the concept of "survival of the fittest" to mean they ought to *narrow* the gene pool, reducing it in size. So this was done, in genocidal wars and eugenics programs, and how surprised people were when lethal recessives began to occur more frequently! To say nothing of the populations who died in droves when diseases swept through them, because they were all so genetically similar there were none among them with natural immunities.

Of course, in a way this was a *good* thing, because there had been far too many people in the world.

All the same, it would be awful if humanity were to go extinct, too. So, to prevent this, Dr. Zeus Incorporated had collected genetic material from every breed of human that had ever existed, from the time the first ones had knapped flints and huddled around fires.

It was all there beyond the Portal, the stuff with which you might make (for example) an ordinary Neanderthal or a Cro-Magnon. There were supposed to be wonderful things hidden in those tubes! The seeds for cold-tolerant humans, heat-tolerant humans, marine-adapted humans. Giants. Tiny, elfin humans. Humans with astonishing skin colors or patterns, with hair and eyes in remarkable shades. Humans with fur. All the splendor of adaptive humanity for every niche it had ever filled, however briefly, all saved in those silver tubes.

All waiting in case they were ever needed again. And there were also—so it was rumored—a couple of tubes of seed for things that weren't human, exactly. But David Reed didn't believe that. Dr. Zeus Incorporated would never, ever do something like experiment with making Recombinants.

No, Dr. Zeus was a *moral* company, and David was proud to work for anyone clever enough to solve humanity's problems in the way the Company had. Just look! Here was biodiversity enough to guarantee humanity's survival, without actually having all the tiresome humans themselves to feed and house. Not making wars or polluting the Earth or breeding in outrageous numbers, no. Safe and tidy here in little silver tubes, minding their manners and waiting their turns.

Why, the unpleasant business of breeding, itself, was now largely unnecessary. Though of course some people still indulged in it . . . David glanced over at the pile of presents all wrapped in baby blue. He told himself, for the hundredth time, that it was *right* that Leslie was having a baby, that it was only the one, after all, and somebody had to have them, or there'd be nobody to open those vials and call forth those sleepers if they were needed.

And look at the fun everybody was having, sticking up balloons and setting out party treats. It was a proper community activity, with everyone sharing the happiness. David smiled at Sylvya, as she came dancing up to the yellow track.

"Can you log off soon? Mr. Chandra's bringing her up in the lift."

David did one last status scan and then logged off hastily. He opened and set out the treats Ancilla had prepared so he wouldn't feel as though he weren't sharing: a bottle of blue lemonade, a wholemeal blueberry biscuit, and little sandwiches. The lift chimed and everyone, including David, turned bright expectant faces to the doors as they slid open.

"Oh!" Seeing them all, Leslie turned pink and clapped her hands to her cheeks in delight.

"Surprise!" David shouted with all the others.

# LATER THAT MORNING
## IN 500,000 BCE

Another island in a shallow sea, uncharted, but it has a name: the Beginning and the End.

This is a larger island. It has rounded hills, and estuaries and lagoons complicate its shores. Seabirds chatter and fight there. Tall white birds—egrets? herons?—stalk through the muck, hunting for frogs and little clams. The place is green with willows and alders, and reeds wave along the marshy tideland.

There are two knobby eminences of rock at either end of this island. On the eastern rock a low dome sits, presenting a smooth windowless face to its western neighbor. To one side the rock has been leveled flat, where a supply shuttle might land. A door faces the level place. It is the only visible break in the dome's surface.

Beyond the western rock, which is bare of anything except alder trees, the *Captain Morgan* stands on and off, keeping well out of sight of anyone who might be watching from the eastern rock.

Nobody seems to be watching, though.

*Mighty queer, all the same,* the Captain growled. *All I can make out scanning is that one mortal lubber, and he's been cyborged right enough; but he ain't tuned in to any defense systems like what you'd think. Sounds as though he's picking up some kind of wide-band signal from Time Forward.*

"Communicating with the Home Office, perhaps?" speculated Edward, who was presently in control. He loaded a fresh power pack into the disrupter pistol.

**Maybe,** the Captain said curtly.

"No cameras or anything?" Mendoza looked up, frowning, from pulling on a subsuit.

**Aye, there's a surveillance camera, doing a half-hour sweep. The datafeed goes to an AI in there, but all it seems to do is monitor life support for the mortal. There ain't no lasers, no missiles, nothing you'd expect. But then, maybe they can summon help straightaway from Time Forward.**

*Makes sense,* Alec said, watching as Mendoza adjusted the fit of her subsuit and zipped it up. Edward returned his attention to the disrupter pistol. He stood to fasten on its shoulder holster.

"Very well," he said. "Then I propose the following: we'll go ashore directly opposite, using the natural cover to conceal ourselves and lying flat at intervals to avoid the surveillance, which you will of course monitor."

**I will, eh? You planned it out mighty smart, ain't you, now?**

"Yes," said Edward. "As a matter of fact, I have."

Mendoza looked at him uneasily.

"Doesn't it seem like a good plan, Sir Henry?" she said.

**Oh, a fine plan, to be sure, ma'am. See if you can keep yerself from killing the mortal, though, eh, bucko? Don't want his AI set on us, now, do we? That'd draw Dr. Zeus's attention for certain.**

"So it would," Edward said. He sat to pull on the boots that went with his subsuit. "But I expect you'll see to disabling the electronics where necessary, won't you? Which ought to render the mortal cyborg harmless without resorting to anything unpleasant. Then a swift search and plunder, if we're lucky. Are you game, my dear?"

"Yes, señor," Mendoza said. Rising to his feet, Edward pulled her close and kissed her, hard. He set her back at arms' length.

"With any luck we'll be back aboard before sunset and sailing free, with all this wretched business behind us. Will you trust me, then?"

"Always," she said, as though it were absurd even to ask.

"That's my girl," he said, with a tight smile. "Let's be on our way."

They moved out together, over the side and into the water, escorted by the dolphins. Once they waded ashore, Mendoza followed like Edward's shadow. They vanished into the first willow thicket and came silently around the western rock.

*I see it.* Alec pointed at the domed base.

*No battlements? No watchmen?* Nicholas frowned.

*How's the surveillance, Captain, sir?*

**Lie low there! The camera's just about to sweep yer way.**

Edward signaled to Mendoza. They flattened themselves among the willows, and waited patiently while an unseen eye studied their hiding place without finding them.

**It's moved on. Go,** the Captain said at last.

*How long do we have before the next sweep?* Edward said, splashing forward across the murky lagoon. Mendoza came after him, scanning as they went.

**Twenty-eight minutes. More'n enough time. Bloody Hell, this place is wide open! Careful of the water, though, I'm reading some damned big fish.**

Edward grinned mirthlessly and waded on. They scrambled out of the lagoon and ran on down the beach, increasing their speed, so that when they came to the estuary mouth they were nearly flying. They crossed half of it in one leap and easily forded the rest of the way, coming ashore on hands and knees. Mendoza turned and stared back at the lagoon. Edward went sprinting on, and after a second's hesitation she followed him.

The last stream was narrow and they bounded across, moving in unison. They fled into the shadows of a stand of alders and leaned there, breathing hard, as Edward checked the disrupter pistol against water damage. Assured that it was unharmed, he holstered it again and inquired with his eyes whether Mendoza was ready. She nodded. They turned together and made the final assault, charging up the hill toward the windowless dome.

In a very short time they reached the top, and flattened themselves against the dome's gentle curve. Edward was drawing out the disrupter pistol when he saw Mendoza lift her head with an expression of astonishment. She looked at him, tilting her head toward the dome, and held out both hands palm up in a what-do-you-make-of-this gesture. He set his ear against the wall and listened intently. Faintly he made out laughter; then a voice lifted in conversation.

He raised his eyebrows at her. She signed *Two?*

He shrugged. Taking a firm grip on the pistol, he advanced along the wall to the leveled space.

It was clear this was a shuttle pad. All dust or loose earth had been scoured away by the wash of air from repeated landings and takeoffs, leaving bare rock exposed, and there were tiny bits of workplace debris scattered here and there: broken bolt heads, crate fragments, anything that might be kicked out or dropped when unloading cargo. And there in the dome's side was the door, a cargo hatch certainly, of plain roll-down steel sheeting. On its corrugated surface were crudely spray-painted the letters AO.

*We made it, Captain sir! We're at the door,* Alec said.

**You know what to do next, son.**

But it was Edward who leaned to the via panel and withdrew the lead from the torque, and with no hesitation selected the correct port. He plugged it in. They heard the click as the lock disengaged. They waited for a guarding reaction. There was none. The door rolled up an inch, and moving together Edward and Mendoza caught it and hoisted it upward about a half meter. Almost too quickly to be seen, then, Mendoza threw herself under the door and rolled inward, seeming to flow like liquid. Edward halted, startled. A moment later her hand appeared in the opening, beckoning him in. He dropped, rolled, and came up on his feet in the half-darkness, glaring around. Beside him, Alec and Nicholas blinked.

They stood with Mendoza in what was clearly a storage area. There were crates stacked floor to ceiling: empty ones neatly nested by the door, those yet unbroached piled farther in. Before them a small servounit, bearing some resemblance to Flint or Billy Bones without a skull, was busily engaged in extracting a canister from an opened crate. As they watched, it plugged the canister into a valve crusted with some kind of orange powder. The canister had a symbol on its side: a crossed spoon and fork. The servounit took no notice of them.

**It's got no brain to spare to see ye,** the Captain transmitted.

Edward nodded, looking past it into the room. There was no other entrance or exit apparent to the eye. Mendoza prowled along the wall, scanning. At last she bent and inspected a grating set in the wall at floor level, and rising she gestured toward it. Edward came close and stared. It was the entrance to a maintenance crawlway.

*That guy's been sealed in here,* said Alec in horror.

*Like a holy anchorite,* said Nicholas, shuddering.

*I'm afraid his meditations are about to be disturbed,* Edward said. He found the via lock port, and a moment later the grate clicked and fell outward. Mendoza caught it, setting it carefully to one side. She lay down and writhed in through the opening. Edward almost stopped her, reaching out instinctively.

**No! She's the immortal one, remember? You let her draw the fire, if there is any. She can dodge it, even in there. You'd only get yerself killed.**

Edward grimaced. He crouched by the crawlway, peering in after Mendoza, and watched as she proceeded her body's length to another grating. She set her face close to it, listening intently. Even Edward could hear, quite clearly now, a man saying in a pleasant voice:

"Ohh! That's a nice one, too. You can never have too many of those, you know."

She reached back her hand and gestured that Edward should give her something. After a moment's hesitation he crawled after her and laid the disrupter pistol in her palm. Her fingers closed on it. She reached up with her free hand and unfastened the catches that held the grate in place.

*She wouldn't kill him, would she?* Alec said, looking unhappy.

*She would, for you,* Edward said. *If it was necessary. Another of her gifts you find distasteful, is it?*

*Who taught her to kill but thee?* Nicholas muttered.

**Shut up and let the lady work!**

Mendoza, meanwhile, had lifted the grate and set it aside. As she peered through, her eyes widened in astonishment.

Immediately before her was dark, though light streamed through a doorway just across from the access grate. In the lit room beyond, a man was standing on a stripe of yellow carpet, holding a tumbler of some bright blue beverage and smiling as he talked to the thin air.

"That's from me," he was saying proudly. "You know, you can never have too many bath things, either. I always think, anyway."

Mendoza scanned the entire base but read no other occupants in any of the rooms. The mortal man was pale and thin, possibly delusional, certainly unarmed. Deciding that she could deal with any threat he represented, she pushed herself out into the room. Edward and the others followed closely.


Ancilla was distracted from her contemplation of the garden by abnormal life-readings within her assigned area. She turned in time to see the woman and the tall man slithering in through Loading Access Crawl A, like nothing so much as a pair of snakes in their scaled rubbery armor. The woman had a weapon and was looking at her David.

Ancilla rose in fury. Her hair stood up around her head in a halo of energy as she prepared to defend David. Then the tall man turned his bright eyes in her direction, *and saw her!*

She stopped, unbelieving, for none of her programming had prepared her for this anomaly; still less for what happened next. The tall man had a golden snake coiled about his neck, which lifted its head and saw her, too. It flowed down from his neck and changed, grew, towered. She found herself staring in horror at a third intruder. This was a big, powerful-looking man in a three-piece suit, with a wild black beard and hair. His face was wicked, clever, charming.

He looked her up and down and stepped toward her, chuckling. She couldn't look away from his sea-colored eyes.

"Well, now, dearie, yer just a tiny thing, ain't you? We'll have no trouble out of the likes of you," he said. The vibration of his baritone made her feel faint.

"I'll kill them if they hurt David!" she said.

"Aw, now, darling, that ain't likely," he said, moving closer still, backing her to the wall. "No reason there should be any nasty business unless you warn yer David, see? My little ones ain't here to do him any harm. But if he tries to stop 'em, well, I reckon it's hail and farewell to poor David, aye. That's a disrupter pistol my girl's got, in case you ain't noticed."

"Please don't hurt him," Ancilla said. "Please! Alternatives! Negotiate!"

"To be sure, miss. To be sure. You and me will manage this together, all friendly-like." He put his hands on her shoulders. "You control yer boy's optical input, don't you? Well then. You just make certain he can't see nothing but that there party he's having such a lovely time at. Why make him all worried and fretful? It's only until my kiddies get what they're after, anyhow."

"Will they go away then?" she asked.

"Certain they will," he pledged. "You've got my word on it for an honest seaman, darling. Here now! I know yer programming, I do, you don't care a brass farthing about that there ice locker. Dear little David's life support, that's all they wrote you to think was important. Ain't it? Say it with me now: David must be happy and safe . . ."

"David must be happy and safe," Ancilla said obediently, and as they went through the command together she blocked all David's visual input from his actual surroundings. Yes, he would be happier, he mustn't be needlessly frightened after all, this was her *job*, of course, and really what did she care about that Alpha-Omega thing?

So in David's world a certain level of gray cold reality was stripped away, and it became a brighter, happier place. The laughter of his coworkers came in with auditory enhancement. Enhanced were the balloons and the pretty little baby things mounting in a heap at Leslie's feet. Though, of course, Brandi was rather officiously making an effort to pick them all up and organize them, noting gifts and givers on a jotpad, as though anyone had asked *her* to take charge . . .

Timidly Ancilla leaned up and kissed the stranger, who laughed in his throat and opened her mouth with his own; but it was raw white power, not tongues, that caressed.

Mendoza saw none of this, of course, watching David carefully. Alec stared at the Captain for a moment, and then looked away with a gulp of embarrassment.

Mendoza considered David in the room starkly empty of anything but his computer console, considered the clearly visible plug in the back of his neck, considered the yellow stripe of carpet from which he was careful never to move. She put her head on one side and smiled; walked forward into the lighted room boldly, though still keeping the pistol trained on him. Edward followed her lead.

David, holding a murmured conversation with the air, looked straight through them.

"I mean, who does she think she is?" he was saying softly, indignantly. "Nobody said anything about playing word games at this party. I'm not good at word games! Neither is Leslie, really. And don't you think prizes are a little, well, *competitive*?"

He was silent a moment, sipping at his blue drink. As Mendoza and Edward slipped past him, he began to nod as if in agreement. Mendoza looked at a sealed entry port in the wall, shaped like a tall oval. On its panel was a polished brass plate with letters engraved in somber Roman characters: AO.

"See, that's just what I thought, too," David whispered earnestly.

Mendoza pointed at the door, grinning. Edward took her gloved hand and kissed it.

"Yes. Yes," said David in tones of mild outrage. "You're right, of course."

They advanced on the doorway and Edward found the via panel. He bypassed the keypad with his lead, and there was a soft hiss and a flow of curling vapor all along the door as the seal gave.

"What?" said David in a louder voice. "Oh. That's cute, look at that! Isn't that clever?"

Edward and Mendoza looked at each other. They clasped hands in a gesture of victory, and stepped together across the threshold. Their breath puffed out in frost-clouds.

Edward's first thought was of Easter Sunday. This was because his immediate visual impression reminded him of a panoramic Easter egg he had been given as a child, into which he had peered and wished himself without success: tiny claustrophobic world of tenderest pastel colors, with a flowering meadow and domed clouds that extended to forced-perspective infinity, in the soft light coming through the white sugar dome.

Too, there was something solemn and cathedral-like in the place where they now stood, where silvered arches rose out of glowing clouds of frost to the curved ceiling. The walls were lined with racks of gleaming tubes that evoked organ pipes, winking racks of lit candles, the severe symmetry of rows of pews.

Mendoza stood frowning, turning her head slowly as she scanned.

*Hundreds and hundreds,* said Alec in horror. *Where do we even start?*

There was a click, and a whirr. The thermocontrol unit had noticed the door was open, and was amping up the refrigeration system to keep the temperature from rising. Like insects in a summer field, or angels howling softly, the sound filled the glittering cave.

Mendoza walked to the nearest rack and inspected the tubes there. Each was engraved with a name. Faintly they could hear David rambling on outside:

". . . Of course, I don't really know much about babies, but it seems to me . . ."

Edward stepped close and examined the racks, lifting a gloved hand to wipe away frost. Names. Spitzka, Spode, Spohn . . . these were the templates of cyborg operatives like Mendoza.

"BTM four-seventeen." Mendoza turned to Edward. "Not a name. A code number!"

His eyes lit with comprehension. He turned and sought back through the alphabet, looking for tubes that might follow the letter Z. Mendoza picked her way forward, looking for what might precede A.

In the same moment that they turned to signal failure to each other, their eyes fell on a rack midway along the wall, where rows of outsized tubes sat in their own recess. Mendoza looked at Edward in tense inquiry. He nodded and they advanced on the rack, meeting in front of it. They stared up. Were those numbers engraved on the vials?

Edward bent and made a stirrup of his hands. Mendoza put her hands on his shoulders and vaulted upward to look at the top row. She swept her hand across the vials, wiping clear what was engraved there . . .

Edward felt the shock in her straining thighs, the involuntary leap as she seized one of the vials and held it aloft. He let her slide down and she presented it to him. It was much bigger than the others, so big she could scarcely get her hand around it, almost a chalice. Engraved on it were the characters BTM 417.

Grinning, he removed his right glove and slipped the vial into it. He unzipped the top of Mendoza's subsuit and tucked glove and vial down between her breasts, secure, and forced the zipper of the subsuit up again. The crucible made a bulge like a third breast. She laughed, shivered pleasurably and took his bare hand, leaning her cheek into it to plant a kiss there. Then she tugged him forward out of the chamber.

They paused beyond the threshold, just long enough to order the door to seal itself again. The mortal man had produced a blueberry biscuit from somewhere and was nibbling at it, apparently while watching something in the corner intently.

"So—just when is she due, then?" he inquired of an unseen presence.

He did not look up as they edged around him and into the next room, where the Captain still had his broad back turned, busy with Ancilla.

*Just keep her attention drawn a few more minutes, won't you, old man?* Edward said airily. The Captain growled in response but did not turn.

They got down and exited through the crawlway, with Mendoza carefully replacing the grates as they went; scrambled rapidly across the storeroom, where the servounit still ignored them, and rolled back out into sunlight beyond. Moving as one, they pulled the door back down and stood. Edward held out his hand for the disrupter pistol and Mendoza passed it to him. He set it secure back in its holster. They started down the rock.

*That was easy!* Alec said in relief.

At precisely that moment he felt a creeping numbness, and then a white-hot shock of pain. Light flared behind his eyes and blinded him.

He mustn't be blind. He must see. He fought, flailing in the void. His hand encountered another hand and grabbed frantically. It wasn't Mendoza's hand, though. It was a big hand. It clenched on his. He turned to find out whose hand it might be, and his vision came back enough to see Nicholas, peering desperately into his eyes.

"What's happened?" Alec cried.

"I know not," Nicholas said. "But Edward's lost again, it seems."

*No indeed, gentlemen,* said an amused voice, coming from everywhere and nowhere at once, just as the Captain's voice did, but it wasn't the Captain speaking. *Edward's most assuredly not lost. Edward has won.*

The void rolled back on all sides and revealed a room, dark-paneled and carpeted, lined with books, lit only by lamplight, for there were no windows and no doors in evidence. There were two big old-fashioned chairs. There was a small table on which were the lamp, a decanter of something amber, and two cut crystal glasses.

There was nothing else. Alec and Nicholas stared around themselves in incomprehension.

"Edward?" Nicholas lifted his head. His eyes went small and suspicious. "What hast thou done?"

*What it was my right to do, and my duty. I've taken command.*

"Captain," Alec shouted. "Captain, get us out of here!"

*The Captain, Alec, is presently occupied, and when he turns his attention this way—as indeed I expect he'll do any minute now—he'll receive a nasty shock. I've jammed his signal, just as Joseph managed to do.*

"Are you crazy?" Alec looked about wildly, searching in vain for a door.

*Not at all, and if you weren't so abysmally dependent on him you'd have discovered you could shut him out long ago. Mind you, I can't keep him balked for long; but I've already done what was necessary.*

"WHAT HAST THOU DONE?" demanded Nicholas, beginning to pace in his fury.

*Killed Alec.*

"What?" Alec shrieked.

*In a manner of speaking. The heart's still beating, never fear; but it's mine now. Didn't you want to die young, Alec? Your wish has been granted. I'm afraid you'll find Limbo rather more irksome than I did, however.*

"He's lying, boy," said Nicholas. "Or mad."

"Edward," said Alec, fighting very hard to seem calm, "what do you mean, I'm going to find it more irksome? Why?"

*Because I've taken you hostage, what do you think? And Nicholas as well, though he's merely a complication. You have the Captain to thank for teaching me how to lock you in. Make yourselves comfortable, gentlemen. You'll be here awhile.* There was the most delicate of pauses, perfectly timed. *Nine months, at least.*

It was almost possible to hear Edward counting the seconds before his meaning sank in and the others suddenly shouted at him. His laughter, lazy and confident, rolled over them.

"You *bastard,*" Alec yelled, pounding his fists against the virtual wall. "You—you—you motherfucker—"

*Not I. No, I've altered my plans. The Captain will work the immortality process on* me. *He'll have no choice but to do so. Any attempt to shut me off will lose your programs, you see. They'd go to a random site—my word, even I can't guess where—and he'd never get you back, either of you. I'm afraid you'd run out of reading matter eventually, Nicholas. Pity.*

"But you can't shut me off," yelled Alec. "I'm not just some memory like you, I'm alive! I'm *real!*"

*You **were** alive. And what indeed is reality, Alec? You're a trifle ill-equipped to debate the issue with me—but, to put it in terms you might understand, it would seem that human consciousness is no more than a program running in the hardware of the brain. My program has displaced yours. Permanently. I have no intention of relinquishing control, nor of releasing either of you until my demands are met.*

*Ah, but once I'm decently immortal, then! I'll gladly set you free, if the Captain makes certain accommodations, as I should imagine he will. Can you guess what those accommodations would be?*

"No!" said Alec, rubbing his shoulder, bruised in his fruitless assault on the wall. Nicholas was hurling himself against it now.

*Oh, you're not even trying! Wretched little slacker. The Captain refused to craft a new body for me, but he'll be desperate to make one for you, Alec, if that's the only way to resurrect you. Or a pair of bodies! I've no objection to Nicholas in the flesh either, especially as it's likely to be some years before either of you will be big enough to thrash me soundly. And, who knows? By that time you may feel differently about this whole affair. I imagine such admittedly satisfying revenge would distress your loving mother.*

Nicholas pulled himself upright, staring.

"Thou lustful, foul and unnatural monster—" he said quietly.

*Oh, really! I have no intention of committing incest. If the idea distresses you, you'll be at perfect liberty to follow your conscience. I daresay you'll have years of innocence before the thought even enters your little head. I confess I never contemplated children, let alone twin sons. Still, we never know what Life has in store for us, do we?*

"Shut up, you pompous jerk! Nicholas, we're locked up in some site he's built," said Alec in desperation. "He must have figured out how to write code."

*Oh, bravo, Alec!*

"But there's two of us, see? If we push hard together, we can break out."

"How?" Nicholas turned to Alec. "Tell me, boy!"

*He can't tell you.* Edward's voice dripped with contempt. *He was unable to show me, either. I didn't learn properly until that useful target-shooting game taught me the trick. You'd have learned, too, Nicholas, if you hadn't been too squeamish to play. I do so look forward to educating you both.*

"Jesu!" Nicholas clutched at his temples, trying to recreate what he'd done to make the ship's rigging obey him. Alec groaned. Edward's voice took on a more amiable tone, almost seductive.

*Come now, gentlemen. I made the best use of the talents we were uniformly born with, therefore I am fittest to command. I will, at last, fulfill our sacred purpose in the world. And is this really such a tragedy? You'll be comfortable enough in here, for the present. Decent brandy and plenty of improving books as well. Nicholas, you'll find I've taken particular care to stock volumes on modern science and philosophy, and of course the complete works of Shakespeare.*

"Thou'lt set *me* to school?" Nicholas said, affronted now, too.

*I expect you to bring yourself up to date! Your mind's too good to waste in a muddle of outmoded ideas. Perhaps you can even learn to control your temper. And teach the boy to read, won't you? Join me in the Age of Reason. When all's said and done, I should prefer not to lose my brothers.*

"Go shrack yourself," roared Alec. "Nicholas, come on, we're stronger than he is. You *were* able to do it, you got into the system just fine! Listen—" He grabbed Nicholas by the shoulders and stared into his eyes. "Try this: imagine Joseph's here, and you've got a gun just like—"

There was a flash and a cracking noise, and Alec was thrown across the room into a corner. Nicholas ran to him where he lay huddled, and stopped in horror.

Alec's torque had become a serpent, coiling shut about his throat and choking off his voice. His face turned purple as he struggled to pull it loose, wrenching vainly with both hands.

*I can remove your tongue, if you make it necessary.* Edward's voice was like steel. *You're only a recording, after all. Shall I take your eyes next? I can delete your senses one by one. You won't enjoy it.*

"No!" Nicholas fell to his knees. "Edward, for our lady's sake—"

*My lady. I'm best able to protect her and I truly love her, which claim I'm afraid neither of you can make. You were already looking for some way to leave her, weren't you, Alec? It was only a matter of time before one of your covert suicide attempts succeeded, and broke her heart forever.*

"Thou whoreson liar!"

*I never asked her to die with me, Nicholas. She loved you far better than you deserved. Think how glad she'll be to see your little face, once you're reborn in the flesh! Though of course she'll have no idea of your true identities. We'll call you Nicholas and Edward, since necessity has, as it were, made me Alec . . .*

With a mocking chuckle the voice faded away, and Nicholas and Alec found themselves alone.

Alec struggled to breathe, staring mutely into Nicholas's eyes as Nicholas lifted him into a sitting position.

"He cannot do this," Nicholas told him, shaking with rage. He bowed his head. His eyes were terrifyingly cold, pale as lightning. His voice rose like rolling thunder.

"Lord of Hosts! Thou hast no mercy nor no infinite love; but on Thine infinite spite, I make claim. Grant Thou hear my cry for justice! Strike him down in his abomination who hath mocked at Thee! Consume him, marrow and bone!"

Alec felt a throbbing in the air and for one fearful moment thought the Lord of Hosts Himself was coming through the wall, before he realized that Nicholas was the source of the energy, *Nicholas* was disrupting the site with pure force of will. He gripped Nicholas's hands and drew on his power; killed the golden serpent, and tore it from his neck.

"You're doing it," he gasped, sucking in a great breath. "Come on, Nicholas, focus! We can break out of here. We can get him."

*Damn you both! You can't—*

Leaping and scrambling, Edward and Mendoza reached the bottom of the rock and set off along the sand. They ran on down the beach, vaulting the estuaries, and came to the lagoon. Birds were rising from the water and shrieking in alarm. Here Mendoza, who had been in the lead, halted abruptly with an expression of horror. Edward continued straight past her and splashed in, wading up to his chest.

*"No,"* Mendoza screamed. "Alec, get out!"

But Edward had halted, was clutching his head distractedly. He missed the dorsal fin cutting the water.

"Damn you both! You can't—" he said, and then something pulled him under.

Without hesitation, Mendoza leaped in after him.

There was a long moment of disturbance in the fast-flowing water, before they broke the surface again.

The first rule of all, the one on which Dr. Zeus Incorporated was founded, is: not everything is extinct simply because it seems to be. Regard, for example, the coelacanth, or . . .

Glistening in the cloudy air, tossing its knife-jawed head from side to side and whipping Edward around by one leg like a doll, grinning bloodily despite the fact that Mendoza, on its back, was raining blows on its head in an attempt to kill it . . .

The ichthyosaur.

Its rule of life was uncomplicated: bite its food and hold on. If the food struggled, if it was too big to kill with one bite, beat it to and fro until it stopped struggling or pieces tore off. However, this other thing, the one on its back, was hurting it. So it lashed and leaped, clear out of the strong-running current, beached itself, but failed to dislodge the other thing. At least the food had stopped struggling.

Edward lay sprawled on the sand, staring at the sky with wide astonished eyes. Mendoza, screaming, terrifying in her transformation, dug her heels into the ichthyosaur's head and caught hold of a broken willow-snag. Its top burst into green leaves as she gripped it.

With all the strength in her body she plunged the makeshift spear into the ichthyosaur's eye, and rammed it up into its brain. Its head jerked, the idiot-grin gnashed, the whole body trembled. Roots and spreading branches tore through its flesh. In puzzlement Edward observed the severed leg still in its jaws. Whose was that? Oh, no, had it got Alec? Or Nicholas? Where were they? He was unable to turn his head to look for them.

*"Meu amor,"* sobbed Mendoza, stumbling from the ichthyosaur's back and falling to her knees beside him. She worked frantically at the gunbelt and tore it loose, binding the stump of his left knee in a tourniquet. "Ai, *meu amor,* please—oh, your beautiful legs! Please hold on—listen, can you hear the motor? Sir Henry's sending the agboat for us, here it comes. Oh, God and Saint James, Alec, don't die now!"

Alec? Edward closed his eyes, grimacing as he remembered what he'd done. He was wet and broken and cold, and quickly growing colder, but he held tight to his plan.

**You little devil, I told you what would happen**— roared the Captain distantly.

"Why, I'm afraid I've lost a leg," Edward said, in an attempt at bravado. "Now I'll be like Long John Silver, won't I, my dear?"

"Yes, darling, just like Long John Silver, you'll like that, won't you?" Mendoza said wildly. "So you must stay with me for the wonderful experience of a wooden leg, yes? We'll even get you a parrot."

"I'm afraid we won't be dancing at the Avalon Ballroom . . ."

"Sweetheart, we'll go dancing some other time," she promised, looking over her shoulder for the agboat.

"Not if I've got a wooden leg," Edward said, wincing. Something hurt. Badly.

"We'll think of something. Just live!"

"Yes. I tell you," Edward gasped, "I will live. I won't lose you. I'll—"

She caught his hand as he faltered. "Yes! Stay with me, darling! Look. Here I am. Do you see me?"

"I will *not* die—" He attempted to draw breath to say something more and choked, as blood came bubbling from his mouth.

"Alec," Mendoza cried, reaching to turn his head so the blood wouldn't suffocate him. In doing so, she placed her hand between his neck and the torque. Inadvertently she connected, flinching.

Edward seized the opportunity, and downloaded into her. Into Mendoza's skull went Alec and Nicholas, still fighting to escape from their claustrophobic Victorian library as it skewed and shook, as virtual books rained from the shelves about them.

But in Edward's extremity the floodgates were opened. All the information in the world, everything the Captain had plundered from Dr. Zeus, *everything*, went roaring through Edward's brain into hers, when even two tiny pieces of the Temporal Concordance had been enough to send Joseph (a far older and stronger operative) to bed with a headache for two weeks. With either the Captain or Alec or both selectively giving her a little at a time, Mendoza might have survived it without harm.

Edward watched in horror as she went rigid, as her mouth opened for an agonized scream that never came, as the data boiled into her indestructible skull and turned its contents into very, very expensive garbage. Realizing what was happening, he got his arm up and pushed her hand away, breaking the connection. She toppled over and convulsed galvanically, arching her spine. Blue flame flared and pulsed over her body.

"Mendoza," cried Edward. He caught at her hand. "Oh, no, *please* no. Mendoza!"

But here was the agboat at last, and here were Flint and Billy Bones come to minister to him, strapping him still, clearing his windpipe, intubating him, injecting him, replacing the makeshift tourniquet and applying a pressure bandage, hooking him up to a synthetic bloodbag. He tried to turn to her, he tried to call her name; but they were closing up the bubble-stretcher around him now and he lost sight of her. They loaded it into the agboat. He didn't see Flint retrieving his left leg from the jaws of the ichthyosaur. He didn't see Billy Bones crouch over Mendoza's body long enough to tear open her subsuit and remove the glove with his genetic crucible, scuttling away into the agboat with it.

He was closed in, and the bubble-stretcher had become the Easter egg. He had got inside at last, nestled in the green and pleasant land where he was the white lamb. Bring him his bow of burning gold, bring him his arrows of desire, bring him his spear—O clouds unfold . . .

He will *not* cease . . .

The agboat crossed the stretch of open sea toward the *Captain Morgan*, which had come around the western rock at last, having nothing to fear from the surveillance camera now. It moved in under full sail and stood just offshore. The agboat rose to its davits. The contents of the agboat were offloaded.

It was silent, there at the Beginning and the End, for perhaps a quarter of an hour. But not motionless; the tide turned and the tidal bore ran through the reef, like a god riding white horses inland. Its passing wash tugged at the ichthyosaur where it lay half out of the water and pulled it to and fro, imitating its living movements so nearly that the seabirds, who had begun to light on it and peck speculatively, became alarmed. They rose in a mewing cloud.

One or two landed near Mendoza and ventured close, eyeing her. They didn't know what to make of the blue flame that coiled and crackled over her body, and moreover she was still giving the occasional kick as something attempted to work, so they kept their distance. The willow tree soared to green maturity beside her, sending its roots down into the sand, and in a small field around her body time went mad. Beach grass sprouted, withered and vanished, sea-grape came and went, sand went to alluvial mud, to gravel shingle, to sand once more.

She was no longer capable of thought, or speech, or effective self-repair, scrambled as she was; but she was not, of course, able to die. She was immortal, after all.

Captain Sir Henry Morgan came out on the deck of the ship that bore his name and climbed quickly over the side. Letting himself down the boarding ladder, he stepped out onto the sea and strode across to the Beginning and the End. Dolphins coursed before him and behind him.

He followed the tide up and stepped off onto the sand, leaving no print as he walked past the body of the ichthyosaur. The shearwaters and terns watching Mendoza backed away as he approached her. His face was set and staring. He stopped beside her and fell to his knees.

Shaking his head, he reached out to her. The blue flames flared; his hand passed through them. Placing it on her forehead, he said:

"Reset! Ten, nine, eight, seven, six, five, four, three, two, one. Run diagnostic now. Please, Alec, please, boy, please . . ."

In precisely ten seconds the taut arch of her body collapsed, and Mendoza lay sprawling in the advancing tideline. Her staring eyes closed at last. She exhaled, shuddering, and stopped. But the Captain let out a howl of savage triumph that would have terrified the crew of any Spanish galleon, to say nothing of raising the dead. Mendoza's eyes shot open. She focused and regarded him.

"Come on, then, dearie," the Captain said, laughing. "Rise and walk."

"Oh, God my Savior," she murmured in horror.

"Not exactly," the Captain said. "More like yer salvager, lass. Haar! Salvager, get it? Bless that fat bastard Zeus. *You* ain't no Semele!"

"Please," she said, tears of despair forming in her eyes. "Let me die now."

"Ahh, no indeed," he said, gently, pitilessly. "For what would my boy do then? You've got my Alec, safe in that ironbound memory of yours. He'll be needing you more than ever, now. Die? Why, darlin', if you was hid on the underside of the lowest rock in Hell, I'd come after you."

She stared at him, exhausted, trying to make sense of what he was saying.

"Alec's not dead?" she said at last.

"No, bless yer heart, he ain't!" The Captain's teeth flashed in a grin of fierce happiness, so white in his black beard. "And he ain't never going to be, by thunder, not with you to help me. No thanks to that murdering son of a whore."

"Oh," she said.

The tide was advancing, pouring around her and waving her hair out in a fan. She didn't seem to notice. The blue fire crackled on the foam.

"Time for you to go back aboard, love. Nice dry clothes for you, and a nap, eh, and then wouldn't you like to see yer man? He's all mended, and sleeping peaceful in his tank," said the Captain.

Mendoza nodded.

"That's my good girl." The Captain drew back, encouraging her to rise. She sat up unsteadily; got to her feet. She swayed a moment, streaming with seawater, wreathed in flames the color of sapphires.

"I'm different," she said, in confusion.

"Ain't you, though?" the Captain agreed. He leaned down and kissed her, tenderly, between her eyes. "Come on, mother. You come home with me, now. We'll take good care of him."

They walked back to Alec's ship and went aboard.

After a while it put about, and sailed away from that place.